Acknowledgements

This book owes special thanks to the following people, who were all the right readers at the right time: Ian Pindar, who built the desk, bought the computer and told me to go for it; Jacky Barrett, the receiver of brown envelopes, who sped through chapters on the bus home and got it through the tricky first trimester; Neel Mukherjee, for generosity, enthusiasm, eloquence and a touch of magic; Judith Murdoch, for giving it a shape and a name; Helen Rumbelow, for wise advice and urging it on; and Catherine Cobain, who asked all the right questions, provided the final push and prepared it for the outside world.

Thanks also to Jaishree Misra, Nanu and Luli Segal, Anna Lawrence Pietroni, and my friends from Cardiff 1995–6, Cornwall 1999, and the turning point of the new millennium.

And finally, love and thanks to my family, in particular my mother, who taught me to look for the right word, gave me some great books, and let me work my way through everything else on the shelves.

For Izzy and Tom

STOP THE CLOCK

Alison Mercer

BLACK SWAN

TRANSWORLD PUBLISHERS
61–63 Uxbridge Road, London W5 5SA
A Random House Group Company
www.transworldbooks.co.uk

STOP THE CLOCK
A BLACK SWAN BOOK: 9780552778183

First publication in Great Britain
Black Swan edition published 2012

Addresses for Random House Group Ltd companies outside the UK
can be found at: www.randomhouse.co.uk
The Random House Group Ltd Reg. No. 954009

The Random House Group Limited supports The Forest Stewardship
Council (FSC®), the leading international forest-certification
organization. Our books carrying the FSC label are printed on
FSC®-certified paper. FSC is the only forest-certification scheme endorsed
by the leading environmental organizations, including Greenpeace.
Our paper-procurement policy can be found at
www.randomhouse.co.uk/environment

Typeset in 11/14pt Giovanni Book by
Kestrel Data, Exeter, Devon.
Printed and bound by
CPI Group (UK) Ltd, Croydon, CR0 4YY.

2 4 6 8 10 9 7 5 3 1

MIX
Paper from
responsible sources
FSC® C016897

From 'Auld Lang Syne'

We twa hae paidl'd in the burn,
Frae morning sun till eve;
But seas between us braid hae roar'd,
Sin' auld lang syne.

Which translates, approximately, as:

We two have paddled in the stream,
From morning sun till eve;
But seas between us broad have roared,
Since long, long ago.

Robert Burns

Prologue

New Year's Eve, 1999

The closer they came to the house, the harder it was to see the way ahead. It was past midnight, and the lane was unlit, and was also obscured by ghostly drifts of fog that clung to the branches of the trees to either side and hung in heavy swirls in front of them. Lucy was beginning to wonder if they'd somehow missed the entrance when Adam said, 'Hang on, isn't that it?' and hit the brakes.

They came to a rest just beyond a pair of big wrought-iron gates. It was just possible to make out the copper-plate lettering on the sign mounted on the wall by the gatepost: *The Old Schoolhouse*.

'Yup, that's it,' Lucy said.

Beyond the gates was a stretch of lawn and a big red-brick, three-storey Victorian Gothic building, complete with parapets, a round tower, an array of steeply pitched roofs and mullioned windows, all of which were dark.

'I thought they were going to wait up,' Adam said.

'I can't see Tina's car,' Lucy said. 'And why would they have locked the gates?'

She rummaged in her handbag – God, there was so much kiddie crud in there! – and fished out her mobile.

'Damn! No signal. Back of bloody beyond. What are we going to do now?'

Adam hit the horn. Lucy nearly jumped out of her skin.

'What are you doing? You'll wake the baby!'

She swung round to check, but Lottie was thankfully still sound asleep.

'Sorry, shouldn't have snapped,' she said. 'I just don't get it. Tina knows we're coming – I even rang her before we left. What if they've had an accident or something? Oh God, they could be lying in a ditch somewhere . . .'

'I bet you anything you like they're down the pub,' Adam said, 'and there's a lock-in and they're in there gossiping and they've lost track of time.'

Lucy thought it over.

'So what do we do?'

'We wait,' Adam said.

In the Black Swan, Tina had told Natalie everything – well, almost everything, and Natalie was doing her very best not to pester for the one crucial detail that Tina had withheld.

Natalie was drunk, and, in spite of her best efforts to take Tina's news in her stride, more than a little shocked. Tina, who was driving, was stone-cold sober, which was a measure of how badly she'd needed to confide in someone; she'd spilt the beans pretty much as

12

soon as they were settled in a snug corner, before she'd finished her first roll-up.

Now Natalie's glass was empty, the bar was finally shut, and the other patrons were heading off, letting in cold blasts of wintry air as they slipped out through the side door.

'I'm not sure it would be a good idea to tell Lucy about this, you know,' Tina said.

'Why not?'

'I think she might disapprove.'

Natalie opened her mouth to disagree, but then realized that Tina was probably right.

'And she wouldn't mince her words,' Tina went on. 'No, I think we should keep this just between you and me.'

'If that's what you want,' Natalie said.

'We should go,' Tina said. 'They'll be here soon.'

As Tina drove them away from the village down the winding lane Natalie reflected that maybe it was a blessing in disguise that her boyfriend was in Singapore, working on a potentially career-making case for his law firm, and would not be joining them to see in the new millennium.

If Natalie's Richard had been there, Tina wouldn't have said anything, Natalie was sure of that – and she was equally sure that Tina had *needed* to come out with it, and felt better for getting it off her chest.

And thank goodness Tina's other friends had different parties to go to, or had bailed out at the last minute. She and Tina would never have had such a heart-to-heart if Tina had been playing hostess to a full house.

How amazing to be bold and reckless and foolhardy enough to lay claim to what you wanted, as Tina had, even if it was so obviously doomed to lead to heartache and a dead end! How good it must have felt for Tina to tell someone the truth, if not quite the whole truth – and how shocked Tina would have been if Natalie had trumped her revelation with one of her own!

But Natalie had kept her own counsel, and probably always would, because what was there to say? Doubts and dreams were not enough to make a secret, and if she didn't act on them, there was nothing for her to tell.

They turned a bend, and there was Adam and Lucy's sensible family estate car, parked and waiting for them outside the gates of Tina's parents' holiday home.

Tina pulled up behind it, and for a moment they both stared at the BABY ON BOARD sticker displayed on the rear windscreen. Then Tina exhaled, slumped forward and pressed her forehead against the steering wheel.

'Oh crap, crap, crap!' she moaned. 'How could they have got here so quickly? Adam must have broken the speed limit most of the way – and he's got a baby in the back!'

She hurried over to apologize. Natalie knew she ought to follow, but as she reached for the door handle she found herself lingering and watching Tina.

Somehow Tina always had the right clothes for any situation. In the city she wore suits and heels and looked groomed, or went out at night in little shiny dresses that got her past the velvet ropes and into wherever she wanted to go; in the country she appeared in old jeans and a padded jacket and was equally in her element.

14

Tina was stooping to talk to Lucy through the car window, and her long blonde hair had swung forward so that Natalie couldn't make out her expression. Then she straightened up, and Natalie saw that she looked as self-possessed as ever.

How did Tina do it?

Natalie knew she'd never be capable of the sort of adventure Tina had told her about in the pub. She wouldn't be able to handle it. She'd feel much too guilty, and she wouldn't be able to hide it.

Once she was outside, the cold air was instantly sobering.

The next day was New Year's Eve. Lucy had forgiven them for not being there when she arrived, and the slight awkwardness of the previous night was forgotten. Tina had always found that staying at the Old Schoolhouse had a pacifying effect; she'd always got on much better with her parents there, on holiday in Cornwall, than back home in London.

At one time, the Old Schoolhouse had accommodated twenty daughters of the Cornish gentry, who learned needlework and a little Latin under the guidance of a maiden great-aunt of Tina's father's. The furnishings and decor were still simple to the point of austerity, and it wasn't exactly homely, but it didn't seem institutional either. It felt sequestered and accepting, as if it was far enough removed from society to take on whatever those passing through chose to bring to it. At a time when she was both excited and unnerved by what she'd just got herself into, it was exactly what she needed.

Tina had invited Natalie and Lucy to stay once before, at the end of their postgraduate year in Cardiff. The three of them had gone on to live in London together and start their first jobs in journalism. But then Lucy had moved out to set up home with Adam, and speed through to marriage and motherhood by the age of twenty-five.

Barmy, Tina thought – not to say anything against Adam, who was obviously gorgeous and the perfect gentleman and made Lucy blissfully happy, but what was the rush? Inevitably she and Natalie had seen less of Lucy since Lottie was born. This little trip was a chance to catch up – though, as she had said to Natalie, Tina had decided that it wouldn't do to tell Lucy absolutely everything.

Luckily Adam seemed to be willing to do his bit with Lottie, who was rising two now, and struck Tina as being jolly hard work. They went to the Black Swan for lunch, and Adam entertained Lottie while the three women got on to cosy do-you-remembers about their journalism course, and the party house they had shared afterwards.

It was inevitable that, having revisited the past, they would start to talk about where their lives were heading.

Tina started telling them how she'd been so nervous on her first day in her new job that she'd spilt her boss's coffee in his lap. Then she realized Natalie wasn't listening, and was looking at Lottie with a sort of muted, hungry longing.

Oh no! Natalie was *broody*. How was that possible?

16

It was bad enough that Lucy had jumped the gun and reproduced already, but why would Natalie want to join in with the nappies and dummies and vomit and poo and endless crying, and getting fat and not being free? Given the choice between a baby and her brand-new secret, Tina knew what she'd go for, no contest.

Natalie inclined her head towards Lottie and said into a sudden silence, 'So how do I get Richard to give me one of those?'

Lucy and Adam exchanged glances.

'Don't ask me. I think Lucy employed witchcraft,' Adam said. Lucy elbowed him in the ribs.

He gave her a sleepy, disarming smile, and then turned to Natalie and said, 'If it's what you want, I'm sure he'll come round.'

'What I want is what you and Lucy have,' Natalie said. 'I want to marry Richard and have his babies. But he doesn't even seem that sure about the idea of us getting a place together.'

'Getting married and having children isn't everything, you know!' Tina said. 'What about your job?'

Natalie shrugged. 'I'm kind of bored of it.'

'Then get a new one,' Tina said. 'Get back on track. You used to want to do news stories with a social conscience. What about that?'

'Just not sure I want it enough to put the work in,' Natalie said.

'You can't give up so easily, not after we've come so far,' Tina said.

'You should do whatever makes you happy,' Lucy said.

'OK, well, here's what's going to make *me* happy,' Tina told them. 'I've got a foot in the door at the *Post*, and I'm going to make the most of it. This time ten years from now I want to have my own newspaper column, with a nice big picture byline.'

'A job can't love you back,' Lucy said.

'Maybe not, but you can love your job, and that's worth something,' Tina said, feeling impelled to defend, not just her ambition, but the other, secret choice she had made. 'Marriage and babies isn't the only thing worth having. It can't be. It's not the only kind of love. And anyway, you can't seriously tell me you don't ever miss *Beautiful Interiors*. You used to be so into that magazine!'

Lucy reached across to take Adam's hand.

'I'd much rather make a beautiful home of my own than tell other people what to put in theirs,' she said. 'That's my ten-year plan. I honestly can't think of any better way to spend the next decade. If we can get this house we've found, I'll have everything I've ever wanted.'

'Yeah, but you are going to go back to work eventually, aren't you?' Adam said. 'To help with the mortgage.'

'Of course, darling.'

And then Lucy started telling them all about the house she and Adam were trying to buy.

'We call it the Forever House, because that's what you call the place you want to live in for the rest of your lives.'

'It sounds like something out of a fairy-tale,' Natalie said.

'For ever is a long time,' Tina said. 'If you ask me, ten years seems quite far enough to look ahead.'

After lunch they went for a stroll on the beach, and Adam got the three women to line up for a photo.

'Just for the record,' he said as he looked through the viewfinder and fiddled with the focus. 'Tina, Natalie and Lucy, on the cusp of the new millennium.'

After a while Lottie fell over and refused to toddle any further, and Adam hoisted her on to his shoulders and volunteered to take her back to the house.

'Let's all go,' Tina said. 'We should stick together. Anyway, it's starting to get dark.'

The light was beginning to fade. The horizon was a deep band of shadow rather than a fine line between the ocean and the clouds, and as they made their way across the sand a chill breeze blew in from the waves. The final night of a thousand years was already rolling in, and the dark, pressing sky, grey sea and icy breeze seemed to harbour the power of transformation, and to be reminding them that change was imminent, inevitable – and already upon them.

1

Spring 2009

Interruption

It was Tina's fault; that was how Lucy thought of it afterwards. If Tina hadn't started writing that silly column, it wouldn't have happened – at least not in the way it did.

But on the morning that Tina's column was to change Lucy's life there was no obvious sign that anything unusual was about to happen, though it did take Lucy longer than normal to decide what to wear. When she was ready she looked herself up and down in the full-length mirror next to the marital bed, and wasn't 100 per cent sure that she liked what she saw.

She had on a long rose-patterned skirt and pink plimsolls – very Boden lady – plus a pink lacy cardigan that knotted under the bust, bought because it looked vaguely artistic, like something a poetess might wear: she'd been charmed by its impractical prettiness. Now she wondered if it just looked dippy.

Of course, the problem wasn't really the clothes – it was her. She was trying to look perky and sweet and wholesome, and she just looked . . . *faded*. The only cure was sex, and that had become a rarity. She felt gorgeous when Adam wanted her, and un-gorgeous when he didn't, which, lately, was far more often than not.

She would have liked to think of herself as a yummy mummy. She'd noticed that women used this as a term of disapprobation, implying criticism of the idleness, vanity and greedy shopping habits that supposedly went with it. But when men described a mother that way, they usually meant they thought she was still sexy.

Lucy had a comfortable lifestyle, a nice house, a family and no job, but was that enough for her to rank as a yummy? Probably not.

There was a stirring of bed linen and Adam heaved himself upright. He had completely overdone it at the fortieth birthday party they'd attended the night before, and she knew he'd be in a foul mood. That was another thing about getting older – hangovers were hell.

'I don't know what you're worrying about,' Adam said. 'Natalie's about to pop. She's not going to be looking her best.'

'I'm not worrying,' Lucy said. 'I just don't want her and Tina to think I look old.'

She decided to brush her hair one last time. Still, with the hairdresser's help, uniformly chestnut brown, it fell to the middle of her back. If she stopped dyeing it, it would probably look eccentric or even witchy. But

Adam had always loved her hair . . . Would there come a time when she'd have to cut it?

'Would you say I was a yummy mummy?' she asked him.

'God, no. No way,' Adam said.

'Oh. Thanks a lot.'

'Well . . . aren't they meant to be rather vacuous? I mean, you're much too intelligent.'

He hadn't meant to insult her, of course not. He just hadn't understood what she was asking, and she should have realized that he wouldn't.

It had been a silly question, but she couldn't explain herself without sounding ridiculously needy. Best Leave It: as useful a motto for marriage as Bless This House.

'You know, the thing that keeps you young is embracing new experiences,' Adam said.

Arghh, no! This could only be a veiled reference to the job in Argentina that he'd been offered a couple of months ago. He had been keen to go, but she had talked him out of it. She had no desire to leave her home, and uproot herself and the children.

She turned to smile reassuringly at him.

'I know it was a tough decision, but we definitely did the right thing staying put,' she said. 'If we'd gone overseas we would have been completely isolated and cut off from all our support.'

'You mean you wouldn't have Hannah to run round after you.'

Ouch! For a moment all she could do was stare at him. How could he imply that her sister was some kind of downtrodden Cinderella, exploited to provide domestic help? Hannah lived in the loft conversion virtually rent-free, and all that was expected in return was a little light babysitting. Adam knew as well as she did that now the children were older, the arrangement was much more for Hannah's benefit than for Lucy's.

Lucy had *rescued* Hannah. And now they were here, in the Forever House. And here they were going to stay.

Maybe she was beginning to lose her looks, but there was nothing tired or worn about her house. Take this room, for example: it was calm and bright and sweet, with lots of white wood and faded blue toile de Jouy. Not too chintzy, out of deference to Adam's masculinity.

'We have to put the girls first, and they're happy here,' she said.

'You can't pretend that my work and the welfare of this family are two separate entities,' Adam said. 'If you want me to carry on bringing home the bacon, you need to support my career.'

His expression was so sulky he suddenly struck her as looking like an aged boy, as if manhood had passed him by and he'd slipped straight from adolescence into the onset of middle-aged decline.

She glared at him. 'I do support your career – just not at the expense of this family. You think that because you're the breadwinner and we are your dependants, we have to do what you want.'

'No, I do not. I mean that what's good for me is good for all of us.'

Lucy turned her back to him and put the hairbrush

down in its place, next to the perfume he'd bought, together with matching shower gel and body lotion, for her last birthday. He had a knack for buying her presents that she liked – got ideas by flicking through her magazines. Never had to ask her what she wanted, and never got anything tacky. She'd always felt a bit sorry for Natalie, who had to give Richard a list.

Why was this desire for change surfacing now? She didn't really believe it was frustrated ambition. He worked hard, but he had always treated his career in marketing as a means to an end, a way of paying for the lives they had chosen: her home-making, the family holidays in the Dordogne or the Algarve or Puglia, the ski-ing trips with his buddies.

'Adam, is everything all right at work?' she asked, but she never got to hear his answer, because at that moment the bedroom door burst open and Clemmie, their assertive seven-year-old, appeared.

'Can't you bloody well learn to knock?' Adam shouted.

'Don't say bloody,' Clemmie said. 'Why are you still in bed, Daddy?'

'I was trying to have a lie-in. I suppose that's too much to ask for around here.'

'It probably is time to think about getting up, you know,' Lucy told Adam. 'Aren't you meant to be playing golf today?'

She took Clemmie by the hand, steered her out and let the door shut behind them.

Hannah was standing in the hallway, studying the whiteboard on which the day's activities were written

25

up, along with times, addresses and contact numbers.

'Did you have a nice evening?' Lucy said. 'I didn't hear you come in.'

'It was OK,' Hannah said, with a self-deprecating grimace.

She was taller and thinner than Lucy, with a short crop of hair that right now was sticking up every which way, as if she'd been dragged through a hedge backwards. Lucy sometimes felt matronly in comparison, but she reminded herself that Hannah's gamine attractiveness was at least partly to her credit.

Hannah was a chain-smoking degree dropout whose boyfriends, like her temping assignments, came and went. But since she'd been living with Lucy in Surrey, in an environment that was as villagey as you were likely to find this close to London, she'd lost the malnourished pallor of the city girl who drinks too much and sleeps too little, and had begun to bloom.

Lucy liked to think her children had something to do with that; they loved Hannah – sometimes, Lucy thought as Clemmie dropped her hand and bowled towards her aunt, almost knocking her over in her enthusiasm, a *little* too much.

Clemmie dragged Hannah into the family room, prattling about the game she wanted to play, and Lucy realized she'd have to get a move on if she wanted to get to Natalie's on time.

Poor old Natalie – Lucy still remembered all too clearly how awful it was getting through those last few weeks in the office, when you were huge and hormonal and bone-tired, and dreading the birth. When she had finished work to have Lottie, she'd thought, Never again – no way I'm going back. And she hadn't.

But it was all worth it in the end. She would love to have a third, if only Adam wasn't so dead set against it. It still wasn't too late – plenty of women hadn't even started their families at her age. Why, look at Natalie, just getting going with her first!

It would be such a treat to have a good long cuddle with little Matilda, when she finally arrived. Babies were so *uncomplicated*. Demanding, yes, and sometimes resistant too, but if they didn't want you to hold them, at least you didn't have to take it personally.

Natalie's house always reminded Lucy of the place they'd shared with Tina when they all first moved to London, before Lucy got together with Adam. Natalie now lived in the outskirts of Clapham rather than Brixton, but it was fundamentally the same three-bedroomed Victorian terrace, just better maintained and with the advantage of central heating.

As Lucy rang the doorbell she could hear Tina talking – except Tina didn't talk so much as deliver. Her voice wasn't posh, exactly, although it was certainly clear and carrying; it was more actressy – unhurried, almost languorous, with a precise, artfully modulated huskiness. It invited attention rather than demanding it, and then made you conscious of listening.

'I meant to be tongue in cheek,' Tina was saying. 'Some of the comments people have made online have been astonishingly vitriolic. I think "bitter old maid" has been about the most complimentary. Someone even posted me a turkey baster. Anonymously, of course. But what am I to do? I was told to write something about being single and childless at the age of thirty-five, and that's what I did. I'm damned if I'm going to go on about how bereft I feel every time I walk past a woman with a pushchair.'

Lucy knocked again, louder this time, and the door opened and Tina stood smiling in front of her.

Not for the first time, Lucy was pained to note that Tina's sharp, dewy prettiness was almost unmarked by time, and she still had the athletic trimness that follows a girlhood spent riding horses and playing tennis. She could just about have passed for a woman at the end of her twenties.

They embraced, and Lucy said, 'Why on earth did someone post you a turkey baster?'

'Because of this!' Natalie said, appearing in the hallway and brandishing a copy of the *Post*.

She looked enormous and swollen, but nevertheless brighter and more cheerful than Lucy had anticipated. They greeted slightly awkwardly – Natalie wasn't a fluent air-kisser, and her belly was a considerable obstacle.

Lucy handed over a pot of her home-grown hyacinths, and as Natalie and Tina admired them and praised her gardening know-how she said, 'Oh, I made these as well,' and fished a Tupperware box of freshly baked brownies out of her basket and passed that to Natalie too.

'You are the domestic goddess,' Tina said.

'The girls helped,' Lucy said, which wasn't strictly

true – they'd only shown an interest once the baking tray came out of the oven.

Then she reached out to take the *Post* from Natalie.

The first thing she saw was the name: Tina Fox, writ large. Next to it was a byline photo, in which Tina looked suitably foxy – sharp and sultry at the same time. She was smiling, but the effect was unnerving rather than friendly, as if she'd just spotted something live and edible, and was about to go for its neck.

There were a couple of hundred words of text, topped by the title of the column: 'The Vixen Letters'.

Lucy immediately had to suppress a stab of jealousy. It was quite unreasonable to mind that Tina had achieved this new success in a field she had long since abandoned.

'Wow! That's amazing – is this a regular column? Tina, why didn't you say anything?'

Tina shrugged. 'Wasn't sure till the last moment I was actually going to get it. I only got the chance because they're cost-cutting and ditching some of the free-lancers.'

'I'll have to have a good read in a minute,' Lucy said, folding the newspaper and tucking it under her arm.

Natalie ushered them into the living room and put the hyacinths next to a large vase of coral-coloured roses on the coffee table. Lucy guessed these were from Tina, as they were the only splash of colour in the room.

The decor was strictly minimalist – too much so, for Lucy's taste – hardwood floors, walls in different shades of off-white, beige blinds. It was all studiously neutral, to the point of feeling like a hotel rather than a home.

A baby, and the clutter that went with it, would do the place good – warm it up a bit.

Natalie started saying something about antenatal classes. Tina perched nervously on the sludge-coloured sofa, as if waiting for an audition, as Lucy settled into an armchair, opened up the newspaper and began to read.

The Vixen Letters

The vanishing women: a mystery story

Have you ever noticed how, soon after a woman tells you she's pregnant, she slowly begins to disappear? The bigger her bump, the closer she is to vanishing. First she stops drinking and smoking and going to parties and bars; she's no fun to go shopping with, since regular clothes no longer fit her, and she has no interest in admiring them on anyone else. If you phone her, make sure to do it before nine in the evening; she eats, she goes to bed early, she sleeps.

Then she goes on maternity leave, and before you know it she's moved out of the city and is going to coffee mornings in the suburbs, and insists that you call her only after the children's bedtime. There's no looking back; she's evangelical about her self-imposed exile – it's for the schools, you know, and the quality of life.

But is it really *her* life . . . or is it her children's? Next time you see her, they are all she'll have to talk about. So what happens when they're old enough to go to school? It will astonish you how much time and energy can go into picking out the right kind of flooring, the best bath taps, the perfect curtain fabric, not to mention dealing with architects and planners and workmen.

But perhaps this dedicated approach to domestic projects should come as no surprise. When a woman has vanished into motherhood, creating the ideal home is a great way for her to convince both herself and everybody else that she still exists.

At this point Lucy cast the paper aside in disgust.

'What happened to you?' she asked Tina.

Tina looked nonplussed. Natalie regarded Lucy with mild anxiety.

'There was a time when you would never have written anything like that. The old Tina was loyal,' Lucy said.

'It's just a series of general observations, exaggerated for comic effect. I didn't intend anyone to take it seriously,' Tina said.

'But it's obviously about me, all the way through,' Lucy said. 'Though maybe there's a bit of Natalie in there too.'

'Look, please, keep me out of this,' Natalie protested.

'Oh, stop sitting on the bloody fence!' Lucy said, and rounded on Tina again. 'Why do you have to be such a bitch? What gives you the right to look down your nose at me? I've got two children, a husband and a home to look after, and you know what? That's a lot harder work than sitting around in an office sipping lattes and occasionally flapping about deadlines. The problem is, you have no idea what it's like to be responsible for someone other than yourself. You know what? I feel sorry for you. I really do. You're on your own, you haven't got a man, and you're running out of time. Another couple of years and it'll be too late for you to have a baby even if you do meet someone!'

Tina stared at her in wounded, watery-eyed shock. Her lips twitched as if she would have liked to retaliate but was too close to crying to trust herself to open her mouth. She dropped her head into her hands and breathed in sharp bursts, as if struggling to restrain herself, then reached for her handbag – could that really be Hermès? Was that what thirty pieces of silver got you nowadays? – and rummaged for a handkerchief.

Then something even worse happened. Natalie snuggled up to Tina, put an arm around her, murmured something soothing and looked at Lucy accusingly.

'Oh go on, turn on the waterworks,' Lucy said automatically. It was what her mother had always said.

Natalie frowned. 'Lucy, please, give it a rest.'

Tina blew her nose and said, 'I'm sorry, I really didn't mean to offend anyone. I've been waiting for this opportunity for so long . . . I just felt I had to go for it.'

'Don't apologize,' Natalie said. 'You haven't done anything wrong.' She looked at Lucy significantly.

Lucy's fury was already beginning to ebb away, leaving behind the horrible feeling of having wildly overstepped the mark – possibly irretrievably. But how could this be? How could Tina have slagged her off (albeit under the disguise of impersonal commentary), and she, having merely stuck up for herself, end up in the wrongdoer's corner?

Yet she had made Tina cry – and Tina just didn't do tears. Natalie, yes, at pretty much any opportunity

– soppy films; weddings (both her own and other people's); one gin and tonic too many – but Tina: no. Not even about men, but then, as far as Lucy knew, she hadn't had a boyfriend since she was a student at Edinburgh, before they'd all met on their journalism course.

And as for what Tina had just written . . . how could anybody send up a friend like that and expect to get away with it?

'All I did was come out with a few home truths. Seems you can dish it out better than you can take it,' Lucy said. She got to her feet. 'I think I'd better go.'

'Oh, this is ridiculous,' Natalie said. 'Can't we all just calm down?'

'Are you going to ask her to go?' Lucy demanded. 'Because it doesn't look like it.'

'I want you both to stay,' Natalie said.

'I'm sorry, Natalie, but you can't please all of the people all of the time,' Lucy told her, and with that she took her leave.

When she got to the car and rummaged for her keys she realized her hands were shaking. God! What a terrible fuck-up. How could she have blown her top like that? But then, how could Tina have written that awful stuff about her?

Or . . . was she just being paranoid and neurotic and chippy? Over the years she and Natalie had helped Tina out with numerous ridiculous assignments, invariably with urgent deadlines. They'd road-tested blackhead strips, gone out and got drunk so Tina could write about what young women talked about down the pub (the reality had been much ruder than the published version), worn blonde wigs for a day to see if men paid them more attention (they did – but Tina, as a brunette, didn't get any less).

There had been an understanding between them that you backed each other up. Yes, Tina had called on her and Natalie more than they had called on Tina, but it wasn't exactly as if Tina's services were needed to enable Lucy to check stockists for a *Beautiful Interiors* photo shoot, or for Natalie to write about the latest early intervention initiative for underprivileged inner-city children. And Tina had been more than generous in return – there had been advance film screenings, goodies purloined from the beauty desk, and drinks in clubs that the other two didn't belong to and had never been invited to join.

Had Lucy just been guilty of taking the game too seriously? Had she read herself into something that Tina had probably put together in a half-hour flurry of desperation? Had she failed to give Tina the benefit of the doubt?

She was halfway to Thames Ditton by the time she realized she'd forgotten to give Natalie her third and final present: the little cushion she'd run up from an off-cut of the toile de Jouy fabric from her bedroom, filled with dried lavender from her garden. Oh well, she would have to post it.

It would be possible to make things right . . . wouldn't it?

It didn't occur to her to let Hannah know she'd be back early. By the time she turned on to the Green the awfulness of the visit had receded, as if it belonged to a different life. She had never been more pleased to see the little circle of prettily maintained Edwardian villas, facing each other across a round expanse of grass planted with cherry trees and silver birch.

Home! As soon as she let herself in she was struck by how welcoming and comfortable it was. The only thing that was missing was a pet – a plump tabby maybe, or a friendly red setter – and that was because Adam was allergic.

She put on her slippers and her feet sank into the hall carpet . . . so much nicer and cosier than Natalie's bare floorboards. She stuck her head round the door of the front room, but there was no sign of Hannah.

She went through to the kitchen. Her favourite part of the house: buttercup-yellow walls, William Morris curtains – lemon, lime and pomegranate – lots of pale oak, French windows leading into the garden, a sofa to one side, in what had once been a play area but was now clear of baby toys.

Still no Hannah.

She would have gone out to take Lottie to Stagecoach and Clemmie to her party, but she should have been back by now. Or had she popped out and neglected to double-lock the front door?

As Lucy started upstairs she heard an animal howl, like a cat doing battle.

She flung open the bedroom door. The smell of sex – visceral, dank, imperative, the opposite of sweet – assaulted her. If it hadn't been for that, she would scarcely have known what she was looking at was

35

real: it was like a scene from the sort of dream that left her feeling vaguely ashamed.

The scene was shocking, yes, but also had the dream-like quality of inevitable revelation.

Adam was fucking Hannah. Doggy-style, on the floor in front of the mirror.

'You stop that right now!' Lucy shouted.

Hannah yelped, and Adam saw Lucy standing behind them in the mirror. His face, which had been flushed and exultant, contorted painfully under the influence of two powerful and precisely opposed forces: the desire to stay exactly where he was and the desire to be a million miles away. He delivered one final, regretful thrust and then, as if with a wrenching effort, pulled out.

Hannah made a dash for the en suite. Lucy noted how smooth her little sister's body was – no stretch marks and no saggy belly. No pubic hair, either, a look that Adam had hinted he might appreciate, but Lucy had been reluctant to provide.

As if surveying a crime scene Lucy took in the steam in the air, the damp towel on the floor, the discarded clothes and the faint scent of her expensive shower gel, the one Adam had given her.

Hannah shut the bathroom door behind her, and Adam grabbed the towel and wound it round his waist, sarong-style. The effect was incongruously camp.

'You absolute fucking prick,' Lucy said.

It was a surprise to hear her own voice – it was a surprise that she was capable of something as everyday as speaking – though it didn't sound like hers: it was harsh and vicious.

He held out one hand to her, maybe to ward her off, or maybe in supplication.

'I'd ask you how long this has been going on . . . but I don't think I'd be able to believe you,' she said.

'It hasn't . . . it hasn't been going on.'

'What – are you going to tell me this isn't what it looks like?'

He stared at her in horror and in shame: it struck her that he would have looked at her in much the same way if he had accidentally killed her. But this had been no accident.

'How could you?' she said.

His face twisted with a spasm of remorse. 'I don't know. She was just there! All the bloody time! Why do you think I was so keen to go to Buenos Aires?'

'Are you in love with her?'

'No. No! No, I'm not – Lucy, you have to believe this, it's you I—'

'Of course. It was just sex. Right?'

'It was . . . it was confusing, that's all, I was confused . . .'

He sat down on the bed, and his back and shoulders slumped.

'Lucy,' he said, and he looked so pathetic now that a small part of her almost pitied him, 'I know I'm a shit and I've just done a terrible thing, but if you can't forgive me, if there isn't even the faintest possibility, I don't think I could bear it. Don't leave me. Please.'

'I'm not going anywhere,' she said, 'you are. Under the circumstances, I think it's the least you can do. I'm going down to the garden now. When I come back in, I want both of you gone.'

He struggled for a moment, then managed to get it out: 'What are you going to tell the girls?'

Lucy paused at the door. 'If you really cared about them,' she said, 'you might have tried to be a little less confused.'

And then she made her exit.

Moments later she was outside in the garden, in the weak spring sunshine. She had a sudden urge to lie down – to feel the earth underneath her, holding her up. And then she was on her back on the damp, cool grass, looking up at the thin clouds and the sky – toile de Jouy blue – and trying not to think about the scene inside the house, the recriminations, the panic, the packing. What would they take? What would be left?

If only Tina hadn't mouthed off in that silly column, if she'd just written about something else . . . But that was a ridiculous thing to think. It had happened, it couldn't be undone.

Somewhere in the house she heard a phone ringing. Oh God – what time was it? Was she late picking Clemmie up?

She checked her watch; it was midday. Clemmie's friend's birthday party didn't finish till one, so most likely it was Natalie, trying to smooth things over. Tina wouldn't – she'd leave it for a bit. Maybe indefinitely.

She would have to pull herself together. She couldn't go under. She had children to collect, washing to do, supper to sort out. She couldn't allow herself to go to pieces. She didn't have time.

What *was* she going to say to the girls?

2

Invitation to lunch

Just over a week later it was Natalie's turn to pick up a copy of the *Post* and see herself unflatteringly reflected in it.

She was on the tube, running late, and worried about how Richard would bear up if the antenatal class started without her. He had gamely signed up to accompany her to ten two-hour sessions, but she knew he was finding the experience intermittently excruciating.

Still, he'd manage. She took an abandoned copy of the *Post* from the seat next to her and leafed past the snaps of celebrity post-baby bodies in search of Tina's column.

The Vixen Letters

Outcast and outclassed

Friends, families, complete strangers, all tend to assume that I must want a ring on my finger and a reason to go to

Mothercare, and are disinclined to believe me when I assure them that I don't. It's a struggle for me to understand that others may yearn for what I so profoundly fear and mistrust, but I have forced myself to accept that other women are much more willing than I am to give up their freedom.

When friends tell me they're expecting – and we're all in our mid-thirties, so this happens a lot – I'm pleased for them, but I'm sad for myself. I can go on safari, loiter at a party or sign up for an improving evening class without a second thought, and if my friends were also still able to do all these things I'd be perfectly content. But once a woman has a baby on the way, the only courses she's interested in are antenatal.

Middle-class women, having got good grades and impressive degrees and professional qualifications their mothers could only dream of – having, in short, out-performed every previous generation of females going back to the dawn of time – tend to have faith in the power of swotting, and approach childbirth as if it were a particularly gruelling practical exam. They go to lessons, they read the books, they watch the videos and do the yoga – they put the work in, and hope it'll pay off. How disconcerting it must be when the gymslip mum down the corridor, whose CV is a desert of underachievement, pops out her offspring in half the time it takes for the ageing graduate to start begging for an epidural.

At this point Natalie folded the paper and put it back where she'd found it.

She didn't want to be annoyed with Tina . . . and she had a feeling that if she read any more, she would be. She knew she should be a good sport, take it with a pinch of salt and remember that Tina didn't mean any

40

harm. But still, she felt somewhat ridiculed. Exploited. Reduced. It wasn't nice to be boiled down to a couple of throwaway lines; to be not so much written about as written off.

No wonder Lucy had been so upset. Obviously Tina had touched a nerve; Lucy must have minded more about giving up work than she had let on. But was it really possible for any friendship to recover from the harsh words that Lucy had flung at Tina in response? *You're on your own, you haven't got a man, and you're running out of time* . . . Of course Lucy didn't know, and probably never would, that Tina had not really been single all these years. If Tina had told her what she was up to, would it have made any difference? If friendships thrived on closeness, not sharing the secret of a long-running love affair counted as a pretty major omission.

Anyway, Natalie was determined not to take sides. She'd always regarded her relationships with both women as perfectly balanced and even-handed, and she couldn't imagine her life without them both in it.

Tina was a passport to a world of members' clubs and gossip and people Natalie vaguely recognized off the telly, a hierarchical, restless, hive-like society in which she was content to watch Tina hold court, and play the mousy foil. Lucy's home territory was also alien, but softer; it was all about sewing costumes for the school play, icing fairy cakes for fêtes, and laying on white wine and nibbles for the Parent–Teacher Association.

Natalie had never felt she could cut it in either environment herself. Sampling someone else's life was all very well, and a change was as good as a rest; but she was much more comfortable pottering round at home with Richard, and trundling into work to compare cute mongoose screen savers with the junior press officer at the next desk.

It was unusual for Natalie to invite Tina and Lucy on to her patch – and look what had happened when she had. At least she'd had a sort of olive branch from Lucy: the little handmade lavender cushion that had turned up, without note or explanation enclosed, in the post a couple of days ago, even though Lucy hadn't returned any of her calls.

The cushion gave off a soft, gentle scent reminiscent of sunshine and bumble bees, and it was hard to reconcile it with the scary harpy who'd laid into Tina. The lack of other communication was definitely odd, and how things stood between Lucy and Tina Natalie didn't know.

She emerged from Clapham Common Underground Station into one of the first nice light evenings of spring. There was a queue spilling out of the posh organic butcher's on the corner, and as she lumbered round the tail end of it she barged straight into a tall blonde hurrying in the opposite direction.

Of all the people . . . It was Tina.

They both apologized and righted themselves. There was a brief mutual hesitation before Tina stepped forward to plant a respectful air kiss as close to Natalie's cheek as the bulge of Natalie's belly would permit, and Natalie let one arm rest lightly across Tina's back before withdrawing it.

Up close, Natalie noticed Tina's perfume, which was sharp, sweet and spicy all at once, grapefruit with a hint of pepper. Natalie wondered if her own smell would give her away. It was probably a combination of fetid Underground, and the raisin Danish and vanilla bean smoothie she'd scoffed on the way: hot and bothered, a little sickly and suggestive of comfort eating.

Tina was as slim and chic as ever, of course. She had on a tightly belted raincoat – designer, probably – whereas Natalie's tunic top and stretchy dress were long, large, and amorphously funereal. Clothes to hide in. Who was she trying to kid? Sure, black was slimming, but even black couldn't make you disappear.

Still . . . OK, she'd put on far too much weight and she was going to have a right battle to lose it all – just that morning she'd tipped the scales at 16 stone – but was there something rather brittle about Tina's thinness that she hadn't really registered before?

Obviously Tina had always been attractive – enough, once upon a time, to pique Natalie's interest in a way that had been confusing and ultimately not terribly helpful, though thankfully all that was well and truly in the past. But what had really appealed about Tina was her confidence, and right now she didn't look particularly at ease with herself. She looked tense, and even though she was smiling, the effect was not one of warmth.

Natalie was reminded of the sharp, rather predatory expression of the byline photo that went with the new column, and a quotation from one of the textbooks they had both studied more than a decade ago came to mind: *If a journalist offers to take you out for lunch, make no mistake, you're on the menu. Become a source, and sooner or later you'll be paying.*

'So how are you?' Tina asked. 'Have you finished work yet?'

'This is my last week.'

'And you're going to be off for how long, six months?'

'I'm planning on taking the full year. Actually, I'm not sure I'm going to go back to work at all, at least not while Matilda's little.'

As soon as this was out Natalie wished she hadn't said it. She hadn't actually discussed it with Richard yet, not as such, and she shouldn't discuss something so important with a friend before she'd been through it with him. Particularly not a friend she was feeling a bit annoyed with, thanks (but no thanks) to that snarky column.

She knew that if she made a halfway decent case for staying at home with Matilda, if she stressed the benefits of one-to-one care and the ludicrous cost of nursery fees and so on, Richard would listen, and ultimately he would agree. What made him uncomfortable was prevarication; she needed to know her own mind first, otherwise it would all end up with her getting worked up about nothing that either of them could explain, and him staring at her in anxious bafflement.

And she didn't really know what she wanted, not yet. She liked her job, more or less – she did, overall, believe in what the Department for Children, Schools and Families was trying to do, and if she was occasionally required to manipulate the facts for the sake of an effective press release, at least it wasn't in the interests of entertainment. There was no real reason why she should have this niggling feeling of having sold out – of being someone other than the person she'd become.

'Oh God, don't tell me you're going to go down the Lucy route,' Tina said. 'You can't. I'll kidnap you and make you come for cocktails.'

'Actually, I'm beginning to appreciate what Lucy's been doing all these years,' Natalie said. 'She put her family first, and now she's got it all: the beautiful home, the doting husband, the two lovely daughters. I think that's quite an achievement.'

'If that's what you want, I suppose it is,' Tina said.

'Have you been in touch with her?' Natalie asked.

'Oh . . .' Tina pulled a face. 'No. Have you?'

'I don't think she wants to talk to me either. Anyway, I should head off. Got an antenatal class to go to. You know what us middle-class mothers are like. Obsessed with swotting up for that all-important practical birth exam.'

She noted with some satisfaction that Tina was at a loss for words. The silence lasted long enough to convey the possibility of a distance opening up between them that neither would find easy to cross. Then, because she could never bear to let hostility hang in the air for long, Natalie came to the rescue by asking, 'So what are you up to tonight?'

Tina lifted up the carrier bag she'd been twisting round, and Natalie saw that it was from Freddlestone's Old-Fashioned Butchershop and contained a small package wrapped in paper, presumably an expensive cut of meat.

'Dinner date,' Tina said.

'Ooh,' said Natalie, 'the Grandee, I presume?'

Tina had never disclosed her married lover's real name. They had continued to refer to him by the silly nickname Tina had first given him in Cornwall all those years ago, when she had explained that he had a certain stature in public life, and his identity would have to remain a secret.

Recently she'd talked about him less and less. The last time she'd mentioned him had been to complain that she never got to see him at Christmas. Natalie, who found that pregnancy made her increasingly inclined to sympathize with all other mothers, including Mrs Grandee, had pointed out that it was only to be expected that he would want to spend it with his family.

'To tell you the truth, I've kind of wound that down,' Tina said, with a forced, ghastly smile that belied her attempt at bravado. 'I'm looking to replace him with a younger model. If it works out, I might even be able to introduce you to this one.'

'Oh God! You broke up with the Grandee? Really? But, Tina, are you OK? I thought you looked a bit . . .'

'A bit what? Down in the mouth? Not me. Us single ladies have plenty more fish in the sea, you know.'

'But – how come? What happened? Did he—'

'Nothing to tell – just fizzled!' Tina said. 'Anyway, I'd better dash. I'm not parked terribly legally.'

She moved in for the farewell kiss.

'Give my love to Richard, won't you? Great to see you!

46

Call me! Good luck with it all, if I don't see you before!'

As Tina moved away she looked back over one shoulder and waved: an airy, undulating little gesture that was simultaneously acknowledgement and dismissal, part salute, part wafting away.

Natalie checked her watch, and realized she was going to have to jog the rest of the way to the leafy side street where Bella Madden, the antenatal class teacher, lived in a large Victorian pile, testament to the success of her private midwifery practice.

Still, she'd never have to rush to the class again. By next week she would have finished work, she'd have nothing to do all day other than lounge round at home, and it would be easy to get there on time. Bliss!

Let Tina slave away at her career! She didn't look as if it was making her particularly happy, but then, she'd wasted ten years of her life on someone who was already taken. Whereas Natalie had worked at things with Richard, and now she was about to reap her reward: the chance to do something genuinely fulfilling with her life.

Motherhood. It was a fresh start, and with it would come new friends: friends who would know only the new, purposeful, capable, maternal, satisfied Natalie.

The end was in sight. Just a few more days to go, and just like Lucy before her, she would be free.

When she got to Bella Madden's she half expected to see Richard loitering nervously outside, but there was no sign of him. She rang the bell and he came to the door to let her in.

'You know what, I kind of wish you'd given it another quarter of an hour,' he murmured as they walked along the cool flagstone-floored corridor to join the class.

They stepped into the hushed conservatory, and she immediately saw what he meant. The other couples had arranged themselves in a loose semi-circle on the floor, and were looking at some bright, shiny, laminated pictures that Bella had cast down in front of them.

All of the images showed the same couple – a weary bearded man and a pregnant woman in a chevron-patterned leotard and leggings – bracing themselves against each other in a variety of testing and profoundly unerotic positions.

'Ah, Natalie,' Bella said carryingly. 'Great that you're here, Richard was just saying he might have to sit this one out. These are positions for labour, showing how the man can support the woman, whether you're in hospital or at home. So would everybody like to take one and give it a try for five minutes, and then swap round?'

Natalie spotted one that didn't look too gymnastic, and involved the woman leaning over a sofa while the man rubbed her back. She grabbed it and turned to Richard. He smiled at her resignedly.

'Well done. I should be able to manage that,' he said under his breath, and dragged a beanbag over to a corner so they could practise as unobtrusively as possible.

Bella Madden was a celebrity midwife – that was to say, she'd delivered the babies of a couple of well-known media personalities, and had grateful signed photo-graphs to prove it. Bella herself looked like Everygran with a thyroid problem; she had curly, stiffly set iron-grey hair, and slightly protuberant, mud-coloured eyes. She was always dressed in readiness for a birth, in com-fortable slacks and tops in pastel polyester, in case one of her clients called.

Unlike her students, she was never disgusted, or defensive, or afraid; she spoke about pregnancy, labour and birth with robust enthusiasm. She was both experienced and knowledgeable, but the real source of her authority was her complete lack of embarrass-ment.

Each class followed a pattern. After the introductions and how-are-you-alls, there was usually some kind of demonstration in the first half-hour, perhaps involving pictures or gynaecological models. A group discussion exercise followed, to lighten the mood and encourage bonding before the mid-session coffee break. The second half usually involved the sharing of empowering medical information, intended to dispel any fears raised by the first.

Natalie hadn't yet made a direct overture of friend-ship to any of the other women – she usually preferred to watch and wait, and let others make the first move. Anyway, she suspected that her favourite, the one she was most interested in watching, was the one least likely to buddy up with her.

At the first meeting Bella had asked them to introduce themselves and suggest some way that other people could remember their names. The woman sitting next to Natalie said, 'I'm Adele. Like the illegitimate dancer's daughter in *Jane Eyre*, the one Jane teaches, the silly little vain girl who likes pretty dresses.'

Natalie had always loved *Jane Eyre* – it was her favourite book – and found this instantly memorable. (She and Richard had failed to come up with any neat ways for people to remember them.)

At thirty-two, Adele was the baby of the group, and she was good-looking, in an unhealthy way – she was pale and often looked tired. Still, Natalie admired her Slavic cheekbones, suggestive mouth, heavy dark-blonde hair, and thin, expressive hands.

Adele was sometimes thoughtful, sometimes flamboyant; she alternated between preoccupied silence and little outbursts that left everyone slightly uneasy. Unlike all the other women in the group, she was unmarried. Her partner, a quiet, stoic older man called Marcus Pryce, rarely spoke, and listened to her without showing any obvious sign of discomfort or embarrassment. Was this acceptance or detachment? Natalie found it impossible to tell.

The group's due dates were scattered throughout April, with Natalie second to last, followed only by Adele. But the day after the positions-for-labour exercise Natalie was sitting at her desk at work, eating the first of her sandwiches, when an email from Adele turned up. The subject line was Paris.

Paris Pryce. Beautiful baby boy born South London Hospital this morning weighing 8lb 3oz.

How could that be? The night before, she'd been trying to imitate the chevron-leotard lady just like the rest of them, but less than twenty-four hours later, Adele had somehow had her baby.

Adele didn't appear at the next class to shed light on this, nor at the next, but sporty Jessie Oliver, who had emerged as the unofficial group leader, reported that Adele had given birth entirely naturally, in five hours from start to finish, and with no pain relief whatsoever.

This news generated a frisson that struck Natalie as being charged with both jealousy and admiration. She wasn't sure whether the reaction was a response to Adele's fabulous birth experience, or to the strange fabulousness of Adele herself.

In the taxi on the way home she said to Richard, 'It was funny the way all the women talked about Adele during the coffee break today, wasn't it? It reminded me a bit of being out with Tina when someone famous would come into the bar, and everybody sat up and took notice. It's like Adele's the celebrity of antenatal group.'

Richard glanced at her warily. 'I suppose she is the sort of person that people pay attention to.'

'Good heavens! Do you know, you're actually blushing – I do believe you fancy her!'

Richard adjusted his glasses. 'Just because I can see how other people react to her, doesn't mean I feel the same way,' he said. 'She seems a bit unpredictable to me, and maybe lacking in the common sense department. If you ask me, Paris is a silly name, especially for a boy, and I have a feeling it was probably her idea. You're not thinking of making a particular friend of her, are you?'

'I don't think she's the least bit interested,' Natalie

said. 'She probably barely knows who I am. I'm just gutted that she's gone and done it. She was meant to be after me. It means I'm probably going to be the last.'

Richard squeezed her hand. 'It's not a race.'

When they got home he ran her a bath, and made some pasta which they ate while listening to the special compilation of Mozart and Brahms they'd bought to play to Matilda, because babies at her stage of gestation were meant to be able to hear quite clearly from inside the womb.

But it didn't lull Matilda; she kicked and thrashed around as if she was wholly fed up of being cooped up inside. It didn't entirely soothe Natalie, either.

The course of sessions with Bella came to an end, the pace of arrivals quickened, and the couples started taking it in turns to host meetings. Natalie and Richard went to a gathering at the Olivers' flat in Herne Hill, which had wall-mounted bikes and an abandoned dumb-bell by the sofa. The small sitting room was filled with proud, exhausted, relieved parents and newborn babies. Natalie felt like a convict who had not yet been vouchsafed a release date, while all around her were former fellows who had already been reprieved.

The rest of that week crawled past. Every day was Groundhog Day, a day Natalie hadn't planned for and didn't know what to do with; the leisure she'd so looked forward to turned out to be an anxious limbo. How the hell was she ever going to muster the energy to give birth? She had not so much slowed down as ground to a halt.

Her due date finally arrived: 27 April – Tina's birthday. Natalie sent a card, but decided not to call – just for once, Tina could ring her. But there was no response. Clearly there was no real reason to remember the date, either for the sake of a fading friendship, or for failing to become her first child's birthday.

A midwife examined her and said it would not be possible to give her a cervical sweep; she was so far from beginning to dilate she hadn't even softened up. Natalie imagined her cervix shut up tight, unyielding, stubborn and petrified. *No way is that thing coming through here.* Nature doing its damnedest not to let nature take its course.

The next antenatal group meeting was due to take place that evening at Adele's Battersea mansion flat. Over her solitary lunch in the silent house, Natalie realized that she couldn't bring herself to go.

She would be the only one who hadn't yet had her baby. She was about to be overdue. She was heading straight for the cascade of interventions that the woman who wants a natural birth must at all costs avoid.

She rang Adele and left a message saying she was very tired and couldn't make it.

The next morning the phone rang and she didn't recognize the number. She picked up, thinking it might be a midwife or hospital administrator.

It was Adele.

'I just wanted to see if you were OK.'

So out of the five other women, it was Adele who had volunteered for the job of following up on Natalie's absence.

'Yes, I'm fine, just a bit fed up waiting,' Natalie said.

'We missed you,' Adele said. 'I've got lots of food left over from last night. Why don't you come for lunch?'

'Oh no, I don't want to intrude.'

'Just come round. You don't have to stay long. It would be nice to see you. I made pavlova, and hardly anybody ate it.'

There was almost nothing Adele could have said that would have been more persuasive. Eating had become Natalie's primary, indeed almost her only, source of physical pleasure – yes, there had been an attempt at sex the other night, with poor Richard toiling under the obligation of trying to induce labour; but that had been inconclusive on both sides, and so hardly counted.

Also, she could never bear to spurn a gesture of friendship. If Adele, with a three-week-old baby, had found the energy to make pavlova, then Natalie had a moral duty to at least give it a try.

'OK,' she said. 'I'll be there at one.'

As she hung up she felt unexpectedly purposeful.

This was what she needed. This was distraction. This might even be *fun*.

When she got to the mansion block where Adele and Marcus lived, she took a moment to lean on the marble reception desk and catch her breath. She had regretted her decision to walk almost as soon as she'd set off. It wasn't far, but she'd been trudging along for more than half an hour.

'I'm here to see Adele Lowe,' she told the concierge.

'Fourth floor,' he said, inclining his head towards the

lifts; his eyes moved over her without registering her presence. She was reminded of what Tina had said: *The bigger her bump, the closer she is to vanishing.*

The lift had a mirror in it. No wonder the concierge hadn't paid her much attention: she was big-bellied to the point of sexlessness. She tried to ignore her reflection from the neck down and concentrated on smoothing her hair.

When she stepped out Adele was coming along the hallway towards her. Her hair was loosely bundled back, and she was wearing a man's plaid shirt, paint-splattered jeans and flip-flops; the red varnish on her toenails was thoroughly chipped, as if she'd applied it in a concession to feminine grooming, then decided to make a point of neglecting it.

She held out her hand and, almost without hesitation, Natalie took it. Adele's touch was dry and cool, and somehow unembarrassing, so Natalie only briefly worried about the potential stickiness of her own.

'Come on in,' Adele said, and led her towards number 21. The door was wide open and beyond it was a corridor, painted white and decorated with dark wooden carvings and large framed prints of mono-chrome photographs: women's noses or bare shoulders next to rotund bits of sculpture, a feathered mask next to a high-heeled dance sandal, a lone tree on a stark cliff edge, that kind of thing. All very arty.

Natalie followed Adele into a sleek kitchen that appeared to have been designed by someone who thought storage solutions were the key to domestic bliss. The only item standing on the glossy white worktop was a gleaming kettle. It was an unfriendly triangular shape, the lid a sharp peak. There was an immense array of cupboard doors, all shiny and cherry-red, devoid of handles and unmarked by fingerprints.

Richard liked tidiness, and Natalie, who was inclined to clutter, had got used to putting things away, but surely this was extreme.

'Take a seat. Do tuck in, everybody brought stuff and we're never going to get through it all,' Adele said, gesturing towards the table in the centre of the room. Made of pale, solid wood, it looked to Natalie like a giant chopping-block on legs, spread with a mad-woman's midnight feast: breadsticks, strawberries, Kettle chips and taramasalata vying with fudge brownies, prosciutto, tabbouleh and Adele's pavlova, which had, indeed, barely been touched.

Natalie started spooning tabbouleh on to a white plate. She felt Adele's eyes flicker over her featureless, bone-obscuring fatness, but carried on helping herself anyway.

The baby wriggled vigorously inside her, then was still.

'Where's Paris?' Natalie asked between mouthfuls.

'Asleep. He sleeps almost all the time – it's fantastic. I've managed to get so much done.'

Like what? Natalie thought, but didn't ask.

Adele sat down opposite her and popped a straw-berry in her mouth, sucked, and swallowed delicately.

'So how are you?' she asked.

Natalie shrugged. 'One way or another, by this time next week it'll all be over.'

'You'll be fine. I mean, it's excruciating – I could never have imagined being in so much pain. It's animal. The sound of women giving birth!' Adele gestured expansively with both hands. 'But you feel very alive. It's very dramatic.'

'Anything's got to be better than hanging round waiting,' Natalie said, and wondered if this was true.

'How are you?' she went on. 'How's the breastfeeding going?'

'It's good,' Adele said. 'It takes up a lot of time – hours and hours! But you can find ways of getting on with things.'

'What, like watching box sets of *Friends*?' Natalie said.

'I don't watch television,' Adele told her. 'I never had one before I moved in with Marcus.'

'Really? How long ago was that?' Natalie said, feeling rather daring, as it was the first time she had asked Adele such a direct personal question, on a subject only indirectly related to maternity.

'Six months ago. We've only known each other for a year,' Adele said.

'Gosh. That sounds very whirlwind.'

'It was reckless,' Adele said. 'I don't think Marcus ever expected to share his flat with a baby and a painter. If he had he wouldn't have chosen white carpet.'

'Oh, you paint?'

'I do. Yes. As much as I can.'

'Is any of your work up on the walls?'

'No,' Adele said, and something about her expression stopped Natalie from asking why not.

57

Natalie attempted some small talk about the other members of the antenatal class, but made little headway; Adele didn't appear to feel obliged to keep the conversation going, and seemed to be happy to sit by quietly while Natalie ate. She gave Natalie a fresh bowl for the pavlova; Natalie tucked in, and then looked up to see Adele watching her with a mischievous smile – the first time there had been any suggestion of teasing in the other woman's behaviour.

'You like to eat, don't you?' Adele said.

'I'm not usually this much of a pig,' Natalie said. 'I've just been ravenous ever since I got pregnant.'

'You'd be wonderful to paint,' Adele said. 'Lots of flesh. Like a Lucian Freud. You should be reclining on a sofa like an odalisque.'

'Well, like I said, there isn't usually this much of me.'

'Have you got photographs?'

'God, no.'

'You should get Richard to take some.'

'I don't think Richard would want to photograph me,' Natalie said.

'Why not?'

Natalie shrugged. 'I can't say I blame him.'

Adele stood up and started moving dishes into a cavernous fridge. 'Come through to the living room and I'll draw you.'

'Oh! No, it's very nice of you, but I should be getting back.'

'You can keep your clothes on, if that's what you're worried about.'

'But I'm wearing a tent.'

'Take it off then.'

'But I'm covered in stretch marks.'

Natalie had never been particularly proud of her body, but at least prior to pregnancy it had been free of scars. Now pink lashings snaked across her hips, breasts and thighs, textured like pastry pulled to the point of rupture.

'Imperfections are what make people interesting,' Adele said.

She closed the fridge and walked off without looking back, and Natalie found herself following her.

She sat for Adele for twenty minutes. The time passed slowly, as it does when one is required to be still, but not tediously; the experience was too novel, too intimate and too gratifying.

Natalie lay on the sofa in the sitting room, naked, propped up on cushions, one arm curved around her jutting belly, which was hard, moon-white and smooth as stone. She had never undressed fully in front of another woman, yet she had not felt awkward or embarrassed. Weirdly, she had felt proud – proud of her own daring; and, stranger still, she had felt relieved.

She had slept badly for weeks now, and was comfortable enough to doze, but Adele's eyes, darting from Natalie back to her drawing and back to Natalie again, made that impossible. It was an impersonal process, scientific, analytical, almost mechanical. Of course it was flattering. How could it not be? To be worthy of such scrutiny, to merit recording? Each glance was an affirmation, and Natalie's skin tingled and glowed as if emerging from obscurity into the cumulative caress of dozens of pinpricks of light.

An hour later, carrying a rolled-up tube of sugar paper secured with masking tape, Natalie stepped into the back of the taxi Adele had called for her.

She felt drunk, or drugged. She'd spent the morning asleep; when the alarm had gone off she'd resisted the summons to wakefulness for as long as she could. She'd been resentful, groggy, sedated. Now she was still out of it, but she didn't feel at all like sleeping.

The taxi drew up outside her house within minutes and she gave the driver a tenner and told him to keep the change. He hadn't tried to talk to her, hadn't broken the spell; that in itself deserved rewarding.

She let herself into the empty house. Richard wouldn't be back for hours. What to do? She stuck Adele's drawing in the back of the wardrobe and ran a bath.

She just fitted in it. Her belly reared up in front of her, enormous, slippery, unavoidable. She couldn't see her crotch. But it was still her body; under occupation, but unsurrendered. She knew it could still be forced into pleasure, in spite of the ordeal that was looming.

Natalie got out and dried herself and hung the towel over the rail to dry. She went into the bedroom and hung back from the window as she pulled the curtains. She sat on the edge of the bed, and then carefully lowered herself down on one elbow until she was lying on her side. She closed her eyes and imagined herself thin, light, supple and implacably erotic.

3

Overlooked

One by one, all of Tina's longstanding office buddies had married eligible men and stopped working at the *Post*. Each one, on leaving, had said, 'I'll miss you,' and Tina occasionally wondered if they ever did.

She certainly missed all of them, but it was necessary to adapt, and so, when her thirty-sixth birthday passed without a card from her colleagues landing on her desk, she told herself it was no surprise; why should anybody remember? It wasn't as if she'd publicized the occasion. What was the point of making a big deal about getting older?

Anyway, a couple of days later there would be another, arguably more important milestone to celebrate: the tenth anniversary of her first day in the office. She knew that wouldn't go by unmarked. Her boss had sent out a department-wide email in advance, suggesting that they commemorate the occasion with a lunchtime drink.

On the morning of the big day she got in at a quarter to nine, the optimum, irreproachable time, just in case anybody who mattered was paying attention. Not so early as to suggest mental derangement, but a safe, professional distance from being late. As she pushed through the revolving doors she felt light years removed from her younger, less certain self, who had passed through this same entrance ten years ago with her heart in her mouth, terrified of making some appalling blunder that would result in her being sent back into the outside world before the day was out, never to return.

The older and wiser Tina Fox had a decent suit and handbag, good shoes, her own column, and a degree of confidence in her ability to cope with whatever the day might have to throw at her. She had not only survived, she'd thrived, while her peers had fallen by the wayside – well, the women among them had, at any rate.

The lobby was in the process of being tarted up, and smelt strongly of fresh paint. The workmen were adding the finishing touches, hanging framed editions of notable front pages on the walls. An older colleague of Tina's, Anthea Trask – a willowy *Post* veteran who'd had five children and still had the figure of a girl – had pointed out that it was usually a sign of trouble when an organization started doing up its reception area. But Tina thought Anthea's scepticism was unfounded. The *Post*'s testy, grumbling persona had such a well-established place in national life that it was impossible to imagine it being abandoned by its readers and falling on hard times.

As she headed towards the lift the front page mounted

on the adjacent wall caught her eye. 'Women warned: "Don't wait to have babies". Scientists reveal fresh insights into the fertility time bomb'.

That was one of the great contradictions at the heart of the *Post* – it liked to give mothers a hard time, especially those who were single, working or in any way removed from a hazy 1950s ideal of domestic bliss, but at the same time, it was uneasy about women who weren't mothers, and it particularly didn't like young females to disport themselves too freely, without fretting at least a little about the potential consequences of their actions.

It occurred to Tina that she had been effectively set up – that if she used her column to acknowledge the downsides of being a thirtysomething spinster, she'd look like a loser, and however much she advocated the joys of the single, childfree life, in the end it would all just come across as so much special pleading. Her readers would conclude that she was lonely and jealous of her more fecund friends, as the letters and online comments she'd received so far had tended to suggest.

It was only then that she noticed Dan Cargill, her office sparring partner, occasional rival and, unfortunately, one-time lover, standing with his back to her and waiting for the lift. Up until that drunken night a couple of weeks ago she would have gone up to him and teased him about the pattern on his tie, or the report about Snookums the baby elephant he'd had in the paper the previous day, or about being in early for once. But she had made a mistake, and now she was just going to have to avoid him.

Even as she veered away she noted the details of his

appearance that most irritated her. Which was worse: the unpolished shoes, the lightly creased chinos, or the rumpled, quite possibly unwashed hair? No, surely the chief offender had to be the jacket, which was one Dan wore often. It was an indeterminate shade of brown reminiscent of nicotine-stained pub walls, its bulging pockets doubtless crammed with notebooks and cigarettes and recording devices.

He was just such a *hack*. Not much of a successor to the Rt. Hon. Justin Dandridge QC, MP (Con.) for Wellerby South and Shepstowe. Justin had always been so dapper – so impeccably well groomed, with his three-piece suits and handmade brogues . . .

How on earth had she let down her guard enough to cry on Dan's shoulder – let alone to tumble into bed with him? Thank God she'd at least retained the self-discipline not to tell him exactly why she was so upset. She didn't imagine for one minute that he would have treated pillow talk as confidential information. If she'd given him even the faintest hint that she'd just emerged from a long-running affair with a married MP, he'd almost certainly have seen it as an opportunity to coax the whole story out of her and write it up as a dazzling exclusive.

She hurried away from him towards the stairs and up towards their office on the third floor, taking the steps two at a time. Honestly, what was the point in getting in early if you couldn't even beat Dan Cargill to it? If he was raising his game, she would just jolly well have to raise hers too. After all, she was the one who had survived the *Post*'s restless newsroom politics, backstabbing and power struggles for a whole decade, and had earned the cachet of her own column. Whereas Dan had only showed up a year ago, fresh from a stint on a medical trade mag; not long before that he'd been covering stories about parking and rubbish collection for a local rag in the West Country. She was an old hand; he was virtually an ingénue.

Which made it all the worse that she had inadvertently slept with him . . . and then, adding insult to self-injury, had deluded herself into thinking that their obviously doomed encounter might be the beginning of a viable relationship! What a fool she'd been . . . inviting him over to dinner, and even going so far as to tell Natalie that she'd met somebody new.

Some date it had turned out to be. They'd barely started on the steaks before Dan began to quiz her about how long she'd worked at the *Post*, and where she'd been before that. She'd filled in the chronology for him happily enough – she'd even been grateful that someone was finally showing an interest in her career. But then, as he continued to press for detail, alarm bells had started ringing, and she'd challenged him: 'Dan, if you want to know how old I am, why don't you just come out with it and ask me?'

'Because that would be rude,' he'd said.

'Why? Do you think I'm old enough for it to be a touchy subject? How old do you think I am?'

'Twenty-eight,' Dan had said without missing a beat.

'Oh, spare me – I'm thirty-five.'

'Really? You look younger.'

She could almost hear the cogs turning: *So she's*

panicking about her fertility, in thrall to her biological clock;
she'll be pushing for at least cohabitation, or preferably
insemination, within six weeks of starting a relationship . . .
tick-tock, tick-tock . . .

'How about you?' she'd asked.

'Me? Thirty-three.'

Then he'd made an awkward crack about cougars,
and she had cleared the table and rolled a cigarette
and he had lit up too, and they had both sat there
smoking and silently cringing. The conversation hadn't
really recovered, and by the time they finished coffee
it was clearly game over. She could see it in his eyes:
the nervousness, the reluctance, the desire to let her
down gently, and then he'd made his excuses (an early
start the next day, to report on a conference about
osteoporosis) and left.

Which was really a blessing in disguise. What if he'd
started snooping? He was a journalist, after all; he was
bound to be nosey. Given half a chance he'd probably
have gone through her drawers, or rummaged in the
wardrobe, and could she really trust him to be discreet
about anything he might find? What if he'd come across
something that could have led him to Justin?

No – if she was going to get together with anyone,
it would have to be someone who was less inclined to
ask questions. So it was just as well that it was all over
before they'd really had a chance to get started.

The only saving grace was that, as far as she was
aware, he hadn't told anyone else at work about their
one-night stand. She certainly hadn't noticed anybody
looking at her differently, or suddenly going quiet when

she turned up in the canteen or approached the water cooler – but if that were to change, she'd make sure that Dan regretted it. Hell hath no fury like a woman spurned – especially if she's spurned because she's deemed too desperate to make use of her ageing ovaries.

She went into the newsroom and saw that her mad dash up the stairs had paid off; Dan was not yet at his desk. She settled down in front of her PC, turned it on and opened her desk diary to peruse her to-do list. A moment later Dan came in. But instead of slouching past her as if she didn't exist, as had become his habit in the fortnight since Agegate, he trudged slowly towards her, as if struggling to make his way through an invisible force field, and came to a halt facing her, for all the world as if he expected her to actually stop what she was doing and talk to him.

Whatever next! He was clearly about to attempt an exchange of words! She looked him up and down with all the superiority she could muster.

'Morning, Vixen,' he said, and attempted a smile.

Oh God, why did he have to go and call her that? It had been Justin's pet name for her – she'd suggested using it as a title for the column as a sort of private joke, hoping that when he glanced through the paper he'd notice it, and be touched, perhaps, or amused, or even a little bit impressed. But no – he'd just become even more preoccupied and unavailable, until she'd finally lost her temper and presented him with an ultimatum. Surprise, surprise, when it came down to it, Justin had opted to stay with his wife, who also happened to be the mother of his children.

Dan waggled his fingers at her as if attempting to break her out of a trance. 'Hello, earth to Tina? "The Vixen Letters" is the name of your column, right? I haven't just walked into some alternate reality where it's called something completely different?'

She scowled at him to let him know he'd been too familiar. Truth to tell, when he said it, she wasn't sure if she liked it. It sounded kind of hard and trampy. Not much like anything worth giving chase to.

'What can I do for you, Dan?' she asked.

'Well, uh, I know things have been kind of awkward the last few weeks and I . . . wondered if you were free at lunchtime, if I could buy you a coffee, or maybe even a sandwich as well, and we could kind of smooth things over.'

'Sorry, I have plans.'

'Oh come on, Tina. Just ten minutes, that's all I'm asking.'

'I'm going to be in the Queen's Head, celebrating my ten years at the *Post*. Jeremy emailed everyone about it last week – perhaps you overlooked it. Maybe I'll see you there.' She glanced at her watch to let him know she had made a major concession just by hearing him out this far, and was really much too busy for any further discussion.

'Oh. Right. Yeah, I remember. Congratulations.'

He was about to turn and move on and she really should have left it there, but she couldn't resist making a parting shot. 'Yes, well, us wizened thirty-six-year-olds have to make the most of our meagre causes for celebration.'

'I guess you do,' he said, and walked on.

Tina glanced down at her notepad, and the list of questions she'd put together to ask the woman she was due to phone any minute now. She knew she needed to focus. Nevertheless, she found herself watching Dan as he trudged towards his desk, which was just as messy and disorganized as you'd expect. Probably a health hazard. He obviously wasn't looking where he was going – hungover? – because he almost walked straight into the fresh-faced Scottish girl who'd just started working on the features section.

Tina had bonded with Julia McMahon, or so she thought. They'd had a chat about Edinburgh University, which Julia had graduated from a decade after Tina, and Tina had hoped that Julia might make a suitable protégée, someone she could take under her wing. She needed a lunch-break pal to take the place of the colleagues who had abandoned her for well-to-do husbands and new lives growing organic vegetables in Norfolk, or bonding with other bankers' wives in Zurich, or making hats in Bath.

There was no doubt that Julia was luscious: she had flawless milkmaid skin and long, thick, heavy, shiny, coppery-red hair, and up until this point Tina had admired these attributes. But as Julia smiled up at Dan her friendly feelings immediately dissolved.

How irritating! Just look at her, batting her eyelashes and shaking out her hair, as if reassuring Dan that he would be perfectly welcome to walk into her any time he wanted to! She might as well just wrap herself up in a big red ribbon and invite him to untie it. Some women were so . . . so unsubtle! Hadn't she figured out that you had to be careful about these things? That an overt flirtation with a colleague was a surefire way to turn yourself into a laughing-stock? Hadn't she realized that Dan, the jack-of-all-trades newshound, was much too low in the office hierarchy to be worth making a play for? Oh well, Julia would learn, by the time she got her marching orders if not before. These young women – they were all so clueless! They all carried on as if they still believed, deep down, that a man really could be the solution to all of life's problems!

Tina forced herself back to her list of interview questions and got ready to make the call. At the other end of the line, a tired female voice said, 'Hello, hello?' as a baby wailed in the background. As Tina introduced herself and reminded the woman about the article she was writing, everything that had bothered or annoyed or troubled her that morning – Dan, Justin, the flirty redhead, the *Post*'s falling circulation, the response to the Vixen Letters, her 36-year-old reproductive system, being single for real after all those years of being surreptitiously attached – all of it just disappeared, like so much audience chitchat silenced by the clarity of a lone performer stepping out on to a stage and beginning to speak.

The interview was for an article about tokophobia: fear of giving birth. This was a new subject for Tina, who had written various articles over the years about the cost to the NHS of women who were too posh to push, but nothing at all about women who were too scared to. When she'd wound up the call and was look-ing through her notes, she was prompted to think of Natalie for the first time that day.

She wasn't feeling great about how she'd left things with Natalie – their last, chance meeting had been kind of weird. Natalie had been pretty grumpy for someone who never usually had a sharp word to say about anyone: *You know what us middle-class mothers are like. Obsessed with swotting up for that all-important practical birth exam . . .*

And the last time they'd got together properly had been a disaster, thanks to Lucy: *Another couple of years and it'll be too late for you to have a baby even if you do meet someone!* Obviously Lucy had been way out of line, but after she'd stormed off, Natalie had attempted to rationalize her behaviour, and had reminded Tina about the thin time of it Lucy had had growing up and the great job she'd jacked in to devote herself to family life. Tina had ended up feeling bad, even though she was the one who'd been attacked.

Natalie's due date had fallen on Tina's birthday, at the beginning of the week. Natalie had sent a card, in which she'd written *Still waiting.* And probably she still was . . . but what if she wasn't?

It could have all kicked off: the baby could be on the way that very moment. Natalie had seemed to have everything under control, what with the assertively written birth plan and the antenatal lessons and the books. She'd certainly done her homework. But when it came to the point of being put to the test, would any of that make any difference?

Natalie's predicament continued to niggle at Tina over the next couple of hours. It was no good – not knowing what was going on was making it impossible for her to concentrate properly. She decided to give Natalie a quick ring and set her mind at rest; if Natalie was there and able to speak to her, then all well and good . . . and if not, like Natalie herself, she would just have to wait.

Tina took her personal organizer out of her bag to check for Natalie's number. Dan had teased her for storing her diary and contact numbers in such a hide-bound format, but Tina liked to have things written down and tucked away. If Justin hadn't had a knack for writing persuasive love letters, she doubted whether their relationship, with its ongoing restrictions and frequent separations, would have lasted as long as it did.

The phone rang for a while before Natalie answered, sounding groggy and half asleep.

'Hello?'

'Natalie! You're there!' Tina exclaimed. 'I was doing this article and it made me think of you and I just had to call. How are you? Is everything all right?'

'If you're phoning to see if I've had it yet, the answer's no,' Natalie said.

'Oh well, I'm sure it won't be long . . . I didn't wake you up, did I?'

Natalie sighed. 'You did,' she said, 'but never mind. How are you? Did you have a nice birthday?'

'Actually, it was pretty crap,' Tina said. 'I ended up staying in and watching telly.'

'You should have come round,' Natalie said, 'we could have watched it together. So have you made peace with Lucy yet?'

'Er, no.' Tina had half hoped that Lucy might get in touch on her birthday, but she hadn't. 'Why is it up to me, anyway?'

Natalie sighed. 'Aren't we a bit old for all this? You've been friends since 1995. Don't you think you should try and sort it out?'

'I will, I will. I've just been kind of busy, what with one thing and another.'

'Oh yeah, the new man. How's that going?'

'Badly,' Tina said. 'I think he likes someone else.'

'And you like him?'

'Well . . .'

'Do you?'

'He's not bad-looking,' Tina conceded. 'But he has a horrible brown jacket.'

'Oh, for goodness' sake, that's hardly a deal-breaker. Learn to love it, or buy him a new one for Christmas. Have you tried actually talking to him?'

'I think it might be too late.'

'Tina, I'm the one who's too late,' Natalie said. 'If I haven't gone into labour by the middle of next week, I have to go into hospital to talk about being induced, which is not how I wanted this to turn out. They'll let me go a fortnight late, and then that's it.' She sighed. 'Anyway. I'd better let you go.'

And then she was gone. It was unlike her to be so terse, but perhaps this was a good sign. Perhaps she had somehow acquired extra reserves of feistiness that would help her get through the approaching ordeal, and emerge restored to her usual gentle, mild-mannered self.

Tina was about to close her personal organizer and put it away when it occurred to her that she might have forgotten something. Something important.

She turned to the diary section and flicked back to the end of March: 20 March was marked by a small red cross. The next week, there had been various evening engagements: the launch of the Dunmore Gallery summer season; the opening night of that Rattigan revival; cocktails in the Oxo Tower with a bunch of telly people.

28 March: Natalie – what a disaster that had turned out to be. 30 March: G. Diary code for the Grandee – Justin. Their last night – an awful, lacklustre conclusion to so many years of hopeful anticipation . . .

The entry for 3 April said: hygienist 8.00 a.m. She distinctly remembered that her gums had still been tender as she sat nursing her gin and tonic in a corner of the Queen's Head after work, and looked up to see Dan coming towards her.

27 April: her birthday. A Monday. She'd planned a quiet drink with an actress friend, but had been stood up – something to do with a shoot for a toothpaste commercial overrunning.

Today's date was 29 April. Which meant she was nearly two weeks late.

Someone cleared his throat, and she looked up from the incriminating diary pages to see Jeremy, the opinion and comment editor and her boss, wearing an unnatural smile and reaching across her desk to present her with a small envelope.

Jeremy was a little terrier of a man who compensated for his lack of stature by barking at people as frequently and aggressively as possible. When she first started working for him Tina had been continually on edge, but she'd come to realize that he was quick to move on and growl at the next hapless passer-by, and there was something to be said for having a boss with a short attention span, who didn't always hang on to your mistakes.

It was Justin who'd advised her on how to handle Jeremy – *someone like that may be tough on you, but if you give him what he wants he'll probably end up being your biggest fan* – and this had turned out to be true; it was Jeremy who had swung it for her to finally get her own column.

'My goodness! Is it presentation time already?' she said, taking the card and opening it. A couple of M&S gift tokens fell out.

'Yes, I've got a meeting at one, so I thought we'd better get on with it,' Jeremy said. 'Congratulations, Tina. You've got through a whole ten years without taking maternity leave. Long may it continue!'

Tina opened her card and glanced through the signatures. There it was, Dan's spiky scrawl, so different to Justin's well-formed copperplate: *Here's to another ten years, I hope they bring you the happiness you deserve.*

What was *that* supposed to mean? She *had* been happy. Still was, come to that. She loved her job – she loved pretty much everything about it. The access; the right to ask questions; the urgency of having a deadline, and the relief after meeting it; the kick of seeing her name in print; the surprising insights into what other lives were like. More than that, she loved the feel and smell of newsprint, and the satisfaction of contributing to something bigger and louder than she was. Why, then, did it suddenly seem as if all this was not enough – too transitory, too ephemeral? An assembly of people who came and went, creating tomorrow's fish and chip paper, the day after's unsearched-for internet archive . . .

She looked beyond Jeremy to where Dan and Julia were standing in the space between the news and features sections, apparently oblivious to everyone else. They were laughing about something, and Julia was pressing her body towards Dan, and his arms were reaching for her as if opening up for an embrace.

'When you're ready, Tina,' Jeremy said, 'let's go, shall we?'

Other colleagues were already mustering behind him: Anthea Trask, freshly lipsticked, smiling brightly; Monty Delamere, the pot-bellied, whiskery parliamentary sketch writer, who'd put his hand on Tina's knee in the taxi after her first *Post* Christmas party, but had taken it in entirely good spirits when she'd turned him down; that week's work experience, bright-eyed, bushy-tailed and eager to please.

Tina closed her personal organizer and forced a smile.

'Sure,' she said. 'Time to get out of here.'

4

The haunted house

A month had passed since Lucy had kicked Adam and Hannah out of the house, and so far she had managed to avoid telling anyone what had happened. She'd headed off potentially awkward questions from the school-gate mums, who were best placed to notice that something was up, by telling them that Adam had been seconded to another office and was away a lot. She had also said that Hannah had moved on. She had avoided mentioning Hannah and Adam in close succession; she didn't want anyone to make a connection between their disappearances.

She was still wearing her wedding and engagement rings. It felt too weird without them on.

If she'd revealed even a fraction of the truth, the reaction would have been overwhelmingly sympathetic. But she wasn't ready yet to lay herself open to others' attempts to comfort her. It wasn't so much that she wanted to keep up appearances, more that she was terrified of what would become of her if she let them go.

Everything had become unreal; it was as if she had turned into a ghost, and nobody else had noticed yet. Force of habit kept her moving, and her shadowy half-life was both less vivid and less painful than being fully alive.

She had decided to ignore other, older friends for the time being, and had even managed not to give away anything to her mother. This was quite an achievement, given that Hannah had pitched up on Ellen's doorstep, and Ellen plainly smelt a rat. Her father was at a safe distance in Spain, and wouldn't expect to hear from her until Christmas.

There were no relatives on Adam's side of the family to worry about. Adam was an only child, and had lost his mother when he was twenty; his father had survived her long enough to hold both his grandchildren, but had passed away soon after Clemmie was born.

She would never forget the look on Adam's face when he first told her about his mother, and the cancer that had killed her. Was it their second date, or perhaps their third? It had certainly been the moment when she had known for sure that she was going to fall in love with him.

It was much harder, now, for her to feel sorry for him; she could no longer trust him to let her make it up to him. She didn't want to tell anyone, ever, what had happened between him and Hannah. However, she knew that there were two people who were owed some kind of an explanation, and who needed it sooner than later.

Her daughters.

And so, when Adam rang one school-day afternoon, she steeled herself to broach the subject.

They were going to have to make it official.

They started with a brief discussion about money. He was still paying the mortgage and household bills; she wanted instead to receive a fixed sum as maintenance each month, and have their family solicitors draw up a formal separation arrangement on her behalf. He said, 'If that's what you want.'

Then he said he had to go away on a business trip over the weekend, and would it be possible for him to see the girls tomorrow evening instead?

'That's fine,' she said, 'a bit short notice, but still, it's fine. They'll look forward to it.'

Something stopped her from adding, 'They miss you,' though this was unquestionably true.

Clemmie, who had always been outspoken, had become downright stroppy – burst into loud tears at the least provocation, and kept having nightmares. Lottie had gone the other way, and was quieter and paler and more withdrawn than ever.

Instead she said, 'We need to talk to them.'

'Oh . . .' He swallowed. 'Do we? What do you think we should say?'

'We have to tell them you're not coming back. As far as they're aware, you've just been staying somewhere else for a while. They need to know it's permanent.'

'Do you really need me there to tell them that?' he said.

'Yes, I do. We need to do it together.'

'If you say so. Sounds like something out of one of your parenting books,' he said.

'It has to be done. We can't put it off any longer,' she told him, but he had already hung up.

After she'd taken the girls to school the next day she finally finished packing up Hannah's stuff.

There wasn't all that much to get rid of, when it came down to it. CDs and skinny jeans showing varying degrees of wear and tear; bedding; a poster of some unhealthy-looking pop star. Hannah wasn't one to set much store by owning things – she'd always spent all her money on going out.

She couldn't help but pick up traces of Hannah's smell: damp denim and smoke and beer, suggestive of all the nights Hannah had walked back in the rain from the station after a night out.

Adam still had a number of shirts hanging up next to her dresses, a squash racket in the under-the-stairs cupboard, a Brand Director of the Year award on the bookcase in the sitting room. But Hannah had been completely purged.

She had told the girls that Hannah had moved in with Ellen, to keep her company. Something about the way she'd said it must have put them off asking any questions. Perhaps she should have arranged some kind of farewell . . . but no. Children needed their fathers, but plenty of people never saw their aunts.

She loaded Hannah's things into the car and drove across London to her mother's.

'She's not here, you know,' Ellen said as Lucy dumped the first box in the grimy hallway. 'She's at work.'

'I know,' Lucy said.

She went back out to the car. Ellen didn't move to help. When Lucy came back in Ellen had folded her arms and looked displeased. She was wearing a man's denim shirt, slightly stained, over grey sweatpants, and her long raggedy hair, which had once been golden blonde but was now rough and grey, hung in loose drifts over her shoulders.

'What if she doesn't want all this stuff?' Ellen asked.

'Then she can throw it away,' Lucy said, dumping a bin bag on the box and turning to go back outside.

'Are you going to come in properly and sit down?' Ellen asked as she came back in with another bin bag.

'Can't, I'm sorry,' said Lucy. 'I've got to be at the school gate at three.'

Which was true. She also couldn't face the old photos of herself and Hannah beaming for the camera.

'It's been a while,' Ellen said. 'How are the girls?'

Ellen had never been the sort of grandmother who babysits on a regular basis, nor yet a spoiler, armed with sweets. Her interaction with the girls was always muted when she was on Lucy's territory, but on the rare occasions when Lucy brought the girls to the flat Ellen became bolder, barking out questions about school and friends and favourite games.

The girls seemed to accept Ellen's foibles – her domestic sluttishness, her strange mix of aggression and defensiveness, the smell of gin that sometimes clung to her; they always seemed more pleased than not to see her. And why not? She was the only grandmother they had.

'Why don't you come round on Sunday?' Lucy said. 'I can pick you up and drop you back if you like. We're free all day.'

She would tell her then. With the girls out of earshot, but still around. That way, Ellen wouldn't be able to probe too deeply.

'That's a possibility, I suppose,' Ellen said. 'Will Adam be there?'

'Er, no. He'll be away. He's been away a lot lately.'

'I know he doesn't want to see me,' Ellen said. 'You don't need to try and hide it.'

Lucy decided not to respond to this either. She came back from the car with the last of Hannah's things: her guitar.

'I do hope she's not going to try and play that thing while she's here,' Ellen said. 'She's a rather selfish girl, isn't she? To be honest, Lucy, I don't know how you stood it for so long.'

'She has her moments,' Lucy said.

Clemmie and Lottie had always loved listening to Hannah play. She put down the guitar next to everything else.

Ellen said, 'When are you going to tell me what's going on?'

'Ask Hannah,' Lucy said. 'Would eleven o'clock be OK to pick you up on Sunday?'

'I suppose I'll have to tell Hannah to keep out of your way when you come,' Ellen said.

'She will,' Lucy said, and made good her escape.

She got back just in time for the school pick-up. Back home, once she'd given the girls a snack and encouraged them to change out of their uniforms and into something nice, somehow it was already early evening and Adam was on the doorstep.

She let him in and ushered the girls into the living room, and made a start on the sad little routine she'd been thinking about for weeks: 'Your dad and I have something to tell you . . .'

There: she'd finally said it. She saw straight away that they knew exactly what was coming. They looked scared, and Adam did too – he'd gone thin and hollow-looking, the way he always did when he was anxious, and his hands were trembling slightly.

She made it through the rest of her speech by staring at the pattern on the Turkish rug.

'Daddy's not going to live with us any more. He's going to see you most weekends, though, and we still both love you very much. We're just not such good friends with each other as we used to be.'

Adam made a slightly strangled, choking noise, and then managed to say, 'And you can call me. Anytime you like. I'll call you straight back, so it won't be on Mummy's phone bill.'

Lucy mustered the courage to look up and saw that Clemmie was furious.

'This is your fault!' she shouted at Lucy through a storm of tears. 'For being so mean. And saying no all the time!'

When Lucy tried to approach her she flinched away

and removed herself to a spot in the middle of the rug, where she continued to sob remorselessly.

Adam said, in a low voice, 'I'm not sure this has helped anything. I'm meant to be taking them out for a meal now. How's that going to work?'

But Lottie went over to Clemmie and settled next to her, and Clemmie relented and allowed Lottie to hold her.

Seeing them together, the older child comforting the younger, Lucy was reminded of herself, at Lottie's age, stepping over Ellen's supine body as she crossed the landing to get Hannah out of her cot and change her. How Hannah had been screaming, soaking wet, red in the face with fury . . . and then, as soon as Lucy had taken charge of her, her crying had stilled, and she had clung to her as if she never wanted to let go.

That night she couldn't sleep, and finally dozed off near dawn. She got back from the school drop-off the next morning to find that Hannah had called and left a message.

'Lucy, it's me . . . You have to know. Mum's had a stroke – I found her this morning. She's still alive, but we don't know how bad it is. I'm at Penge Hospital with her now. Please come as soon as you can.'

She's still alive. Did that mean she could die?

Lucy's legs went weak and she found herself sitting at the kitchen table. Resting on the surface in front of her were both her hands, still clutching the phone: square, capable, practical hands, unmanicured, made for doing. Hands she'd inherited from her mother.

She had spent most of her adult life trying both to impress Ellen and to be different from her in every possible way. If she lost her, how on earth would she know who to be?

Her engagement ring caught the light and the diamond glinted.

The symbol of for ever. But all you could really lay claim to was now . . .

And then, somehow, she was moving again, returning the phone to its cradle on the dresser, gathering up handbag and keys, locking up, going out to start the car.

She had to get to Ellen as fast as she could. She mustn't be too late.

The hospital was a warren of a place, a long, low, irregular structure that could never have been planned, but must have just been added to, bit by bit, over the years. There was scaffolding up in the reception area, and as she skirted round it someone called out, 'Can I help you?'

It was a tall old man with a shock of white hair, who was sitting at a plywood table next to a wall-mounted map of the premises.

She hesitated, and he smiled at her encouragingly. His eyes were a milky pale blue; they looked as if they might be capable of otherworldly visions. He wore a neatly pressed check shirt with a lapel badge that announced he was a volunteer.

'I'm looking for the stroke ward,' she said.

He pointed to the map and directed her, and she thanked him and set off briskly, although she was less sure of the way with every step. As she walked on she felt herself undergoing the strange transition that afflicts anybody who enters a hospital, whereby personal history fades and becomes inconsequential, and the designated role – whether visitor, patient, worker or volunteer – takes over.

Somehow she came to the right ward. She pressed the buzzer next to the entrance. And then she was in.

She stumbled up to the nurses' station and was told that Ellen was stable, that tests had been scheduled, that the consultant would be round soon.

'Your sister's here. Lucky she found her,' one of the nurses told her, trying to be reassuring.

There was nothing for it but to go on.

She walked past a bedridden young man attended on by a sorrowful girl, who stroked his hand and murmured urgently; a heavy old man in striped pyjamas, who had turned his back on everyone; a couple of cubicles with drawn curtains; and two old ladies who were sitting, fully dressed, next to their beds. One was watching TV and the other was being told something in low, admonishing tones by a middle-aged woman. Her daughter, Lucy concluded; only a daughter would speak with such irritable intimacy.

And then she came to Ellen, who was lying on her back, slightly propped up, with a drip connected to her hand, seemingly deeply asleep. Hannah was sitting beside her.

Lucy leaned over and brushed Ellen's cheek with her lips, and murmured, 'Hello, Mummy.' But Ellen's only response was a snoring intake of breath, followed by a wet-sounding exhalation. As Lucy straightened she saw that Ellen's mouth was slack and twisted, and damp with spittle.

Throughout Lucy's childhood she had been aware that her mother was a beauty; it had been obvious not just from the pride Ellen took in grooming herself and dressing well, but in the special attention she attracted when dealing with tradesmen, Lucy's friends' fathers, the neighbouring husbands, and the other males who entered her orbit.

But then, when Lucy was ten and Ellen was forty-two, Hannah had come along, and the girls' father left them and Ellen gave up.

Now, even in repose, she looked deformed; one side of her face sagged as if the skin had been frozen in the process of melting and sliding away from the bone. She had always been, like Lucy, a fleshy sort of woman – in her day, a curvaceous siren, and in old age, shape-lessly substantial – but for the first time she struck Lucy as gaunt. The arms protruding from the sleeves of her nightie were sinewy and fleshless, and yet they were suggestive not of frailty, but of reserves of endurance.

Hannah said, 'This is my fault. I told her what happened. She told me I was a bloody fool. Said I was lucky you hadn't gone for me.'

Lucy looked up and saw that Hannah's grey-blue eyes – so like Ellen's – were small and bloodshot with crying.

'Why did you do it?' she asked. 'The only reason I can think of is that you had a chance to take something that was mine. So you took it.'

Hannah shook her head. 'I just . . . I knew it was wrong. I just gave in.'

'Oh, Hannah,' Lucy said. 'When are you going to learn that just because somebody wants you to do something, it doesn't automatically mean you have to go along with it? I might be able to forgive you, one day. But I don't think I'll ever be able to forgive what you've done to my children.'

Hannah began to cry again, but the sound was distant, not anything Lucy could reasonably be expected to deal with. She was overwhelmingly aware of the movement of her own breath, her heartbeat, the skin on her hands, the raised blue lines of blood beneath the skin: everything accelerated, but still working as it was meant to, for now at least.

Then Hannah said, 'I think she might be waking up.'

Lucy looked down at Ellen and saw that Hannah was right; Ellen was stirring.

She touched Ellen's hand. 'Mummy, it's me, Lucy. Can you hear me?'

Ellen's eyes opened wide. They were as clear and lovely as ever, but their expression was remote and unfamiliar. Was there recognition there, or acceptance, or indifference? Lucy felt that Ellen was looking through rather than at her, as if what Lucy might say or do was of symbolic interest, but was otherwise irrelevant.

And then the moment passed, and Ellen's eyelids drooped, and she drifted back into unconsciousness.

The next day was a Saturday, and Lucy brought the girls to the hospital with her. They squabbled infuriatingly all the way in the car, but when they reached the entrance to the ward they both fell quiet.

Lucy said to Clemmie, 'Now, there are lots of poorly people here, and I don't want you being noisy, or making any loud comments about what they look like, because it will hurt their feelings. OK?'

Clemmie pulled a face that was expressive of extreme displeasure and distaste, much as she did when presented with a meal she found particularly repulsive.

Lucy glanced at Lottie. She was staring into space with the flat resolve of a child waiting to enter the haunted house at a fairground, who has some idea of the dangling spiders, jiggling skeletons and strange mirrors that may lie ahead, and is summoning up the courage to cross the threshold.

'Is this where people come when they die?' Lottie asked.

'No, it isn't,' Lucy said firmly. 'I mean, it might be, sometimes, but Granny isn't dying. She's getting better, though she's still very ill. You'll see.'

They went in, and there was Ellen, and there, too, was Hannah.

Lottie hung back, but Clemmie rushed up to her aunt. Lucy could almost, but not quite, bear to watch: at the last moment, before Clemmie and Hannah embraced, she looked away.

Her mobile beeped, and she remembered that she ought to have turned it off. She got it out of her bag and saw that Natalie had just sent her a message.

Still nothing doing. Due to go into hospital to talk about induction on Wed. Not long now till I get to see Matilda face to face. Richard and I are both really looking forward to hanging out with her!

'Good luck with that,' Lucy muttered.

The impulse behind her response was jaded and cynical: *Just you wait! Your marriage is never going to be the same again!* But once spoken, the words sounded like an innocent, impersonal plea, made on behalf of all of them; as if the stagnant hospital air had softened them and stripped them of bitterness, and transformed them into a genuine benediction.

5

Induction

Natalie's appointment was scheduled for 2.30 p.m. She arrived at the maternity ward clinic at two fifteen and found Richard already there, his briefcase at his feet, working his way through a stack of papers.

Two thirty passed, then two forty-five, then three, by which time she had finished with *Wow!* and, rummaging for something else to pass the time with, came across Wednesday's copy of the *Post*. She rifled through in search of Tina's column.

The Vixen Letters

The price of pleasing Mother

Whatever the compensations, I have to admit that there are times when being single is no fun at all. Other people's weddings can be relied upon to provide at least a few highly uncomfortable moments. I've lost count of the times an older woman has established quickly and pitilessly that I don't have an other half tucked away somewhere out of sight, and then told me, 'Never mind, dear, I'm sure your time will come. Don't give up hope!'

Having a degree, a diploma and a career just doesn't cut it with the senior lady. On the whole, my mother's generation believes that women can't be truly fulfilled without marriage and babies, and cannot conceive of being happy in old age if their daughters fail to reproduce.

Yet when I and my friends were in our twenties, we regarded the prospect of pregnancy as a disaster to be avoided at all costs. It was challenge enough to find a job and a place to live, and then hold down the job, and pay the rent, and work out what to do on Saturday night. We hoped that one day one of our frogs would turn out to be a prince, but we saw true love as a goal in itself, not as a passport to something else. We certainly weren't in any rush to embrace family life — after all, we'd only just managed to leave our own families behind.

I'm sure the near-constant headlines about egg-freezing and IVF play their part in whipping thirtysomething women into a frenzy of broodiness, but I have a theory that the so-called biological clock is really powered by a force that is much more personal and universally effective than the media. It's a ruthlessly efficient mechanism for ensuring the survival of the species, a failsafe that comes into its own now that the dominance of men has been undermined: *Most women do not want to disappoint their mothers.*

'What's she on about this time, then?' said Richard, peering across at the paper.

'Complaining about the pressure to produce grand-children,' Natalie said. 'I don't think her mother's going to be very happy about this.'

'Has her mother been dropping hints?' Richard asked.

'Probably not, but she wouldn't have to say anything for Tina to know that's what she'd like,' Natalie said. 'I think Tina's got a point. Nothing else I've ever done made Mum quite as happy as the news that I was having a baby. That we are, I mean.'

'That's because it's the first,' said Richard, whose older sister already had three children. 'Sounds to me as if Tina's protesting a bit too much. She's probably secretly insanely broody.'

'Oh no, I don't think she is at all.'

'Why shouldn't she be? Remember how you got when Lucy had Lottie? You were champing at the bit. It seems to be contagious.'

'It just makes you think when your friends do these things, that's all,' Natalie said. 'I mean, come on, you're exactly the same. I know that when your sister had hers it got you wondering about what it would be like to have your own one day. At least a little bit.'

'Yes, but they're my family,' Richard pointed out. 'There's no real reason for what Lucy does or what Tina does to have any kind of effect on you. And yet you've all got this stake in each other's lives, even though you're all quite different and you've gone about things in very different ways. It's like you're all looking over your shoulders to check what each other's up to.'

'It's no different to you keeping tabs on all your

contemporaries from law school, to see how far up the greasy pole they've got.'

'Yes, but I don't care if they've got married or had children,' Richard said. He pushed his glasses up to the bridge of his nose and went back to reading through his paperwork.

As time passed the waiting room seemed to fill up rather than empty out. Eventually, at three ten, Richard said, 'Shouldn't you go and check they haven't forgotten you or something?'

She checked. They hadn't. She sat back down again.

At three twenty her name was finally called and a midwife led her to a small office where she was asked a few routine questions and told to strip off for yet another awful examination. Natalie thought of herself as a good sport and not particularly prissy or coy, but having her recalcitrant cervix prodded was, she thought, pretty much a zero on the fun scale. She was relieved to get back into her clothes and pull up her sleeve for a blood pressure reading.

The midwife pumped the blood pressure cuff till it was tight, and then studied the gauge. She said, 'It's a little on the high side.'

'My blood pressure's been fine all the way through,' Natalie said.

The midwife tried it again. 'It's still high,' she said. 'Do you have your specimen?'

Natalie handed it over. The midwife took off the lid and stuck a stick into the pot. The stick turned black.

'You have protein in your urine,' the midwife said.

'I've had just a trace before,' Natalie said.

'This isn't just a trace.'

The midwife took the blood pressure reading again. 'It is definitely too high,' she said, and sent Natalie back to the waiting room.

By now Natalie's heart was pounding, as if she'd just screwed something up in front of an audience. *If I can just calm down it will be all right and they will let me go. Please God just let me get out of here.*

'What's going on?' Richard asked.

'My blood pressure's high.'

'I'm not surprised. Mine probably is too. Anybody's would be after waiting in here for an hour and a half. So what does that mean?'

'It means we have to wait.'

'Well, that'll help,' Richard said.

Natalie tried to focus on drawing air slowly into her lungs and then gradually expelling it. Her heart continued to race.

Richard went to get them both a cup of tea from the machine. He came back with two cans of Fanta.

'Nothing seems to be working out today,' he said as he handed hers over.

At four thirty Natalie's name was called again. She was taken to another office where a curly-haired woman sitting on the other side of a desk introduced herself as the registrar on duty and took her blood pressure again, and then pronounced sentence. She was to be induced straight away. No, she could not go home. It was too dangerous. She had pre-eclampsia. Somebody else would have to pick up her things and bring them.

Once things had progressed sufficiently, she would be given an epidural and the labour would be augmented with syntocinon.

Bella Madden had encouraged them to question medical professionals, to ask why certain steps were necessary, or what might happen if you didn't take them. But it was quickly apparent to Natalie that there was no way out.

She stood to leave; the registrar also got to her feet and followed her. At the door to the office the registrar touched her lightly on the back and said, 'Sometimes it is hard to be a woman,' and walked quickly away along the corridor.

Natalie went back to Richard and told him the news. He said, 'They'd better know what they're doing,' and she knew he was trying to sound bullish, but he looked too terrified for the comment to come across as anything other than fearful.

Richard hurried home to fetch Natalie's things and Natalie was taken into a lift and along a corridor and left in the labour ward waiting room.

It was full of women, with not a single father-to-be in sight. Where were all the partners? Was this how it was, outside Bella Madden's conservatory? Natalie found a spare seat between someone who was sitting with her eyes closed, as if trying to nap, and a pale teenager who was leafing through a magazine.

The teenager put her magazine aside, stood up and shuffled out. Her bump looked all the more enormous for being the only part of her body that curved. She was dressed in a filmy top over knee-length leggings, and a pair of sloppy ballet shoes that came off her feet with every step.

And then yet another woman came in. She got her mobile out of her handbag and started making a call. It quickly became apparent that she was in exactly the same situation as Natalie, and had been told she couldn't leave the hospital and go home, and was asking the father of her child to bring in the things she needed. It was also obvious that he wasn't at all keen on the idea.

'No, they're not going to let me out,' she said. 'Yes, I know it's bloody annoying. Nappies, babygros, wipes. OK, then ring your mother. Get her to sort it.'

The teenage girl reappeared in the doorway and shouted: 'What's happening? What the fuck is happening to me?'

She had brought with her a stink that was as strong as shit or sex: a rank, sharp, insistent smell that did not belong in a public place, in front of strangers. A clear, viscous fluid was oozing down her legs, soaking the shabby fabric of her shoes and puddling on the floor.

The woman sitting next to Natalie opened her eyes. She had the subdued, exhausted look of someone who makes her living on her feet – a shop assistant or waitress, someone resigned to crap pay, tedium, rude customers and bunions.

'Your waters just broke, that's all,' she told the girl. 'It's a good sign. It means it's all happening.'

She got up and guided the girl to a seat, then went off to fetch help.

The girl's head and arms dropped towards her belly,

as if she were imploding, and she rocked forwards and backwards in her seat and groaned.

'If you want to see this baby being born, you'd better get it together and get over here,' said the woman who was on the phone.

The girl was sitting upright again. Droplets of sweat had sprung out on her forehead.

The other woman put her phone away. She looked at the girl with resigned sympathy.

'It'll be over soon, and you'll forget all about it,' she said. 'You're young, and that's all to the good. It'll be quick.'

The woman who had gone for help reappeared with a midwife, who led the girl out. As the door was about to shut behind them Natalie saw a plastic carrier bag under the chair where the girl had been sitting. It was full of baby stuff, and a tiny all-in-one with Tigger on the front had fallen out.

Natalie leaned down and made a grab for the bag, shoved the contents back in and went after them.

She caught up with them a little way down the corridor and held the bag out to the girl.

'You left this,' she said.

The girl turned to look at her. Her eyes were big and dark and shocked and fearful. She didn't say a word. She took the bag, and the midwife swept her away.

Natalie went back to the waiting room, where all that remained of the girl was the puddle of amniotic gloop by the door.

'Wonder how long it'll take them to send someone to clear up,' said the woman who'd made the phone call.

Nobody replied. The room fell restlessly quiet, and the tired woman shut her eyes again, and Natalie wished that Richard would hurry up.

If only she could have her things, she might feel a little more ready for whatever was going to happen next. What on earth was he doing, anyway? He was certainly taking his time.

Someone came with a mop and gave the floor a desultory once-over to get rid of the traces of the girl. The woman who'd made the phone call was called away to a delivery suite. Her partner still hadn't showed up.

But Richard did reappear, finally, looking panicky and overwrought. He'd changed into jeans, and was dragging Natalie's pull-along suitcase.

'I'm so sorry it took so long. There'd been an accident; the traffic was horrendous,' he said.

'Did you bring the CD player?' Natalie demanded.

'Oh no. I'm sorry. I forgot.'

'Oh well. No whale music,' Natalie said.

'I'm really sorry it took so long,' Richard said, settling next to her and squeezing her hand. 'Are you all right? I can't believe you're still here. I thought I'd find you surrounded by beeping lights and flashing monitors and staff in surgical masks. Are you sure they haven't forgotten about you again?'

'They didn't forget about me last time,' Natalie said. 'They're just really busy.'

She went to check anyway. No, they didn't know how much longer it would be, but if she started seeing shooting stars she should definitely let them know.

Back in the waiting room Richard opened the suitcase,

took out a document folder and tried to read. After a few minutes he said, 'I can't do this. I can't concentrate.' He sounded genuinely shocked that his ability to work had deserted him.

As Richard stared into space Natalie rummaged through the tiny nappies and babygros and cotton wool in the suitcase and found the small cushion stuffed with lavender that Lucy had sent her. She pressed it to her nose and sniffed. Her heart continued to batter away. Still, the scent was comforting; it was redolent of the kind of vintage femininity Lucy's home and lifestyle paid homage to. Natalie was beginning to see how the prettiness and sweetness of well-ordered domesticity might come to serve as an antidote to the brutal impotence of biological womanhood – and was even, as practised by Lucy anyway, assertive, a triumph of the will over muddle, helplessness and mess.

Shortly afterwards her name was called ('I think they did forget you, till you went and reminded them,' Richard muttered) and she was taken off by a friendly-seeming but very young midwife wheeling a machine on a trolley. The midwife seemed to be looking for something, or somewhere, and after they'd been traipsing around for a while it occurred to Natalie that it was proving difficult to find a space to put her in. Eventually the midwife gave her a pair of blue plastic shields to put over her shoes and took her past a door marked SLUICE to a little curtained lobby with a hospital bed and a couple of cupboards. She had a furtive expression, as if she was doing something that was common practice, but might not be officially approved of.

100

She fixed a grubby strap round Natalie's belly, flicked a couple of switches and studied the display. 'OK, we need to see whether anything is happening yet,' she said. 'I'll be back in twenty minutes. Don't go any-where. Theatre is just down the corridor; that's why you have to have the covers on your shoes.'

Then she took off, and Natalie lay back and tried to relax, and stared at the display and willed it to kick into life.

The midwife returned thirty-five minutes later and studied the printout from the machine. She didn't look particularly impressed, but she didn't look wholly dismissive either. 'There's something going on,' she said, 'nothing regular, but some kind of activity,' and Natalie padded after her down the corridor again, until she said, 'Oh, you can get rid of those now,' whereupon Natalie took the blue plastic shields off her shoes and was delivered back to the waiting room.

As she went in Richard shot her a look of mute male suffering that said, loud and clear, *I'm out of my depth.*

Not so very long ago he could have cleared off to the pub across the road and nobody would have thought any the worse of him. She could picture it quite clearly, him sipping half a lager to quell his nerves, watching sport on a large TV screen even though no sport interested him and he would much have preferred the news. Maybe, for him, that would have been better – but then she would have been completely alone.

Soon afterwards they were admitted to a delivery suite. Natalie was given to understand that this was a special privilege – if anyone came along who was in more urgent need, they would be turfed out. Richard, who had not accompanied Natalie on the tour of the labour ward, looked round in confusion.

'Where am I meant to sleep?' he asked.

The midwife indicated a green armchair. 'It reclines.'

This, too, it seemed, was a privilege.

Richard went off to the hospital canteen to buy some sandwiches, and the midwife poked a prostaglandin pessary as close as possible to Natalie's unripe cervix.

'Try to sleep,' she said brightly, 'you're going to need it. Have a good rest, and then you'll be ready to wake up tomorrow and have a baby!'

Then she went off, leaving Natalie to her own devices. What to do? She was alone in a windowless delivery suite, not in labour, with a television and telephone unit that didn't work.

Richard came in with some sandwiches. 'I got some for you as well, just in case what they bring you isn't very nice, or isn't enough,' he said, putting the food down on the wheeled table that could be used for someone in the bed to eat from.

God, am I really that greedy? Natalie thought. Yes, I am.

'Thanks,' she said.

Richard perched at the end of the bed and opened up one of the packets of sandwiches.

The room fell silent. Natalie picked up the other sandwich and tore it open.

After a sleepless night spent listening to Richard's snoring the morning examination revealed that Natalie was still not much further along than she'd been the evening before. The new midwife on duty didn't believe on stinting on the pessaries and went for a double dose. 'That'll get you going, you wait and see,' she said. 'It's a lovely day. Why don't you go out for a walk?'

It was strange to be allowed out into the sunshine when the previous day she'd been forbidden to leave the hospital. When you were powerless the whims of those in charge had an inordinate effect. And indeed, strolling along the walkway besides the Thames, for all the world like an ordinary couple, did seem to speed things up. Periodically she fell quiet and Richard waited discreetly for the pain to pass before carrying on.

When they got back to the ward the midwife who'd sent them off examined her.

'Well done,' the midwife said, 'you're on your way,' and Natalie felt she was beginning to redeem herself.

As the afternoon wore on the pain became more vicious and Natalie was allowed to try out the gas and air. God, it was good . . . Within minutes the whole scene was transformed. She was riding queen-like on the bed, clasping a mask to her face, she and the bed were high and enormous, what was the French for it, oh yes, *s'accoucher, je m'accouche*, Bella had told them, it was Louis the Wotsit started the vogue for women giving birth in bed flat on their backs, *elles s'accouchent*, Louis liked to perve on his mistresses in labour through the spy hole, watch coming out of them what he had put in . . .

But Richard wasn't really watching. He could hardly bear to look at her. Miserably uncomfortable – well, perhaps that was preferable to being titillated? And anyway he was distant and very small, poor Richard, terrified, hating every minute of it, doing his best, it was hopeless really, not fair on him . . . His nerves, his fears, a dark bubble of tension on the far side of the room, and there was nothing she could do to reassure him or make it up to him, to make it right, he had done what he came for, he was superfluous now, but still required to be here.

All that effort, all that senseless worry, should they, shouldn't they, moving in together, getting engaged, the wedding, starting a family, each fresh stage eliciting a fresh bout of doubt from Richard, while she cajoled and reassured and waited, hanging on to him for dear life, trying to convince him that it was the right thing, that she was right for him, that he was right for her . . . She had believed that Richard made her safe, but now it was apparent this was not so, he was a bit player, and she was undergoing this extraordinary, this astonishing torture . . . as Lucy had done, twice – good God – and Natalie's own mother, who was so modest: Natalie had never seen her undressed . . . Lucy's mother, the difficult one, the drunk . . . Tina's mother, Madam Chairman, fundraiser for good causes, the lady of the house. All those other mothers: clinging to branches during hurricane and flood, on planes, tube trains, Underground platforms during the Blitz, medieval bedsteads, the floors of caves . . .

The price of pleasing Mother. But no, that wasn't it . . . it was the secret price of life. So this was it, this was what it cost, this was the charge every single person walking on every single street had exacted before they had even been born.

The door opened and a man in a white coat walked in at the head of a short retinue. She recognized the curly-headed woman behind him from the maternity clinic. *Sometimes it is hard to be a woman.*

White Coat addressed a few words to the latest midwife, who passed him Natalie's notes to survey.

'Ah yes,' he said, 'the pre-eclampsia case.'

He studied Natalie's notes and addressed a few questions to her. Somehow she answered. As she did, she felt the pace of the pain slacken and die away.

A belt was run round her belly and White Coat examined the display on the machine.

'Not much going on there,' he observed.

He told her what would happen next. The anaesthetist would give her an epidural; she would be induced on a syntocinon drip. The belt monitoring her contractions would need to remain in place from now on. A blood pressure cuff, too.

And with that he swept out, followed by his attendants.

The latest midwife muttered, 'Well, that was a waste of time, wasn't it?' and Natalie realized that this was how her attempt at labour could be seen: pain for no purpose.

She began to say something to Richard, but was silenced by a final desultory pang. Like a last crack of heartbreak from a love affair that never had the chance to progress.

*

The anaesthetist was glassy and calm, and set about working his magic with the benign assurance of one whose ministrations are always welcome. Afterwards she found herself small again, shrunk back down to size, hooked up to the epidural, the blood pressure monitor, the contraption that kept track of her contractions and a catheter bag; paralysed from the waist down, and watching the jagged peaks and troughs that represented her contractions, spewed out on a printout. She supposed she ought to be grateful.

Richard settled in the green chair next to her and ate another hospital sandwich. He looked pale but relieved. *At least this way you'll be safe.* 'We'll check on you in four hours and see how you're doing. Try to sleep. You're going to need all the strength you've got,' this latest midwife said and disappeared.

But of course Natalie couldn't sleep, and once again the dark hours ticked by to the soundtrack of Richard's snoring, broken, once, by screaming from the next room. There goes another one, Natalie thought. Lucky thing; at least for her it's over. She tried to think of happier times but it was a struggle, and she found she had to go back – a long way back – to find a memory that was bright and strong enough to face down her fear.

No, not the honeymoon in Florence, nor the dinner at Pierre Victoire when Richard had finally proposed. Not even the ring shopping, or the pure gratification of finally being able to tell her mother she was getting married. No, not the takeaway pizza they'd ordered on their first night in the house they'd bought together, nor the exchanging of contracts or signing of the mortgage . . .

Her home life had been comfortable, convenient, steady, reassuring . . . There had been consolidation, but not much adventure. Not since she'd jacked in her job and gone off travelling just after the millennium, spurred on by Tina's insistence that she should take control of her life and do something for herself. And look how that had turned out!

Oh God, what had she been thinking, she'd been such a fool – leaving Heathrow for Auckland after the goodbye kiss with Richard, feeling so pleased with herself, setting off to visit her brother and spend a couple of months sightseeing on her own. And what had she gone and done? On the other side of the world, she had allowed herself to be someone else. To be with someone else.

One night only, in a cheap white room over a red pub in an old gold rush town in the middle of nowhere. It wasn't a place she had chosen to be. She was only there because she couldn't get a bus out till the next day. She was just waiting for her connection . . .

It was outside of backpacker season and the hostel had been virtually empty, a little creepy it was so deserted. Jerry-built too: the door handle to her room felt as if it might come off if she turned it too fast; one tap dripped and the other gave nothing away; the walls seemed thin, insubstantial; a breeze whipped round the window frame as if hinting that anybody who wanted to could get in. The pub next door at least seemed solid and enclosing, even if it was ersatz – a traditional

British boozer, dim and high-ceilinged with brassy mirrors and crimson walls and ornate mouldings, in an un-English, flat, dusty, remote no man's land of a place. But the job of any pub is to allow you to forget that sometime soon you'll have to leave and go home, and it fulfilled that . . .

She'd played a couple of games of pool. She only knew how because Lucy and Tina had taught her. Her opponent was a girl with bright blonde hair that was dark at the roots and a pack of Gauloises in her back pocket. Nobody had noticed when Natalie left with her; nobody had turned a hair.

The girl's room smelt of sandalwood, her skin was soft, her ribs, her hipbones, her spine were hard and apparent, there was nothing redundant about her, no baggage. She had a mole on her left breast. It was a fight for something and yet she was accommodating and it was real, and then it was over, it was morning and Natalie was being nudged awake, 'Didn't you say you have to get your bus?' and she was rushing dazed to the flimsy room she hadn't slept in, half surprised to find her things were still there, gathering them up and running for the stop and the bus was still there, waiting, and she got on and the bus moved off and the town disappeared behind her, and there was no reason why she would ever return.

When she saw Richard six weeks later, the first night she got back, spacey and strung out with jetlag, she had been astonished by how much she coveted him. He was so gentle, so unsure of himself, so visibly trying to hide it. She wanted him to hug her and soothe her and assure her it was all right, but of course he couldn't, because she told him what had happened and he was shocked and he cried and she cried too and then it became possible to wish in earnest that it could all be undone.

They held each other and he left. She hurt him and they broke up and they didn't tell anybody why. Everybody wanted them to get back together, and eventually they did . . . But slowly, slowly . . . and who could blame him?

Those doubts were over. There was nothing there for her; it wasn't where she lived and it was nowhere she could stay. What was left behind was a sort of shadow, an unease, the ache of something that had been excised and refused the chance to grow.

How was it possible to be happy once you knew your future was restricted and you had made it that way, and your bed was well and truly made and now you had to lie on it?

It had happened a long time ago; nearly a decade. Wasn't living in the past what old people did? Ignoring all the interim, returning to the clarity of youth?

But when you are trapped and waiting and afraid, what else is there to do?

At 4.00 a.m. she was examined by another midwife, a big, easy-going woman with an air of calm and expert authority. A youngish doctor came by afterwards and informed her that she would be allowed another four hours. He made it sound like a significant concession.

'Patti's been doing nights on the labour ward for twenty-two years,' he explained, 'and she says she thinks you're about to start dilating, so I'll give you the benefit of the doubt.'

Natalie had been reprieved by the Queen of the Night.

Richard went back to sleep and she waited, and she remembered that there had been a time when she had been free and had not known how free she was.

Walking on the beach by the Old Schoolhouse on the last day of the old century. She hadn't realized that she was happy at the time. What she had felt was anticipation: as if the machinery of time was inexorably grinding towards a great transition, taking them all with it. It was an ominous sensation, and yet also a liberating one. It was not a day like any other, a day of mundane deeds, repetition and limitations; it was a day on which it was possible to believe in the imminence of unknown and unknowable change.

Richard stirred and, finally, she felt the ghost of an urge to push.

She rang the bell. Richard was at her side, willing but terrified. Another examination. She couldn't feel it.

'You can start to try to push if you like,' the latest midwife said. And she tried, but it was like trying to read the very smallest row of letters during an eye test. She could hazard a guess, but she couldn't read the signs.

A doctor examined her; blonde, female, doubtful. 'How long has she been pushing? Twenty minutes? Well, nothing very much is happening at all. You've got forty minutes left,' she told Natalie.

Her time was nearly up. And so Natalie, with the encouragement of the latest midwife, and slightly more hesitant encouragement from Richard, began to push in earnest.

When Richard shifted down the foot end it crossed her mind to tell him that he shouldn't, that it was a mistake, but then the next contraction was clearer and she shoved back against it as hard as she could and yes, she was making progress finally, she'd show the lot of them. The doctor quickly snipped her open and she felt a tugging as the ventouse was applied to the baby's head, but no, no good, someone noticed the syntocinon was running out and started running round like a mad thing looking for another bag, oh shit, and the next contraction was slower and less sharp and the one after that weaker still. She really absolutely genuinely was running out of time, and then there was another spasm and she shoved and the doctor pulled with the forceps and she could feel the baby being lifted up and out of her. Richard stepped nervously forward to cut the cord, as per the birth plan, and then, also as per the birth plan, the baby was dumped on her chest and covered by a sheet, and she looked into her daughter's cloudy blue eyes.

'Welcome to the world, Matilda Rose,' Natalie said, and burst into tears.

6

Theatre

The heart of the courtroom was an empty space. It was a modern facility, square, windowless, airless, the colour of dull metal. Tina was sitting overhead in the press gallery, watching the proceedings as if in the stalls at a particularly uncomfortable piece of contemporary theatre. Below her, the witnesses and lawyers were seated around the four sides of the chamber, facing each other.

To the left were the parents of Alice March, whose death at just nine months of age was the subject of the inquest. On the right were the medical professionals who had tried and failed to save Alice's life. And directly beneath Tina, opposite the coroner on the far side of the court, was Kelly-Ann Rose, the eighteen-year-old nursery nurse who had made the mistake of giving Alice food that she shouldn't have eaten, after which Alice had suffered an allergic reaction, turned blue and stopped breathing.

The proximity of the grieving mother and the girl whose mistake might or might not have contributed to the baby's death filled the courtroom with an electrical charge that had nowhere to go until the verdict was announced and the inquest was over. The atmosphere was intensely claustrophobic, exhausting, deadening. Kelly-Ann looked grey and stiff, and the bags under her eyes were the colour of weak tea. Mrs March was the dry, worn white of old stone, as still and composed as a carving of a good wife on top of a medieval tomb. One was the picture of remorse, the other the picture of grief.

Accidents happen, Tina told herself. Anyone can make a mistake.

Whatever they had taught her at St Birinus School for Girls, the bundle of cells currently multiplying inside her was not a life.

She had resisted the morbid temptation to look up the extent to which it, the invading cell-bundle, had adopted human form, although she imagined that it probably looked amphibious, like a newt, something from a previous stage of evolution, crawling towards land. They had told her over the phone that an ultrasound would be necessary to establish how many weeks pregnant she was, but she wouldn't have to see the scan.

Surely nobody ever wants to look, she'd said.

You'd be surprised, the woman from the clinic had told her. We're all different, and we all have different reasons for the choices we make, and different ways of coping.

Tina had seen Natalie's birth plan, a mission statement

113

for Natalie's desire not to be at the mercy of her body, but to direct what happened to it. The opportunities for Natalie to stamp her will on the natural process were limited, but still, she had set out what she wanted: gas and air, no interventions, water birth if possible.

And by now, more than a fortnight past Natalie's due date, it must be over. Tina had texted to see if there was any news, and hadn't yet heard back. She told herself that all was bound to be well, and found it was a guilty relief to put her concern about her friend to one side. The idea of Natalie as a new mother, settling her new-born at her breast, was a painful one, for reasons Tina didn't particularly care to examine.

Tina, too, had had to select from a limited range of options. She had been guided primarily by the desire to have it over with as quickly as possible. So: a phone consultation, to be followed by a surgical procedure, in and out on the same day. No general anaesthetic, no sedation; that way she'd be able to leave as soon as she felt ready to walk. It would take all of five minutes, and then she'd be able to go home and crawl under her duvet and hide there until Saturday morning. When she would have to get up, put a brave face on it, and go to her father's seventieth birthday party.

She was dreading what she had to do, but she was also resigned to it . . . though if the coroner didn't reach his verdict soon, they'd all be back here again in the morning, and she'd miss her appointment. She'd almost forgotten what a time-consuming business reporting could be. She wouldn't normally have been here at all, except they were short-staffed, and she was meant to be using it as the basis for a long article about the increasing prevalence of allergies, as well as producing a news story for the next day's paper. Anyway, it would be thoroughly unprofessional to regard it as a junior, demeaning assignment. She was a staff writer; she wasn't just a columnist. Plus it never hurt to keep your hand in.

She was half listening for facts or quotes that she might need, but most of what was emerging was clarification rather than wholly new information, and her note-taking had ground almost to a halt. They'd all been shut in together for the best part of two days, but still the coroner was taking his time, going back over some of the evidence from the previous day, asking for further details from the GP, the paediatrician, the paramedic, the A & E consultant.

Only Mr March, the baby's father, had not been called upon to speak. His features were boyish, but shock and loss had robbed him of youthfulness, and he looked tired beyond either anger or despair. He was sitting very close to his wife; sometimes they held hands.

Tina had never seriously entertained the idea of telling Dan, or Justin, about the fix that one or other of them had got her in. She knew perfectly well how they would react if she did: there would be dismay, a desire to disbelieve, followed by concern – concern that she should get rid of it as quickly as possible, and terror that she might not. There was no point in lying, in telling either one that he was the only candidate for paternity – neither would want her to bear their child.

And why should they? If you wanted to have a child

with someone, you went out with them, you lived with them, you got married. You didn't hook up with them just the once after having a few too many down the pub and then move on to someone younger. And you didn't keep them at your beck and call – but at a safe distance – for the best part of a decade, playing an occasional part in a long performance that had all the props of a love affair – the letters, the lingerie, the secret rendez-vous, the intense reunions, the reluctant separations – and yet, at its heart, was all about what wasn't there.

She had to face facts, she just wasn't the mothering kind. Mothers were either staunch and dedicated like Lucy, or mild, gentle souls like Natalie. They were not bony-kneed, bitchy bigmouths like herself.

Finally! The verdict.

Time to concentrate. She might need to include something from the summing-up. She sat with her pen poised on her notebook, ready to start scribbling.

Accidental death.

Accidents happened. Even the law made allowances for that.

So why did she have this feeling that after she'd gone through with what she had to do tomorrow, she would never forgive herself?

Getting back to her flat was a relief, but a qualified one. Lately she'd become uncomfortably conscious of how badly she'd neglected the place, and as soon as she walked in through the front door it struck her as tatty and uncared-for.

How wonderful it would be, like the heroine in *A*

Little Princess, to return to her garret one evening to find it warm, cosy, magically transformed. The fading paintwork, the heaps of books and papers, the dust: these were things that a month ago she would have been oblivious to. Now it was as if she'd lost her immunity, and there was nothing to protect her from seeing that her home was unloved.

The flat occupied the top two floors of a big Victorian house, with the living space and kitchen area upstairs in the converted attic, and a downstairs bathroom and bedroom. After she'd let herself in, the first thing she did was head to the bedroom and take off her work clothes: blouse, skirt and tights, which were de rigueur at the *Post* – opaques in winter, 10 denier in summer. Women in trousers, or with bare legs, were frowned on, whatever the weather, as were men with rolled-up shirt-sleeves, or no tie. These were irksome restrictions, but Tina had spent seven years in the pea-green and dung-brown uniform of St Birinus, and the *Post*'s unofficial dress code was zany freedom in comparison.

Having stripped down to her underwear, she went over to the full-length mirror she had bought soon after starting at the *Post*, not for vanity, but as an act of professional self-protection. She used it to check for drooping hems, see-through shirts, fresh ladders and VPL – anything that might remind male colleagues to speculate about her body parts, or elicit a raised eyebrow from one of the artfully groomed lovelies on the fashion desk.

She turned sideways and examined her belly. A bit bloated, yes, but not too obvious. What would it be like to do this – to check for evidence that you were beginning to soften and swell – if it was a transformation you actually wanted? What if you had a man beside you, who wanted it too, who might even be proud of you? How blessed you would feel! But no . . . she couldn't afford to think like that; it was much too close to self-pity. She'd brought this on herself, and now she had to square up to it like a . . . well, like a woman.

She turned again, and looked at herself head-on. Was her face beginning to look fractionally fuller? She was almost spilling out of her bra, and her breasts looked eerily creamy, as if milk was already blooming beneath the skin . . .

Ridiculous. It was a late period, that was the way to think of it, an escalation of hormones.

She rummaged in the chest of drawers for an old T-shirt and one of her looser pairs of jeans, pulled them on and opened up the wardrobe. She was a hoarder of clothes as well as of books and papers and photos, and it was beginning to look like a badly organized archive. There was plenty there that she hadn't worn much lately – particularly among the going-out clothes, the sheer or shiny or brightly coloured tops and the short skirts and trousers from previous seasons.

There was the vampy stuff, too, a legacy of her relationship with Justin. Sooner or later she would have to have a clearout. She couldn't think of another living soul in whose company it might be possible to wear leather hotpants, or a bustier, or an elasticated minidress that squeezed and squashed her into shape with all the efficacy of an old-fashioned girdle.

The top shelf of the wardrobe was given over to hats. The Ascot fascinator, the classic straw boater for Henley, and an array of others that she thought of as her disguise hats, used for her trips to Justin's flat in Pimlico: the fur-trapper, the big knitted beret, the baker boy cap, the fedora.

There had been a time, years ago now, when Justin had been willing to come to her place. She'd made quite an effort to clean and tidy back then, and had bought a wrought-iron, king-sized bedstead that cost much more than she could afford, imagining it was the sort of thing a proper scarlet woman would recline on in order to ensnare her lover. She'd even gone to the trouble of getting a new cooker installed, so she could prepare seductive feasts. But then he had decided that regular visits were too risky, someone might recognize him, and it would be better by far for her to go discreetly to the studio he referred to as his bachelor pad, and cook dinner for him there. And so she had resigned herself to spending her evenings at home alone, and sleeping without companionship in the new hard, cold and spiky bed.

It had been all the excuse she needed to let things slide. Nobody else ever came round; when your friends were coupled up, and particularly when they had children, it was automatically assumed that they would be the hosts and you would be the visitor. And it hadn't been difficult to dissuade her parents from coming – why on earth would they battle through the traffic to get to Clapham when she was more than happy to head west, away from central London, and visit them in Barnes? Anyway, she worked long hours . . . liked to keep fit . . . and, until very recently, had gone out a lot. She didn't have time to nest.

She moved the Stetson sunhat to one side and took out the old wooden box that was hiding behind it.

The box had been made by a long-dead relative to store needlework, but it didn't quite have the status of a family heirloom – it had been kept, not because it was valued for itself, but because it had a scrap of her father's Great-Aunt Win's handwriting glued to the inside of one of the inner lids, and that made it too personal to throw out.

Tina had found it in the loft as a teenager, and her mother had been surprised that she wanted it, but happy for her to keep it. Tina liked it precisely because of that hidden remainder of Winifred Fox. She'd been attracted to concealed mementoes and secret messages even then – had bought, second-hand, a heart-shaped, empty locket, before realizing she didn't have a photo to put in it; kept a diary that opened with a key, and stored the diary, not quite in plain view, but on the bookshelf, inside the pages of the *Children's Encyclopaedia*, while the key was in her jewellery box, with the cross she didn't wear.

The lid of Great-Aunt Win's box depicted a ship at sea, picked out in intricate marquetry, though the wood was so dark and scratched it was difficult to make it out. Inside was a top layer of small, individual compartments, each lined with red velvet and fitted with its own carefully wrought lid. Some still contained ancient cotton reels, buttons and embroidery silks, none of which had been touched for decades.

She lifted out the lid of the central compartment. On the reverse Great-Aunt Win had stuck a strip of paper, now brown with age, on which she had written, in spindly, copperplate handwriting, her name, the date – 1875 – and a declaration: *Made by I alone.*

Underneath was the pay-as-you-go mobile phone Justin had given Tina a year earlier, when he'd decided it was too risky to keep on contacting her on a number that someone might be able to trace. She still kept this phone switched on and charged up, and occasionally checked for messages. But he hadn't called.

She put the phone away and lifted out the whole top layer.

The body of the box was tightly packed with letters; mixed in with them were the dried heads of half a dozen red roses that he had sent her after their first date. The petals were drier now than paper, the colour of old blood.

Then she had carefully hung them upside down so they would keep their shape. Now she thought: Only six?

She picked out an envelope at random. She didn't know quite what she was looking for. Well, she did. It was the sign-off: *love* . . .

At first he had written to her often, but as time went on and he became more nervous about exposure he'd increasingly relied on the phone. Still, it had always reassured her to look back, to be able to hold something his hand had touched, to have something of him to keep.

She had looked in the box whenever she'd doubted him; as she grew older and began not only to realize that he really was never going to leave his wife, but also to suspect that his insistence on caution was just a means of maintaining control, his letters had restored her faith in him. And she had looked again when the strategies and ruses that were once heart-rending and thrilling in equal measure had become first a drag, and then habit and routine.

His handwriting was beautiful, of course.

Dear Vixen,
There's no point being alive if you're not prepared to take risks. Calculated risks, by all means, but still, what's the point of anything if there's nothing worth taking chances for?

Well, he would say that. Wouldn't he?

But there was no way she could keep this baby. Was there?

She put the letter back into its envelope and tucked it away – gently, as if putting something to sleep – replaced the top layer, put the box back in the top of the wardrobe and went upstairs. It was time to eat, whether she felt like it or not.

Usually she treated cooking for herself as a worthwhile investment in her wellbeing. After all, she needed to maintain her health and energy levels in order to perform well at work. But ever since she'd seen the blue line come up on the pregnancy test – and then on the next one, and the one after that – she hadn't felt like bothering with her favourite recipes. So it had been noodles, pizza, takeout all the way, fast food, stodge that would satisfy her hunger.

She'd let her exercise schedule lapse, too. Normally she swam three times a week, religiously, literally religiously, given that she'd become a keen competitive swimmer at about the same time she'd experienced a slow dawning of scepticism, a gradual awakening into what she thought of as reason, though her mother regarded it as a foolish, self-spiting rebellion, a wilful rejection of the self-evident truth of Father, Son and Holy Ghost. (Her father, more subtle about these things, said only that if Tina was ever sorry about turning her back on the Church, it would probably be too late.)

Swimming hadn't been thought much of at St Birinus – too individualistic, apart from relay races. Hockey was the sport in which excellence was most highly prized – team-spirited, and potentially punitive to boot. Still, Tina had scored a couple of trophies, and she'd kept up the habit when she left home for university and stopped going to Mass. What she liked most about it was how, after fifty lengths, you were conscious only of your body, and when you got out, you felt as clean and clear as if you'd just been forgiven.

It wasn't just her good habits she'd given up since she'd found out she was pregnant; she'd been giving her vices a miss, too. She'd had to chuck out the best part of a bottle of white because it had been in the fridge too long, and even smoking had lost its appeal.

While her pasta was simmering she wandered over to the framed photo montage displayed on the chimney breast, composed of old pictures of her friends. Right in the middle was the one of her with Lucy and Natalie on the beach on New Year's Eve, 1999, all fresh-faced and hopeful. There was no sign of the typical posed group photo awkwardness. They were huddling together for the photo as if they were happy to be close to each other.

Beneath the photo montage, standing on the mantelpiece, was the ormolu carriage clock her parents had given her as a housewarming present, quietly and relentlessly keeping time.

What was it she had said that night?

'This time ten years from now I want to have my own newspaper column, with a nice big picture byline.'

And Lucy had said, 'A job can't love you back.'

The phone rang and she rushed to pick it up, thinking it might be Natalie, then realized too late that it was her mother.

'Hello, darling, I didn't think I'd catch you!' Cecily exclaimed. 'Are you all set for Saturday? We're both very much looking forward to seeing you.'

Tina responded with brittle civility, and made an excuse to get off the phone as soon as she decently could.

After she'd wound up the call she turned off the pasta, rolled herself a cigarette and climbed out of one of the dormer windows on to her unofficial balcony, the narrow ledge between the roof and the parapet wall.

It was quite safe; the parapet wall was chest-height, just right to lean on as you lit up and looked out pensively across the rooftops of Clapham towards the green rim of Battersea Park. You couldn't fall. Well, you could, but you'd have to be very reckless, or very determined, which would make it a jump, wouldn't it?

She lit her cigarette. But the smoke didn't taste right, and as she stubbed it out she realized it was because she was ashamed.

She finally heard from Natalie the following morning, when she checked her mobile in the taxi on the way to the clinic, and saw that she had a new text message.

Matilda Rose Carswell arrived safely at the South London Hospital on Friday 8 May, 8 pounds 1 oz. We're all home now and doing well. Love Natalie, Richard and Matilda xxx

Tina was about to attempt to compose a congratulatory reply when she realized they were nearly there. The message would have to wait. She put the phone back in her bag and directed the taxi driver to a side road off Brixton Hill.

She'd been so nervous about getting snarled up in traffic and missing the appointment that she now had three-quarters of an hour to kill before her appointment. She could, of course, pass the time in the waiting room . . . but she hated the thought of sitting with a group of other equally miserable women, trying not to meet their eyes, knowing only too well what they were all there for.

Teenagers, students, married mums who'd slipped up, girls who would be getting on a plane back to Ireland as soon as they were able . . . She had no doubt that there would be all sorts, all ages, all backgrounds, and just as she would be briefly distracted from her own plight by wondering about theirs, they, too, might spare a moment to speculate why a woman in young middle age, who looked healthy and not too badly off, would choose to terminate a pregnancy, even if she didn't have a ring on her finger to legitimize it.

She paid and got out. She didn't allow herself to hesitate as the taxi drove off, but set off straight away in the direction of the main thoroughfare, even though she didn't quite know what she was going to do next.

The area was still familiar from the time she'd spent living nearby, first with Natalie and Lucy, then with Natalie alone, and then with Natalie and Hannah. It was a network of Victorian terraces that estate agents referred to as 'Brixton Village'. Back then it had been relatively cheap, and also had the advantage of being completely unlike anywhere else Tina had ever lived.

She cringed at the memory of the three of them attempting to limbo dance at the Pineapple Bar, while the otherwise black clientele turned an indulgent blind eye, tolerant of their small white incursion. They had been like tourists in the middle of an illuminating but occasionally threatening adventure, trekking down the hill together each weekday morning to catch the tube, past the thin prostitute on the corner, who always asked if they could spare a cigarette and then listlessly looked away when they refused. Behind her was the big church with the red neon cross and the sign: 'God so loved Brixton He gave His only son', illustrated with a hand-drawn Jesus, his arms emphatically outstretched.

The next landmark had been the clinic. Once they'd seen a thin man with a dark beard down on his knees in the driveway, praying, with a rosary in his fingers. Tina had been infuriated, as if his presence was a personal attack. There was just so much else to pray about if you were the praying type: what about the yellow incident signs? The hooker? But still, the sight of him had made her feel oddly guilty.

She could perhaps have tried to book herself in elsewhere, but this was close, and they'd been able to fit her in on a day Jeremy, her boss, was willing for her to have off, so . . . Anyway, it didn't really matter where she had it done. She just had to get it over with.

She should go to a café. There was one on Brixton Hill they'd always favoured, with a Spanish name, or perhaps it was Portuguese. The scene of many morning-after fry-ups –perhaps it was still there?

On the way she witnessed an altercation. A young black woman was sitting on the ledge of an open first-storey window, her back to the road, as music pumped out from inside the room. An older black woman stopped to berate her: 'What you think you doing with your backside hanging out into the street like that! You ought to be ashamed of yourself!' The younger woman showed no sign of taking any notice and the older woman showed no sign of giving up. Tina skirted round them, kept her head down, and kept moving (*don't get involved, stay out of it, stay out of everything*).

A big fat white man with bad clothes and a receding hairline shuffled towards her. 'I need some money . . . I need some money . . .' he announced in a plaintive, singsong drone, as if stating a universal aspect of experience rather than begging for cash. She ignored him too, and walked quickly on.

El Desayuno was still there. She sat in a corner and sipped a cup of tea, and admired the lovingly cornrowed hair of the little girl sharing a bun with her mother at the next table. But there was no point getting sentimental about the care other people lavished on their children. She'd made her choice.

She opened up the copy of the *Post* she'd brought with her and flicked through till she came to her report about the inquest. It was illustrated with a photo of the Marches at home that Tina had arranged to have taken after the end of the first day in court. She'd felt awful, approaching them to ask about it; however often she had to do this kind of thing, it still bothered her to break the taboo against intruding into other people's grief. But still, it was necessary to remember that often the bereaved wanted to tell the story of their dead. The Marches hadn't minded; they had looked at her trustingly, gratefully even, and offered up a phone number, and she said the *Post*'s photographer should get in touch.

The photograph showed the couple sitting on a sofa; Mr March had his arm round Mrs March, and she was holding a small white christening gown on her lap. Their expressions were sombre and direct, neither solicitous of sympathy nor fearful of the public gaze; it was the look, Tina thought, of those who have been touched by death, and show the mark of it, whose hearts will always turn, from time to time, away from the living and towards the past, the lost, the what-might-have-been.

There it was, staring her in the face: courage. And here she was, carrying a last-chance-saloon baby that she was too afraid to have.

Her phone rang. Her first, uncharitable thought was: Oh no, please don't let it be Natalie. I really can't hear her birth story, not now . . . But then she saw it was work calling.

Shit! Had the Marches complained about her story? She'd been so careful. What could have gone wrong?

'Tina.' It was Jeremy. 'Where the fuck are you?'

'I'm on annual leave. You signed it off.'

'Yeah, well, more to the point, where's your bloody column?'

There was a brief, stunned silence while Tina lurched from guilt and apprehension to panic. It took her insides a moment to catch up with what was happening, as if she'd just plunged downwards in a lift.

'I emailed it to you from home on Tuesday night,' she said. 'Are you sure it didn't get caught in the spam filters or something?'

'Even if it had, do you seriously think I've got time to faff about with the pissing IT department? You've got till half past to sort it out. If you can't cope with doing an occasional bit of proper reporting as well as banging out the opinion stuff, it's a poor bloody show. I thought you women were meant to be good at multitasking!'

And with that he was gone.

Tina took a deep breath and checked the time. Just gone eleven.

What the hell was she going to write? It was a complete lie that she'd sent something in earlier in the week. It had crossed her mind, once or twice, but she'd put it off. And then she'd found herself at the inquest.

Jeremy had a point: it *was* a poor show. She'd screwed up. The column represented the culmination of a decade's hard slog and ambition, and she'd forgotten to write it. She'd been distracted . . . no, worse, distraught. In the courtroom press gallery she had felt a sadness that was not only to do with the case, but was her own, inside her, at her core, the gathering weight of anticipated loss.

Just when her professional life was finally what she had always wanted it to be, her personal life had risen up and stabbed it in the back.

She got a notebook out of her bag, found a biro and started to scribble. Three paragraphs later, she decided she'd got the nub of what she wanted to say.

The Vixen Letters

Why the ideal husband is a . . . house

Who needs a husband, if you can have a house? On the whole, women are pragmatic creatures, who, in the style of Scarlett O'Hara, understand the primary appeal of land. We may indulge in romance, but in the end, security is what we fight for. We've even turned the patrolling of our territory into an art form – home-making is a definitively feminine pursuit.

I don't have a husband, but thankfully, I do at least have a flat. Over the years, it's given me shelter; it's gone up in value; and it's always there for me. Is there any husband that could claim as much?

Boyfriends, spouses, lovers come and go, and man is born to trouble as the sparks fly upward; but we patient Penelopes need somewhere to work on our tapestries while we wait for our heroes to show up. In the meantime, we may well have other suitors, and we prefer to entertain them in a modicum of comfort.

It took her a little while longer to pad it out and round it off, and by the time she'd finished dictating what she'd scrawled to the copytaker she was already quarter of an hour late for her appointment.

What next?

Should she call the clinic?

Well . . . probably. It would be the polite, the right thing to do. If she didn't, they'd probably contact her . . . actually, she was kind of tempted to just turn the damn phone off.

But first of all she would text Natalie. *Great news! Can't wait to see her!* Something like that. And then she was going to order something to eat . . . something with some vitamins in it . . . a steak, perhaps, with a tomato salad. Maybe pudding, too . . . She was suddenly famished.

The prospect of a leisurely afternoon had all the allure of unexpected freedom, and she was surprised by how happy and relieved she felt, as if she'd just had an unexpected reprieve. A great feeling of peace settled over her, as if, for the first time in as long as she could remember, she had all the time in the world.

7

Sunnyview

'So,' Lucy said, 'I have some news.'

She had Matilda on her lap and was feeding her a bottle of formula. The light, warm weight of the baby resting in the crook of her arm, and the blindly trusting appetite with which Matilda was gulping down the milk, reminded her of how it had been when Lottie and Clemmie were small and looked to her for everything. It had been tiring, of course, and monotonous, but from time to time she had known with absolute clarity that her love was being returned, and that the mutual flow of tenderness was sustaining her too.

She could hardly remember now what Lottie and Clemmie had looked like as babies – each stage of their lives seemed to supersede the last, and it was always hard to picture them any other way than they were at the time. But she did recollect what she had felt for them, and the memory, which was bound up with the smell of milk and baby skin, gave her the courage to finally broach the subject she had been avoiding.

She had talked about Ellen's stroke and partial recovery and move to a nursing home, and Tina and Natalie had sympathized; she had explained that Hannah was living in Ellen's flat and had found a lodger to join her, and they had accepted that without question. Probably everybody thought it was about time for Hannah to have a more independent existence.

Lucy had thought it was bold of Natalie to risk getting them all together after the last time, and Tina had been a little quiet, but perfectly friendly and not at all resentful. Probably Lucy should have said sorry first, but in the end it had been Tina who had made the first move, by ringing to apologize. Lucy had immediately reciprocated, and it seemed that a mutual decision had been made, at least for the time being, to pretend that nothing had happened. Besides, there was nothing like a new baby to sweep away old animosity.

Natalie and Tina were looking at her with surprise and pleasure. Oh God – they thought she was about to tell them she was pregnant.

'Not good news,' she added quickly. 'Adam and I have separated.'

And now she was reminded of Clemmie and Lottie again at the moment when she had explained to them why Adam was no longer living in the house. Natalie and Tina were horrified, and she felt culpable, as if she had hurt them and let them down.

Natalie was the first to respond. She looked tired and pale, and there was a faint reek of Savoy cabbage in the air from the frozen leaves she'd been using to cool her swollen breasts; she'd had problems nursing the baby.

'But, Lucy, this is dreadful,' Natalie said. She was sitting next to Lucy on the sofa, and turned towards her and rested her hand on Lucy's, which was cradling Matilda's head.

Lucy was suddenly conscious that she still had her rings on. But why not? Adam had given them to her. He might have gone, but they were still hers.

'When did this happen?' Tina asked. She was the picture of disbelief; eyes wide, eyebrows raised, mouth open.

'Soon after I last saw you, actually, back in the spring. But it's all very amicable.' Why did she feel the need to reassure them? But she did. 'Obviously, it's been an awful time, but we're getting through it. He's seeing the girls most weekends, he's letting me keep the house and the car, he's supporting us financially, we're all coping. So please don't worry – at least, not *too* much.'

Tina gazed at her wonderingly, and then shook her head. 'I can't believe how well you're dealing with this. You're sure you don't want us to come round and cut all the sleeves out of his suits or something?'

Lucy smiled in spite of herself. 'He's already retrieved most of those,' she said, 'and taken them off to Ollie Merrick's. Remember Ollie? That's where he's staying, for now.'

'OK, but if there's anything else I can do,' Tina said, 'vindictive or otherwise, you let me know.'

She looked well, Lucy thought. Better in fact than the

last time they'd met – rested, and relatively relaxed, for someone who tended to run on nervous energy. There was something slightly different about her too, a coy, gratified, sensual quality, Mona Lisa-like, suggestive of physical fulfilment . . . Was it possible that she could be pregnant? But no, surely not.

'Is it definitely over?' Natalie asked.

Lucy hesitated, but only for a moment.

'Yes,' she said. 'It's a dead love, and I'm grieving. But I can't bring it back to life.'

She thought about this later, on the drive back to Thames Ditton to pick up the girls from their playdate, and realized that it was true. Her marriage was history. But whatever the state of their union, Adam still somehow had to be lived with.

She saw him the next day, in the Royal Festival Hall. In the end he was only fifteen minutes late – not too bad, in the scheme of things – but she was fuming anyway. It wasn't for herself that she minded, it was for the girls, so painfully hopeful and waiting, and then so delighted when he arrived.

Of course he was pleased to see them too – who wouldn't be, greeted by such enthusiasm? But she was cool to him, and he looked wounded, as if she was somehow the one in the wrong . . . and then she had to turn her back on all three of them and walk away.

Seeing him always threw her and made it difficult to concentrate. Once she got to Waterloo it took a while for her to work out which platform she needed to get to the Sunnyview Nursing Home, which was round the corner from the hospital where her mother had recovered from the stroke.

As her train pulled away from the station she thought how nice it would have been to spend a summer afternoon pootling round sightseeing with the girls on the South Bank. Instead, she was going to be incarcerated in Sunnyview.

But it served her right; Ellen had accepted that she was not well enough to return home and that Hannah was not around enough to look after her, but she rarely missed an opportunity to hint that Lucy might have seen fit to take her in. This had occurred to Lucy too, but no – with Adam gone, sooner or later she was going to have to go back to work herself; they were getting by for now, but she had to look to the future. And Ellen was still so sick, she needed round-the-clock care . . . and it didn't come cheap.

She had made this point during several painful conversations with her mother, and eventually Ellen had agreed that they could let out her flat to cover the cost, but only if Hannah was one of the tenants, and kept an eye on the newcomer. Luckily, Hannah had been up for this and had spruced up the place a bit and found a friend of a friend to move in with her, so, from a financial point of view at least, Ellen's needs were taken care of.

Ellen was quite capable of saying things like, 'I'm so sorry to be a burden to you, dear. I know you wish I had died.' Lucy knew that if she had to listen to such provocations on a daily basis, in the end they would turn into the truth. It was much easier to persuade herself she was a good and loving daughter when she only saw Ellen once a week, and could summon up the energy to jolly her along.

To distract herself from these uncomfortable thoughts, she fell to eavesdropping on the conversation going on behind her. A girl was telling her friend, 'I just really want to *do* something! Let's do something, yeah? I don't care what it is, let's just go somewhere, have a little adventure, you know?'

The girl's voice was slightly husky, as if she'd only recently taken up smoking, and was pitched at a volume that refused to acknowledge everybody else's right to be indifferent. Lucy didn't want to turn and look – overhearing was one thing, staring was quite another – but thought she was probably listening to someone who was prettyish, but not pretty enough to command attention without trying, and in her last summer before leaving home, perched on the cusp of womanhood.

How wonderful to be eighteen, with a future that was expansive, featureless and there for the taking – to be able to just *do* something!

When Lucy had left home for Bristol for the first time she'd gone by train. She had worried about leaving Ellen and Hannah behind, but she had also felt quite dizzy with freedom.

Thank God you had no way of telling what was coming. She'd had big plans: to get a good degree and become a solicitor and earn stacks of money. But by the end of her first term she was already finding her law degree crucifyingly dull, and she'd fallen hook, line and sinker for the boyfriend who would go on to dump her just before finals and get together with one of their mutual friends, prompting the rest of their circle to close ranks and leave Lucy stranded.

And if she had known that one day she'd walk in on her sister having sex with her husband she would never have allowed herself to fall in love again.

Romantic love was so all-absorbing, but for a limited time only. Where did it go? All that fierce desire to know and be known, to belong, to own and be owned? You might escape, for a time, from the quotidian drudgery of family life, with its more or less suppressed tensions, its unfairly allocated chores, its competitiveness and collusions, its rows, sulks and hissy fits, its occasional moments of transcendent happiness . . . but somehow, sooner or later, you found yourself back where you'd started.

She was well and truly back in the old order now: regulated by duty and guilt and loss. If only she could summon up another kind of love, that would be patient and forgiving, and redeem everything . . . maybe then it would finally begin to change.

The narrow ground-floor bedroom in which Ellen now lived was painted a particularly nasty shade of pink, the colour of the inside of a moist, open mouth. There was one small window, which looked out on to a steep bank of lawn. No sky. The window was open, but there was no breeze. The furniture was minimal, but still took up almost all the available space: a single bed, a small unit with a kettle on it, a chair.

Lucy found Ellen sitting next to the bed, on the

chair, with her back to the window, facing the door. Despite ill health and disability, she had not lost the power to dominate her surroundings, and, if anything, in this confined, institutional, unremarkable space her presence was all the more overwhelming.

'Hello, Mum,' Lucy said and stooped to kiss Ellen on the cheek. She still hadn't quite got used to Ellen's changed appearance, and wondered if she ever would. Had Ellen? Was it possible to get used to something without accepting it?

The only clue to Ellen's lost glory was the grey-blue of her irises, the colour of a calm sea on a wintry day. It was still possible to imagine that a man might once have gazed into those eyes in search of reciprocal adoration or desire. Now, however, they were gloomy and reproachful.

'Come and find me if you need anything,' said Joy, the care assistant who had let Lucy in, and went off leaving the door open.

'Close that, would you? I don't want to see any more of this place than I have to,' Ellen said. Her speech was slower and less clear than it had been, hampered by the paralysis of her face, but it was as emphatic as ever.

Lucy shut the door and sat down on the bed. She'd bought Ellen new bed linen to use here; Ellen had always slept in a double bed, long after she had anyone to share it with, so the duvet she'd left at home would be no use at Sunnyview.

Ellen had been aggressively grateful: 'Very kind of you, when you're so busy and have so much on your plate. I expect they could have given me something, though it might have come off the bed of someone who had died.'

'She seems nice,' Lucy said, inclining her head in the direction of the door Joy had just passed through.

Ellen made a sound that was the closest she could manage to a snort.

'Did you see her fingernails?' Ellen said. 'I'm surprised she's allowed. Not that I should be surprised by anything any more. At least she's alive, I'll give her that. More than you can say for most of the people round here. House of the Living Dead, that's what this is.'

'Oh, Mum, they're not all that bad. Joy took me through the lounge and some of them were sitting watching an old film and having a laugh with the carers. They all seemed quite cheery.'

Ellen made the snorting noise again. 'Most of them can't hit their mouths with a spoon, let alone hold a conversation. Even if they did still have all their marbles I wouldn't have anything in common with them.'

'I read something in the paper the other day about a couple who got married in an old people's home.'

'We had a man turn up just after you last came, and they've already taken him out feet first. They don't last long, you know. Especially in the heat. That's one of the things people talk about here – the ones who can talk, that is. Who's going to be next.'

'I saw some fun social things up on the noticeboard. Something about a quiz night.'

'Did I tell you they play music at mealtimes? All the wartime hits. Vera Lynn and the white cliffs of bloody Dover. The big band sound. I'm the youngest one here,

140

you know. There's more than a few that are old enough to be my mother. Thank God she didn't live to end up in a place like this.'

'I'm sure you could put in a request for the Beatles if you wanted.'

'I take it you didn't bring me a bottle of gin.'

'No, Mum, I didn't.'

'I don't know what you've got to be so high and mighty about. You're not the one who's stuck here. Not yet anyway.'

'It's a nice day. I'll take you out for a walk.'

'You'll get to meet I-want-to-die.'

'Sorry?'

'There's a woman here who sits in the hallway and stares out of the window and says "I want to die, I want to die." That's all she ever does.'

'Oh dear. Poor thing.'

'I hate her.'

There was a short silence.

'It's good you didn't bring Clemmie and Lottie this time,' Ellen said. 'It's no place for children. I can tell when they're here that they can't wait to go, and I don't blame them.'

'Actually, they're with their father today,' Lucy said brightly.

Ellen looked puzzled. 'He's back now, is he?'

'No, he isn't. He's not coming back. He's still staying with a friend.'

'I should think his welcome's wearing pretty thin by now, isn't it?'

'No, actually, that's not a problem.'

'No need to bite my head off. I'm just concerned, that's all. You can't trust him. Not after what he's done. What if he meets someone else? Has another child? It's not like you've kept your career going.'

'I might meet someone else myself.'

'Yes, but it's a lot less likely, isn't it? At your age. It's a great shame you didn't stick with law, if you ask me. If you'd got a good job with a law firm, you'd be set for life by now.'

There was another short silence. Then Ellen said, 'Hannah came last week. She's looking very thin. Seems to me that man's destroyed all of us. Since it was the shock of it that put me in here.'

'Mum, I don't want to talk about it,' Lucy said.

It was suddenly hard to breathe. She got to her feet and murmured something about needing to use the loo.

'It's very difficult not having an en suite,' Ellen observed. 'But there we are, I know it's too expensive, and you've done your best. You have to cut your coat according to your cloth, don't you?'

Lucy went out, shutting the door behind her. The bathroom was down the corridor and round a corner. Like Ellen's room, it was unpleasantly pink. It was equipped with a handrail and an emergency cord that dangled to the floor.

There was a mirror, but no window, and so no natural light to soften the reflection – a combination Lucy could have done without. She saw that she looked pasty, worn out and old. She thought that she looked like death.

*

Thankfully, Ellen's mood seemed to lift as the afternoon went on. In due course they made their way down the corridor past I-want-to-die, a shawled, nodding, mumbling figure slumped in a lobby in front of a window. ('She isn't very clear, but I promise you that's what she's saying,' Ellen told Lucy.)

Ellen hobbled with a stick, leaning heavily on Lucy's arm. Lucy left her sitting in the reception area and went off to find Joy and ask for a wheelchair. Joy moved to lift Ellen into it, and Ellen said, 'No, no, I want to get into it myself.' Joy smiled and carried on regardless, and Ellen seemed to acquiesce.

'Not too long,' Joy said to Lucy once Ellen was in the chair, 'remember dinner is at six. Do you have a blanket?'

'I don't need a blanket, it's the middle of summer,' Ellen protested.

In the end Lucy draped the blanket over the back of the chair, as a compromise, and they set off round the square.

'I doubt the dinner will be worth rushing back for,' Ellen said when Joy was safely out of earshot. 'It's always bland and mushy. Like baby food.'

But as they walked on Ellen fell quiet, and Lucy knew she was content. Seen through her mother's eyes, the sunlight falling on dusty leaves was a reminder of another world.

An hour or so later she returned Ellen to her room, reminded her that she had to collect the girls from Adam at the prearranged time, interrupted Ellen's opening plea for her to stay a little longer, and took her leave.

As she walked away she was surprised to find that her legs still worked, that it really was that easy to escape. At first she couldn't shake the feeling that her mother was jealously watching her, though she knew full well that Ellen was stuck in her viewless room. But once the nursing home was out of sight, as each step put a little extra distance between them, she felt herself growing stronger. One foot in front of the other, that was all it took to break free of Ellen's gravitational pull . . .

And yet as her mother's physical presence faded Lucy felt the stirring of an old, long-buried desperation. The impulse to get off her head; to be completely out of it . . . The desire for release.

When Lucy was finally home and Clemmie and Lottie were both in bed, the house took on the special pall of quiet know only to mothers who are home alone at night: a suspenseful, empty silence in which every ordinary creak speaks of a potential intruder, and the absence of any protector. As Lucy sat in the office, browsing the Boden sale, she had to try her hardest not to listen out for the sound of footsteps on the gravel or a tread on the stairs.

Adam had often been away, of course, but this was different. This time he wasn't coming back.

She finished her glass of Sauvignon Blanc. Just the one. So refreshing after a hot day. The way condensation misted the outside of the glass when it was fresh from the fridge. The taste of summer.

The office had always been Adam's territory: sparse, with an eighteenth-century map of the world on the wall by the desk. She'd replaced the map with one of the nice professional photos they'd had done of the girls last year.

Along with the map, Adam had also taken the mug with the lady who turned naked when you put hot coffee in it, the sound system with the fancy speakers, his drum'n'bass CDs, the photo albums from his childhood, the laptop, his skiing gear and his golf clubs.

He'd left the big PC – just as well, because she would have struggled to set up a new computer.

A yellow envelope had appeared in the bottom right-hand corner of the screen. She opened up her inbox and saw that the message was from Adam. No subject line.

I'm sorry to bring bad news. I was going to tell you today, but everything was so rushed, and with the girls around it didn't seem the right time. I've just been made redundant.

'Oh shit,' Lucy said out loud.

And then she tiptoed downstairs, got the wine out of the fridge and filled her glass to the brim.

8

Girls' night out

'Natalie? Your parents are here!'

Natalie was down on her knees in a corner of the third bedroom, which was currently an office, mainly Richard's, but with a corner for Natalie. Soon it would be Matilda's, when they finally moved the cot out of the marital bedroom, which Richard had abandoned some time ago for the guest room. Then Richard would go back to sleeping with Natalie. At least that was the plan, though Natalie wasn't in any rush to put it into action.

She had a pile of back issues of *First Educator* on one side and some yellowing copies of the *Post* on the other, and a large cardboard box in front.

'It's a bit of a funny time to be having a sort-out, isn't it?' Richard said.

Natalie checked her watch. 'I didn't expect them till twelve.'

'Well, they're obviously very keen to see you.'

That was new: the note of slight irritation with her

parents. He'd always been quite happy to see them before. But then, in the past they had never visited quite so frequently, whereas in the three months since Matilda's birth they had come every couple of weeks.

Usually they came for the day, but tonight they were staying overnight so Pat, Natalie's mother, could help Richard look after Matilda while Natalie went out for the evening. Natalie knew that Richard was grateful not to be left on his own with the baby, but was also not thrilled about spending most of the weekend closeted with his in-laws.

'I just thought, you know, while Matilda was napping, I ought to take advantage and make a start,' she said. She started putting the magazines back into the box.

'I hate it when you flinch like that,' Richard said.

'Like what?'

'When I came in just then. You visibly flinched.'

'You just startled me, that's all.'

'I'd been yelling up the stairs for the last five minutes. It can't have been that much of a surprise,' Richard muttered. He picked up one of the old copies of the *Post*. 'What have you kept this for?'

Natalie took it from him and flicked through till she came to the story she was looking for. 'Speed-dating? Speed-hating, more like . . .' Next to the headline was a large photograph of a noticeably younger Tina Fox, smiling in a sheepish yet self-satisfied fashion, and wearing a short skirt that showed off her legs.

She held it up to show him, and Richard said, 'She was rather attractive, wasn't she? It's funny that she never found anybody. You don't think she might be . . .'

He looked tentatively at Natalie. 'I don't know, gay or something?'

Natalie willed herself not to sound exasperated. 'You can be single without being gay,' she pointed out. She folded the paper and put it away. 'Anyway, she was seeing someone, on the quiet, until quite recently.'

'Oh, that. What was it you used to call him? The Grandee. I always wondered if he was a bit of an excuse.'

'For what?'

'I don't know,' Richard said, 'I just thought it was a very strange thing for her to do, this long relationship with someone who wasn't free to be with her. I mean, why would you do that? It can't have just been about the sex. It seems to have gone on for a lot longer than some marriages.'

'Who knows,' Natalie said.

She put the last few issues of *First Educator* back into the box – it was the title she'd worked for until she'd gone off travelling, just after the millennium. Though really that had been more of an extended holiday; she hadn't saved enough to keep going.

She shoved the box back in the corner and followed Richard downstairs.

Natalie knew that Richard felt invaded by his in-laws' recurring presence in the house, but she was still enjoying the warm glow of her parents' approval. She'd been overshadowed by her older brother throughout her schooldays. He'd been outgoing and sporty and bright, and a shoo-in for head boy; she'd been anxious and bookish and shy, and hadn't even made prefect. Then she'd gone off to Reading to study history, with her parents' rather unenthusiastic blessing; 'If that's what you want,' Larry, her father, had said, 'though I can't see the point of it, myself.' At some point during every phone call home, whichever parent she was speaking to could be counted on to start talking excitedly about David's medical career, but she found it quite impossible to be as pleased about it as they were.

Then, just after she'd started her journalism course, David had dropped a bombshell. He had announced his decision to move to New Zealand. For good.

After he'd gone Larry and Pat continued to speak of him with pride, but it was tempered by sadness. Larry said often that it was good David had left because Britain was going to the dogs, and Pat, who hated flying, planned their annual trips to New Zealand with an attention to detail that struck Natalie as borderline obsessive. She herself had gone out there much less frequently – just twice since the post-millennium trip, but then, David usually came over to Britain once a year anyway.

And as for David himself . . . When she'd been staying with him in Auckland back in 2000, he'd taken her out early one morning to fish for red snapper. It had seemed as good a time as any to bring it up, so she'd told him, 'Mum and Dad do miss you terribly, you know,' and he'd looked away from the boat and stared out across the water to the horizon and said only, 'The thing about being out here, Nat, is that you can do things like this. I know that they're upset, but it's my life.'

David's departure shook both his parents – whatever

they tried to think of it, Natalie knew they felt it as a rejection – and since he'd gone, Natalie found that everything she did attracted attention and concern. Pat worried about David too, but impotently; she worried about Natalie with a purpose. And when Pat worried, Larry worried too, because they were that kind of couple: they were almost indivisible, and rarely expressed different points of view.

Natalie had often thought: Thank God for Richard. They loved Richard; she could hardly have found a son-in-law more guaranteed to please them. They were delighted with their first grandchild, too, but that didn't stop them fretting. There was still plenty that could go wrong, and they wanted to do everything they could to ensure that it didn't.

Almost before Pat had got her coat off she was asking when they were planning to move Matilda into her own room, and was she still disturbing them at night and how was Richard coping with that and his heavy workload, and had Natalie managed to get Matilda into a proper routine yet?

Meanwhile, Larry went from room to room to see if there were any DIY jobs that needed tackling – another feature of Richard's perfection as a son-in-law was that, like Natalie, he wasn't particularly handy, and Larry was, and this meant he could make himself useful.

Then Larry asked whether their preference was to trade up or extend, whereupon Pat said, 'Move right out of London, I should think,' and Natalie didn't hear Richard sigh, but suspected that he wanted to.

Richard needed to stay in or near London for work,

and Natalie had grown up in Home Counties suburbia and didn't particularly want to go back. When they got married in central London, she'd hoped to send out a signal – *we are cosmopolitan now, and this is home* – but it seemed likely that both their families were going to continue to call this into question.

For lunch Natalie washed a pre-prepared salad and heated up a shop-bought quiche. She felt that this was a bit of a poor show (Lucy would have cooked something nice, even with a three-month-old baby), but although she'd planned to master lots of new dishes while she was on maternity leave, it hadn't quite happened yet.

After helping to load the dishwasher Richard escaped to the office on the pretext of doing some work and Larry settled in the most comfortable armchair (usually reserved for Richard) with the *Post* Sudoku. Pat cuddled Matilda, who was, as ever, soothed by her grandmother's air of calm, sensible authority. Natalie made a bottle of formula.

'Have you given up on that awful breast pump, then?' Pat asked.

'I have,' Natalie said.

'That must be a relief,' Pat said. 'I expect you'll start to get your figure back now. I think lots of women find they carry a bit of extra weight while they're feeding.'

Natalie saw the anxiety in her mother's face and realized that this was something Pat was particularly concerned about. Maybe she thought Natalie's post-baby bulk would make Richard vulnerable to temptation? Natalie felt herself reddening, and turned her back on

Pat while she screwed the top on the bottle and shook it vigorously.

They went into the sitting room, where Larry was already dozing, and Pat gave Matilda her bottle, and asked Natalie, a little hesitantly, 'Any more thoughts on whether you're going to go back to work?'

'I'm going to take the full entitlement, which is a year,' Natalie said.

In her view, this was a major concession. Her ante-natal group acquaintances were all planning to return to work in the autumn, when their babies were six months old.

'And your employers are happy with that, are they?' Pat asked.

'They made the rules. They can hardly object if I take advantage of them.'

Pat sniffed. Neither she nor Larry were admirers of the Government, and they found it strange that Natalie made a living out of attempting to justify its actions, although they always noticed if there was a spokes-person's quote from the Department for Children, Schools and Families in the *Post*, which was their paper of choice.

'And what about after the year's up?' Pat asked.

'I'm thinking about going back part-time.'

'They're so important, these formative years. It's time you don't get back, you know.'

'Did you enjoy it?'

'Beg pardon, enjoy what?'

'Being at home with me and David when we were little.'

'You have to remember it was jolly hard work back then. There were no disposable nappies, and we didn't have a washing machine, let alone a tumble-dryer. I'm not sure enjoyment is what it's about, really. Children aren't a hobby.'

'They certainly aren't,' Natalie agreed.

Pat looked down at Matilda, who was drifting back off to sleep. 'But they're what it's all about. Aren't they? Who knows, maybe seeing you with your little one will make your brother re-evaluate,' she said.

David's partner, a consultant radiologist at the Auckland hospital where David also worked, was a youthful forty-five to his thirty-eight. By choosing to cohabit with an older woman, and one with such a high-flying career at that, David had signalled his lack of interest in reproducing, while still leaving his parents a glimmer of hope that one day he might wake up brimful of the desire to propagate himself and move on to a nice girl in her twenties.

'I kind of get the impression David's happy as he is,' Natalie said.

'Happiness isn't everything,' Pat said. 'Happiness doesn't mean you're immune to regret.'

Natalie felt faintly reproved by this. But then she got out the latest batch of photos of Matilda so Pat could choose which ones she'd like copies of, and Pat said, 'Oh, she's gorgeous – she's so like you were,' and the awkwardness of the return-to-work conversation was forgotten.

That evening, once Matilda was down, Natalie squeezed into the black top and trousers and sequinned cardigan she'd decided to wear for her night out with the other mothers from antenatal class. They were pre-pregnancy clothes she was just about able to get back into. When she checked out her reflection she thought she didn't look too bad; at least she had a waist again.

She went into the office to say goodbye to Richard, and he said, 'Have a good time. You deserve it. You should make the most of it. Say hello to them all from me.'

They exchanged a dry kiss and she went downstairs and into the living room, where Pat and Larry were watching the news.

'Oh, you look lovely,' Pat said. 'Doesn't she, Larry? Natalie, I do declare, motherhood suits you.'

As Natalie's taxi moved away she reflected that perhaps Pat was right; maybe after all those years of feeling inadequate and restricted, she was finally going to come into her own.

After so many evenings spent at home attempting to breastfeed Matilda and worrying about mastitis, it was bizarre to be out after dark, in a cocktail bar, knocking back margaritas. Natalie guessed that everybody else was finding it slightly strange too, because they kept talking about their babies, as if that would compensate for the unfamiliarity of not being with them.

Adele was the only one who hadn't made an obvious effort to dress up, and yet she was the clear winner in the style stakes. She was wearing a little yellow cotton sundress that looked as if it might well have come from a charity shop, and yet showcased her suntanned limbs and long, honey-coloured hair as if made to measure. The effect was insouciantly leonine; she looked as if she'd barely made an effort, but would be terrifying if she did.

More than once, someone said, 'But we must all keep in touch. We will, won't we? We must do this again,' and Natalie wondered if they would, once they were all back at work and scattered across London. Pretty much everybody seemed to be planning to move to bigger houses in outlying parts of the city, apart from Natalie and Richard, and Marcus and Adele.

After her second cocktail she felt ridiculously sleepy – too much to drink after too many broken nights, and she wasn't used to alcohol any more. It would probably be as well to get home before too long, anyway – Matilda still often woke a couple of times during the night, and refused to let Richard comfort her; only Natalie would do.

'So, who's up for another drink?' said Jessie Oliver, who had organised the get-together. 'Nat, how about you?'

'I think I'd better pass, actually,' Natalie said. 'I'm probably going to head off soon.'

'You sure? How about you, Adele?' Jessie said.

'I'm going to make a move too,' Adele said.

'Oh dear oh dear, this will never do. It's only half past ten! OK, before you guys go, I'd like to propose a toast. To our babies.'

They clinked their empty glasses, and there was a round of goodbye embraces, through which Natalie moved self-consciously but sincerely; whether or not these women were going to turn out to be part of her future, they had already been through a lot together.

Then she and Adele were out of the warm, perfumed, over-eager babble of the bar and striding quickly through the surprising coolness of the summer night. Adele was wearing a thin white cardigan over her frock, and Natalie wondered if she was warm enough, but then she concluded that Adele was not the type to feel the cold, or to admit to it if she did.

Neither of them spoke for a while, and Natalie found herself hurrying to keep up. She glanced at Adele's profile and saw she looked both determined and pre-occupied, but couldn't deduce whether she was angry, or sad, or both.

'I'm sure there's a mini-cab office somewhere along here,' Natalie said, but Adele ignored her.

Try again. 'It was a nice evening, wasn't it?' she ventured. 'I hope we do it again soon.'

'I don't suppose we will,' Adele said. 'It was nice while it lasted, but we were all just going through the same thing in the same place, and now we've done it and everybody's moving on. It takes more than liking people to make the effort to stay in touch. There has to be something else.'

Then she took Natalie firmly by the hand and led her a little way down a quiet side street.

Natalie giggled.

'What are we doing now?' she asked.

Adele stopped and squared up to her. She shifted closer so that her body was pressed up hard against

Natalie's. Then she planted her mouth on Natalie's and kissed her.

After a while she withdrew.

'I've been wanting to do that for a long time,' she said.

'I guess it had crossed my mind,' Natalie said. 'I mean, once or twice. I'm a bit new to this kind of thing. Not totally new, but mostly new.'

Adele took her by the hand again, and Natalie felt something that shocked her – a distinct crackle, a tug of energy passing from palm to palm.

'Come back to mine,' Adele said. 'I've got the place to myself. He's taken Paris to his mother's.'

'I should be getting back.'

'When are they expecting you?'

'Oh, I don't know. Midnight?'

'Then come home with me, and I'll call you a cab.'

Surely that was a harmless suggestion? Sensible, even.

'OK,' Natalie said.

They kept holding hands as they walked along. Natalie stumbled and lurched towards the pavement and Adele pulled her back upright. Natalie giggled again and realized that she was drunker by far than she'd expected to be. She also realized that she didn't care.

9

Publish and be damned

Tina's upbringing had instilled in her a range of values that she was able, with a little effort, to ignore: chastity, truthfulness, willing self-sacrifice, and so on. It had also taught her one guiding principle for which she had enduring respect: May as well be hung for a sheep as a lamb. And so, once her pregnancy was so advanced that it was not going to be possible to keep it secret for much longer, it was inevitable that she'd be tempted to use her column to announce it.

She hadn't piled on the weight, but there was only so much you could do with tunic tops, empire-line dresses and forgiving jackets. Her hair had the implausible bounce and vigour of a celebrity's crowning glory in a shampoo ad, she'd gone up from an A cup to a C, her belly button was no longer an inny and she had a weird black line bisecting her belly from her navel to her pubes. The smell of cooked cabbage made her want to vomit, and after every lunch break she had to fight the urge to crawl under her desk and nap.

The changes weren't just physical, either. She had discovered a perturbing ability to cry; it had turned out to be a very bad idea to watch that film about unmarried, institutionalized mothers in 1950s Ireland. Yet her response to stress had slowed down; deadlines didn't fill her with adrenalin as headily as they once had. Perhaps she just didn't care quite as much. The baby thrashed around and pummelled her insides so insistently that it was impossible to forget how much her life was about to change, and while her old priorities hadn't been swept aside entirely, they seemed to have been suspended.

She carried, in her wallet, the printout she'd been given after the twelve-week scan, showing a smudge of white curled against shades of grey. If you didn't know what it was, you couldn't have guessed; it looked like the ghost of a bean. But she had been told it was a boy. Her son! At the twenty-week scan – a couple of weeks ago now – she'd been startled by the array of bones he had sprouted, all as sharply visible as the remains of a dinosaur exhibited in a museum: the spikes of ribs, the limbs, the skull. She was gestating something as hard and enduring as a fossil, something that was, if not yet visibly human, at least obviously animal . . . and much too big now for its life-size image to fit easily into a wallet.

She knew from her baby books – her current guilty pleasure – that he was now growing toenails and fingernails, had capillaries blooming with blood beneath the skin, could hear her heartbeat, her voice, the grumbling of her stomach before mealtimes. So far, nobody had said, 'So when's it due?' or offered her a seat on the tube, but surely it wouldn't be long. When she was in her swimming costume the real reason for her enhanced embonpoint was immediately obvious, but so far she'd managed to avoid bumping into anyone she knew in the pool.

She fancied that, just lately, she'd been the focus of sidelong, calculating glances from some of her female colleagues, most notably Anthea Trask, the lissom mother of five, but also, lately, Rowena Fix, the fearsomely efficient features editor, and even Julia, Dan's girlfriend, who seemed to be surviving in her position as Rowena's general dogsbody. Maybe they were trying to work out if she'd had a boob job. It was sod's law that now Tina finally had a cleavage worth drawing attention to, showing it off was the last thing she wanted to do.

Dan had barely looked at her at all. Soon after she had decided to keep the baby she had bumped into him coming into the building with Julia one morning. After that she kept seeing them together, usually at lunchtime, when they paraded up and down the road outside the office, holding hands, and laughing at each other's jokes, and looking like the picture of young love. Once she'd even walked in on them in the basement room where spare back issues were kept – though mercifully they'd been doing nothing more intimate than gazing into each others' eyes.

She knew it was unreasonable to be hurt, and yet . . . She told herself that what she missed was the bantering, flirty friendship she'd once had with Dan, and she'd wrecked that as soon as she'd slept with him – it wasn't really Julia's fault. It did occur to her to wonder whether Julia knew that something had happened between her and Dan and had put an embargo on any further contact, but she dismissed that as self-aggrandizing; why should Julia be jealous?

She kept going back to that awful conversation . . . *'Really? You look younger.'* So humiliating. But thinking about it now, hadn't what he'd said actually been rather innocuous? Couldn't it even be interpreted as a sort of compliment? To be sure, it had been an awkward moment, but was it possible that that was more to do with her own feelings about having been left behind in the race than anything he had said?

But then . . . it was irrelevant now whether or not he'd been put off because she was at an age where she might want to chivvy things along towards commitment and reproduction. She *was* having a baby, and it might or might not be his. There was no way that was going to be welcome news.

Mulling it over, she realized how little she knew him; she found it impossible to predict his reactions. Would he be angry? Upset? Would he push her to have a paternity test done as soon as possible – even though she had decided she wanted to wait until after the baby was born, because testing in utero carried a small risk of miscarriage and now she had decided to have this baby, she really didn't want to lose it? Would he press her to tell him who the other candidate for paternity was, even if she said she couldn't? Would he say the magic words – 'Whatever you want, I'll support you' – or would he accuse her of wrecking his life?

Justin's response was much easier to foresee. He had forbidden her to contact him, so from the outset he would be angry, but coldly so, and his first concern would be for his reputation. He would warn her to keep him out of it. He would hint darkly that embittered ex-girlfriends tended to come off worst if they attempted to go public about their relationships with powerful men. And he would wash his hands of her and make sure she knew that she was on her own.

Which was how she felt: alone, with only the growing baby for company. Surely that was the best, the safest, the least complicated way. She didn't want anything from anybody else. She didn't need anything from anybody else. All she wanted to do was keep her head down, hang on to her job and her sanity, and stay healthy. And so she drifted along in a soporific, self-contained state, lying low, biding her time, knowing that sooner or later she would have to cope with the reaction to her news, but not yet quite ready to invite it.

She would have liked to tell Natalie, and Lucy too, but she could hardly go to her friends before she'd brought herself to disclose her pregnancy to her parents or her former lovers. She felt bad about keeping a bit of a distance from them, given that Natalie was trying to adjust to life with her new baby, and Lucy was having an awful time, with Adam gone and her mother in a nursing home. But right now, she needed to focus on looking after herself . . . and although she felt very sorry for Lucy, she still hadn't *quite* got over the showdown over her column back in the spring. *You're on your own, you haven't got a man, and you're running out of time.* She was glad they'd patched things up, but the words couldn't be unsaid.

It hadn't actually been all that difficult to avoid her friends – so many people were away in July and August, or expected you to be. And somehow, so far, she had got away with it. She'd gone out with Megan Morton, her actress pal, but Megan had been too busy going on about her planned reality TV debut, and checking to see if anyone had recognized her, to join the dots between Tina's virgin Bloody Mary and mystery weight gain. A weekend with Lucilla Gordon in Norfolk would have been trickier to manage, but at the last minute Lucilla's baby came down with chicken pox and Tina was able to stay home with a clear conscience.

Her parents had been more of a problem. After getting through her dad's seventieth back in May, she'd felt she'd earned a couple of months' reprieve. But Cecily had had other ideas, and Tina had been obliged to make a string of excuses to get out of going home: deadlines, summer flu, press trips, friends who needed her support. She'd just about managed to wriggle out of going down to Cornwall for the August Bank Holiday weekend, as she was due to work on the Monday. But actually, saying no had made her feel sad. It was more than a year since she'd stayed in the Old Schoolhouse, and she missed it. Now, more than ever, it would be good to be reminded that her childhood was not just an increasingly distant memory, and that the scene of all those long-ago summer holidays was still essentially unchanged, and could be revisited any time she was free to go.

Even before she got her own column, Tina had noticed that the articles she wrote were umbilically connected to how she felt about whatever was going on in her private life. After she'd started seeing Justin she had found herself writing repeatedly about political mistresses, and middle-class career girls who were apparently respectable but nursed dark secrets, such as heroin or cocaine habits, which they somehow fitted in round office hours and funded with weekend lap dancing.

In the last few months just about everything seemed to have been about mothers and babies. Her latest assignment was a feature about women's experiences of childbirth, which she suspected was not going to be reassuring.

She did the first case study interview with the editorial administrator, an unflappable, pragmatic woman who was currently on maternity leave, and who, under cover of anonymity, spoke candidly about her desire to suffer as little as possible, and how it came to be thwarted.

They said to me, Have you made a birth plan? I said I'd like an epidural please, and the ventouse. They said you can't have that, it's too stressful for the baby. I said, Well, if you're going to tell me I can't have what I want, what's the point of me making a plan?

When Tina reviewed her notes after finishing their phone conversation, she decided she wouldn't bother with a birth plan either. Going by Natalie's experience, they seemed to be pretty pointless, except as a psychological sop. Anyway, it would be fitting for an accidental conception to be followed by an unplanned birth.

She looked up to see Julia approaching her. God, she was slim! Admittedly it was quite a nasty pinstriped shirt she was wearing, but at least she had a waist.

Julia came to a halt at a slight distance from Tina's desk. She looked rather upset – bad day, perhaps. Julia's boss, Rowena Fix, was a hardened marathon runner who was known to expect similar feats of endurance from her underlings, so it wouldn't be surprising.

Tina attempted a smile, and Julia's lips twitched in what might have passed for a friendly response, if she hadn't looked quite so miserable.

Julia said, 'I just picked up a call from reception for you. There's a woman down there who says she's your mother,' and hurried off.

It was a quarter to one. Lunch, or at least a brief conversation, was unavoidable. Tina shouldered her handbag, took a deep breath, and went downstairs to meet her maker.

Cecily was sitting in one of the modish armchairs provided for waiting visitors, just in front of the framed and wall-mounted front cover that warned women not to wait to have babies: 'Scientists reveal fresh insights into the fertility time bomb'. She was flicking through a complimentary copy of the *Post*, and for a moment Tina was able to see her as a stranger might: as a conscientious, comfortable older woman who cared about appearances, and was doing her best to keep the ravages of time at bay.

Cecily's skin had a buffed, healthy sheen suggestive of regular exercise, good lunches and quality moisturizer, and her immaculately bobbed hair was tinted blonde, a shade or two lighter than Tina's own. She was dressed in a cotton blazer, T-shirt, slacks and pumps in shades of white, cream and beige, with a narrow scarf in copper and bronze silk wound round her neck – to disguise lines and droop, perhaps, or to add a dash of panache, or both. Somewhere under the scarf, Tina knew, was the small gold cross that Cecily always wore.

Then Cecily looked up, and Tina was reminded that her mother's face was softer and rounder – more motherly, in fact – than her own, which had her father's sharpness.

Cecily's expression was tense and anxious. For a moment, for the split second in which she spotted Tina coming towards her, the fretfulness gave way to unthinking pleasure, only to be replaced, in rapid succession, by conjecture and assessment, diagnosis, shock and dismay. From the sudden tight set of Cecily's mouth Tina deduced a suppressed question that would almost certainly spill out before very much longer: *So what about the father?*

Cecily looked away first. She tucked the free copy of the *Post* into a John Lewis carrier bag – she must have been shopping round the corner, as a pretext for popping in – and got to her feet. Even though Tina had the advantage of an extra couple of inches, she suddenly felt very small, and she was sure that she was blushing.

She knew the natural thing to do – the behaviour the receptionist would expect – was to attempt some sort of embrace, and peck her mother on the cheek. But somehow this was not possible.

'Well,' she said, and her voice sounded unexpectedly shrill and nervous, 'this is a surprise.'

'It is,' Cecily agreed.

'You should have told me you were coming.'

'If I had, I imagine you wouldn't be here,' Cecily said. 'Is there somewhere we can talk?'

That night Tina did not sleep well. She worked herself up into an impotent fury with Cecily for being so judgemental . . . so resolutely undelighted . . . so *ashamed*. For heaven's sake, it was the twenty-first century! Tina had every right to bring a child into the world on her own if she wanted to. Perhaps some of Cecily's more devout friends would disapprove, or be pitying, as if Tina had let the family down, but damn it, this was a new life, a first grandchild – surely it wasn't really something to pull such a long face about?

OK, so perhaps Tina hadn't handled it very well. She should have taken control, managed the disclosure, faced both her parents down at a time of her choosing. The truth was, she hadn't told them because she'd been scared of how they would react. Oh, she knew they would come round, especially when the baby arrived; she knew she should give them time to adjust, and make allowances for their beliefs about family life,

167

according to which there was a right way to do these things, which involved matrimony, and a wrong way, which was everything else. They might manage to love the baby, but they would never ditch the beliefs, which meant that, in their eyes, she was a failure.

Even if something good – something worth cherishing – came out of her shortcomings, it would always be qualified; her child would never be a straightforward cause of celebration. She knew that both her parents would behave as if they had something to forgive, as if their acceptance of her son was a badge of virtue; but love provided with such reservations would be mortifying. She thought that outright rejection, unmixed with goodwill, would be less disheartening.

As the night wore on her resentment turned to misery, and she cried for the child that even she had not entirely wanted. Eventually, sometime after 2 a.m., she turned on the light and read a bit of a history of women's lives in seventeenth-century England. That did the trick; things could have been worse – had been, in the past. She was woken after what seemed like a couple of minutes' sleep by the alarm and the recollection that she'd promised to break the news to her father.

'I think it ought to come from you,' Cecily had said, firmly but kindly, and probably she was right; Tina was a grown-up, she shouldn't need Cecily to intercede on her behalf. But then Cecily's parting words had been, 'Goodness only knows what Daddy's going to say. I'm afraid he's going to feel rather let down,' and Tina had realized that, as usual, the tough love, the real chastisement, was going to be left to her father to deliver. And she didn't want to accept it. Cecily being wounded was one thing, but Robert being outraged was quite another.

The prospect of ringing home, and Robert answering the phone, and the conversation that would follow, was just too appalling to contemplate.

'No, it's actually you I wanted . . . I've got something to tell you . . . No, I'm not involved with the baby's father, and no, I don't actually know for sure who he is, and he, whoever he is, knows even less than I do.'

No. She couldn't submit to that. She had to go down fighting. There had to be another way.

That was when the idea popped into her head, and it was so mischievous, so disrespectful, so downright naughty, that her initial response was incredulity at her own devilishness.

Then she started to laugh.

Why not? Why shouldn't she explain herself? She had the chance to justify what she'd done, and why she'd done it, on a grand scale. Presented with such an opportunity for vindication, who could resist?

She was going to have to tell work sometime in the next couple of weeks. So why not kill two birds with one stone? Anyway, she was clean out of ideas for this week's column – what the hell else was she going to write about?

Maybe it was only a temporary reprieve, but for now, at least, the guilt and regret Cecily had prompted had completely disappeared.

*

When she got into work the next morning she saw Dan, as usual, waiting by the lift. He was on his own, and no one else was in earshot.

It wasn't really a conscious decision. She'd got out of the habit of taking the stairs anyway – didn't have the energy any more. Somehow she found herself standing next to him.

The lift doors opened and he stood back to let her go in first. The doors closed and the lift started to ascend, and she said, 'How are you? How are things with the lovely Julia?'

'Oh . . . didn't you know? We broke up.'

'I'm sorry to hear that,' she said.

He glanced at her. 'So are you going to start talking to me again now?'

'Me? You were the one who wasn't talking to me.'

He sighed. 'Well . . . whoever started it, I think we can agree that we've been pretty silent lately.'

The lift hit the third floor. The doors opened, but nobody got in. Tina hit the button, the doors closed, and they went up again.

It was now or never.

'We need to talk,' she said. 'Properly, not like this. Are you free for lunch?'

'Yes, I suppose so, but—'

'How about one o'clock, in the café in John Lewis?'

'Why there? Nobody ever goes there. Isn't that where all the mums and babies go?'

Fourth floor. The bell rang.

'Please,' Tina said as the doors opened.

She stepped out and round Monty Delamere, the

rotund parliamentary sketch writer, who was waiting, cigs in hand, to go down for his first smoker's break of the day.

Monty brandished his cigarettes at them and declared, 'It's no good. I shall never give up. I just can't make a start without them.'

Monty was known for his booming voice, which was echoed in the hectoring tone of his writing. Tina only just heard Dan say, 'OK.'

When she got to the café at lunchtime Dan was already there.

'Aren't you going to have anything to eat?' she asked him, setting her tray down on the table – she was starving.

He shook his head.

'Too nervous,' he said. 'So . . . what did you want to talk about?'

She got a single sheet of paper out of her handbag, pushed it across the table towards him, and tucked in to her chilli con carne while he read.

The Vixen Letters

A secret too big to keep to myself

Nobody's perfect, according to the famous final quip from *Some Like It Hot* – but some are more imperfect than others, and some inflict their imperfections on their offspring and drag the whole lot of us down into the gutter. This is the lot of the single mother, or so many of the political class and my fellow columnists in the media would have you believe.

Single mothers have a lot to answer for, don't they? Street crime, social breakdown, happy slapping, pretty much any petty act of violence perpetrated by hoodie-wearing thugs . . . Who'd have thought that a bunch of mostly middle-aged women (the average single mother is thirty-seven), who are by definition lumbered with sole responsibility for looking after at least one child, and therefore likely to be somewhat preoccupied, would have the energy to generate so much restless violence? It's phenomenal, isn't it? I've always had a lot of respect for the resourcefulness of my gender, but this supposed ability to change nappies with one hand and lay waste to civilization with the other strikes me as truly incredible.

Time for me to declare a vested interest: I'm five months pregnant, and well on the way to becoming a single mother myself.

Accidents happen, and who knows how many of us wouldn't be here if they didn't? Sometimes accidents are blessings in disguise. I am very happy that I am having a baby; scared, honoured, intimidated, but mainly happy.

Some will take the view that my interesting condition is a moral and social failure, and if I wasn't relatively well off financially, many more might be inclined to agree with them. But then, a couple of hundred years ago, many of our forebears genuinely believed in witches, and thought it was quite proper to prosecute them with the full force of the law. We're never as far ahead of our ancestors as we'd like to think, and however we try to move forward, the bad old desire to find a scapegoat will always pull us back. And so we keep finding ourselves in the gutter, and looking for someone convenient to blame.

Dan read it, then read it again. She finished eating and watched him and waited.

Finally he looked up. His face was stiff with shock and discomfort, as if he'd just sucked on something horribly sour, and couldn't get over the taste of it.

'Am I the father?' he asked.

'I can't be sure. There was someone else. We'll have to wait until after the birth to find out.'

'Who is he?'

'I can't tell you that. I can't tell anyone that.'

There were smile lines around his eyes, which were a clear bright blue, the colour, she'd once read, most likely to be deemed trustworthy. He wasn't smiling now. He was contemplating her with such forensic attention that she was suddenly acutely self-conscious, and felt herself beginning to itch.

Finally he asked, 'Has anybody else seen this?'

She shook her head. 'I haven't filed it yet.'

'Why are you showing it to me? Are you warning me, or asking me for my permission?'

'I think I'm asking for your blessing.'

'Can you keep my name out of it?'

'Yes,' she said.

'I never told Julia what happened between us,' he said. 'She kept asking, though. People might figure it out.'

'I can live with that,' she told him, 'but I'd prefer to leave them guessing for as long as possible.'

'Then let's,' he agreed. 'But go ahead, do your thing. I don't want to censor you. It's not for me to give you permission, anyway.'

'I'm sorry,' she said.

'About what?'

'About . . . putting you in this position. Springing it on you like this.'

He swallowed. 'Well . . . It's a new life, Tina. That's what matters, in the end, isn't it? So I guess congratulations are in order.'

She opened up her handbag, and he said, 'Oh God, you haven't got another column in there, have you?'

'No, something much better,' she said. She got her wallet out and found the scan picture and passed it to him.

He gazed at it for a while, and then passed it back. The expression on his face was quite unfamiliar, and it took her a moment to see it for what it was: a kind of awe.

She was due to file her column by noon on the following day, for publication on Bank Holiday Monday. She saved it in Jeremy's copy folder at ten to, and rewarded herself by making a cup of camomile tea. (To her astonishment, she had managed to give up caffeine.)

When she was back at her desk, her phone rang. It was Jeremy.

'Well well,' he said. 'I must admit, I thought you'd been looking a bit porky lately.'

'I wouldn't make that kind of comment if I were you. I might get terribly hormonal and upset.' She looked around to check who was in earshot, and then remembered that everyone was going to know soon anyway.

'You do realize, don't you, that you're going to have to

174

tell me this officially? Much as I admire your disregard for standard workplace protocol.'

'I don't actually have to notify you for another couple of weeks, you know. This is just me jumping the gun, in the interests of the column.'

'So when's it due?'

'Christmas Day.'

Jeremy gurgled with laughter. 'You're kidding me. That is just perfect. That is too good to be true. So should I expect a big star and a couple of wise men?'

'I'm afraid the only stars will probably be the ordinary ones, and I think wisdom is a rather subjective quality.'

'But I presume you're not actually laying claim to an immaculate conception. Is there anybody you ought to give advance warning before this goes to press?'

'I haven't libelled anyone, or invaded anyone's privacy. I'm well within my rights. Publish and be damned.'

'So, er, Tina, between you and me . . . who's the daddy?'

'Watch this space,' Tina said. She let Jeremy hang up first.

Over the next few days the news of Tina's pregnancy began to fan outwards from the subs' desk. Perhaps it was paranoia, but she detected a thrill of speculation following her as she moved around the office – she wasn't waddling yet, not exactly, but she certainly couldn't sashay, and much as she wanted to appear to be in control, she knew that she probably came across as increasingly clumsy and burdened.

That week's work experience congratulated her in the

loos, Julia looked more upset than ever, and Anthea Trask told her she looked 'positively blooming': 'The second trimester's wonderful, I always think – so much energy! You will make the most of it, won't you? It doesn't last, I'm afraid. As you know, I've got five of my own, so if you ever want any advice, do feel free to ask.'

The weekend came as a relief, as it involved no personal contact with anyone. She ate, slept, swam, read and shopped online for maternity clothes – now that she was about to out herself, she could embrace elasticated panels, expandable waists and flat shoes. It was easy enough to ignore the accusatory vibrations given off by the telephone: her mother, still waiting for Tina to call and tell her father.

Saturday was fine, and she packed a picnic lunch and took it to Clapham Common, but was plagued by swarming ants and wasps enjoying their last hurrah. At dusk on Sunday she went out for a stroll and smelt an autumnal chill in the air, redolent of approaching bonfires. The sky was clear, and there was a huge, low, foreboding harvest moon, a reminder that the season of cold and darkness was on its way.

On Monday morning she was at her desk, finishing off the feature about women's experiences of childbirth, when her mobile rang. *Mum and Dad.* She decided to let her father leave a message; it might be as well to allow him some cooling-off time before they spoke.

She had known he would see it. Her parents took the *Post*, not because it was really their kind of paper – they were broadsheet people – but out of loyalty.

They didn't necessarily read everything she wrote, but usually at least checked to see that she was still in there. Tina suspected it was her picture byline, not the words that went with it, that gave Robert most pleasure. *My daughter.*

She listened to the message.

Tina, I'm afraid I have to tell you that I'm very disappointed in you. You've upset your mother and embarrassed both of us. I must ask you to reconsider your approach, if not for our sakes, then for the sake of our unborn grandchild.

Click!

Tina put her head in her hands and fought the impulse to curl up into a foetal ball in her chair. Thankfully the office was quiet, it being a Bank Holiday, and the corner she shared with Monty and Anthea and the work experience was empty, so there was no one close enough to lean over and ask her if she was all right.

Very disappointed in you . . . It wasn't the first time he'd said it. There'd been that time she got into a muddle with her finances during her journalism course, and had to ask for an additional loan . . . Or back further still, when she got caught with some cigarettes in her bag, and was nearly suspended from school . . . It wasn't the words so much, though they were bad enough, it was the chill in the voice. That voice! It had dominated all the dinnertimes of her youth: discussing, questioning, encouraging, and, of course, prevailing.

Of course both her parents probably still believed, deep down, that a woman's name should appear in the papers only when she got engaged, married, gave birth, and died. If they had tolerated and even encouraged her career as a journalist, it was at least partly out of relief that she'd dropped the idea of becoming an actress, which would, had she succeeded, have been even more exhibitionistic and amoral. She'd compromised early on, by applying to do a degree in drama and English rather than trying to get into RADA or LAMDA or Central or Guildhall . . .

She pictured the scene back home: her mother banishing any conflicting feelings by keeping busy, stewing apple for the winter's crumbles or boiling up a great vat of plums for jam or chutney, while her father harrumphed over the *Record* crossword in the dining room.

Don't care! Don't care was made to care! A small, mean, miserable sense of satisfaction stole over her. This was the rebel's reward; if you invited punishment, it lost at least some of its sting.

By eight o'clock that evening she was lying on the sofa in her new, large, drawstring-waisted pyjamas, grateful for the sudden cool that came with sundown, enjoying, if truth be told, the smooth, taut, alien protuberance of her bump, and watching *Friends*, which had become her proxy social life. Then she heard the phone Justin had given her working its way through its default ringtone.

She padded downstairs, fished the phone out of Great-Aunt Win's box and listened to the message. He would call back in ten. He did not sound anxious, or angry. He sounded . . . professional.

Now feeling thoroughly unrelaxed, she put the phone away, carried the box upstairs and set it down on the coffee table.

Her mobile beeped. It was Lucy: *Well, well, well, you are a dark horse! Congratulations. It makes a change to hear some good news, for once.*

What a nice response! She remembered Dan saying, *It's a new life, Tina. That's what matters, in the end, isn't it?* Perhaps Justin would be sympathetic too . . . concerned . . . interested. He was, after all, not without fatherly feelings – on and off, over the years, he'd mentioned his children quite a bit.

Feeling encouraged, she opened up the sewing box, lifted out the top layer and picked out an envelope.

To my dear little Vixen –
Please, no more sulking: you know as well as anyone what the British public are like where affairs are concerned. This is the most hypocritical nation on earth. Its appetite for smut is almost unlimited, and matched only by the pleasure it takes in shaming anyone who is less than perfect. The man in the street doesn't have the opportunity or energy or resources to sin as thoroughly as he would like, so he takes what satisfaction he can from reviling those who are more fortunate, but who are unlucky enough to get caught. If we were French, we would not have this problem; I could take you to the Ivy and hold your hand between courses on as many consecutive nights as you could wish. But as it is, we must be wily, we must be strong, and we must take our chances where we can.

But it is very dreary and bare without you, Vixen.

She put the letter back.

Right on time, the phone he had given her rang again.

'I'm glad to have caught you,' he said.

'It's not hard, these days. I haven't been going out much.'

'You're wise to take it easy. You're going to need your rest. I saw your column today, of course.'

'I thought you probably had.'

'I shall look forward to following your progress. Perhaps you'll end up with a book deal. Maybe even a television mini-series.'

'I'll be lucky if I hang on to my job, the way things are going. You know they got rid of Flora McNamara. Ten years of uselessness, and finally she gets the axe.'

'Nonsense. You're a favoured daughter. Even if you are a prodigal one at present. Just don't let anyone see you smoking.'

'I've given up. I can hear traffic. You're not in a phone box, are you?'

'You know what your brethren are like, and it's very important for me that this conversation should remain private. I'm relying on your innate good breeding not to allow matters to get out of hand. I simply cannot afford to have my name attached to some is-he-isn't-he hokum scandal concocted by your rag.'

Tina didn't know whether to laugh or be insulted.

'Your name is safe with me,' she said.

'It's a good idea to counterbalance ambition with restraint, as you know. And there's no point making enemies unless you absolutely have to. Sometimes it's best to ignore short-term advantage in favour of long-term peace of mind.'

'That sounds suspiciously like a threat. Are you planning an accident for me if I step out of line?'

He chuckled. 'You're keeping well, then, I take it.'

'Not bad, thank you for asking.'

'You have everything you need?'

'If you mean, do I need money, then no, I don't.'

'Well, Christina, I wish you well, and rest assured that I'll be thinking of you fondly. Don't expect me to be in anything like regular contact, though. I'm sure you'll appreciate that I need to keep my distance.'

'Well, go on then. Ask me who I think the father is.'

'Oh, my dear girl. I was just coming to that. I have some news for you, too, you see. I'm afraid it can't possibly be me. I had a vasectomy a couple of years ago. Ginny suggested it, and I thought it would be for the best. You did seem very focused on your career, but I know that women have a way of conjuring up babies when they decide they want them, and it seemed to me that it would be a very bad idea to put myself in a position where I might be used in that way.'

If he had been there, she would have slapped him. It probably wouldn't have helped. Outbursts of temper amused him. He was impervious to other people's negative emotions; sometimes this was a good quality – and sometimes it was absolutely enraging.

'Then you lied to me. You lied by omission. We talked about this. You asked me if I wanted children, and I said I probably would one day, and you said you never ruled anything out.'

'I think if you're honest with yourself, you'll realize I haven't broken any promises. I didn't see any point

181

in letting some vague worries about the future spoil a perfectly satisfactory present.'

'You told me things would be different when your children were older.'

'My children are older, Christina, and so am I, and so are you.'

She caught her breath. Did she really want to end this screaming and shouting? But then, did she have any dignity left to preserve?

'It was good, you know,' she said. Mustn't cry. That would be the worst, most futile thing she could do.

'Not all of it,' she added – attack, within reason, was the best form of defence. 'But definitely some of it.'

'I know. Of course it was. But now we both have to look forward rather than back. There may be some things that you would like me to have, for safekeeping, as it were. I thought I would send Dilys round to pick them up. One evening this week perhaps. Or in the morning – she's quite close to you, she could call by on her way in. I wondered when would be convenient.'

Dilys was Justin's secretary. Her devotion to him would have baffled Tina if Tina hadn't built so much of her own life around him. As it was, she did occasionally wonder if they had ever had an affair, and if Dilys's calves had been slightly less sturdy she might have been positively suspicious.

'Are you telling me you want your letters back?'

'I'm going to trust to your good judgement, Christina, and your goodwill.'

'I'm not going to sell you up the river, you know.'

'I need peace of mind about this. Please.'

'OK. If that's the way you want it, I suppose it's all the same to me. Tell Dilys to be here at seven thirty tomorrow morning. She can have the lot.'

'Thank you. I appreciate it. And, Christina, if I may, I'd like to offer you some advice. You are now in the business of selling yourself, and you're doing quite a good job of it, I might add. But you're not just selling yourself – you're selling other people, too, and sooner or later, if you are successful, demand will outstrip supply, and then there is more than a passing risk that you will lose control of what you put on the market. Let me remind you of a wise old saying: Be careful what you wish for, because you might get it. And here's another thought for you: those whom the gods wish to drive mad, they give what they want.'

'Then I don't think I'm in much danger of going crazy. This is most definitely not how I wanted my life to turn out.'

'Perhaps not,' he agreed, 'but I think you want to take what you can. Which is understandable. But you can't just take what you want and pay for it. We all take. We all pay. And we all want attention, but it can be very uncomfortable when you can't escape it. Goodbye, Christina. And good luck.'

She pressed the button to end the call, then muttered, 'Anyway, vasectomies don't always work, you know,' as if he might still be able to hear her.

She sat for a while without moving.

The landline rang, but had gone dead by the time she picked up. It was Natalie.

She'd left a message: *Oh my God, Lucy just told me your*

news. You're in the club! That's fantastic! If you ever want a second-hand breast pump, I've got one I'd be very happy to see the back of.

Tina went to the photo montage hanging on the chimney breast. Back to happier times . . . Tina, Lucy, Natalie, and Richard, fourteen years ago in the Plasnewydd Arms, postgraduate students in Cardiff, their faces smooth and bland with youth. Apart from Richard, they were all smoking, even Lucy – that was before she'd turned into an impeccable wife and mother who baked her own ciabatta bread.

Karaoke night. It had been fun – the kind of fun you have when you know you're only going to be in a place for a year, and you've deferred the *Reality Bites* moment of knuckling under and getting a job. Even Richard, who was rarely parted from his law conversion course textbooks, looked as if he was enjoying himself. They had spent hours in the pub back then, talking about nonsense, talking about themselves . . .

Usually she wasn't aware of the tick of the clock on the mantelpiece, but at that moment it struck her as obtrusively loud.

She had to tell Dan. She would. But . . . she didn't have to do it here and now, did she? The moment she did, he would have rights. Rights over the baby . . . and since she and the baby were currently indivisible, wouldn't that give him rights over her too?

She turned away and moved about the flat, collecting the things she needed: brown parcel paper and tape, scissors.

Then she sat down again, opened the box, picked out

184

the lid of the largest compartment, and ran her finger-tips over the strip of paper glued to the inside.

Winifred Fox, 1875. Made by I alone.

She slotted the lid into place and closed up the box. For the first time it struck her as an ominous object, ill-starred, and she wondered if it would seem so to him. Would he feel rebuked by it? Would he see it as a token, a final lover's gift? Would he give it any thought at all?

Great-Aunt Win had never married. As far as Tina knew, this was all that was left of her. Tina had acquired the box as a child mainly because no one else had wanted it. Now what would become of it?

Made by I alone.

She set about wrapping up the package for Dilys. When she'd finished she tidied up, rinsed out her mug and went downstairs to bed. She left the parcel unlabelled, sitting alone on the coffee table in the dark.

10

Pumpkin

Lucy hadn't seen Hannah in the flesh since the first days of Ellen's stay in hospital, but as summer turned to autumn the image of Hannah rutting with Adam intruded at odd times, throwing her off track. It kept coming back, unbidden, taunting her, haunting her . . . She tried to keep busy, and the odd glass of wine (or two, or three) was a helpful analgesic, but nothing could diminish the power of what she'd witnessed.

Perhaps seeing Hannah face to face again would bring about some kind of exorcism, but she preferred not to risk it. She'd managed to hold on to her dignity at the hospital, but that was no guarantee that she wouldn't lose the plot next time, and launch herself at Hannah and try to wring her neck.

They were in touch more or less weekly via email, so that they could arrange separate visits to Ellen and swap notes on how she was – that way, they could both avoid each other and ensure that Ellen had contact with the outside world at regular intervals. Hannah always asked after the girls, and Lucy answered, briefly, as if responding politely to a faraway acquaintance.

The teachers, the mums at the school gate, her friends; pretty much everybody now knew that Adam had gone for good. They had been shocked and sympathetic, but it had not taken long for them to become matter-of-fact about the separation, as if it had become normal. Whereas Lucy lived in a house filled with memories of both her husband and her sister, and could not imagine that life would ever feel normal again.

She didn't want the girls to feel that way, however, and she tried to keep them busy over the summer, with playdates and trips and tennis and swimming. Then, in September, Clemmie went back to St Katherine's and Lottie started at her new secondary school, Caldecott Grammar.

In the old days, Lucy would immediately have sought to establish herself as an active and committed parent, but she decided to keep her head down. It was all she could do to keep track of Lottie's homework, and try to find out about her new friends.

Now the summer holidays were over and the girls were back at school, she had no excuse for not cracking on with her job hunt. Adam had been sending her a third of his salary; he now didn't have one, and didn't plan on having one, at least not on a comparable pay scale. He said he was burnt out and didn't want another corporate job; he was going to do a TEFL course and then go travelling. Drifting round the globe having sex with gap year students . . . she could picture it all too easily. He should probably have done it years ago. When he was gap year age himself.

Still, he'd handed over a lump sum of several thousand pounds from his redundancy payment. She couldn't look to him for anything more. She needed to find work, and soon.

She'd applied for a couple of promising jobs, school hours only of course, but so far she hadn't even had an interview. She had gone for a part-time job in the admin office at Lottie's school, but hadn't even heard back, and the constant headlines about the poor state of the economy were endlessly discouraging.

She had trimmed their expenditure, of course. She was buying wine in bulk now; it was so much more economical. It was really her only treat, now that she'd given up clothes shopping and cancelled her magazine subscriptions. It was helping her to cope, just in the short term – it was the ritual of it, as much as anything. The creak of the cork as she levered it out and the glugging sound of the cold fluid splashing into the glass were not enough to lift her spirits, but were certainly soothing. If she felt rough the next day, well, what was new? Waking up alone was rotten anyway, and a hangover was a welcome distraction.

Her anxiety about the sleight of hand required to keep on balancing the family finances came to a head in the run-up to Clemmie's birthday party. She'd booked it – Clemmie wanted an interactive show from Salt'n'Pepper Theatre, the same as her best friend Elspeth Morris had had for her birthday party back in the summer, the day that . . . the day Lucy had rowed with Tina about her column, and come home just a bit too early.

Despite her worries, she always crashed out without any difficulty at night – the wine helped with that – but one morning she surfaced in the early hours in a blind panic. Would she really be able to handle a group of twelve seven-year-olds on her own? She'd always had Hannah to help her before. And also . . . she'd made the down payment, but what about the balance? What if her cheque bounced? She got up and checked her bank account online, and what she saw kept her from going back to sleep.

There was nothing else for it. She would have to do anything, anything at all. She'd walk up and down with a placard advertising root beer, or golf clubs. She'd go door to door asking householders what gas tariff they were on. She'd work in a call centre! On a checkout! Clean offices! Walk dogs! Babysit! But to start with, she would call round the agencies she had registered with, and she would do it as soon as she got back from taking Clemmie to school. It was Friday, a good day for picking up assignments for the following week; she remembered that from temping after Cardiff.

Having decided this, she finally dozed off. She didn't feel too good when the alarm went off, but luckily the girls pretty much got themselves ready these days, and Lottie took herself in to Caldecott Grammar on the school bus. Lucy just about managed to drop Clemmie off at St Katherine's without talking to anyone, though only by waving apologetically across the playground at Jane Morris, Parent–Teacher Association president and mother of Clemmie's friend Elspeth, before rushing off as if she had an urgent appointment to get to.

Jane almost certainly wanted to confer about the forthcoming fundraiser. Oh well, maybe by afternoon pick-up Lucy would be in a suitable frame of mind to worry about knives, boards and Bath biscuits. Was she really still going to help organize, and duly attend, a cheese and wine evening? Was she still capable of making polite chitchat about different varieties of Brie, and, when that subject ran dry, about tutors and builders and cleaners?

Back home, Lucy briefly contemplated tackling the kitchen floor. She hadn't had a cleaner since the children were small, preferring to do the chores herself; she had thought of the house as her job, and had been scrupulous about putting the effort in. There was no reason to let her standards slip now.

But first she forced herself to pick up the phone and ring Nicky from Red Apple.

'No, I've got nothing at all next week, I'm afraid, but do keep on trying,' Nicky told her. Then someone interrupted her, and Lucy could hear them conferring: 'Marta from Barris Hume? No, I haven't heard from Tamsin, no. Well, she could have phoned, couldn't she? OK, tell Marta we've got someone on the way.'

Now Nicky turned back to Lucy. 'Hello? Are you still there?'

'Yes, I'm here.'

'Do you know what, Lizzie, it must be your lucky day, because we may have something for you after all. It's for the whole of next week, but you need to be able to start today, as soon as possible. It's the Kingston office of Barris Hume, I expect you've heard of them?'

'Er . . .'

'The estate agents. I'm looking at your form right now and I see that you're just round the corner and you have your own transport, is that right?'

'Well, yes, but—'

'Word processing, web editing, Excel?'

'Er, yes.'

'And shorthand too – that's an unusual one these days! Marvellous. I think you might be just what they're looking for. Our contact there is called Marta, she's absolutely lovely, and she's off on holiday next week. She's very keen to get someone up and running before she goes. Unfortunately, we've just been let down by the temp who originally had the booking. But we can rely on you, can't we, Lizzie?'

Lucy stifled the guilty knowledge that her web-editing skills consisted of once, eleven years ago, choosing three paragraphs from *Beautiful Interiors* for the designer to put online, while she had failed her 80 wpm shorthand at Cardiff back in the previous millennium.

Perhaps she'd get to nose through the details of some nice houses. She'd always enjoyed helping to flatplan the property ads for *Beautiful Interiors*; all those Chelsea townhouses and moated seventeenth-century mansions in the Cotswolds.

'Of course,' she said. 'I like to think I'm an extremely reliable person. And my name's Lucy, by the way.'

*

But by two o'clock in the afternoon she was still nowhere near completing the task she had been set on her arrival, and as she was due to leave at half past, she was beginning to realize that her chances of finishing were nil.

Nicky from Red Apple had grudgingly agreed that it would be OK if she left in time to pick Clemmie up from school, as long as she didn't take a lunch break, and sorted out arrangements for the following week that would enable her to stay until five. But how the hell was she going to do that? Lottie could become a latchkey kid, but she couldn't let Clemmie walk home on her own.

Her only option was to do some serious begging of favours from the other St Katherine's mums, which was not a pleasant prospect: she hated the feeling that she'd gone from being a provider to a needer of services. Once capable and managing – a safe pair of hands, a runner of cake stalls and stalwart of committees – would she now come across as flaky, importunate and visibly struggling? But first things first: to start with, she had to get through the rest of today.

She had in front of her an Excel spreadsheet and several windows of an website content management system, and was finding them all inhumanly baffling; everything operated with a feverish, frustrating, ob-fuscating dream logic, like trying to play croquet with flamingos. She couldn't bring herself to ask for help from Marta, who was young, dressed in an impeccably professional trouser suit, brisk and busy. Such a request would only make it obvious she didn't have a clue what she was doing.

It had all been such a rush that she had not had time to make herself a sandwich, and was subsisting on some raisins and banana crisps she carried round in her handbag as emergency snacks for the girls. Her hunger had dulled now, becoming a persistent niggle rather than a warning signal, blending with other physical symptoms of unease: aching upper shoulders and back, dry, tired eyes and fluttering heartbeat.

The fluorescent strip lighting, the artificiality of being seated at a desk in front of a computer – half forgotten, but as familiar as an archetype in an old folk tale – and her inept struggles with the work had conspired to lull her into a state of timeless, impotent anxiety, like those dreams in which you turn over the exam paper and realize that you can't answer a single question, but are nevertheless obliged to sit there and suffer indefinitely.

When the phone on her desk rang it took several moments for her to come to and realize she ought to answer it.

'Who's that?' said a belligerent male voice.

'My name's Lucy Dearborn. I'm temping here today. Can I help you?'

'That would make me your boss. Paul Maddox speaking. I rang earlier and spoke to Marta about you. I gather you've got shorthand.'

'Yes.'

'Unusual these days. Well, Lucy, I don't think we're actually going to get a chance to meet. I'm going to have to go to Europe next week. It's a shame. I was rather looking forward to giving you dictation.'

Lucy had absolutely no idea how to respond to this,

so kept quiet, and Paul went on, 'Of course that means I'll be all the more reliant on you. Put me on to Marta, would you? Oh, and Lucy?'

'Yes?'

'Company policy is to answer before three rings.'

Lucy craned her neck to peer through the tinted glass of Paul's corner office. Marta was in there with the door closed, sorting out brochures for a mail-out.

Marta had told Lucy how to transfer a call, but now Lucy came to look at her notes they didn't make much sense. She screwed up her nerves and punched a couple of numbers on the telephone key pad. The line went dead; then, almost immediately, the phone rang again.

'Lizzie? It's Nicky from Red Apple. How's it going?'

'OK, I think.'

'Great stuff, that's what I like to hear. OK, Lizzie, I'm just phoning with a personal message for you. Your sister called. Hannah. She is also registered with us, incidentally, so you're keeping it in the family! She said can you please give her a very quick call about your older daughter, but not to worry as everything is under control. Apparently your mobile is off. OK then, I'll let you go. Don't forget to fax over your timesheet! Have a nice weekend!' And Nicky rang off.

Lucy fished her phone out of her handbag. Oh God, the bloody thing had switched itself off; the screen was completely blank. Sure enough, it was a bit on the old side; back in the spring Adam had suggested several times that she should replace it, but she knew how to work it so . . . Well, she knew how to text, and nobody

194

phoned her on it very often . . . How the hell did you get into voicemail?

A-ha. Finally. Three messages.

First message. Lois from the Caldecott Grammar School office, to whom she had, not so long ago, addressed an unsuccessful job application.

Oh God, it was Lottie, Lois had called to tell her that Lottie was ill, and she'd been stuck here, completely oblivious . . .

Second message. Lois again:

Mrs Dearborn, just to let you know that as we were unable to reach you we've been in touch with your sister, as she's named as the primary emergency contact in Charlotte's personal details file.

The next message was from Hannah herself.

Don't worry about Lottie, she seems fine now, I've picked her up and we're back home. I still have my key, so I thought that would be best. I saw the agency card next to the phone and I've had some dealings with Nicky myself, so I just gave her a call and I think she's going to try and get in touch with you. If I don't hear from you, I'll pop out to get Clemmie from St Katherine's – don't worry, I'll double-check with her teacher, just in case you've made arrangements for her to go home with someone else.

End of messages.

Hannah! Of course, she had filled in all the paperwork

back in the spring, when the school confirmed that Lottie had been offered a place . . . She had never updated the form.

She had never been quite so pleased to hear her sister's voice, and the thought of Hannah being back inside her house was, under the circumstances, a relief.

She rang her home number, and Lottie said, 'Hi, Mum. Where are you?'

In the background Lucy could hear Hannah saying, 'Who is it? Is it Mummy?'

'I'm so sorry, darling, my stupid mobile isn't working, it turned itself off,' Lucy said. 'Are you OK? What happened?'

'I got my period,' Lottie said.

There was a short silence.

'What happened?' Lucy said.

'I got blood on my skirt. The teacher sent me to the nurse and she gave me a sanitary towel. My tummy aches. Mummy, where are you? Why is it taking you so long?'

'I'm just on my way home now, darling. I'll be with you very soon.'

Out of the corner of her eye Lucy saw Marta emerge from the corner office and bear down on her, carrying a stack of letters. Lucy shook her head without looking up and gestured sharply with her free hand. *Not now.*

'Let's talk about it when I get home, shall we?' she said to Lottie. 'Tell Auntie Hannah I'm going to pick Clemmie up from school, and then I'm coming home. I'll see you soon.'

She ended the call and dropped the phone in her bag.

When she looked up Marta was standing right next to her, hands on hips.

'If you've quite finished?' Marta said.

'Yes, sorry, urgent personal call. My daughter's not very well. I'm afraid I'm going to have to go.'

Marta didn't reply. She moved round to stand behind Lucy and leaned over to peer at the computer screen. 'Look, you've left a non-breaking space in there. And what's that down in the bottom? It's in the wrong style.'

'Oh dear. So sorry.'

'OK, I'm going to have to have another look at these. I spoke to Mr Maddox, by the way. I gather you cut him off. He managed to get through to me eventually, however. He wasn't best pleased.'

'Sorry. I got a little confused with the phone system.'

'I gathered.' Marta sighed heavily. 'You'd better go. Don't shut down. I'll sort it out. Which means I'm going to have to stay late. I'll be in Mr Maddox's office when you've done your timesheet.' And with that she went off.

The one thing you must never do in the office is cry. Lucy hurried off to the ladies' and locked herself into a stall. As she perched on the toilet seat the urge to burst into tears receded.

'What on earth am I doing here?' she said out loud.

She came out and went straight back to the office without looking in the mirror. She knew her reflection was unlikely to boost her confidence.

Marta was on the phone in Paul's office, but hadn't shut the door.

'You're going to have to send another one on Monday,' she was saying. 'Not this one, OK? Send someone else.'

Lucy went back to her desk and sat down to fill out her timesheet.

After tax, her pay from Barris Hume would almost, but not quite, cover the balance of payment due for Salt'n'Pepper Theatre.

She hoped that Clemmie would appreciate it, but thought it quite possible that she wouldn't.

Lucy had fully intended to ask Hannah to leave the minute she got back home, but somehow it wasn't that easy with the girls around, and when Hannah offered to help out at Clemmie's birthday party, some crazy, masochistic, stupidly forgiving impulse prompted her to say yes.

In the end, when the day of the party came round, she was glad of the help. She even found herself able, despite everything, to treat Hannah fairly normally; it was difficult to sustain feelings of murderous rage while surrounded by excited small girls in polyester dressing-up clothes.

The party package Lucy had booked for Clemmie was designed for a group of twelve children. There were six parts – Cinders, Prince, two Ugly Sisters, Wicked Stepmother, Fairy Godmother – and eleven carefully vetted little girls, plus Clemmie herself, to play them. (Lottie had agreed to come along, but only as a spectator.) Vicky and Rufus of Salt'n'Pepper Theatre allocated the roles in rotation, in order to ensure that no one child enjoyed the glory of being Cinders, and none was condemned to remain an Ugly Sister in perpetuity.

So it goes, Lucy thought, as she helped Clemmie into

Cinderella's bridal gown for the final scene. She herself had gone from contented bride to bitter reject, and didn't much fancy her chances of another turn in the limelight.

Salt'n'Pepper Vicky pressed a button on the CD player and the Wedding March started up. Lucy withdrew to join Hannah and Lottie behind the counter that separated the kitchenette from the rest of St Margaret's Church number one function room. They had already cleared away the paper plates, half-chewed cocktail sausages, untouched diced carrots and crumbs of mini strawberry tarts: the remains of the feast the girls had scoffed during Cinderella's third and final ball appearance. There was nothing left to do but look on as Rufus declared Clemmie and Elspeth Morris man and wife.

A big dirty fantasy about money. That was the secret of the Cinderella story's enduring appeal. Who wouldn't like to hook a super-eligible bachelor on the back of a few choice costume changes and some chemistry on the dance floor? But then, when the dancing and the magic was over, all you were left with was rodents, a pumpkin – and rage.

The music moved on to Lucy's pre-approved, age-appropriate disco selection, and the girls tried to follow the dance moves modelled by Vicky and Rufus.

'Look, some of the mums are here,' Hannah whispered. 'Shall I let them in?'

'Sure,' Lucy said.

Hannah opened up and the waiting mothers filed in. A general hubbub broke out. Some of the girls helped

Rufus and Vicky tidy the masks and props into their trunk; others rushed to their mothers; a few chatted excitedly to each other. Lucy steered Clemmie towards the box of party bags standing on the counter.

Jane and Elspeth Morris came forward and Clemmie handed over a party bag. Jane wished Clemmie a happy birthday, and her voice was so kind and concerned that it was obvious she was thinking about Adam, and wondering whether he'd been in touch. And the answer to that was: no, or at least it would have been if Lucy hadn't lost her nerve at the last minute and reminded him to phone.

Lucy gave Jane and Elspeth her brightest smile. In accordance with the formula for these occasions, she murmured the satisfying phrase, 'She's been very good. I think she's enjoyed herself.'

'I'm sure she has,' Jane said. 'You always give lovely parties. You should go into business.'

'Oh, it's just a bit of fun, but thank you,' Lucy said graciously.

As Jane and Elspeth left she reflected sadly that she could have set herself up in some genteel freelance occupation – interior design, perhaps, or making pretty knickknacks, or flower arranging – if she had still been able to count on the support of a well-paid husband. But while she still had the salaried spouse, she would never have felt the need.

Now it was too late. The time for dabbling in the production of prettiness had passed. She needed hard cash, and plenty of it, in a predictable, regular supply. And soon.

But she wasn't offered any more temping assignments in the weeks that followed – she'd rather blotted her copybook with Red Apple, and kept drawing a blank with other agencies too. So she put all her energy into Clemmie's school's cheese and wine evening, approaching it with the kind of fastidious foresight she'd put into planning her own wedding.

She mapped out a careful arrangement of tables for the food and drink, and commissioned Jane Morris's husband, Ian, who was good with iPods and things, to sort out the background music: All Saints and so on, hits from the late eighties and nineties, when most of those middle class enough to support such an event had been young.

Usually a certain level of attendance during the first hour or so was almost guaranteed, as the school governors, class reps and other Very Important Parents felt obliged to put in a token appearance; but by nine o'clock the hall was still full, and Lucy decided she could afford to congratulate herself.

It had all been worth it, and she felt she made a rather fetching mistress of ceremonies. As soon as Adam's latest payment had come through she'd splashed out on a pair of black high-heeled suede court shoes (Hobbs sale), which she shouldn't have done, of course, but you had to have some pleasure, didn't you? Her hair was pinned up in an artfully casual chignon, her cleavage was modestly displayed in last winter's Monsoon party dress, and the shoes, which finished off the ensemble perfectly, hadn't given her blisters, despite being half a size too big. Just about every conversation she'd had kicked off with some kind of congratulation. In a way, it was easier without Adam standing in a corner somewhere, wearing a fixed grin and deigning to make conversation, but obviously hating it and wishing he was somewhere else.

She drank two glasses of Chilean Chardonnay, which she normally detested, in quick succession while listening to Tim Sturrock, one of the few dads active on the parental scene, bore for Britain about the strengths and weaknesses of the local state secondary schools. Finally she excused herself to go to the loo, where she admired her reflection before returning to the hall. Her eyes were bright and her cheeks were rosy. Her hair was a little dishevelled, but it struck her as looking rather sexy.

Someone called out to her, 'Lucy, come and say hello, or we'll think you're ignoring us and get upset.'

It was Tessa Grier, whose daughter was in the same class as Clemmie. Tessa was one of the naughtier mums. She had a tattoo of a dolphin on her ankle, and had got drunk at her fortieth birthday party – the last social event Lucy had attended with Adam – and started talking about her rubber dress collection. Also, Lucy had seen what Tessa packed in her daughter's lunchbox: an apple, half a ham sandwich and four different kinds of biscuit.

Tessa was sitting with a small group that had commandeered a semi-circle of chairs next to the French wine table. They looked as if they'd all been laughing and guzzling the best booze, and she suddenly wanted very much to join them.

'Come on, Lucy, take a load off. You've been on the go all evening,' Tessa said, and Lucy saw that she'd eased off her very small red stilettos. Suddenly Lucy's feet ached in sympathy. Or maybe they had been aching all along.

'But where shall I sit?' Lucy said, looking from face to face and not seeing a vacancy.

'Sit on my lap if you like,' Ian Morris said.

Lucy tucked a stray curl behind her ear. 'I'm much too heavy,' she demurred, 'I'll do you a damage.'

'Nonsense,' said Ian, who was quite sturdily built himself; he had the look of a former rugby player. 'It would be a pleasure. I'd be delighted to be of service.'

He patted his thighs, and suddenly sitting down struck her as a very good idea indeed. She dropped down on to him with all the delicacy she could muster.

Jane flashed into orbit, quick as a red kite dropping from the sky to peck at road kill.

'Lucy,' she hissed, 'would you mind not sitting on my husband's knee?'

Lucy jumped up. 'So sorry, just a bit of fun, no offence.'

'None taken,' Jane said, and then, as Lucy made a show of studying the few bottles that still contained anything more than dregs, 'Don't you think you've had enough to drink?'

'You're right, I don't feel too well,' Lucy mumbled, 'I'm on antibiotics. I think it must have interacted. I'll just go and get some air.'

As she turned and stumbled towards the exit her foot came right out of her shoe. She slipped it back on, looked round, and saw that Mr Dalston, the headmaster, was watching her with an expression of puzzled concern.

Chin up! She walked out with all the nonchalance she could muster, as if this sort of thing happened to her all the time – hell, it could happen to anybody; there was just no relying on shoes.

Hard on the heels of the cheese and wine fundraiser came another event that called for an investment of Lucy's flagging maternal energy: Hallowe'en.

The morning after she woke early, with a start; it was as if an intruder, wishing to alarm her, had suddenly switched on the lights, though her bedroom was still pitch dark. Her mouth tasted dry and sweet, and her head throbbed. Oh God, she was heading towards forty, alone, and broke, and she had lost Adam; these things could be put to one side in the evening, but in the morning, which always began too early for comfort, they recurred like a fresh insult.

She was still wearing yesterday's underwear. She got up, found her pyjamas and dressing-gown and put them on instead. Then she tiptoed downstairs – she wasn't quite ready to face either Clemmie or Lottie yet – and put the kettle on.

The Hallowe'en pumpkin was still sitting on the kitchen windowsill, baring its grinning teeth at the world, a burnt-out candle in its hollowed-out belly. Sad. Like a Christmas tree on Boxing Day, or a row of greetings cards the week after the birthday they were meant to celebrate: out of time.

Hallowe'en had been a washout, she had to admit it. Lottie had refused point-blank to participate, and had retreated to her room to listen to God knows what and read *Twilight*. Clemmie still wanted to go trick or treating, but Lucy didn't want to leave Lottie alone in the house, and didn't like to impose by asking one of the neighbours to take Clemmie with them. So instead she and Clemmie had dressed up, bobbed for apples and read *Room on the Broom*, but really it had been a poor show, and she knew Clemmie knew it.

She had dreaded the moment when the doorbell would ring and an eager little crew of green-faced, fang-wearing, black-hatted marauders would demand their fistful of Celebrations – would Clemmie cry, protest, demand to know why she was being kept from collecting as much candy as they? – but in fact, what had happened had been worse; nobody had come at all, despite the message of welcome she had hoped to transmit with her carefully positioned pumpkin.

Maybe, not having seen her out and about with the girls in costume, the neighbours had assumed she'd turned her back on the tradition. Or was it a sign of something more ominous – evidence of how, without a man in the house, she and her daughters had become inconsequential and thus invisible, or at least, easy to overlook? Did they think she would feel threatened by people calling at the door under cover of darkness? Or, which was perhaps more likely, had they all just had somewhere better to be – some event to which she and the girls had not been invited?

She unlocked the back door so she could take the

pumpkin out to compost. But the door was unlocked already, or had been, and must have been left that way overnight, and she'd just locked it.

Damn! What had got into her? Since Adam had gone she'd become as absent-minded as a new mother. Milk-brained, they called it. But how could she have forgotten to lock up? It had always been her job – she'd never trusted Adam to oversee the security of the house. Burglaries were not uncommon in the houses on the green; they were assumed to have wealthy inhabitants.

Still, no harm done. She turned the key in the lock again and took the pumpkin out into the drizzle. It was cold and still very dark. She prised the lid off the composter; a few flies buzzed at her. She dropped the pumpkin on to last week's rotting potato peelings and tried not to breathe in. Why did decay always smell sweet – toxic and curdled and sour, but still sweet? She slammed the lid back on and hurried inside.

Carving the pumpkin had been one of the things that Adam always did. Lucy hadn't found it easy going, but the effort had paid off in the delight on Clemmie's face when the pumpkin was ready, and the candle inside it was lit. The effect had not been spooky or creepy at all; the fat little orange lantern had looked cosy and welcoming, an undaunted sign of life, a round glowing beacon warning the ghouls to keep their distance, and summoning the goodwill of absent friends.

11

Café Canute

Natalie had not begun to feel guilty until the morning after her kiss with Adele. The kiss, and the skirmish on Adele's sofa that had followed, had taken her somewhere out of time. It had not occurred to her to think ahead, only to feel, and she had felt privileged, and suffused with wellbeing, and grateful.

She had not been herself, and yet she had been more herself than ever – as if all her previous selves, all the memories locked in her body, had been brought simultaneously to life: the mother, the jealous child, the uneasy student, and the young woman who had found a companion in Richard and, once, in a flimsy room on the other side of the world, something even more powerful than the comfort of friendship.

It was an encounter she had not looked to have, and she passed through it without expectations, and while she knew it was not safe – you felt safe in a place where it was possible to remain, and she knew she could not stay at Adele's for long – at the time it did not seem dangerous, either.

It was only as she waited for the taxi that Adele had called for her that she remembered what her mother had said: *Happiness isn't everything. Happiness doesn't mean you're immune to regret.*

After the ride through the night, she let herself back into the dark house and crept upstairs, past the spare room where her parents were, got into her nightie, pulled Matilda's covers back up, and laid down next to Richard, who stirred and went on sleeping. He would go back to the guest bed the next night, after her parents had gone, and she knew this would be a relief to both of them.

She fell asleep without difficulty. When she came to it was morning, and Richard wasn't there. She immediately remembered that she had done something she ought not to have done, and could not undo.

Matilda was pressing a button on her cot toy that made a wheel spin round, and chattering to herself. Natalie reached down to lift her up and held her close, and breathed in her smell as the baby melted into place, head against chest, knees and feet tucked up, her bottom snug in the crook of Natalie's arm.

There was something matchlessly consoling about the way her baby's skin felt pressed next to hers. In its way, it was completely satisfying.

Days passed, and she resumed the gentle, humdrum routine that she had established to keep herself busy and Matilda entertained: Tumble Tots, baby music and other excuses for getting out of the house alternating with cleaning, food shopping and the making and clearing of meals.

She couldn't tell Richard. She had confessed to him once before, and it had finished them, and they had only got back together because she had assured him it was a completely isolated incident, a folly; that she had needed to get something out of her system, and now it was gone. Why should he believe that a second time? Could she even believe it? She didn't know, but one thing was for sure: she couldn't imagine her life without him in it.

Yes, Adele had been a mistake, another mistake, never to be repeated. Clearly, she could not see Adele in that way again . . . and she wasn't sure if she was ready to meet her in the cold light of day and act as if nothing had happened. She'd left a cardigan in Adele's flat – had completely forgotten it when her taxi showed up – which could have provided a reason to get in touch; but no, better to leave well enough alone.

She was invited for coffee at the Thameside penthouse owned by Zeb and Soraya Mitchell, the trendy designers from the antenatal group. Her heartbeat went rather wild on the way over, but when she got there Soraya showed her into an open-plan living room that did not have Adele in it, and it transpired that Jessie was the only other member of the group who was free to come.

Natalie felt something very close to disappointment, but distracted herself by admiring the cream and orange colour scheme and the kitsch 1960s lamps and the view of the river. Soraya did mention Adele later on, but only to comment that she was very hard to get hold of, and Natalie told herself that this was just as well.

As the nights drew in and the leaves changed and began to fall, that summer night's adventure with Adele began to seem quite unreal and dreamlike. But then, when she'd finally more or less come to the conclusion that she was never going to see Adele again, Adele sent her an email.

Hi! How's it going? I've been settling Paris in at nursery. It's dreadful! Today he screamed the place down the minute we got in the door. Back to work next week, so I'm just having to harden my heart and tell myself this is how it has to be. Will be in touch soon. Maybe we could catch up over coffee sometime. Hope all well with you xx.

Natalie forced herself to wait a day or two before sending a brief, formal reply: *We're all fine, thank you. Good luck with the return to work.* She allowed herself to sign off with a single kiss.

As she had half expected, there was no reply.

She rang Lucy up, and they chatted for a while about Tina: the public revelation of her pregnancy; how gutsy she was and how well she seemed; how tough it was going to be having a baby on her own. Lucy said, 'In a way, maybe it'll be more straightforward. She can just worry about the baby; she won't have to keep a man happy as well.'

Was it Natalie's fault if Richard was unhappy? She had assumed that his discontent was mainly to do with his failure to progress as fast as he would have liked in his career. A couple of cases had not gone well; contemporaries were doing better. It occurred to Natalie that besides Matilda, and their middle-of-the-road, small-c-conservative, keenly aspirational parents, the most important attribute she and Richard had in common was frustration.

There was so little intimacy between them, physical or otherwise: that must be getting him down too, even if he hadn't said anything. And he wouldn't say anything, because if there was one thing Richard would avoid at all costs, it was being drawn into an analysis of their moribund sex life.

Natalie made a determined effort to be a better wife. She prepared fiddly meals (none of which quite came off), she enthused about weekend trips to petting zoos and soft play centres, she even watched some of Richard's *The World at War* DVD with him, and rested a hand on his knee; but he told her warningly that he was feeling tired, and she took it away again.

She realized that these token attempts to foster togetherness would not be enough to break their drought, and that perhaps their only hope of becoming close again was for her to be honest; but she could not bring herself to risk it.

Richard was, as he kept reminding her, tremendously busy, but still, as 5 November drew closer, she extracted a promise from him that he would make it home in time to join her and Matilda at the Clapham Common fireworks display. She had always thought of Bonfire Night as belonging to them; it was the anniversary

211

of the moment, back in Cardiff, 1995, when, under cover of darkness, watching bright flowers and sizzling spirals and shooting stars form and fade in the black sky, they had brushed against each other, and Richard had reached out to squeeze her fingers. First contact: to be followed some hours later by their first kiss, a tentative, beer-enabled articulation of lips and tongues and teeth outside the Plasnewydd Arms.

It would be good, Natalie thought, to reaffirm that moment of connection, to wrap up warm against the cold and huddle together and acknowledge the fireworks' spectacular but ephemeral protest against the onset of winter. This time they would have Matilda with them, too; the living legacy of that long-ago moment when Richard had taken her gloveless hand in his to warm it.

But it was not to be. That morning Richard called her from the office and told her that something urgent had come up; he would have to work. Yes, she said, of course she understood; that was absolutely fine.

Later that afternoon, while Matilda was napping, the phone rang and she grabbed it in a sudden flurry of hope – maybe he had changed his mind, was going to come after all.

'Hello, you,' said an assertive female voice, and she realized it was Adele. 'I have your cardigan. Black, with sequins. You left it at mine after our illicit evening. Did you not miss it?'

Natalie hesitated. 'I guess not,' she said finally. 'I mean, I hardly ever wear it.'

'You should, it suits you,' Adele said. 'A bit of sparkle.

When are you free? It's high time I gave it back to you.'

Natalie told herself there was no danger; nothing was going to happen. Adele obviously just wanted to ensure that they left things on an amicable footing; otherwise she would not have waited so long to get in touch.

'I'm around most days,' she managed to say. 'When's good for you?'

'No time like the present. How about tonight?'

They agreed to meet near Clapham Common, set a time and a place, and said goodbye.

Natalie told herself this wasn't some kind of amoral rendezvous, it was a cardigan exchange, a chance to restore normality; all perfectly above board. She'd pitch up to meet Adele, and afterwards she would go straight home – there was no point watching fireworks on her own, and if Adele was going and suggested Natalie join her, she would just say no. She'd keep it short and sweet, and then she'd bury the bloody cardigan in the back of the wardrobe and put it all behind her.

At half past six that evening Natalie bundled Matilda into her all-in-one snowsuit and put her in the pushchair. She locked up, and then they were off, abandoning the empty house and trundling through the dark cold streets to the prearranged meeting point: Café Canute, just off Clapham Park Road. It was a small place, painted an electric shade of blue, in which, from lunchtime onwards, local mothers were often to be found, either keeping themselves awake with coffee, or sedating themselves with large glasses of wine.

She arrived first. Matilda had dozed off, so Natalie

decided to distract herself with the café copy of the *Post*, and flicked through in search of Tina's column.

The Vixen Letters

Trust me . . . I'm a journalist

I decided to train as a journalist after university because I thought I'd be good at exposing wrongdoing in the corridors of power. I had no idea that I'd turn out to be useless at investigative reporting, or that I'd end up writing almost exclusively for the women's pages, and, ultimately, about myself. But it's a lot easier to say what you think than what you know.

I hope my baby will inherit the more attractive traits of my profession – wiliness, pithiness, stubbornness, curiosity, a reluctance to accept statements at face value, the gift of knowing when to ask questions and when to listen, a perverse interest in the truth. I trust that the traditional journalistic shortcomings – bullying, sloppiness, backstabbing, hypocrisy, self-indulgence, manipulating the facts – are not genetically transmissible.

Natalie told herself she wasn't being self-indulgent or backstabbing – not this time. Maybe she and Adele would end up becoming friends . . . just as she and Tina had. After all, it would be fair to say that when she'd first met Tina she'd been – not attracted, obviously, that was much too strong a word – *impressed*. Those legs! They were definitely coltish, whereas Natalie's were made for plodding along, like a dumpy little pony. And that swishy long blonde hair! The milky, lightly freckled skin, and those quick greeny-grey eyes! The astonishing lack of shame with which Tina, in the journalism institute canteen, had held forth about the crushes she'd had on other girls at her rather intense-sounding school! But . . . no. It was obvious that those teenage attachments had been no more than a temporary diversion, and that, if Natalie were to develop similar feelings for her, she would not reciprocate.

With Tina, Natalie knew – had known, really, right from the start – that their connection was a friendship, not a romance, and that this definition meant there were certain boundaries and, ultimately, the boundaries would prevail. But ever since she had stripped off for that drawing – which was still tucked away in the depths of the wardrobe – she had been aware that Adele wasn't much of a respecter of boundaries . . . yet it was also true that Adele had been the one who had called Natalie a taxi and sent her home. What had happened would never had happened if Adele hadn't instigated it; it had only been possible because Adele was calling the shots.

Before Adele, before the girl in New Zealand, before Richard, there had been other chances: the woman she'd got talking to about *Possession* and other favourite novels in a bookstore café; the friend of a friend she'd met at Reading Festival, who ran a crystal healing stall in Camden . . . Both times, and on other occasions too, she'd felt the same sudden pull of implied potential.

But if she had been bolder, if she had explored these tantalizing but alarming connections, she would never have had Matilda. And she had needed to have Matilda, for reasons that were not really reasons, but were all the more powerful for being obscure; that were to do with wanting to make something of herself, but were also to do with believing she had something to give.

She went back to the *Post* and was part-way through an article about workplace romances gone wrong, by someone called Julia McMahon, when she looked up to see Adele at the entrance, pulling at the stiff door to open it wide enough to accommodate her three-wheeler. Natalie jumped up to help, but too late; Adele was already manoeuvring the pushchair into the space next to Natalie's table. Her eyes were darting round the café as if she was looking for someone else, and she did not seem especially relieved or cheered to see Natalie; she looked flushed and flustered, far removed from the self-assured diva who had emerged from the evening of cocktails in @happyhour.

Paris, who was still awake, didn't look especially happy either, and Natalie wondered how long it would be before he started crying.

'Sorry I'm late. Paris seems a bit off colour, so I don't think I'll be able to stay long,' Adele announced, pulling off her coat, which was fake fur (at least, Natalie assumed it wasn't real), a slightly darker shade of blonde than her hair.

Underneath the fur, she was wearing a paint-splattered sweatshirt and jeans. Natalie remembered the large canvas propped up against the wall in Adele's living room – she'd only paid attention to it once her taxi was on her way, and it was nearly time for her to leave.

The painting showed a life-size female form taking flight, with great wings rearing up and away, powerful as an angel's, black as a crow's. Underneath the woman stood a little girl in a pink nylon fairy outfit, watching her go.

Adele had been defensive about the painting. 'It isn't finished.'

'Oh,' Natalie had said, 'but it looks as if it is.'

'It isn't quite,' Adele had told her. 'It will be finished when there's nothing more to be done.'

Natalie was still on her feet, half anticipating some kind of embrace. But Adele promptly settled down and picked up a menu, leaving her hovering. Natalie slid back into her seat.

'Poor Paris, I'm sorry to hear he's not well,' she said.

Adele didn't look up. Natalie decided to venture a question.

'How has it been, going back to work?'

'Dreadful!' Adele said, casting down the menu. 'You're so lucky to be in a position to take this extra time – you really must make the most of it.'

'But I thought you liked your job.'

Adele shrugged. 'Believe me, if I thought I could just sit around painting and taking Paris to swimming lessons, I would. But I need the money. I have to be able to keep a roof over our heads.'

'What about Marcus?' Natalie asked. She would not have anticipated making any references to the father of Adele's child during this particular meeting, but then she was a long way from clairvoyant when it came to predicting Adele's moods and behaviour.

217

Adele sighed. 'We're not getting on very well. I don't want to rely on him. I'm not sure how long it's going to last, and I won't let myself become too dependent on him.'

'Maybe you should talk to someone. Go to Relate or something,' Natalie said, and wondered if it was hypocritical to suggest this to someone you'd kissed, even though both of you were meant to be with someone else. Adele could quite justifiably tell her to follow her own advice. Perhaps she should. Except that discussing what had happened with a professional would rob it of the secrecy that allowed her to carry on living with it – and with Richard.

Adele shrugged. 'Maybe,' she said. 'Right now the person I really want to talk to is you. Is everything all right between us? I don't mean to say that I'm sorry about what happened. But it was naughty of me. I've been worrying about how you might have felt afterwards.'

Natalie decided it was imperative to play it cool, and act as if she was more than capable of taking whatever it was that had happened – a seduction? Fumble? Betrayal? – in her stride.

'Of course everything's fine,' Natalie said.

'I'm not a very nice person,' Adele said, 'and believe me, I am not the right person for you to be spending much time with right now.'

Natalie was tempted to ask why, but didn't, and Adele sighed and looked away.

'I've got your cardigan, anyway,' she said, and bent down to rummage underneath her three-wheeler. She brought out a carrier bag and handed it over, and

Natalie peered inside – what a strange, silly thing to do, as if she doubted whether Adele had really put anything in there, or expected her knitwear to have been transformed into something else. But there it was, looking just as Natalie remembered it, with one or two of the sequins coming loose. She thanked Adele, hung the bag from the handles of her pushchair and wondered what on earth to say next.

Well, there was the weather, their babies' health, the news . . . the paper right in front of her.

'I've just been reading something by one of my friends,' she said, gesturing to the copy of the *Post* in front of her on the table. 'I think I told you about her. She's having a baby too, now. I only found out she was pregnant from her column, so I like to keep up with it, in case there's any other unexpected announcements.'

What was she really trying to say? *You might not be interested in me, but remember, I do have other friends, and some of them are really quite high profile?*

'That's hardly worth writing about, is it?' Adele said. 'I mean, it's not exactly news. Someone having a baby. What's the big deal?'

'It's all in the context. It's a surprise. Man bites dog is a news story; dog bites man is what you expect to happen, so it isn't,' Natalie explained. 'This is man bites dog.'

'I still don't see why anybody should be interested. My mother had six children and nobody thought that was a remarkable achievement. Quite the opposite, in fact. Anyway, isn't *Man Bites Dog* a film?'

Natalie was stumped. What to talk about next? The

magic of their last meeting seemed to have well and truly vanished. This was hard work. She was reminded of the date she'd had with that gorgeous French exchange student when she was still at school: the mutual incomprehension, the laborious translations, the anxiety of being out of one's depth, the conscious effort of treading water.

Why did it always have to be like this? Why was she forever watching what she said, treading on eggshells, minding her manners? Why couldn't she bring herself to just say what she wanted to say? Why couldn't she be a bit more like Tina Fox?

'I had a dream about you the other night,' she told Adele. 'I was kissing you, and I could feel that you had this hard little erection. Then we stopped, and you took a purse out of the front of your trousers and opened it, and it was empty, and you laughed and threw it away.'

Adele looked genuinely startled, and that moment was almost (though not quite) as satisfying for Natalie as their original kiss had been.

Then Adele smiled. 'Maybe I'm not the one who should be talking to a counsellor.'

A waitress hovered to take her order, but Adele carried on regardless: 'Anyway, I'm glad to hear you've been dreaming about my cock.'

For a moment the waitress looked shocked. Then her professional expression, a mask of polite, patient willingness to serve, clicked back into place.

Outside a fierce crackle built to a fast crescendo and exploded, and Paris started crying.

Natalie told the waitress they needed a bit more time,

but as she watched Adele attempting to comfort Paris she realized there was nothing to be gained from staying any longer.

It was time to go home and lick her wounds – if that was what they were, because even though the meeting had been difficult, and she'd made a fool of herself, she somehow felt more resilient than before. As if it had become possible for her to draw on a source of strength she had forgotten she had.

A week or so later Natalie was on her way back from playgroup, carrying Matilda on her front in the sling, when it began to pour with rain. She ducked into Café Canute for shelter. The windows had steamed up, and it wasn't until she had entered that she saw Adele and a man she didn't know sitting at a table together.

'Natalie! How lovely to see you! You must come and join us,' Adele said, jumping to her feet and kissing Natalie on the cheek. She was wearing work clothes: a long grey cardigan, tightly belted, over a white shirt and black trousers. Natalie hadn't seen her dressed for the office since the earliest days of the antenatal class. It made it much easier to treat her formally, as if they were barely acquainted. Still, Natalie noted that Adele's dirty-blonde hair was loose, and her face was as prettily flushed as a doll's.

'Greg, this is my friend Natalie, we met at antenatal class,' she went on. 'Natalie, this is Greg, and this is his son Max, who is friends with Paris at nursery.'

Greg smiled and held out a hand for Natalie to shake; she took it and he pumped it briskly, then released her and went off to find her a chair. His shirt was open at the neck, revealing an impressive thatch of chest hair, and he had the stocky build of a sportsman. He was almost grey with fatigue, but seemed relaxed, as if weariness was something he had come to accept.

Natalie had to admit, the beaten-up-by-life, down-trodden-dad look was not unattractive. Greg looked crumpled and pummelled and stoic and benign.

Without taking Matilda out of the sling she eased herself down into the chair he offered her – it was like being pregnant again – and asked the waitress for hot chocolate. Was it the same waitress who'd overheard Adele that other time? That typically loud, I-don't-care-who-hears-me, be-shocked-if-you-want-to-be comment. *I'm glad to hear you've been dreaming about my cock.*

'I reckon I've got about five minutes before this descends into chaos and I have to go home,' Greg said, retrieving Max's dropped breadstick. Max promptly dropped it again. Natalie wondered how old Max was. Nine months? A year? Young enough to ensure that Greg and Adele had plenty in common; old enough to give Greg a slight head start in the parenting game. She imagined Greg offering Adele useful advice with the authority of one whose child was just a few developmental milestones ahead.

Natalie saw that Adele had already finished her espresso, and Greg was halfway through a café au lait. Paris was snoozing in the three-wheeler next to Adele. There was no food on the table; their meeting had clearly been conceived as a quick pit stop rather than a long leisurely session.

'So what are you both doing here?' she asked.

'Working from home,' Greg said.

'The nursery's closed because of swine flu,' Adele explained. 'I just had to take Paris into a business meeting! Luckily, he behaved like an angel.'

Natalie cast round for something to say.

'So how are you finding Happy Zoo?' she asked Greg.

'Fine, apart from the awful name,' Greg said. 'Sounds like the children are caged animals.'

'Oh well, at least they're happy caged animals,' Natalie said.

'Actually, it's a very good nursery,' Adele said. 'Paris has really bonded with his key worker. I think it's absolute nonsense to suggest it does them any harm.'

Natalie decided not to observe that Adele had been much less positive about the nursery the last time they had met. To suggest that Adele was capable of blowing hot and cold, of shifting from one position to its exact opposite, would sound much too much like an accusation. And perhaps that was what it would be.

'How's full-time motherhood treating you?' Greg asked Natalie.

'Very well, thank you. I am going back to work, though, just not yet.'

'It's such a terrible wrench, but now I'm so glad I've done it,' Adele said.

Max started banging his juice cup on the table. Greg swapped it for a set of keys. No wedding ring; used to dealing with his son on his own. Single dad?

'So how did you find modelling for Adele?' Greg

asked Natalie. She stared at him in horror: how had that been reduced to currency for flirtatious gossip?

'I only ask because she wants to draw me,' Greg went on, apparently oblivious to Natalie's reaction. 'I have to say though, I have my doubts. I really don't think I should expose my love handles to public view.'

'It wouldn't be to public view,' Adele said, 'it would be to me.'

'Maybe you could improve me? Like Photoshop. You could just edit the bad bits out. Or you could obscure my face. You'd have to spare my blushes somehow.'

The waitress set down Natalie's hot chocolate, slopping a little of it into the saucer. Natalie glanced up at her for a sign of recognition and saw she was being watched with a steady, impersonal detachment, as a driver at a jammed intersection watches the oncoming traffic for the next move.

'I think you'll find that sitting for Adele is an illuminating experience,' she said to Greg. 'Besides, you don't strike me as the blushing kind.'

But then she noticed that Greg's neck above his collar had turned a distinctly girlish shade of pink.

12

The birth partner

'I brought my mother here after she found out I was pregnant. She was not impressed,' Tina said. 'With me, I mean, not with John Lewis, which is beyond reproach.'

'How's that going?' Natalie asked.

'Resigned martyrdom seems to be the order of the day,' Tina said.

'Don't knock it,' Lucy told her. 'It's got to be better than out-and-out rudeness. I've lost track of the number of reasons my mother's come up with to explain why my husband leaving me was actually all my fault. Of course I can't actually be rude back, because I feel terrible about her being in a home, rather than in my home being looked after by me, and she knows it.'

The three of them were in the café on the top floor of the department store that Cecily Fox had found so much less disappointing than her daughter, and where Tina had told Dan that he might be on the way to becoming a father. It was the first time Tina had seen

Natalie and Lucy since meeting Matilda back in the summer. Back then, it had still been possible for her to get away without disclosing her pregnancy – although Lucy now claimed she'd suspected something at the time. This time, William's due date was less than six weeks away, and her bump was keeping her a distance from the table.

They had got together, at Lucy's suggestion, to ensure Tina bought a cot, plus a short list of other items. Not for the first time, Tina was grateful for Lucy's willingness to organize other people's lives for them. It wasn't as if anyone else was champing at the bit to go shopping for babygros and nappies and a car seat with her. Dan would have come if she'd asked him, but buying baby stuff together struck her as much too couply, and anyway, she suspected he wouldn't have been much use. Her mother, who was the other obvious candidate, hadn't exactly washed her hands of the whole business, but still sounded hurt and sad whenever Tina spoke to her, and was keeping her distance.

The shopping was now done and would be delivered sooner rather than later, at Lucy's insistence, and they were sitting next to a window with a decorous view of Chelsea. They were surrounded by women. At the table next to them, a mother and daughter were discussing an acquaintance whose Caesarean had been followed by unstoppable bleeding and a life-saving hysterectomy. Despite the gory subject under discussion, they were both, like the rest of the clientele, cheerfully feminine, and sported nicely groomed hair, pretty earrings and jolly sweaters.

It struck Tina that neither of her friends quite fitted in. Lucy's floral shirt was creased, and she smelt faintly of cigarette smoke; the dark shadows under her eyes gave her a louche, night-owl look, and she'd stopped wearing her wedding and engagement rings. Natalie, meanwhile, seemed to have made an almost deliberate lack of effort with her appearance, as if she didn't want to put temptation in anybody's path, and thought this could be avoided by hiding away in a shapeless black hoodie, wearing no make-up and scraping her hair back from her face.

And as for Tina herself . . . she would have welcomed the chance to disappear, as she had once accused all expectant mothers of doing; but instead her vulnerability seemed to make her conspicuous. Could strangers somehow tell that she lacked a male protector? Did she give off an unconscious signal that she was undefended and alone? When other women sized her up, she was reminded of the time in adolescence when she had begun to attract the attention of men. There was an unnerving implied aggression in such assessments, and she would have much preferred to be invisible.

'I can't believe you work ten minutes from here, and you've never so much as set foot in the baby department until now,' Natalie said.

'That's because she's been in denial,' Lucy commented.

'It would be great if denial worked as a kind of natural anaesthetic during labour,' Tina said. 'You know, mind over matter. This can't be happening to me, ergo I can't feel it. I don't suppose it does, though.'

'Personally, I think if you describe anything as

natural, it's a way of saying it's not all that great,' Natalie said. 'People bang on about natural childbirth, but what's natural about choosing to suffer more pain than you have to? How about natural tooth extractions, or natural amputations? Abscesses and gangrene and septicaemia are all natural, but that doesn't mean you want to experience them.'

'I'm sure Tina will have a perfectly straightforward delivery,' Lucy said warningly.

'Personally, I'm seeing the chance to try some new drugs as one of the few potential upsides of the birth experience,' Tina said. 'I don't imagine I'm going to get that many more opportunities to try out new mind-altering substances, especially not ones that are provided by the state.'

Natalie giggled, but Lucy said, 'Tina, I hate to say this, but has it occurred to you that you might just not be taking this seriously enough? Have you been to any antenatal classes?'

'I don't have time, and anyway, I don't want to be the only single mum in the group. Everybody'll think I'm after their man.'

This time Natalie didn't laugh; she looked away, towards the view of cold, dank, wintry Chelsea, and Lucy said, 'Oh, for heaven's sake, you're paranoid. Nobody's thinking about things like *that*, given the circumstances. So who are you going to have with you at the birth? What about the fathers?'

'You make me sound like a gay couple's surrogate. There's only one.'

'Well, yes, but you don't yet know who he is, do you?'

228

'Actually, yes, I do,' Tina said.

Now she had both her friends' full attention.

'Without going into sordid details,' Tina went on, holding up both hands as if to ward off too much scrutiny, 'it came to light that there was only really one potential candidate after all. Someone I know from work. He's called Dan. Dan Cargill. He's not really awful or anything, but we're not together, obviously.'

She had broken the news to Dan back on one of those balmy September afternoons when the leaves are on the turn, but the skies are blue and cloudless; at her suggestion, they had met for a walk on Hampstead Heath.

Dan had looked both cornered and unfathomably pleased. He had asked her how she could be sure, and she had told him she had been involved with a married man who had only revealed that he'd had a vasectomy after he'd found out she was pregnant. He had said, 'What the hell kind of relationship was that, when you didn't even know he'd had that done? What a bastard.'

'Is Dan single?' Lucy wanted to know.

'For goodness' sake,' Natalie said, 'why haven't we met him?'

'Look, don't start thinking of him as some kind of love interest,' Tina told them. 'I made the decision to go through with this on my own, and that's how I plan to carry on. He seems to be interested in seeing the baby when he's born, so we'll see how it goes.'

'Is Dan going to be your birth partner?' Lucy asked.

'Ladies,' Tina said, drawing a circle in the air with her hands and then bringing them together as if to silence an orchestra, 'back off. Nobody's going to be my birth

229

partner. I'm not having one. I certainly don't want Dan watching me scream and swear and shit myself.'

'Well,' Lucy said, 'what about us?'

'How can you? Natalie's got a baby, and you've got two children to look after.'

Lucy rolled her eyes. 'Look around you. Do you see them? We are capable of doing things without them, you know.'

'Yes, but that's only because they're with their fathers, by prior arrangement. And it's taken for ever to sort out,' Natalie objected. 'Plus Richard's already texted me once asking when I'm going to be back. Lucy, don't look at me like that. I'm just being realistic. Anyway, I don't think I'd be much use. I'm very squeamish, remember?'

Lucy sighed. Suddenly she looked very tired, and seemed to have run out of fight.

'This conversation isn't over,' she told Tina, and then, in a further admission of defeat, went off to the counter to buy another cup of coffee.

'Do you still see much of your antenatal group friends?' Tina asked Natalie. 'There was one you really got on with, wasn't there? I've forgotten her name – Annie, or something like that.'

'Oh. Adele. No, not really, not any more.'

'So much for making lots of great new friends through antenatal classes. Go on then, tell me, what was it like?'

Natalie looked shocked and guilty, as if she'd been caught out doing something dreadful. What on earth did she think Tina meant?

'Giving birth, I mean,' Tina added quickly.

'Ohh . . .' Natalie looked momentarily relieved, and then thoughtful. 'You do realize it's different for everybody,' she went on, picking her words carefully. 'I was induced, so it was all quite artificial.'

'Natalie, for a recently practising press officer, you are not a very good liar,' Tina said. 'But it can't be that bad, on balance, or women wouldn't choose to do it more than once, would they? Are you going to have another one?'

Natalie folded her arms and looked away and mumbled something non-committal. Clearly not a question she was happy to answer. Maybe they were trying already, and nothing was happening?

'Look, I just want to have some idea of what I'm up against,' Tina said. 'Is it like breaking a bone, for example?'

'I wouldn't know, I never have.'

'Really? You are a cautious beast.'

Natalie sighed. 'I suppose I am.'

Lucy returned to the table, and Tina said, 'Can I ask you both a favour? Could you keep it under your hats about Dan, at least for the time being? It's just that other people in the office don't know, and we're trying to keep it under wraps, just for now at any rate, to give us a bit of a breathing space. Plus, I haven't told my parents yet. I'm worried my dad'll get his address and go over with a shotgun. It's kind of easier to keep everybody in the dark.'

'Who would I tell?' Lucy said. 'I seem to spend most of my life talking to four walls at the moment.'

'And I may be a lousy liar, but I promise you, I'm very

231

good at keeping quiet,' Natalie said. The smile she gave Tina was almost conspiratorial.

Tina had hoped that the John Lewis trip would awaken her dormant nesting instinct, or at the least enable her to feel prepared. But somehow, even when she had a kitten-patterned changing mat, a pile of bedding and the components of the cot lurking in the tiny second bedroom, the flat still didn't feel like somewhere a child was going to live. She did manage to pack her hospital bag, but it took her longer than she thought because handling and folding the tiny babygros left her feeling so out of her depth she started crying, and then it was difficult to stop. It was like assembling the costume for a part she was going to have to play even though she didn't know what it was, or even when or where the performance was due to begin.

She'd been all for working right up until Christmas Eve, but Jeremy had told her he'd prefer not to have her wandering around like a disaster waiting to happen and then making an unseemly mess on the carpet. So she had arranged to start maternity leave in mid-December, although she'd still have her column to file every week; the work Christmas party would be her swansong.

The prospect of spending time at home, alone, in the depths of winter, did not appeal. Sure, she could file all her old bank statements, sort out her childcare and kit out the nursery – but what then? And as for Christmas . . . She wasn't into Christmas at the best of times. Justin had always spent it with his family, and she had always spent it with hers – back in Barnes, with her parents, trying to avoid the subject of why she hadn't gone to Mass. She was a Scrooge who refused to give her spare change to carollers and wouldn't give house room to so much as a table-top tinsel tree. Christmas Past was unsatisfactory, Christmas Present was terrifying, and as for Christmas Yet to Come . . . well, maybe she would learn to enjoy it, for the baby's sake, but that prospect still seemed far off.

Perhaps Lucy had been right and she should have gone to antenatal classes, and summoned up the energy to inveigle some other new mothers into a maternity-leave friendship fling. It was silly to be shy after she'd revealed so much about herself to the readers of the *Post*, but in a way, the column made it even harder to go out and hawk her social wares in person. All anybody had to do was type her name into a search engine, and then come to their own conclusions, which might very well not be favourable. And besides, pretty much everybody else would be part of a couple. And it would be like being back at school; seeking friends out of necessity, rather than choice.

Perhaps, too, she should have accepted Lucy's offer of companionship at the birth, but it was just so *embarrassing*. How the hell would she ever be able to look Lucy in the face again? She'd considered asking her mother, but Cecily had elegantly pre-empted her by making it very clear that she was very happy to come and help out *after* the birth . . . judiciously making no mention of before. Or during.

Dan raised the subject of the birth a couple of weeks after she'd talked to Natalie and Lucy about it, after a stroll round Richmond Park. They'd met up outside of work several times during the course of the autumn, for weekend walks – it was a chance to talk without having to worry about being overheard by colleagues. She was careful to avoid inviting him to her flat, and politely declined when he suggested lunch at his place. After all, they weren't *dating*, they were just *meeting*. The conversations they had while strolling along were mostly polite, getting-to-know-you chit-chat – as if the baby was an invisible chaperone, keeping them from any untoward behaviour.

So she now knew that he was originally from the West Country, though he'd dropped the accent and refused to demonstrate it for her; he'd once been heckled off stage during an attempt at stand-up at Leeds University student union; his brother was a radiographer and thought it was hilarious that Dan had a degree in philosophy and worked for the *Post*; his best friend from home was in the army; and he had only just managed to stop smoking, even though he'd been trying, on and off, ever since his dad had died of lung cancer a couple of years ago.

They had not, however, talked much about the baby. He broached the subject in the tea-house that had been Bertrand Russell's childhood home; he had a slight catch in his voice, and she could see that he had steeled himself to say his piece.

'I've been thinking about the birth. I know you said you didn't want me around – just wondered if you'd had second thoughts?'

He looked guiltily relieved, but also slightly crestfallen, when she told him she absolutely definitely didn't want him there.

'I think I'd prefer to leave you with happy memories of my perineum – if, that is, you remember it at all,' she said.

And then she broke her private vow not to drag him into the kind of things that an expectant father might do for someone he actually had a relationship with.

'But there is one thing you could do for me . . .' He began to look nervous. 'You could come and put the cot together. You men are all genetically predisposed to be handy with an Allen key. Aren't you?'

He smiled and replied, 'So I don't get to see you give birth, but you get to laugh at me as I struggle with a flat-pack. Well, I guess that's a fair enough exchange.'

They arranged an evening for him to come round, and she found herself looking forward to it. Even more surprisingly, she started to tidy up the flat a bit. And, some days in advance, to start planning what to cook.

When the agreed day came round she woke early from a graphic and really quite convincing erotic dream, and couldn't quite shake off the part Dan had played in it. But even then, she didn't consciously decide to attempt to seduce him. It wasn't until she had left work, and was on the train back to Clapham Junction, that the vague hypothesis – could she? Would he? – occurred to her. She immediately told herself it was ridiculous – she was due to have his baby in a month's time, for heaven's sake – but still, the notion did not entirely disappear.

She'd left the office in good time – early enough to get home, jump into the car, drive round the corner

235

to Freddlestone's and pick up some good steak before it closed. When she got back home again she let herself in and slowly mounted the four flights of stairs to the top landing.

There was much about her future that was difficult to imagine, but the role those stairs would play was already clear to her; she was bound to suffer endlessly from the Sisyphean torment of carting wailing child and pushchair from street to flat and from flat to street, and rue the day she'd turned her nose up at the garden flat in the same building. She'd told the estate agent, as if it was something to be proud of: *I don't garden!* Of course she didn't. She was a career girl with a complicated, secret love life, or had been. Grubbing round in a designated square of earth was a pastime for the settled, and, until now, settling had never appealed.

She would have to move. She would have to bloody move, on her own, with a baby, and it would be hell, and despite her desire to remain independent she would doubtless end up begging for help from Dan or her parents or her friends. But there were so many other hells to get through first there was no point worrying about that one.

Time to focus on dinner. She'd settled on stir-fried beef in oyster sauce: quick, meaty, exotic, not too heavy. She bashed the meat with a rolling pin – always a good way to relieve a bit of nervous tension. Then she seasoned the meat and left it to marinade, and went to choose her outfit.

She knew what *not* to wear – no leggings, no scary maternity tights, nothing with elasticated panels;

Bridget Jones in her mummy pants was as Brigitte Bardot in her heyday compared to Tina in her stretchy-sided jeans. But what was the magical outfit that might tempt Dan to regard her as an early Christmas present in need of unwrapping, despite the fact that her belly was now, by quite a margin, her most conspicuous feature?

By the time her doorbell rang she'd settled on a sweater dress with bare legs and felt slippers. Maybe he'd think she looked cuddly. She left her hair in a pony-tail. She could always take it out later.

She buzzed him into the building and he made it up to the entrance to her flat a few minutes later, slightly out of breath. Maybe he'd started smoking again, on the sly. He handed over a bottle of fizzy cordial and a bunch of lilies. (Lilies? Wasn't that rather funereal? Was he trying to tell her something?) She thanked him and led him up to the attic.

She stuck the flowers in the sink and put the cordial in the fridge, which still looked like a single girl's, apart from the fact that half the booze was alcohol-free. Otherwise it was almost empty, apart from the end of a loaf of bread, a sliver of cheddar, milk, Dr Pepper, and the pak choi for tonight's date, if you could call it that. Soon, no doubt, it would also be accommodating breast milk and jars of orange baby food. The single mother's fridge.

She sorted out a vase for the flowers, then turned to Dan and said, 'Now, what can I get you? Wine? Beer? I got the kind with alcohol in.'

'Better not. Not if you want that cot to hold up,'

Dan said. She noticed he made no move to take his jacket off. He looked slightly nervous, which was to be expected, but also shifty, and she wondered with a pang of jealousy whether he was seeing someone else . . . someone new, rather, since they weren't actually seeing each other. Not in that way.

That was one thing they'd never discussed on their weekend walks: his love life. In theory, of course, he was quite within his rights to have one. What if he'd got back together with Julia? Or had been seeing her, on the quiet, all along? Julia didn't strike her as the sort who would accept an exes-with-benefits arrangement, but people did sometimes make strange compromises in order to get their needs met . . . as she, of all people, should know, after all those years with Justin.

It wasn't unreasonable to be jealous, she told herself; well, not entirely. Right now, whether for good or ill, she wanted him to want *her*, at least for . . . maybe . . . a kiss or something. If he was still expending his romantic energies on Julia, or on A. N. Other – presumably someone with regular-size boobs and a normal waist-line – what chance did she have?

'Oh, the cot'll be fine,' Tina said breezily. If she didn't get Dan at least slightly inebriated, what chance did she have? She was beginning to wish she'd never mentioned the flipping cot – anyway she was sure she was perfectly capable of putting it up herself. 'Probably go up all the easier with the help of a quick drink. Go on, what can I get you? Or would you like some cordial?'

'Actually, can I have a look at the cot?' Dan said. 'Might be an idea to tackle it before we eat.'

'OK,' Tina said. Perhaps if they got the cot out of the way . . . but it did seem like a bit of a passion killer.

She took him downstairs to the little second bedroom, where the constituent bits of the cot were leaning, still wrapped in polythene, against a wall, next to the pristine kitten changing mat and a plastic bag full of baby clothes. It definitely didn't look like a baby's room – it looked like a spare room that was being used for storage.

Dan got to work, scanning the instructions and laying out the bits of slatted wood, and she hovered like a spare part until he asked her to hold part of the frame in place for him while he secured it with the Allen key.

'There, just like that. Don't strain your strings,' he said, and she said, 'That was it! That was your West Country accent. Wasn't it?' and he said, 'All right, Miss West London, you got me, I let it slip.'

After a while she said, 'Don't you want to take your jacket off?' and he said, 'Are you kidding? It's freezing in here. Aren't you cold?'

She realized he was looking at her bare legs. Was that a good sign?

'Oh no. You know, right now, I'm finding I don't really feel the cold. Shall I turn the heating up?'

'Don't bother on my account,' he said, 'but you might want to think about turning it up a notch once the baby arrives. He'll be in with you at first, won't he? Do you want me to move this into your room when it's done?'

This cot-building lark was all very well, Tina thought, but it was getting less erotic by the minute.

'Maybe another time,' she said. 'It can stay in here for now.'

Eventually the cot was done. It looked convincingly sturdy and robust, and Tina was rather impressed; she hadn't had Dan down as particularly handy, given his lack of ironing skills, and the moss growing in the window seals of his car. They put the mattress in, and just like that, the room was transformed into a space that was waiting for a child.

'I think I decided on a name,' she said. 'William. William Fox.'

'William Fox,' he repeated. 'That's good. I like it. So what about the birth certificate? Do I get to go on it?'

'Yes,' she said, 'for the record, I suppose you do. Come on, I'm starving – let's go and eat.'

They went upstairs and she gave him a beer and got stuck in to making dinner, warming the noodles and stir-frying the beef. You couldn't fail with this recipe; it smelt amazing. It turned out just right . . . but once she'd served, and was tucking in, she saw that Dan was sitting opposite her pushing his food around his plate like a WAG with a salad.

'What's wrong?' Tina said. 'Spit it out. I know my cooking's not that bad.'

Dan shrugged. 'It's just . . . It's all so real.'

Any remaining hope that they might end up making love in an abandoned fashion on the sofa was finally done for.

'I mean, don't get me wrong, I've always thought I'd like to be a dad one day,' he said. 'But I was thinking maybe in a decade's time, you know, when I've settled

240

down, bought a house, got married . . . And now it's about to happen. I mean, it could literally be any day now. Couldn't it?'

'It's a bit late to suddenly get cold feet,' she said. 'Are you with me on this or aren't you? Because I don't need a waverer on board.'

Dan looked both hurt and ashamed.

'I'm just trying to tell you how I feel,' he said.

'Well, don't,' Tina said. 'I'm the one who's got to give birth to this . . .' She gestured towards her belly. '*That's* real. That's pain. That's not just . . . *feelings*.'

'Yes, and you don't want me to be there,' he said. 'You've never even asked what *I* think about that.'

'OK, then, go on, tell me, I'm all ears. What *do* you think about it?'

'I don't know,' Dan said, 'I don't know what to think.'

'Well, that was worth asking, wasn't it?'

Dan pushed his plate away.

'I'm sorry,' he said. 'I shouldn't have said anything. But I don't know who else to talk to about it. I mean . . . to say something like that, to someone else . . . it would seem like a betrayal.' He stood up. 'I think I'd better go.'

'Then you better had,' Tina said. 'You can let yourself out.'

She pulled his plate towards her and helped herself. She sensed rather than saw him hesitate at the door, but didn't look up, and then it clicked shut.

What would he do now? Go to the pub, probably, and nurse a pint and tell himself she was half mad with hormones and had been totally unreasonable. Maybe he'd even indulge in a packet of cigarettes. He'd said that he'd given up, and he never smoked when he was with her, but she suspected him of occasional lapses; she still sometimes picked up the smell on him.

While she ate, she thought about all the people who would have preferred it if this baby had never come along. Justin. Her parents. Her boss . . . It was all very well now, when her column was attracting a pleasing amount of web traffic, but what was Jeremy going to say when someone gazumped her nanny and she missed a deadline, or the kid came down with a string of freak infections contracted at some plague pit of a nursery?

And here was Dan, wanting to do the right thing but doubtless wishing, deep down, that it had never happened.

There was a difference between fathering a child and becoming a father. Was Dan capable of turning into a parent? Was she? Could she evolve into someone who was not wary of proximity, stickiness, love; who was nurturing, reliable, dependable, in for the long haul, willing to stick around no matter what? Inevitably she would be clueless, ignorant and wrong-footed; she would be way out of her depth; she would fall short and she would fuck up and she would fail.

But maybe she would surprise herself, too . . . For the baby's sake, she hoped so.

She moved the hand that wasn't forking meat into her mouth on to her belly and rested it there. Maybe she was seeking reassurance, maybe she was providing it; maybe both.

*

Despite its reputation for stuffiness, the *Post* threw very good Christmas parties. There was always a reassuring press of bodies, plenty to drink and lots of enticing nooks and crannies. The venue was usually an avuncular club, somewhere designed to suggest a blend of one of the smaller stately homes and an unusually comfortable boarding school, and the party was a chance for everyone to celebrate making it through another year without being summoned to walk Stab Alley (the corridor leading to the editor's office, and to dismissal). So long as you were naturally cautious, or some kind old hand had warned you not to let your hair down before ten o'clock, when the senior management traditionally left the building, it was likely that you'd make it through at least until January. (It was a generally held belief that only left-wing papers fired people just before Christmas.)

It was also wise not to wear a low-cut or strapless cocktail dress, or any other garment likely to reveal what was best left to the imagination, especially during enthusiastic bopping. It was, however, acceptable to wear a skirt that rested some inches above the knee, though it was necessary to be sporting about any excitement that resulted.

Tina usually judged the success of her Christmas party outfit by the number of older, married hacks and executives who propositioned her each year, but on this occasion her shape was well past disguising, and the dress she was wearing (empire-line, knee-length, not too plunging at the neck) was flattering only in comparison to the drawstring-waisted pyjamas she'd be putting on as soon she was safely back home.

By half past nine, a mere hour after arriving, she was propping herself up against the wall near the end of a sweeping staircase, close to the exit for the ladies'. She was determined to avoid sinking into one of the large Chesterfield sofas scattered around the margins of this hall and the upstairs reception room that the *Post* had hired for the disco. Once she sat down, she'd be stuck. She was already feeling the lack of her usual social agility. She'd never normally have settled on the outer edges of the action.

She checked her watch and suppressed a sigh. She'd had far too many conversations with female colleagues who were already mothers, none of which had been reassuring. Meanwhile, the brief chats she'd had with her male co-workers had been brief, tense and jocular, and involved them looking at her bump with pink-faced pride, as if they, rather than Man Unknown, were responsible, and would shortly be priming a fine cigar and selecting something from the cellar with which to wet the baby's head.

Monty Delamere passed by in pursuit of the waitress with the top-up bottle of fizz and paused to greet her.

'Tina, how lovely that you're still here,' he said. 'Marvellous. Absolutely marvellous.'

He made a full-bodied gesture with both hands, intended to mimic the circularity of her frame.

'Motherhood, always such a wonderful thing for a woman,' he went on. 'My wife took to it like a duck to water. She used to work here, you know. One minute she was all sharp elbows and vaulting ambition, the next she'd thrown herself into baking pies and knitting booties, and she was as happy as Larry. Mother Nature is just extraordinary. I must say, though, you've played your cards very close to your chest, haven't you? Are you planning to share all with your faithful readers after the birth?'

'I'm not going to go into all the gory details, if that's what you mean. I don't want to put anyone off their cornflakes.'

Monty looked at her as sharply as he could, given that he was too pissed to focus, and had a slight squint at the best of times.

'No, no, I meant the paternity question. Who the lucky chap is. We've all been speculating, you know. All sorts of wild rumours. I've heard at least one law lord mentioned, and a cabinet minister. But a little bird tells me he might be closer to home, and a bit less of a catch.'

Then he narrowed his eyes and pressed his lips together as if he'd just finished snacking on a particularly large and tasty canapé, and was availing himself of the last trace of flavour.

'Sometimes what you leave out is so much more powerful than what you put in,' Tina said, and gave him the smile that was intended to convey her willingness to bite if necessary.

'Now, now, I only meant to tease. Why is it that the fairer sex struggles so with humour?' Monty said with an evil stare, and went off huffishly.

Tina's fellow columnist Anthea Trask passed by.

'Not long now,' Anthea said sympathetically. 'Can I get you anything from the bar?'

'No, thanks,' Tina said. 'There's only so much orange juice I can take.'

'I do hope you've had at least one glass of champagne. I should think this would be pretty unbearable otherwise.'

Tina shook her head. Anthea smiled pityingly.

'Word of warning to the wise,' she said. 'I wouldn't take the latest guidelines too much to heart if I were you.'

'I'll bear that in mind,' Tina said as Anthea moved on.

She was just wondering how soon she could make her escape when Julia McMahon saw her from across the room and bore down on her with the righteous anger of a victim seeking redress. Must be Dutch courage – in the office, she avoided Tina as much as possible. It was obvious to Tina that Julia had fallen hard for Dan back in the summer, and it must be equally obvious to Julia that something had happened between Tina and Dan. If Julia had put two and two together, then . . . oh dear.

'So when are you coming back?' Julia demanded. She had interpreted the dress code faultlessly – she looked decorative but demure, with just a hint of fun. Close up, though, her dark eyes had a dangerous, champagne-fuelled glitter.

'I'm not really going away, strictly speaking,' Tina said. 'I'll still be writing my column every week, and generally keeping my hand in. But I'll be back full-time in June.'

Julia's lip curled. 'It's a long time.'

'I've been working here for a decade,' Tina said. 'If

you look at it in terms of a whole career, six months is not a big deal. On the other hand, if you look at it from the perspective of someone who only started a year ago, I suppose it is.'

Julia turned red. Her mouth puckered as she rummaged round for something to come back with. Tina thought for a moment that she was about to apologize. Then Julia's gaze settled on Dan, who was standing, glass in hand, next to Monty, and attempting to banter with him.

'Well, where would you old hands be without some fresh blood?' Julia said.

'If you want him, I'm sure he's all yours,' Tina told her.

'He's not an office chair. You can't bequeath him,' Julia snapped.

Dan chose that moment to excuse himself and amble over. Either he'd had nothing more to do with Julia since their break-up and had an entirely clear conscience – or he was blind drunk and wanted everybody to love each other because it was nearly Christmas.

'What are you two talking about so intensely?' he asked.

'Julia was just about to tell me the ways in which you are not like an office chair,' Tina said.

'I think I'll leave you two to it. You obviously have rather a lot to talk about,' Julia said with a pointed look at Tina's bump, and marched off.

'What was all that about?' Dan said.

Tina sighed. 'You know what, I think I'm going to go home.'

'Oh no, no, don't do that. Let's find a sofa somewhere and sit down. I want to talk to you. I've been feeling awful about the way I behaved the other night. I'm so sorry, Tina. I shouldn't have said what I said. I *am* with you, I'm completely with you, whenever you want me to be that is, and when you don't, then, phhht! I'm gone.'

Yup: blind drunk.

'OK, Dan, I appreciate that. Don't worry about it. I shouldn't have bitten your head off. Great party, isn't it? You have a good evening – I'm just off to get my coat.'

But Dan grabbed her by the hand. 'Please don't go, not just yet. I've been thinking about you so much, and there's something I want to say to you.'

Monty, now in conversation with Jeremy, was staring at them both as if considering a gentlemanly intervention.

'Not here,' Tina hissed. 'People are staring.'

'So what?' Dan said. 'They're going to find out sooner or later and when they do it'll be a ten-minute wonder and then they'll get over it. Why are you so obsessed with having secrets?'

Jeremy detached himself from Monty and descended upon them with the melancholy assurance of the senior colleague who knows his underlings have to at least pretend to like him.

'Evening all,' he said. 'Enjoying the largesse?'

'Dan, please,' Tina whispered, and Dan let go of her hand.

'We are, very much,' she said to Jeremy, 'but I'm actually heading off now. Dan's very kindly offered to help me on my way. The coat check's down a few too

248

many stairs for me – I'm getting to be like a little old lady.' She got the ticket for her coat out of her evening bag, and Dan took it and went obediently off.

Jeremy watched him go, then turned back to Tina.

'I suppose that was what they call inappropriate behaviour,' he said. 'Wasn't it?'

'He was just getting a little carried away with the festive spirit, I guess,' Tina said. 'Marvellous party. I thought they might scale it down a bit this year, after the redundancies.'

'Different budget,' Jeremy said. 'You know how companies like to compartmentalize these things. Well, we all do, don't we? It's human nature, isn't it? But sometimes it's hard to keep it going. You know, Tina, you've done a great job so far, but I'm genuinely curious to see how you're going to manage when you've got a screaming infant keeping you up all night. And they do, believe me. Women moan about men, but children are infinitely more trying.'

'Yes, well, men are meant to be adults,' Tina snapped.

'You're going to have to be careful. The powers-that-be don't like the chaotic mum thing.'

He gave her the full benefit of his disturbing smile: a mouthful of true hack's teeth, stained with a lifetime's heavy reliance on nicotine, beer and coffee. Then he walked away.

She leaned against the wall and wished herself in bed, and then Dan appeared with her coat.

'Let me see you into a taxi,' Dan said.

'Oh no, I'll be fine, I don't want to take you away from the party.'

'You'd be doing me a favour,' he said. 'Look, I'm really sorry. That was all I really wanted to say, and now I've got even more cause to say it.'

She gazed at him, took in the worried frown, the oh-so-trustworthy blue eyes, and suddenly thought: He really means it.

'All right,' she said, 'then let's go.'

As they walked out their arms somehow aligned so that his hand was just underneath her elbow, barely touching, but ready to catch her if she stumbled and fell. The warmth and hubbub of the party followed them down the corridor and out of the entrance into the night. They were leaving it in full swing.

Outside it was freezing; their breath hung and plumed in the air. But she barely had time to feel the cold before he spotted a black cab and stepped out into the road to flag it down. The cab did a U-turn and halted in front of her, and she got into the back seat and he shut the door. He stooped to smile at her and drum his fingers on the window and wave as the car moved away.

13

Moving on

Adam had a girlfriend. Lucy suspected as much when she rang him one morning to confirm arrangements for dropping off the girls and heard what sounded suspiciously like a feminine giggle in the background. She told herself she was imagining things. But a fortnight later, he cancelled a day out with the children at short notice, pleading a dose of flu. She rang him the evening before he was next due to see them to check he was better, and then he broke it to her: he'd moved on.

He dropped it in at the end of the conversation, after the discussion about when he was coming (twelve noon, on the dot) and where he was taking them (for pizza). She checked whether he'd Amazoned the Christmas present suggestions she'd given him (he had), double-checked that he was still happy to see them on Boxing Day but not on Christmas Day itself (he was), and was about to ring off when Adam said, 'Er, Lucy . . . there's something you should know. I'm seeing someone.'

'Really,' she said.

'I don't think it's serious,' Adam said.

'Then why are you telling me?'

'Well, you know, I just . . . I didn't want you to hear from someone else.'

'Like who? It's not as if we have any mutual friends any more. Your buddies aren't exactly beating a path to my door to pass on the latest gossip.'

'Oh come on, it's not as if your mum friends have made any effort to stay in touch with me. And as for Tina and Natalie, I've known them for years, and neither of them have bothered to make contact.'

'Yes, well, I imagine they have other priorities. So who is this person you're seeing?'

'She's called Emily. She did TEFL with me, and she's doing a bit of work at the language centre.'

'So that's why you haven't gone abroad yet. I knew it. I knew you'd end up dating a student.'

'Actually, she was one of the older ones on the course,' Adam said, 'and she's a very nice person.'

'Good for her,' Lucy said. 'I'll see you tomorrow.'

She ended the call before he could come out with the line she could tell was on the way: 'You know, if you two met under different circumstances, I think you'd get on . . .'

The girls were in bed, and the house seemed very quiet. She opened a bottle of wine and sat down in front of the television, but found it difficult to concentrate. She was plagued by the unkind questions that women whose husbands cheat on them are told to ask themselves: *Could it have been my fault? What did I do wrong? Was there anything I could have done differently?* The questions were much more obvious than the answers, and after she'd got through the wine she had to console herself by popping outside to finish off her pack of ten.

She came to with a start in the middle of the night, alone in the double bed, in sheets that were damp with sweat, although the air was cold.

'Mummy! Mummy! Mummy!'

It was Clemmie. Another nightmare! Lucy turned on the light, hauled herself out of bed and rushed to offer comfort, banging her hip on the chest of drawers as she went past. Another bruise to add to the collection. She was covered in them, all at varying stages of repair; if she'd had a resident husband, she might have been taken for the victim of a brute.

Ellen had been the same. She was beginning to remind herself of Ellen more and more: puffy-faced, bitter, erratic, forgetful, emotional by night, irritable by day, and, every evening, always with a drink on the go.

Clemmie was sitting bolt upright, the whites of her eyes wide and round in the gloom. Lucy sat down next to her and pulled her into a hug; Clemmie was stiff but unresisting.

Lucy asked what the bad dream was about. Clemmie was initially reluctant, but after a bit of cajoling she murmured, 'I dreamed you didn't love me any more.'

'What a silly dream! Of course I love you. Try to go back to sleep now.'

Lucy lay down and patted the space next to her. Clemmie snuggled back under the covers and rested her head on the pillow, her face up close to Lucy's. Lucy reached out to stroke her hair. So soft! Being horizontal felt a bit better. Pounding headache, nausea . . . she really shouldn't have finished the bottle.

'Mummy,' Clemmie murmured, 'you know Grandma gave me that money for Christmas? Do you think I could use it to get a Talking Walking Pet Wolf?'

'We'll talk about it tomorrow, darling. Go to sleep now,' Lucy said.

Ellen had refused Lucy's offer to buy the girls presents on her behalf, and had rustled up a crumpled fiver for each granddaughter, posted to them right at the beginning of December in cards that must have been written for her by one of the nurses. But a fiver would not go far towards covering the cost of the animatronic wolfhound toy Clemmie had spotted advertised on TV, and had been pestering for since November.

Then Clemmie said, in a quite different tone of voice – wide awake, sharp, and rather critical: 'Mummy, you smell funny.'

Lucy jerked upright.

Was it the booze Clemmie had noticed? Or the cigarette smoke?

'Don't be so rude, Clemency. I'll see you in the morning.'

Ignoring Clemmie's protests, she left the room, shut the door gently but firmly behind her, and went back to bed.

Four fifty a.m. In a little more than seven hours she'd come face to face with Adam. And she'd be looking knackered, hungover and haggard. It wouldn't even be a battle. She was heading for wipeout.

254

At midday, bang on time, a sleek grey Mercedes pulled up outside the house with Adam in it. In the driving seat sat a young blonde woman Lucy had never seen before: Emily.

Emily glanced up at the house rather fearfully, as well she might, because Lucy, who had spotted her from an upstairs window, was already storming down the stairs like a Fury in pursuit of vengeance.

Lucy flung open the door just seconds after Adam had pressed the bell. He looked at her with mild astonishment. Had he had his teeth whitened? He certainly had a new hairstyle – was that gel in it? – and a new leather jacket. Oh God – his new woman had given him a youth-over.

'What is that woman doing outside my house?' Lucy hissed.

'For God's sake, Lucy, keep your hair on,' Adam said. 'What was I meant to do, drop her off round the corner so she could cower in a hedge and you wouldn't have to see her? I did tell you about her.'

'You didn't tell me you were planning to invite her round to my house. You said you'd bonded because she was one of the older students on the course!'

'She is. She's twenty-six.'

Exactly the same age as Hannah.

'You are just so fucking predictable!'

'Lucy, calm down. You're making a scene. It's embarrassing.'

'I take it that's her car. Presumably she's got a rich daddy. Is that the attraction? She looks like a Sloane.'

'Sloanes haven't existed since 1988. You're showing your age, sweetheart.'

He caught her hand before it slapped his face.

'I wouldn't do that if I were you. The children are watching.'

She looked over her shoulder and saw Lottie and Clemmie hovering shyly in the corridor.

Adam let go of her wrist.

'You'd better borrow Clemmie's booster seat,' she said.

'If you really think it's necessary.'

'I do.'

She clicked the key to unlock her car for him, then pulled the front door to, stepped back into the hallway, took Clemmie's anorak off the banister and started helping her into it.

'Daddy's brought a special friend to meet you, isn't that nice? Would you get your coat on, please, Lottie? Are you going to wear your boots? Clemmie, you can do those yourself, can't you? Chop chop, Daddy's waiting.'

She ushered them out and they trotted towards the car. Emily was standing next to it, watching Adam from a slight distance as he put the booster seat in the back. She had on a good quality coat. Navy blue, princess cut. Cashmere, probably.

Adam withdrew, looking flushed, and the girls climbed in.

'I want them back by five,' Lucy said. 'And your friend had better drive carefully.'

She locked the car, went back into the house and shut

256

the door. She heard the Mercedes slowly turning and pulling out on to the road. Then it was deathly quiet.

With the girls gone, the house was suddenly enormous, echoey and unreal. More than ever, it struck her as somewhere it would not be her luck to stay; it seemed as if it might vanish at any minute, like a mirage, or one of those folk-tale mansions that disappears when you make the wrong, morally faulty wish.

She was tempted to have a little hair of the dog, but no, it really was a bit too early. Instead she decided to pop out for more cigarettes. The walk, in the fresh, cold air, would do her good.

She made her way to the newsagent's near the station. The Lemon Brasserie, where she and Adam had gone for most of their anniversary and Valentine's dinners, was decked out with tinsel and fairy lights, and the shop windows displayed reindeers and Santas and spangly snowflakes. It was bitingly cold, but as she came out of the newsagent's she saw three girls strolling along arm in arm, all dressed almost identically, and quite inadequately, in thin jackets, tiny skirts and stripy tights, accessorized with fur-trimmed Santa hats. They were loudly discussing a miscreant boyfriend.

'You should dump him!'

'I know, but I already got his present, and I don't want to be on my own at Christmas.'

'Oh come on, what better time to meet someone else? Get yourself under the mistletoe!'

She had to step out into the road to pass them. Yet she found them charming – they looked so united. Was that how she and Tina and Natalie had been, once upon a time: impervious to the elements and the world around them, confident in the belief that while men might come and go, they would always have each other for back-up?

In some ways, now that Natalie had a baby, and Tina had one on the way, she was closer to them than she had been for years. But while motherhood was now common ground, their experiences of love and marriage remained poles apart. How could Natalie, safely hitched to reliable Richard, understand what Lucy was going through? How could Tina, who was so self-contained, and seemed to be quite happy to live a life free of romantic entanglements?

Maybe it was unfair to hold their lack of under-standing against them when Lucy hadn't really tried to explain, hadn't told them exactly what Adam and Hannah had done to her – but even if she did, even if she could bear to relate the story of her humiliation, they would never be able to return to the intimacy and frequent contact that had bonded their younger selves. They had children, which meant there would never be time. And, in the end, her friends could not give her what she was missing.

What was she going to do with herself till the girls got back? There was Christmas stuff she could be getting on with, but she really wasn't in the mood. Usually she approached Christmas as a great labour of love: making the pudding and the cake and the pies; hunting down the right presents for everyone; dressing the tree with the treasured ornaments that hibernated all year round in the loft waiting for their brief, magical lease of life.

But this year she was cutting back, doing less, paying lip service; it would look more or less like Christmas, but it wouldn't be the same – it would never be the same.

No, she should check all the job sites she was registered with. And once she had got that out of the way, she would investigate setting herself up on Facebook. She had to face facts; she was lonely. Putting herself out there would take the edge off her isolation, remind her that she was not without connections, and give her the chance to present her life in a way that would come across as positive, even to herself.

She had a quick smoke in the garden, then trudged upstairs and settled down in front of the computer. Before getting started, she checked her email. Nothing – just a message from Hannah.

Mum seems happy with the Christmas plan, though she did ask if I'd drawn the short straw coming for both Christmas Eve and Boxing Day (!). She said that at least you taking her out on Christmas Day means she's in with a chance of getting a meal that doesn't taste of mush.

Everything is fine in the flat, the boiler is bearing up under the strain and I am managing to keep the dreaded black mould at bay. It would be lovely if you felt like popping round some time when you are over this way to visit Mum and then you can see for yourself.

Well . . . why not? But if she was going to finally meet Hannah, wouldn't it be better to do it on her own territory?

Lucy replied to say that yes, she would like to have a look round the flat sometime. And in the meantime, she knew it was short notice, but what was Hannah doing the following day – would she like to come for Sunday lunch, and see the girls?

As she pressed send she couldn't quite believe that she was able to contemplate with relative equanimity the idea of inviting Hannah back into her house. No, it was more than that. She was almost looking forward to seeing her.

When the girls got back from seeing their father Lottie was paler and quieter than usual, and Clemmie was demanding and fractious. By now Lucy was familiar with these reactions. Lottie would thaw out in a day or so, and Clemmie would have a big tantrum about something completely unrelated before reverting to her normal bouncy self.

The next morning Lottie stayed up in her room, probably writing in her secret diary (which Lucy had so far been very disciplined about not reading – she figured that Lottie needed a safe, private space in which to vent, and her schoolfriends, who were into pop and ponies, might not be mature enough to provide it). Clemmie slept in, and the first thing she said when she came downstairs was, 'Emily said she'd take me to the hairdresser's to get braids put in. Can I do that today?'

Lucy opened her mouth to speak and found herself clenching her fists. She forced herself to relax and took a deep breath.

It wasn't Clemmie's fault. It wouldn't be right to take

it out on her. She'd have to have a word with Adam about not letting Emily make promises she couldn't keep – especially ones to do with hairstyles.

'No, because Auntie Hannah's coming for lunch,' she said. 'Won't that be nice?'

She had the meal all planned: a bottle of decent white wine; a chicken to roast; and she'd make a trifle. You had to push the boat out for the return of the prodigal sister, and Lucy suspected there was nowhere else Hannah could get a decent home-cooked Sunday lunch.

The girls turned up their noses at Lucy's trifle, predictably – Lucy was engaged in a constant battle with their stubborn preference for the pre-packaged. Lucy let them go off upstairs to play on the computer, and Hannah carried on gamely eating.

She was looking unfairly well: slim, but not gaunt, fresh-faced, possibly even make-up free. That was what being twenty-six and childless did for you; you could just roll out of bed, shower, pull on jeans and a T-shirt and look, if not quite radiant, then at least relatively pretty, and certainly presentable.

Actually, in a way, Lucy could see why Adam had developed some kind of crush on her . . .

This thought led to a certain insincere rigidity in Lucy's face as she returned from clearing their plates, and said to Hannah, 'It's so lovely to have you here.'

Hannah glanced at her nervously.

'It's nice to be here,' she said.

'I know the girls are pleased to see you,' Lucy told her. 'Also, I want you to know I really appreciate what you've

261

done to fix up Mum's flat, and keep an eye on her and everything.'

Hannah nodded, folded her arms, crossed her legs, pressed her lips together, stared at the tablecloth and waited. Perhaps this was how Hannah had presented herself at all the numerous interviews where she'd failed to land a permanent job? She looked as if she didn't want any part of what was happening, or what might follow next.

It hadn't occurred to Lucy before, but perhaps Hannah viewed the afternoon she'd taken off work back in the autumn to get Lottie from school, and the birthday party help, and even coming here today, as penance: acts of contrition that were necessary to redeem her guilt over having let Adam seduce her?

'So how's work, anyway?' Lucy said. 'Have they forgiven you for having to shoot off early that time?'

'Oh, yeah, I'm somewhere else now. I've got an interview coming up for a six-month contract, though.'

'Really, where's that?'

'Admin job. Department for Children, Schools and Families.'

'You should get in touch with Natalie, ask her about it,' Lucy said. 'You know she works there.'

'Oh, I expect I'll manage,' Hannah said.

'No, seriously, you've got to make use of every possible advantage. She's still on maternity leave, but she's going back part-time in the spring. You should phone her. She won't mind.'

Hannah looked troubled. 'Well, but . . . have you told her what happened?'

'What, you mean, did I explain that I caught you shagging my husband? No, I didn't.'

Lucy realized too late how aggressive she had sounded. Hannah's expression was startling: it was fear, pure and simple, and Lucy suddenly saw, with all the clarity of a revelation, how she must look from Hannah's point of view: tired, overweight, drunk, wounded, angry, demanding and unpredictable.

And suddenly Lucy had the odd sensation of being back in her mother's pink room at Sunnyview, but in her mother's chair, looking at herself.

'I was thinking about asking you if you'd move back in,' she said. 'But you won't, will you?'

'I don't think I can,' Hannah said. 'But if it would help, if you ever need a breather, I'll babysit any time you like. You wouldn't have to pay me, obviously. I'm usually free these days. I'm not going out so much as I used to.'

'You've toned down your social life a bit, then,' Lucy said.

'Yes,' Hannah said. She looked at Lucy very directly and added, 'Cut down on the drinking, too.'

'That's good to hear,' Lucy said. 'Well done you.'

She got up and went out to the kitchen to stack the dishwasher. It was odd; she felt that she had been defeated, and at the same time she was relieved.

She didn't expect to have much cause to take Hannah up on her offer of babysitting, as her social life was pretty much a non-starter, apart from the occasional pizza with other mums from school. But that evening she got an email from Tina, and it included an invitation.

> *Everybody keeps telling me I'm going to be late, so I'm fully expecting to still be pregnant on New Year's Eve and wondered if you fancied coming over to celebrate it with me, if you've got nothing else on? Can you believe it's the tenth anniversary of my millennium house party? Natalie and Richard have got something else on but might be able to pop in for a quick one, and I promise to get in some decent champagne even though I can't drink it, though surely it can't make too much difference at this stage . . . You're very welcome to bring the girls if you like.*

Lucy promptly sent a message to Hannah to ask if her newfound love of staying in extended to New Year's Eve, though she was careful to emphasize that she expected that it wouldn't. Somehow she'd lost the appetite for inflicting any further guilt trips.

Then she decided to browse a couple of internet dating sites, just out of curiosity, before starting to hunt for special offers on Clemmie's Christmas present of choice, the Talking Walking Pet Wolf.

It couldn't hurt to try, and it was amazing the deals you could find online if you looked hard enough.

14

Nativity

Natalie had been looking forward to her first Christmas as a mother. She hoped it would help her to put the slip-up with Adele behind her, and affirm the choices she'd made: Richard, marriage, Matilda. It was a time for families. It was time for her to be happy, because what could be more affirming than that?

And she *was* happy – in snatches. She was happy one afternoon in late December, when she took Matilda out, wrapped up against the cold, for a walk on Clapham Common, and saw the lights come on in the houses they passed as they walked home, illuminating a series of variations on the domestic Christmas scene: greetings cards, fireplace, evergreen and holly, baubles, candles and gifts.

Being outside, and able to see so clearly the appeal of inside, reminded her of what she had read about space travel, that what was most remarkable about going to the moon was not the moon itself – a cold, pale, lifeless lump of rock – but the sight of home from a distance, glowing in the darkness like a perfect round jewel.

She was happy, too, to see Matilda lying, in her red Santa babygro, on her sheepskin rug beneath their own lit-up Christmas tree, like the best present of all; and to take Matilda to the children's service on Christmas Eve, and sing, 'O little town of Bethlehem, How still we see thee lie, Above thy deep and dreamless sleep, The silent stars go by . . .' and to feel connected, for a moment, to centuries of winter darkness in which new mothers had held their babies close, and been grateful to be sheltered and safe.

Yet somehow, none of these moments of happiness included Richard. She could see that he was having his own, separate, special Matilda's-first-Christmas times – at least it looked that way: dandling the baby on his knee; feeding her turkey-and-parsnip mush; helping her open her first ever Christmas present from Mummy and Daddy, a little tinkly piano keyboard that played festive tunes . . . but somehow, she was always watching his experiences of happy fathering, and was never party to them. She was glad that he was getting the chance to spend some time with Matilda – he usually only just made it home for her bedtime. But when Richard and Matilda were together, she always felt at one remove, as if she was being granted the chance to see that they could function perfectly well without her.

She had hoped that Christmas would bring them together as a trinity: Mum, Dad, Baby. But instead, she feared that their family was not so much a unit as two pairs, joined together by the practicalities of living under the same roof: Mum and Baby, and Baby and Dad.

She and Richard had not yet broached the subject of whether Matilda would lose out as an only child. But Richard was still sleeping in the spare room, and they had somehow still not quite got round to sex since that half-hearted attempt in the run-up to the birth. So the creation of a sibling seemed a remote and hypothetical prospect.

This worried Natalie, but she was so preoccupied with looking after Matilda that it was easy to put off thinking about whether or not she would ever have another baby – easier, at any rate, than it would have been to force herself to think the whole thing through, and ask herself exactly why sex with Richard had become something she was content to do without.

They spent Christmas Day at Natalie's parents' house, where her brother David and his partner were also staying. She and Richard slept in the twin guest beds in her childhood bedroom, which still had the same old pink flowered curtains, and it felt quite normal for them to be entirely chaste.

She knew that it meant a lot to her parents to have their children and grandchild all together under one roof, but she found it as claustrophobic as if she was a teenager chafing to leave home. She escaped by taking Matilda out in the sling, accompanied by varying combinations of family members.

On one such stroll David fell in step beside her. They had a perfectly innocuous conversation about fishing, which he loved and she knew next to nothing about, and then, out of the blue, he said, 'Natalie, are you OK? Are you sure there's nothing bothering you? Is everything all right?'

Thankfully no one else was in earshot, and she reassured him that she was fine, and he didn't pursue it. Later, she wondered how he would have reacted if she'd confided in him: 'I committed some kind of adultery with another woman; now I feel guilty and I'm doing my best to be a better wife and mother, but I'm still as miserable as sin.' But no, it was unthinkable. She couldn't confess all to the golden boy. 'You see – I really am the gay daughter Mum and Dad never wanted!' She didn't want his enlightened response, his professional concern; there was nothing for him to fix, and still some pride left for her to lose.

Next came the visit to Richard's parents and sister in Norfolk. She was acutely aware of being required to play a part, and the pressure to fulfil her role convincingly was increased by the knowledge that the audience, though accepting, was not automatically predisposed to take her side if something went wrong and the show ground to a halt. She and Richard were expected to share a bed, which was uncomfortable, but they did manage to sleep, and got through it with the minimum of touching. Richard's mother did comment on how nice it would be if Natalie had a boy next time, but only once; perhaps the stony-faced reaction from both her son and her daughter-in-law persuaded her to keep her thoughts on the subject to herself.

Richard's sister Amanda made a cake to celebrate Natalie's birthday on 28 December, and his nieces, who were aged three, five and eight, helped to blow the candles out. What an inauspicious start – arriving in the anticlimactic lull between Christmas and New Year, between birth and rebirth, when everybody was heavy and slothful and everything was suddenly half price.

Richard gave Natalie a surprise birthday present and watched her hopefully as she opened it. She schooled herself to look delighted – usually he stuck to the list she'd given him, he was obviously trying to be spontaneous – and smiled and thanked him when it turned out to be an imitation pearl necklace she definitely wouldn't have chosen for herself. She'd have liked . . . maybe something a bit different, something *bold*. But still, she was touched that he'd made the effort. As she tried it on, and the nieces made admiring comments, she wondered how often she ought to wear it. Once a week? A couple of times a month? Less?

By New Year's Eve she, Richard and Matilda were all back home, and the visiting season was over. Richard promptly came down with flu and retreated to bed. They'd been invited to a black-tie cocktail party at the large Dulwich home of one of his more successful colleagues, and while he agonized about cancelling, she could tell he was secretly relieved – any social event that involved waiters and canapés made Richard slightly nervous. She was surprised to find that she was disappointed, even though she, too, had been a little intimidated at the prospect of snacking on deep-fried tempura while making fluent small talk with people it was necessary to impress.

Anyway, she still had an excuse to get her sequinned cardie out, and put her black silk frock on, and at least she'd be able to have a proper chat with Tina and Lucy, and wouldn't be obliged to rush off.

When the time came for her to leave, Matilda was tucked up in her cot and sleeping soundly, while Richard was lying on the sofa under his duvet with his pyjamas on and a box of tissues to hand, watching more of *The World at War* on DVD.

She perched next to him, and said, 'Are you sure this is all right? I feel rotten leaving you.'

'Do you know what,' Richard said, 'I'm actually feeling a little bit brighter. Don't worry about me. New Year's never really been my thing, you know that.'

'That's true,' Natalie agreed.

'I haven't always been much fun for you, have I?' Richard said. He looked at her wistfully – his glasses had the effect of always magnifying his expressions. 'You should go out and have a good time. Don't feel you have to hurry back. We'll be fine here, me and Matilda. I'm probably going to turn in soon anyway.'

He reached for a tissue and blew his nose, and she stood and planted a motherly kiss on his mild, balding forehead, and went off to get her coat.

Natalie was a nervous driver, and avoided using the car as much as possible; but she knew it would be difficult to get a taxi back, and decided there was really no other option. Luckily, she was able to find a space big enough for her less-than-adroit parking right behind Tina's new, sensible, family hatchback. Natalie knew that

Tina had been sad to sell on her little sports car, and her sympathy was mixed with self-pity and resignation. That was how it was when you had a child; you had to try to be practical, and plan ahead, and not indulge yourself.

Tina had told her that Lucy was coming too, having arranged for Hannah to babysit. Natalie thought this was particularly selfless of Hannah, who was still, after all, in her twenties, and might legitimately have had plans to get dressed up and go out clubbing, and taking drugs, and pulling; Natalie gathered that, despite being such an obviously sexually attractive person – louche, lanky, slouching, with a sort of boyish insouciance – Hannah was still inexplicably single. But then, perhaps Hannah felt guilty for having moved out just as Lucy's marriage fell apart; though Natalie thought that, from Hannah's point of view, it was probably best that she had. Natalie would never have said so to Lucy, but she had wondered for some time how healthy it was for either sister for Hannah to be lodging in Lucy's attic as a sort of au pair.

It was obvious that Lucy had decided to make the most of her evening off. As Natalie settled on Tina's sofa she noted that Lucy was talking a little too fast and a little too loud, and tucking in to what was obviously not her first glass of champagne.

Natalie glanced at Tina, hoping that Tina would give her a look back that said something like *I know, just humour her, I'll try not to top her up too often*, but Tina didn't seem to be paying much attention to either of them. She was struggling to crack a walnut, and looked grumpy and withdrawn.

Natalie remembered the bad scene back in the spring, when she had been heavily pregnant, as Tina was now, and Tina and Lucy had ended up virtually trading blows across her bump. Was tonight going to be a case of out of the frying pan and into the fire? For a moment she almost wished herself back home with Richard, who just didn't do drama, and was only ever harsh towards himself.

Lucy was complaining about Adam cancelling arrangements to see the children at short notice, or turning up late. Then she told them about Adam's girlfriend.

'It won't last,' she said with grim satisfaction. 'It's obviously just sex, and when that burns out, he'll find out they've got nothing in common. And anyway, she's twenty-six, and before long she's going to want to settle down, and I can't imagine that he'll want to start another family. She seems to have been nagging him to get a proper job, though, so I suppose I ought to be grateful to her for that. Anyway, what's sauce for the goose is sauce for the gander. I've decided I'm going to try internet dating.'

'Are you sure that's what you want?' Tina asked. 'Not that I've ever done it, apart from for an article, but I got the impression it can be a bit of a ruthless meat market. Mightn't you be . . . you know . . . a bit on the rebound? Maybe you should give yourself some more time. You don't have to move on just to show Adam you can do it too.'

'After what I've been through, do you really think a bad date or two is going to hurt me?' Lucy said. 'I'm just looking for a bit of fun, that's all. I'm not looking for a soulmate.'

'It's just that in my experience, sometimes, when you're upset, you do things you think will make you feel better, but actually just leave you in a worse mess than the one you were in to start with,' Tina said.

'We can't all be as self-sufficient as you are, Tina,' Lucy said. 'Honestly, I don't know how you've managed it, being single all these years. Didn't you ever find it lonely? Because I'm so lonely it's killing me.'

As soon as she'd said this she looked quite taken aback by her own frankness – and Tina looked stung.

'I was lonely, sometimes,' Tina said.

'But you were always so busy at work,' Lucy said. 'And you seemed to go out an awful lot. I don't suppose you had much time to think about it.'

Tina straightened and sighed, and when she spoke it was with regret.

'I was having an affair with a married man,' she said. 'It wasn't just a fling. It went on for years. I got together with him just before the millennium, and we broke up in the spring.'

Lucy stared at her aghast. Then she screwed up her face in concentration and began to calculate.

'So . . .' She opened her eyes wide. 'Did you think he might be the father of your baby?'

'I did.'

'But he isn't.'

'No.'

'Who was he?'

Tina shook her head. 'I can't tell you,' she said. 'I've never told anyone. He has a certain profile in public life.'

Lucy swung round to face Natalie. 'Did you know about this?'

'Um. Yes,' Natalie said.

'For heaven's sake!' Lucy rounded on Tina. 'Why didn't you tell me?'

'Look, I'm not proud of it, and it's over,' Tina said. 'It doesn't matter any more.'

'Of course it matters! You had this massive thing going on in your life, and I had absolutely no idea.'

'I thought you'd disapprove,' Tina said. She looked rather hangdog, and had both hands clasped protectively around the base of her belly.

'Of course I would have disapproved! How could you? How could you do that to another woman? It's a dreadful thing to do. What on earth possessed you? I can just about see how somebody could make a mistake, but to keep on deliberately doing it, that's something else entirely.'

Tina shrugged. 'I thought I loved him,' she said, and then added, 'Also, to be honest, it fitted in with work, as we couldn't see each other all that often.'

'It fitted in with work,' Lucy said. 'What sort of reason is that for a ten-year relationship?'

'Would anybody like some more tortilla chips?' Natalie said, but Lucy ignored her.

'Adam had been at Carlosto International longer than you've been at the *Post*, and they made him redundant just like that,' she said to Tina. 'A job isn't for life any more than a marriage is. But I hope you never have to find that out.'

Natalie said, 'Everything's so insecure, isn't it? Even the Department for Children, Schools and Families is going to be making some cutbacks—'

'Natalie,' Lucy said, 'don't try and change the subject!'

She rounded on Tina again.

'It's women like you who make it impossible for the rest of us,' she said. 'Women who are prepared to sacrifice anything and everything to get what they want.'

'Then the only difference between us,' Tina said, 'is that you were willing to sacrifice yourself.'

And then Lucy began to cry. She didn't make a noise; the tears slid from her eyes and splashed on to her novelty snowflake jumper and caught in the wool.

'I did,' she said softly. 'I know I did. And it still didn't work. I did the absolute best I could, and it wasn't enough.'

Natalie, who had become warier than ever about physical contact with other women, tentatively put an arm around her. Lucy didn't recoil.

Tina said, 'I'm so sorry,' and got up and squeezed on to the sofa on the other side of Lucy. She took a box of tissues from the coffee table and offered them to Lucy, who took one and blew her nose.

'I found them, you know – Adam and Hannah,' she said, 'in our bedroom. They couldn't have hurt me any more if they'd sat down and deliberately decided to destroy me. And in a way I think they have. I know

275

I'm a mess . . . barely holding it together. I'm drunk every night . . . Right now I can barely see straight. I wanted my children to have a better time than I did. And somehow it's all turning out exactly the same.'

There was a short, shocked silence, broken only by the ticking of the clock on the mantelpiece and the sound of Lucy trying to stop crying. Natalie saw in Tina's face a reflection of her own sudden appalled understanding. So that was why both Adam and Hannah had gone; that was what Lucy had been going through, and hadn't felt able to talk about. So much damage. The family undone, the home irrevocably broken.

Tina caught Natalie's eye and grimaced as if to say, 'Adam and Hannah – what a revolting pair!' Natalie realized that Tina had already revised her impatience with Hannah and reluctant acceptance of Adam into loyal contempt for both of them. Lucy looked up, and her big brown eyes were wet and bleak and squashed-looking. Tina reached out to squeeze her hand.

'I just can't help but ask myself,' Lucy said, 'where did I go wrong? Did I choose wrong? But you don't choose, do you? Not really. You fall for someone who fits, and sometimes they fit in bad ways as well as good ways.'

'But what happened was not your fault,' Tina said. 'I think you've been amazing! I mean, my God, you let him come round all the time to see the children . . . and somehow, you're still talking to Hannah – how do you do it? I think you're a saint. A slightly tipsy saint, maybe, but definitely possessed of super-human powers of forgiveness. How can you stand it?

276

If anybody deserves to find internet-dating happiness, it's you.'

'I'm just window-shopping, really. I don't want to get involved with anybody . . . ever again,' Lucy said.

'Don't say that,' Natalie said. 'You've got so much ahead of you. And you've done so much already – look at us, playing catch-up.'

'Remember how, at the millennium, we all talked about what we wanted out of the next decade?' Lucy said. 'I wanted my dream house. Do you remember? Well, I got it – and look how that turned out.'

'But you've still got it,' Tina said. 'Haven't you?'

'You wanted to have a column,' Lucy said. 'You got that.'

'Starting to think it's been more trouble than it was worth,' Tina said.

'What did you wish for?' Lucy said to Natalie.

Natalie's arm was still round Lucy's back. She cautiously withdrew it.

'I wanted to get married to Richard and have a baby,' she said.

'The millennium wish fairy strikes again,' Tina said.

And then Tina reminded them about the mad flatmate Lucy had lodged with while they were doing their journalism course, who had maintained that she believed in fairies – or was it angels? – and claimed she could see people's auras: Tina's had been lilac, Natalie's was indigo and Lucy's, apparently, was green, but with a tinge of yellow. The conversation moved on to other reminiscence: how, when they were in Cardiff, Tina had enjoyed the luxury of living alone, even if in a poky

277

bedsit that looked straight out on to a brick wall, while Natalie was stuck with the smallest room in a large house filled with other students.

By and by Tina talked more about the Grandee, and Lucy explained how she had slowly come to re-establish contact with her sister, and make a kind of peace with her. The time ticked by towards midnight, and Natalie realized that for both her friends the mood had lightened, as if something had been lanced, or purged . . . as if a crisis had passed. But it wasn't over yet; it wasn't nearly over. How could they not see that? How could they be so oblivious? She had the oddest feeling, almost an out-of-body experience, as if she was slipping away from the room, leaving them there, talking and laughing and feeling, while she was no one . . . nowhere . . . vanishing.

Tina said, 'Do you remember the first time we met? The game of pool?'

'Oh yes. I thrashed you, I seem to recall,' Lucy said.

'I'd noticed both of you before,' Natalie said.

The other two looked at her in mild surprise. Most of their stories of the past were well rehearsed, but neither of them had heard this one.

Natalie said to Lucy, 'I saw you smoking outside the front of the journalism institute. I was a bit surprised, because you looked so wholesome and kind of clean-living. And I remember you' – she turned to Tina – 'in the canteen one lunchtime. You were talking to Terry the anarchist, the one with all the hair, but actually quite a lot of people were listening to you, especially the men, though they were trying not to show it, not that you would have cared anyway. You were describing your school. You said that if you went to a school like yours, there wasn't much option but to have crushes on the other girls. Unless you were into nuns. I'll never forget that. I'll never forget the way you said it. You sounded so . . . free.'

For the first time that evening she found herself the centre of attention.

'I met this woman . . . in my antenatal group,' she went on. We had this . . . this encounter. It was just a one-off. But it made me sad. It made me sad because I wanted it. And because I can't have that . . . and have Richard and Matilda. Which means I can't have it at all.'

'My God – Natalie,' Tina said. 'Are you telling us you think you might be gay?'

'I'm telling you I've decided I can never find out,' Natalie said.

'But you love Richard,' Lucy said. 'Don't you?'

And suddenly Natalie was rooted back in the room, in her body. She could even feel an itch behind her eyeballs, as if of tears.

'I haven't told him,' she said. 'I mean, he knows – he knows I had doubts, once. Something else happened, a long time ago – when I went travelling. After the millennium. That's why we broke up. I told him it was a mistake. I promised him. I can't tell him about this.'

'But . . .' Tina said. 'You've been . . . happy with Richard?'

'In bed, you mean?' Natalie said. 'We were . . . I don't know how to say it, really. We were never the kind of lovers who can't keep their hands off each other. I

279

wasn't with him for that. It was . . . reassuring. But now it's gone. It went pretty much as soon as I got pregnant. We've just completely dried up.'

'But lots of couples go through dry spells,' Lucy said. 'Long dry spells, too. Natalie, I know you will have thought about this, but how about speaking to a counsellor? You don't have to tell Richard. You could just go on your own. I could mind Matilda for you if you liked.'

'Or I could,' Tina said.

'But what would be the point?' Natalie said. 'I've made up my mind. Now I just have to get on with it.'

'But you make it sound like a punishment,' Tina said.

'Whatever I do, I'm going to struggle to live with it,' Natalie said. 'So I might as well do what's right. Don't you think?'

'Oh, who says what's right?' Lucy said. 'Who decides? Natalie, you've always been a dark horse – but if there's one thing I know about you, it's that you always try to do the right thing. But that shouldn't mean that you have to sacrifice yourself.'

The carriage clock on the mantelpiece began to chime midnight.

Tina said, 'It's time! We have to make a toast. Right now.' She leaned forward to get her glass from the coffee table.

'I rather think I've had enough,' Lucy said, but she picked up her glass too, and Natalie followed suit.

'To old times,' Tina said.

'And to new times,' Natalie said.

They clinked glasses, and the clock fell silent.

280

Natalie's phone beeped, and she got it out of her bag and saw the message was from Richard: *Happy New Year my dear. Give the others my best. R xxx*

Tina winced, and said, 'I'm sorry, he just kicked me,' and then, 'Oh God – I think I just felt something go pop. Oh my God, I'm just going to go to the bathroom. No, don't come with me. I have to be on my own for a minute.'

She went out to the stairs and disappeared from view.

Lucy reached out and took Natalie's hand.

'Everything will be all right in the end,' she said, 'whatever happens.'

Tina was gone for just long enough for them to ask each other whether they ought to go and check on her. Then she came back upstairs and told them yes, her waters really had broken. Would they mind sticking around while she rang the hospital, and if she had to go in tonight, would it be possible for Natalie to give her a lift?

By the time they set off, Tina, who was sitting next to Lucy in the back, had stopped timing her contractions; they were so close together that it was not reassuring. Lucy had sobered up enough to help Natalie with directions, although Natalie would have much preferred it if Lucy had been in a position to do the driving herself.

It was a fraught journey, given Natalie's fear of negotiating central London, but also an otherworldly one. She remembered what it had been like in the early stages of labour, walking with Richard alongside the Thames – how their surroundings had been both

281

vivid and remote, imbued with the fleeting clarity of a memory or dream. Now she could see the familiar London nightscape through Tina's eyes, and take it in with the sad affection of an émigrée who is on the way somewhere completely different and unknown, and has no idea when she may be able to return. The dark wet streets, the glowing windows of pubs and bars, the drunk, short-skirted girls staggering companionably, would all carry on, magical and oblivious, while Tina was drawn into a fast-narrowing tunnel, with no way out other than onward, and Lucy and Natalie stood by and waited for it to be over.

Tina hadn't asked them to stay, but Lucy had insisted that they would, assuming that Natalie would be equally gung-ho at the prospect of providing moral support to the bitter end . . . and Tina hadn't put up much resistance, had seemed glad to have the offer of help. Matilda would be fine with Richard, and Lucy had Hannah at home, so there was no need to rush back. And things seemed to be moving along pretty fast, judging by the regularity of Tina's contractions. If it did turn out to be a protracted labour, Tina would need them there all the more. Perhaps they could do shifts – though Natalie was actually very relieved to have Lucy there.

She couldn't really admit to it, but she wasn't sure she was cut out for this. Her own experience had been so passive. She'd contributed a bit, but other people had mostly made it happen for her. She hadn't given birth; birth had been taken out of her, like gallstones, or a perforated appendix, or cancer. It was difficult for her to conceive of the moment of delivery as miraculous or special; it was all about the patter of gushing blood. So how could she possibly cheerlead someone else to the crisis point? And besides, she was rather squeamish. Gore, horror movies, scenes of torture weren't her thing. It had been bad enough going through it all herself; given half a chance, she'd never have opted to witness someone else's suffering.

They stopped at the entrance to the car park and Natalie wound down her window and took a ticket. The barrier rose. The maternity wing loomed up in front of them, ghostly white concrete striped with the shine of glass, the futuristic vision of yesterday's men.

Natalie did a careful circuit, found a space and nosed into it. She killed the engine and exhaled.

'How are you doing?' she asked.

'I think your upholstery is going to be spared,' Tina said.

Natalie got out and took Tina's bag from the boot. Lucy took Tina's baby car seat. This was one of the items she had insisted Tina should buy when they met up back in the autumn to make sure Tina was properly kitted out. Seeing it reminded Natalie of the question Tina had asked her that day, which Natalie had failed to answer: *What was it like?*

Tina got out of the car and shut the door, then stopped and leaned against it. Natalie waited. She offered Tina her arm, but Tina shook her head. She straightened and made her way towards the bright sliding doors. Lucy quickened her pace to walk alongside her, and Natalie followed.

Inside they found a reception desk with an empty chair. There was a buzzer on the desk, and a small notice: 'Please ring for assistance'.

Lucy rang. They waited.

Nobody came.

'I actually don't know where we're meant to go,' Tina said.

'You sit down,' Lucy said.

She steered Tina towards a row of seats bolted to the wall and went off. Natalie settled down next to Tina.

'She seems to have sobered up nicely,' Tina commented. 'Must be the mother instinct. Ability to snap out of a drama when confronted by a crisis.' Then she stiffened and fell silent, and Natalie found herself wincing in sympathy.

Lucy reappeared and led them to a midwife who took the brown folder with Tina's medical notes, asked a couple of desultory questions, and sent them all through to the waiting room.

It was empty. So this was what it looked like! It was so much more innocuous than Natalie remembered. She thought of it as drenched in fear and bodily fluids, but actually it was a banal, dull sort of place, with worn, institutional flooring and plastic chairs.

They sat in strained sympathy while Tina suffered and drew breath, and suffered and drew breath. Tina had been told that all the delivery suites were full, and it was possible that she'd come in too early, and would be sent home. In the lapses of time between bouts of pain Lucy kept up an encouraging patter, affirming that Tina was doing brilliantly, everything was going just fine, and all was going to be well, and Natalie, listening to her, almost felt reassured herself.

Then Tina was taken off to be examined, and Lucy said to Natalie, 'Don't look so scared. She'll be OK. Just stick up the head end, and if she ends up having a caesarean I guess they'll chuck us out anyway.'

'I just don't know how I'm going to cope with the gruesome bits,' Natalie said. 'When I had Matilda, I couldn't help but be aware that it was pretty grisly for Richard. He just sort of withdrew. He was horrified. I don't want to be Tina's Richard.'

'So don't be,' Lucy said.

Then they fell to swapping birth stories – Lucy's two caesareans to Natalie's one ventouse-and-forceps-and-episiotomy – and Natalie was reminded of the conversations she'd had along similar lines with her antenatal group. Such exchanges had a compulsive quality; you could see, when a woman talked about the experience of having a baby, that she was remembering a time when she had not been herself, and trying to reclaim it.

Tina came back in, accompanied by a midwife.

'Guess what, it's a miracle!' Tina announced with a rather forced smile. 'They've found room at the inn!'

The midwife confirmed the good news: Tina could stay, and so could both her friends.

Lucy said, 'Oh, thank God for that!' and Natalie, who had been secretly hoping that only one companion would be permitted – in which case she would have been off the hook – agreed that it was a great relief.

They all went up to a tiny room on the fifth floor, with a narrow bed, a bedside cabinet and a window looking out on to the black sweep of the Thames and the lights of the city beyond.

'Bathroom's down the corridor,' the midwife said. 'This is the postnatal floor, so don't be surprised if you bump into someone who's already had her baby.'

She closed the door. Tina waited for another contraction to pass, unzipped her bag, rummaged and said, 'OK, I'm too hot, and I'm going to get changed.'

There was a rustling of clothing.

'You can look now. Chocolate?'

'Wouldn't mind,' said Natalie, taking a square.

Tina perched on the bed. She was wearing a loose white nightie with a frilled neckline and buttons down the front: the sort of thing a voluptuous virgin might wear as a B-movie Dracula pressed his fangs to her neck.

'What do you think?' Tina said, posing with hand on hip. 'Demure, but rather fetching, I thought.'

But an hour later Tina was not so cocky. She begged one of them to ring the bell, and when the midwife appeared Tina grabbed at her arm and pleaded: 'Help me . . . Help me . . .'

The midwife gently but firmly detached Tina's hand, went off and returned with a syringe, which she sank into Tina's backside.

'There, that should give you some relief,' she said. 'In a couple of hours, when it wears off, we can see about getting you an epidural. Ring the bell if you feel the head.' And then she left again.

Watching Tina moaning and contorting on the bed as if an invisible corkscrew had been driven through her and was being mercilessly twisted, Natalie was struck

286

by the impassable gulf between witnessing pain and suffering it. Tina was in her own private hell, and she could not share it; and Tina had anyway turned away from both of them and withdrawn into the struggle.

The sight of Tina, who had always been so self-possessed, writhing like a clubbed seal was shocking, and also a little shaming, but it was compelling too. The carefully maintained carapace of Tina's social mask had disappeared. Here was a woman for whom words were currency, reduced to wordlessness; groaning as if she'd been bludgeoned and left for dead by the side of the road, yet with no wounds, no blood, no bruises to show for it – not yet, at any rate.

'Oh God! Help me! I can feel something, I think it's the head,' Tina cried out. 'Ring the bell!'

Lucy rang and kept on ringing until the midwife reappeared and thrust her hand up Tina's nightie like a vet inspecting a cow.

'You're nearly fully dilated,' she said. 'Don't push yet. I'm going to see what they want us to do. We might have to deliver the baby here.' She used the phone mounted on the wall to call for instructions.

'I told you you'd pop it out in a couple of hours,' Lucy said to Tina. 'Speedy Gonzales!'

A faint glimmer of something close to a smile crossed Tina's face before it and her body contorted again.

The midwife hung up and turned to Tina. 'They want you in a delivery suite,' she said. 'The porters are coming to take you down.'

And so Natalie found herself running alongside Lucy behind Tina screaming on a trolley, panting past the

287

horrified face of a dressing-gowned mother-to-be on the stairwell, and so down in the lift into a windowless room with a muted frieze of peach and aqua flowers bordering the ceiling, a frieze at which Natalie found herself staring as Tina, screaming now like a reluctant sacrifice, was dumped on to another bed, examined, and instructed not to push until the baby's heartbeat had been checked. A belt was strapped round Tina's belly. It picked up nothing. A new, apparently senior midwife struggled and shoved between Tina's legs like a removal man trying to get a particularly bulky sofa through a door.

Natalie didn't know what to do with herself, but didn't want to get in the way, so stood back a little, feeling like a spare part, and worse than useless. They all seemed to be in a panic . . . where the hell was this going to end? Would Tina suddenly be wheeled off to theatre? Surely, if your body had done its job and sped through to the transition stage without so much as a prostaglandin pessary, you'd earned the right to escape being cut?

But Lucy had somehow found a space by the head of the bed, between the various bits of alarming monitoring equipment, and was leaning forward, saying something over and over again, a little mantra, six words in the face of potential disaster: 'It's going to be all right.'

'I've done it, I've clipped the monitor on to your baby's head,' the senior midwife said. She waited for a moment and watched a display.

'OK, I've got the heartbeat.' She pulled the stem of the monitor free. 'You can push now. Don't scream. Push.'

A doctor bustled in and Tina cried out, 'Help me! Help me!' and the doctor said, 'Yes, I think we will help you,' and selected a pair of scissors and cut Tina open. Natalie didn't look but she couldn't help but hear the sound of metal snipping flesh, and then it was tuned out by a high electric buzzing gathering force, and she glimpsed Tina's face purpling and heard Lucy scream, '*Push!*' and the red ball of baby hurtled out into the doctor's hands. Minutes later the great steak of the placenta was held up for inspection and that was it, the final straw, the buzzing was a swarm, an approaching whiteout, and in the end it was a relief to yield and go under.

Coming to was much more painful than being out. Natalie was down on the floor, someone was leaning over her, and everything was bright and loud and brutal. She got to her feet and the midwife hustled her back down the corridor to the waiting room and told her to keep her head between her knees till she felt better.

It was some time before she felt sure enough of herself to straighten up and make her way out. She had to explain herself to the woman at the reception desk, which was mortifying, though she could hardly make more of a chump of herself than she already had. The woman shook her head in amused contempt, told Natalie the delivery suite number and buzzed her through.

She knocked gently at the door, heard nothing, knocked harder. Thought she heard 'Come in.' Pushed the door open, a little way at first, then wider.

Tina was sitting propped up, pale and stunned, with

Lucy perched on the end of the bed. It was dim and quiet, and Natalie couldn't see anybody else.

'Where's the baby?' she asked.

Tina gestured towards the far side of the bed. 'He's asleep. Come and have a look.'

Natalie shut the door behind her and went to see. The baby was lying in one of those awful hospital cots that Matilda had refused to settle in for the duration of Natalie's three sleepless nights on the post-natal ward – a cabinet on wheels with a thin mattress on top and a clear plastic rim.

But, just as Tina had said, he really was sound asleep. A red triangle of face – two lines for eyes, a small flat nose – was just about visible between his little white hat and the sheet he'd been swaddled in.

'He's gorgeous,' Natalie said. 'Congratulations.'

'He looks like his dad,' Tina said.

'I'm so sorry about what happened,' Natalie told her.

'What, that you passed out at the sight of my placenta? Honestly, I don't blame you. I wouldn't have minded being unconscious myself.'

'I was worse than Richard,' Natalie said. 'At least he didn't pass out.'

'You did fine,' Lucy said. 'You got us here, which is more than I could have done. If I'd tried to drive I'd have probably got myself arrested, and I don't think we'd have had much luck getting a taxi at two a.m. on New Year's Day.'

'So how are you feeling?' Natalie asked Tina.

'Compared to an hour ago, absolutely bloody fantastic,' Tina said.

Natalie noticed, on the stand that had been pushed down to the end of the bed, an empty cup of tea and a plate with some cold-looking toast.

'You seem so calm,' she said. 'I can't get over it. It's like it was all in a day's work, and now you're sitting there having your tea break. I have to hand it to you. No gas and air. No epidural. No nothing.'

But maybe an epidural wouldn't have been such a bad thing. Had she been deluded in her disappointment over the way her own labour had turned out? Perhaps there wasn't really any right way for a birth to go . . . or maybe any and every way was right, as long as nothing went permanently, unfixably wrong.

There was a knock on the door and the midwife walked in.

'They're ready for you on the ward now,' she said.

Tina swung her legs over the side of the bed and stood up. Natalie saw that the white nightie was splashed with red at the hem.

'You'd better put something on your feet,' the midwife said.

Natalie fished a pair of espadrilles and a dressing-gown out of Tina's bag and Tina put them on. Then she shouldered the bag and Lucy picked up the car seat. The midwife led the way, pushing the baby, followed by Tina, who shuffled along with Natalie and Lucy behind her.

Despite their slow progress, it struck Natalie as a triumphal procession. It was a victory over something – over what, she wasn't quite sure; biology, perhaps, or birth, or death? – that Tina, bloodied but no longer bowed, was back on her feet.

At the entrance to the dark ward the midwife said, 'No visitors allowed at this time, I'm afraid, so it's time to say goodbye.'

Tina turned to Lucy and Natalie and said, 'Thank you. I'm not planning on getting him christened, but if I did, you two would definitely be the godmothers.'

'We're honoured,' Lucy said.

Tina flashed them a smile of relief so intense it was not far off elation.

'Happy New Year! I think this beats the millennium.'

Then she allowed the midwife to usher her and the baby on to the ward.

A moment later, a newborn – maybe Tina's? – started crying.

'When they stitched her up she couldn't stop shaking,' Lucy said. 'I think she might have been in shock. If they'd sent her home, you and I would have ended up delivering that baby.'

'You mean you would.'

'Oh, for heaven's sake, stop putting yourself down,' Lucy said. 'It takes guts to face up to something you're afraid of. It's a hell of a business, isn't it? And that's what it's like when it works. Anyway, I don't know about you, but I'm just about ready to get out of here. It's so stuffy! I've got the most appalling headache.'

Natalie hesitated, and then decided to be brave. She had avoided inviting people round to her house for months. During the day it was all right, but not when Richard was there. But she had to at least make the offer, and Lucy could make of it what she wanted.

'Do you want to stay over at mine?' she said. 'I don't think you'll have much luck getting a cab.'

'Are you sure? I don't want to intrude.'

'No, you're very welcome,' Natalie said, and realized this was true. 'As long as you don't mind the sofa. And a bit of a weird atmosphere. Richard's been sleeping in the guest room.'

'Natalie,' Lucy said, 'you look white as a sheet. Are you OK to drive?'

Natalie nodded. She didn't quite trust herself to speak; she thought she might cry.

As they made their way to the lift she found herself humming: 'Once in royal David's city, Stood a lowly cattle shed, Where a mother laid her baby, In a manger for His bed . . .' and she noticed for the first time that the hospital had Christmas decorations – shining paper streamers, purple, silver and gold, in the shape of Chinese lanterns, gleaming in the artificial light – and some of them were still up.

15

The gift

Sometime during William's first morning on earth, Tina checked her phone and saw a message from Dan: *How are you? Would love to see you and William as soon as you're ready.* She replied, *All well. Come soon – but not just yet. Will let you know.*

Despite the inevitable ambivalence he felt about becoming a father, Dan was desperate to see his son. She would have been touched by this, if she hadn't already been feeling so overwhelmed.

She wasn't allowed to use her phone on the ward, but she also wasn't allowed to take the baby anywhere else. One of the midwives had agreed to keep an eye on William as long as she was quick, and she had nipped into the corridor outside. But she had to wait for what felt like ages before someone responded to the buzzer and let her back in to the ward, and the midwife who was supposedly keeping tabs on William was nowhere to be found. He'd woken up and was crying – again.

She'd had some idea of what to expect – the tiredness, the discomfort, the crying – but she hadn't realized that William's thin, keening wail would panic her like nothing else. Nor had she expected to find his face so endlessly fascinating that watching him would distract her from sleeping – not that there had been much opportunity for that so far.

It had been about five in the morning by the time she said goodbye to Natalie and Lucy and was installed on the ward with William. Every time she'd drifted off, somebody else's baby had started wailing, and then it had been seven o'clock, the ward lights had gone on, and a succession of people had felt entitled to fling aside the curtain and burst into her cubicle.

The lady who filled up the water jugs, the one who brought round and collected the lunch menus, the pert little researcher who'd left her a questionnaire to fill in about pain . . . probably all very necessary and useful in their way, just not what she needed right then and there. If only they would all just leave her alone – but at the same time she was terrified of being left alone with this tiny baby's life literally in her hands.

She had been told she would be discharged that day, but just as the hospital had been reluctant to admit her, it was slow to let her go; and even though she was scared of going home with a child she had next to no idea how to care for, she didn't want to linger any longer than was necessary in the Hades of the postnatal ward, and chafed at having to wait round for her paperwork to be signed off so she could escape.

She toyed with the idea of getting a taxi home; her

friends had done their bit, and she sure as hell didn't want her parents to show up and collect her, as if she was a shamed child being released from a correctional facility. Dan would come like a shot if she called him, but he had drawn the short straw, the New Year's Day Bank Holiday shift, and was working. She didn't want him to have to come up with a pretext in order to leave the office and collect her; she didn't want to oblige him to come to the rescue.

But in the end, she decided she couldn't face the prospect of lugging everything to the lifts, and down to the taxi rank, and she suspected she might get short shrift from the staff if she asked for someone to carry some of her stuff. It was quite a haul: her bag, William, the car seat, and the strange plastic bag of promotional gubbins that all new mothers apparently got, which it seemed rude to refuse. Probably she could manage it, but her stitches were going to pull with every step, and things she would normally not think twice about had become insurmountable challenges; even going to the toilet was a big deal.

So she rang Natalie and did something that did not come naturally, but that she suspected she was going to have to learn to do more often; she asked for help. Natalie came quickly, did not object to sitting round waiting with her until she was finally given her discharge letter, and carried everything up the four flights of stairs at the other end without complaint. She offered to stay, but Tina said she should get back to Matilda; Tina's parents were already on their way over.

Tina couldn't remember the last time her parents had

been to the flat. Visitors of all kinds, whether intrusive or more usually confined to their own territory, were another feature of new motherhood that she had not anticipated.

There was this to say for a stay in hospital, however short; it made you appreciate having a space to call your own. She'd come to see the flat as a bit of a tip, a dumping-ground for her eyes only, but now it struck her as bright and light and full of things she liked. The big wrought-iron bed, the piles of books and papers, the photo montage of her friends, the ormolu carriage clock . . . nothing was impersonal, everything was hers. She was no longer a numbered patient on a ward; she was Tina Fox, mother of William Fox, and she was home.

When Cecily and Robert arrived it was immediately obvious how pleased and relieved they were – almost pleased and relieved enough to overlook the misfortune of her single status, but not quite.

Cecily put pink roses in a vase and filled the freezer compartment in the top of Tina's fridge, plus two of the shelves beneath it, with portions of home-made lasagne and Bolognese sauce and shepherd's pie. She'd brought a cake, too – chocolate – and Tina, still baggy-bellied but too ravenous to care, asked for an indelicately large slice and wolfed it. Meanwhile Cecily settled on the sofa and ceremonially held her new grandson, and Robert submitted to Cecily's gentle admonishments and held him too.

Robert didn't look very sure of himself. He looked as

if he feared being unmanned, but was moved in spite of himself by cradling this tiny scrap of his own flesh and blood, his unforeseen and probably only descendant. Perhaps it was this that prompted Tina to say, 'There you are, Dad, a male heir to carry on the Fox name. It's funny how things turn out, isn't it? You see, there are some advantages to me not being married.'

The fond look on Robert's face gave way to irritation. 'I don't think it's something to be flippant about, Tina.'

'Robert,' Cecily murmured, 'remember what we talked about.'

'Well, has his father even seen him yet?'

'Dad, I only just got out of hospital.'

'Plenty of time for all that,' Cecily said, and Tina was grateful that her mother was defending her, but would have preferred it if Cecily had looked a little less pained.

She had told her parents a little about Dan: his name, his profession, where he lived, his West Country roots. She wanted Robert and Cecily to think well of Dan, so she had assured them that he wanted to be part of William's life and was keen to contribute financially, money that she had reluctantly decided to accept. However, she also didn't want to get their hopes up, and so she had told them that she wasn't in love with him and never had been.

'Boys need their fathers,' Robert grumbled.

'And daughters don't, I suppose,' Tina muttered.

That did it. Robert was not inclined to engage with her, or William, any further, and occupied himself with the newspaper and the crossword.

Cecily, saddened, as on many previous occasions, by her husband's penchant for stubborn, sulky moods and her daughter's willingness to provoke them, busied herself with housework. She found an apron and some rubber gloves to put on, and these accessories contrasted oddly with her silk blouse, well-cut slacks and trim, elegant frame, as if she'd pulled them on to rehearse a part in a play. It was an unfamiliar sight, because for many years Tina's family home had been kept spick and span by the help, but it quickly became apparent that lack of practice had not diminished Cecily's cleaning skills.

While Tina bathed, Cecily moved the sofa and vacuumed, unasked, the curdled dust that had collected underneath it; and when Tina awoke from a deep sleep, more a bout of unconsciousness than a nap, to find that it was pitch black outside, the whole flat smelt of lemon bleach.

She was half relieved when her parents left, but felt, too, a strange tug of sadness, as if she had just been abandoned. This was it, this was really it; she was on her own.

But, damn it, there was a whole world out there, and she was still connected to it. She was not just a woman home alone with a newborn baby on a cold, dark winter's night; she was not confined to these four walls.

She got William off to sleep and settled him into the cot, then checked the *Post* website. They hadn't yet put anything online to say she'd had the baby, though she'd sent Jeremy a message about it. But everything was probably out of sync because of New Year. It didn't

299

mean that her column was no longer regarded as of interest.

As sometimes happens when you go looking for confirmation of your well-earned place in the scheme of things, she stumbled across something that made her feel even more at sea.

It was a photo. *The Rt. Hon. Justin Dandridge QC, MP enjoying the New Year's Day brass band parade in Shepstowe's market square, at the heart of his north Devon constituency, accompanied by the fragrant Mrs Virginia Dandridge.*

Justin and Ginny were pictured standing close together, wrapped up warm against the cold. Presenting a unified front to the world? Or genuinely united against possible affront – including the threat that Tina might once have presented?

The fragrant Mrs Virginia Dandridge! But Ginny did look as if she probably smelt rather good – fresh and floral – and was not, like Tina at that particular moment, emanating a bitter, iron-heavy undertone of dried blood.

William started crying again, and Tina was grateful to be needed – although, as the night wore on and he fed and fed and then demanded to feed some more, she was drained beyond astonishment that anyone could need her quite so much. He had dozed so sweetly most of the day, but now, like a vampire, he wanted blood: milk from her blood, the milk that she wasn't yet producing, but that, if he persisted, would eventually come in, replacing the insubstantial fluid he was getting from her now.

The hours passed in dark fits and starts, snatches of

sleep broken by crying that was quieted by suckling again. And that was the end of Friday, the first day.

By noon on the second day the community midwife had been and gone, she still wasn't up and dressed, her parents were about to return and Dan, who wasn't working and was free to come any time, had already rung twice.

The third time, she picked up the phone, and said: 'No. Not now. My parents are coming.'

'Ohhh . . .' He sounded heartbroken. 'But I'll only stay five minutes. I won't be in the way, I promise. Maybe I could make it before they turn up.'

She gave in and told him to head on over, but to make it quick. Then her parents were early – Cecily obviously anxious and eager, Robert uneasy and forbearing – and Dan arrived soon afterwards.

He showed up all bright and hopeful and clean-shaven with a ridiculous blue heart-shaped helium balloon and an ostentatious bouquet and a teddy bear that was bigger than William was. He held William fearfully, but with an expression of proprietorial, incredulous pride; and he set about making small talk with Cecily as if it was perfectly normal for him to be hanging out in Tina's flat, chatting to her mother about the weather and Cornwall and Christmas – as if he belonged there.

Then Cecily said, 'So have you given any more thought to having William christened?', directing the question to both of them.

'It's no good asking him that,' Tina told her. 'He's a

confirmed atheist. He's very tolerant, though. He takes a sort of anthropological view of it all.'

'I'm sure Dan's quite capable of speaking for himself,' Cecily said.

'Thank you, Mrs Fox,' Dan chipped in.

'Oh – Cecily. Please.'

'Thank you, Cecily. Well, I would say that the christening thing is up to Tina. Whatever she wants, I'll go along with.'

'That's a very generous approach.'

'Mum, please don't nag. I've said I'll think about it,' Tina said.

She knew it would upset her mother terribly if she failed to have William baptized, and to her surprise, she could foresee her opposition ebbing away . . . it seemed feasible that some sort of wholly irrational homing instinct would kick in, and eventually she might think, Well, after all, why not? But not yet . . . not just yet.

When she took William back there was a definite tang of Dan's aftershave clinging to him. It was as if William had been marked. It was a woody scent, not unpleasant, but also not wholly familiar, interfering with the sweet baby smell of William's head.

It was all too much . . . and William wanted feeding, so she took him downstairs to her bedroom, away from the conversation Dan and Robert had started having, with Robert trying to find out if Dan was interested in rugby or cricket, and Dan tentatively mentioning Bristol Rovers.

She sat on the bed which she had never shared with

Dan, and tried to latch William on. It didn't work. He jerked away from her nipple as if it revolted him, and started wailing again.

Then Dan barged in without knocking, and she exploded into a histrionic, tear-spouting rage and told him to leave. He reacted as if she'd gone insane. She put William over her shoulder – he was still screaming – bundled Dan towards the front door, opened it and pushed him through and out down the stairs.

Cecily appeared and said, 'Is everything all right?'

'It's not all right! It'll never be all right!'

And so it seemed. But Cecily took William from her, and half an hour later she tried to feed him again and the magic she'd already come to rely on, her physical connection to her son, was restored.

Then even Robert's muttered comment – 'That young chap's obviously trying to do the right thing, and you're not making it easy for him' – didn't bother her. Why not be magnanimous? She left Dan a message of apology, and put the teddy in the cot, and tied the silly balloon to the rail – not that William could even focus on it, or make out the colour.

That night William fell asleep at the breast and she stirred and he abruptly came adrift. His parted lips were glossy with milk, and in the glow of the nightlight she saw herself eject a fine spray of white droplets that came to rest, glistening, on his cheek.

Wasn't that the myth of the origin of the Milky Way – a stray spurt of sustenance from the lactating mother of a god?

There was much she hadn't done for William; he

didn't have a freshly wallpapered nursery with a frieze of jolly animals and a stain-resistant carpet, or a doting father living under the same roof, or any hope of a wholly devoted, stay-at-home mum. But for now, there was one thing he wanted more than anything else, and she could at least give him that.

On the third day she was calm and heavy and languorous, as if sated. Cecily and Robert came again – how quickly they had settled into a kind of routine! Robert had his newspaper, and Cecily, who had run out of cleaning to do, had brought the bootees she was knitting.

But just as Tina had begun to get used to having them around, it seemed that her parents were beginning to tire, if not of her and William, then of all the to-ing and fro-ing required to see them. Cecily dropped some hints about her needing to get a bed for the spare room, for overnight guests.

'But that's going to be William's room, when he's old enough to go in on his own,' Tina objected.

'Maybe some kind of put-you-up or sofabed,' Cecily suggested.

'I can't see Dad settling for that,' Tina said.

'I was thinking more for me. I'd love to come and stay and help out. But Daddy needs his rest, and he's such a light sleeper. I'm not at all sure how well he'd cope if he was disturbed at night,' Cecily said with a circumspect little glance in the direction of her husband, who was still stoically reading.

They agreed that since Tina appeared to be coping, Cecily and Robert would not return until the fifth or sixth day.

The fourth day was very cold. The *Post* ran a series of pictures of the hoar frost: glazed white fields and crystallized trees, the sun a delicately tinted disc floating in a sky of fog, exuding, not light, but a pale umbra of colour – lemon and rose diffused by milk.

On the fifth day it snowed, and she couldn't venture out. She finished Cecily's chocolate cake, and, at midnight, microwaved the last portion of lasagne.

On the sixth day she was reduced to eating from tins. She decided to leave the chickpeas till last. The snow was still thick on the ground, and she was due to file her column. She had a stab at drafting it, but the sentences refused to follow each other, or make sense.

She was glad to be interrupted by a phone call. It was Lucy, who arranged to come and see her on the tenth day. She sounded excited – something about a job interview. Tina tried to enthuse, but was aware of sounding rusty and lacklustre, as if she was beginning to lose the power of speech.

After she'd chatted to Lucy her head was clearer. She hunched over her computer with William lying on a pillow on her lap, feeding, and kept on typing until she reached the necessary word count.

Lucy must have got in touch with Natalie, because on

the seventh day Natalie came round and refilled Tina's freezer, and brought her a pile of glossy magazines, more flowers, and another cake.

By the eighth day William's navel had healed, he was back up to his birth weight, and it was hard to believe she'd ever been nervous about bathing him or changing his nappy.

His eyes were blue. She knew all newborn babies had blue eyes, but she was sure she could see beyond the slight haze in his to a colour that was bright and abiding, more like his father's than the greeny-grey of her own.

The flowers Cecily had brought her were past their best, but the snow had dwindled enough for delivery services to be resumed, and a bouquet turned up from work. After the traditional congratulations, the message went on: *Oh go on then, put those feet up! But don't forget there's a desk here waiting for you!*

It was reassuring to see that whatever else had changed, Jeremy's communication style hadn't.

A couple of cards arrived in the post. Nothing from Justin . . . but then, everything was still at sixes and sevens, and it was early days. There was still time for him to make some small gesture to acknowledge her transformation.

She was glad to have left the life that had him in it behind her, but still, the break with the past would be cleaner, more absolute, if she could know for sure that she had finally earned his respect.

*

On the ninth day Tina was on her best behaviour. Dan came, and so did Cecily, on her own.

They all tried to stick to neutral topics of conversation, which was not a straightforward exercise. Tina was reminded of those medieval maps of the world, with vaguely recognizable land masses surrounded by seas embellished with ornate monsters, and warnings at the margins: *Here be dragons.*

Cecily attempted current affairs, but soon faltered, and resorted to reminiscing about Tina's babyhood, much to Tina's discomfort. It was bad enough to hear the familiar sigh, and 'Of course, I would have liked to have more children . . .' but to have Dan quizzing Cecily on what Tina had been like as a child was just infuriating. Dan duly heard that she had been the most strong-willed, demanding, vociferous little girl in Barnes, and looked smugly amused – as if this somehow proved him right.

They got on to the subject of holidays, and Cecily said, 'You can have the Old Schoolhouse at Easter if you like, Tina. I mean, you can have it to yourself . . . and invite anyone you want to go along with you, of course.' (At this she gazed almost flirtatiously at Dan.) 'We won't be there,' she added, 'Robert's booked us on a trip to Venice, to celebrate our anniversary. It's our ruby wedding. I'm planning to give a little family party sometime in the spring. Dan, dear, I do hope you'll come.'

Tina looked pointedly at her watch to hint to Dan that he should begin to think about moving on; they had got through thirty minutes, surely there was no need to push their luck. Still, it was all good practice for the likely awkwardness of Dan's mother's first visit . . . to which she had agreed in principle, although she was being a little evasive about the date.

But then William, who was strapped into the little cloth-coloured rocking cradle Lucy had bought him, opened his eyes and began to whimper. Dan said, 'Is it OK if I take him out?'

'Sure,' Tina said, so emphatically that it was obvious she would much rather have done it herself.

Dan fiddled awkwardly with the catch on the cradle strap, and she reached down to undo it. He smiled at her and said, 'Thanks to the expert,' clumsily scooped William out and settled back on to the sofa with him.

Dan looked down into William's face and William's hand wrapped tightly round Dan's finger.

Cecily said, 'Well, he definitely knows who his daddy is.'

'Mmm,' Dan said non-committally. Then he glanced up at Cecily and said, 'Do you know what, I think he might have a look of you.'

'Do you think so?' Cecily said, and Tina knew she was pleased. 'I know people love to make out these resemblances, but I have to say I'm not convinced. How can a tiny baby possibly look like a sixty-three-year-old woman? I don't look like my own self at that age, so I fail to see in what way he could be said to look like me.'

'It's the high forehead, and something about the set of the eyebrows,' Dan said.

'Well, I'll defer to your expertise,' Cecily said, and Tina thought: Sold.

The doorbell rang, and Cecily said, 'I'll go.'

They sat without speaking as Cecily's tread retreated down the stairs. Then Dan said, 'So, you were a pain in the backside when you were little. That makes sense.'

'I bet you were an absolute toe-rag,' Tina countered.

'I was an angel, actually,' Dan told her. 'So do you think you'll take him to Cornwall at Easter, then?'

'If you're angling for an invite, forget it.'

'I just kind of like the idea of introducing him to the seaside.'

'Not going to happen.'

'I think your mum approves of me.'

'She's only sucking up to you because she's hoping against hope that you'll redeem me from being a scarlet woman.'

'No she isn't. She just wants you to be happy,' Dan said, and then added, 'Mums always like me.'

Tina hit him over the head with a cushion. He held up his arm to keep her at bay and complained that she shouldn't hit a man with a baby. But she kept pelting him . . . if only to ward off the strange, lurching urge to lean forward and kiss him.

The game halted abruptly as Cecily came back in, carrying an armful of parcel.

'I expect it's another present for William,' she said, handing it over to Tina.

'It's addressed to me,' Tina pointed out.

She did not recognize the handwriting. The post-mark: Barnstaple.

She put the parcel on the dining table, fetched the scissors and cut through the brown paper to reveal a layer of bubble wrap and, beneath it, dark wood.

'Oh my God,' she said.

She picked the parcel up and turned it round. There was a return address. It was not a place she'd ever been, but she'd seen its name written at the head of so many letters, and heard it referred to with such affection, that she felt as if she knew it.

She pulled away the rest of the paper and bubble wrap, and there it was, as if it had never been away.

'Isn't that Great-Aunt Win's sewing box?' Cecily said.

'It is.'

'I'd forgotten you had it. I thought it was in the loft.'

'I rather like it,' Tina said. 'I think it's admirable. Romantic.'

She ran her fingers over the lid, took in the scratches, the dark wood, the image of the ship. There was a loud rushing noise in her ears; it could have been blood, or the sea, or the hum that precedes a faint.

She opened the box and lifted out the compartment lid with the inscription: *Made by I alone.* The compartment was empty.

'I don't see what's romantic about it, I must say,' Cecily said.

'I just rather like to think of Win living defiantly by herself, with her sewing box for company,' Tina said. 'She'd obviously been let down in love.'

'Well, yes, dear, but you know she didn't actually live alone,' Cecily said.

'But I thought she never married.'

'Well, no, she didn't, she may have had some disappointment in that regard, but she did find a companion in the end. Miss Glennie. They lived in a little cottage in Port Maus, you know – it was after Win closed the school, and let the house to Arthur Symonds, the watercolourist. Next time you're in the Black Swan, you ask about Miss Fox and Miss Glennie. They're still remembered – they're part of village folklore. They were quite inseparable. They even slept together. Of course it was completely innocent, which people find hard to believe these days, but there you are. They were like sisters, and it was perfectly normal for sisters to share a bed back then.'

Tina lifted out the whole of the top layer and saw what she had not seen for many years, the box's red velvet lining. There was nothing inside apart from the dried roses, and a single letter.

She heard her mother asking her why somebody had just posted her Great-Aunt Win's box, but she didn't reply. Instead she muttered something – more an apology than an excuse – snatched the letter and rushed down to her bedroom to read it.

The envelope was the familiar shape and size, and inside was the same thick, creamy, headed paper, but the handwriting was familiar only from the address on the parcel.

Northcourt Farm
Shepstowe
Nr Barnstaple
Devon

Dear Tina,

We've never met, and I hope we never do, as however I try to rationalize the part you've played in my life, the thought of you arouses strong feelings, and I am not certain of my ability to control them. Nevertheless, even though I have never seen you face to face, I know far too much about you for my own good. You also know a little about me – I prefer not to think about how much.

Until I came across this box, I knew about you in two ways. First and foremost, I knew you as the young woman with whom my husband had been conducting a lengthy, passionate, but very discreet love affair. Although I did not know your age or name, I deduced that you probably had a successful, demanding career, maybe in law or the media.

Lately, I had begun to suspect that this relationship had come to the end of its natural life. These days, my husband seems unusually grateful, as if he has repented, and decided on a fresh start. However, while you may have faded from his thoughts, you have continued to inveigle your way into mine.

As a mother myself, I wondered whether you would ever want children, and whether you understood that whatever he said, my husband had no intention of leaving me – us – to be with you. I wondered what your own mother would say to you if she knew. I wondered

312

what I would say to my own daughter if I found out that she was doing what you did for so many years that I had almost (but not quite) got used to your presence in our lives, which usually manifested itself in the form of my husband's absence – not in physical terms (his work took him away constantly, I was used to that) but an absence of mind, even when he was here with me.

I wondered, were you jealous, guilty, thwarted, bitter, hopeful? I certainly was.

Over recent months, I have also come to know you as many other readers do – as a writer of occasionally droll prose in a popular national newspaper. Today, by chance, I had the opportunity to put together the two versions of you with which I was already familiar, and find out exactly who you are.

I read your letters; I read every single word. It was a painful process, as you may be able to imagine, but an illuminating one. I discovered that you are someone who makes a public show of honesty, but has lived, for years, with a lonely lie.

The letters. Ah, the letters. Dear Vixen, do you imagine that he treasured them? They were in the garage, underneath the toolbox, next to the snow shovel that we never, in the normal way of things, have cause to use.

I think he intended to burn them. I don't know why he had put off doing it, and I haven't asked him. Sometimes, when you love someone, it is necessary to take on burdensome tasks that they cannot manage alone. And now all those words are ash.

The letters were stored in an unusual wooden box

that I presume is a family heirloom of some kind, and am now returning to you. Sooner or later, he will realize it is missing. Will he then have the courage to bring the subject into the open? I must admit, I am curious, and for that I must thank you: after so many years of marriage it is exciting to find that one's spouse is not entirely predictable.

Inconstant he may be, but he is far from inconsistent. As you may have realized, he finds pregnancy and its aftermath unattractive; he started his first extramarital relationship when our son was two months old. Even if he had not taken steps to ensure you could not conceive his child, the demands of childbearing would almost certainly have ended your affair.

As for the box, I trust you will be able to find a fresh use for it. I am returning it to you because it is not in my nature to destroy something that belongs to someone else.

Yours sincerely,
Virginia Dandridge

William was crying . . . again. She felt the hot needling in her breasts that meant she had milk to give him. It was an almost instant reaction, like the prickle of perspiration in response to stress. She would have to collect herself, go upstairs, sort him out . . . but then there was a gentle knock on the door.

She folded the letter and stuffed it back into the envelope.

'Mum, no . . . Please, just give me a minute.'

But it was Dan who came in. He was holding William very carefully, as if jolting him might cause an explosion. He moved slowly across the carpet towards Tina, passed William into her arms and sat down on the bed next to her.

She yanked up her T-shirt and jammed William on to the breast. Dan didn't speak, didn't ask what was wrong, didn't even look at her. She took his discretion for granted. It wasn't until later that she realized his presence hadn't bothered her at all.

On the tenth day Lucy came, and brought Clemmie and Lottie with her. Lucy held William for a long time, and was reluctant to hand him back. The girls were soon bored of him, tired of the entertainment they'd brought with them – a DVD, some toys – and started roaming round the flat, looking for ways to pass the time while their mother and her friend talked about birth.

Tina let Clemmie try on her hats and shoes and parade round in them, but Lottie hung back, too self-conscious to take part in dressing up.

Clemmie took a particular shine to the Ascot fascinator – a silly concoction of feathers and net – and Tina said, 'You can keep that if you like. I don't think I'm going to wear it again.'

Lucy protested, but Tina overruled her. She tried to persuade Lottie to accept a straw boater, which did look rather sweet perched on her dark hair, but Lottie politely declined.

Clemmie continued to preen herself, and Lottie wandered around the flat, inspecting Tina's CD collection, the photos, the books, finally coming to rest in front of the old wooden box, which was still sitting on the dining table.

'What's this?' she said, running her hand over the surface of the wood.

She opened it, lifted out the lid of the largest inner compartment, and studied the scrap of paper glued on the inside: *Made by I alone.*

'It's a sewing box,' Tina said, 'but I'm not very good at sewing, so it's empty.'

'It must be very old,' Lottie said.

'It is,' Tina said, 'see, there's a date on it, 1875, so that makes it a proper antique. You can have it if you like. You can keep anything you want in it. I was thinking of taking it to the charity shop anyway, when I got round to it.'

Lucy didn't look at all sure about this, but Lottie looked so pleased that she eventually acquiesced. And so Lottie got her wish, and carried off a receptacle ideally suited for the storing of secrets from her mother.

When they had all gone Tina felt lighter, but also hollow and sad.

But then, when William started to suck, the past retreated, and the present lulled them both.

The Vixen Letters

Nature's way? Oh, please. Spare me

Well, I've done it – and I'm glad that it's unlikely that I'll be called upon to do it again. This is one upside of being a single mother – there is no social expectation that you will provide your little dear with a sibling, whereas respectably married ladies, my own mother among them, are forced into defensiveness about having an only child.

All only children live with the prejudice that they are lonely and selfish. When I was little, I was completely uninterested in my peers – I was precocious, and preferred the attention of adults, which I retained by being provocative if necessary. Will William grow up to suffer from a similar blend of prickly detachment and self-importance? If he does, and then goes through life both demanding a wider audience and pushing me away, it will serve me right.

My friendships are as close as I'll come to sibling relationships. I think it would be fair to say that I'm neither a nurturer nor a peacemaker; I'm a limelight-hogger who is sometimes insanely cagey. Selfish and lonely, in other words. But I won't persist in seeking to blame my reluctance to play co-operatively on my lonely only status – after all, my shortcomings are not my family's, but my own.

Being kind and tactful souls, my friends didn't really tell me about their experiences of giving birth till I'd done it myself. I am given to understand that if you get a group of mothers together, even if they don't know each other well, even without the lubrication of a glass of wine, they'll start swapping birth war stories. I imagine such gatherings as meetings of so many Ancient Mariners, compulsively retelling the tale of the terrible voyages they made, and were somehow able to return from.

One of my friends very nearly managed to do it nature's way, first time round; she laboured for twenty-four hours, but to no avail. At least the baby escaped more or less unscathed – apart from the scratch marks on her head where the midwives had struggled to turn her so her mother could push her out. After this emergency caesarean, my friend wanted an elective caesarean next time round, and got it, despite strong opposition – caesareans are, after all, more expensive, and major surgery brings its own risks.

I always wince on her behalf when I hear the phrase 'too posh to push'. Too posh to undergo a second round of what you recall as torture? I don't think so. How about 'too smart to suffer unnecessarily'?

I did it nature's way, and I shouldn't really complain – it was fast, it was straightforward – but still, it struck me as pretty awful. I would say it's badly designed, if it wasn't obvious that no guiding intelligence has had a hand in the process, and it's simply the blind product of evolution – unless, that is, you belong to the punitive school of thought that regards the pain of birth as punishment for Eve's rebellious sampling of the apple. Perhaps even that is more honest than the contemporary desire to pretend the whole thing is absolutely wonderful, and needs only the addition of a smelly candle and some whale music to bring you to a state of bliss.

Another friend didn't end up with a caesarean, but did lose as much blood as the victim of a car crash, and was catheterized and paralysed from the waist down for the first twelve hours after the birth – which didn't stop the midwife snapping at her when she asked for help changing the baby's first dirty nappy. 'If you want that done, you'll have to do it yourself!' She couldn't stand up, and had no idea how to do it anyway, so the baby was left dirty until a new shift came on to the ward.

She found the time she spent in hospital exhausting, stressful and oppressive – she managed about three hours' sleep in five nights — but that moment of unkindness was, she says, the lowest point. She was not cared for; she was monitored. A midwife occasionally barged in to dole out pills and check her blood pressure, and advice on breastfeeding was available on request, but that was about it.

These days, the orthodoxy is that new mothers should have their babies at their sides in hospital all the time, right from the start. In practice, that means you may well be left to cope with a fractious and unsettled infant without rest or respite, in a space that is filled with the crying of other newborns.

My mother remembers when the approach was very different, and all babies were taken away overnight to be cared for in a night nursery, and brought in for breastfeeding – no more than fifteen minutes – every four hours during the night.

What was lacking, then as now, is a willingness to be flexible, to listen to what individual mothers want and need. Surely, as one of the richest nations on earth, we can strike a balance between neglecting our new mothers on understaffed wards, and forcing them to acquiesce in rigid routines that separate them from their children? Or are we secretly in thrall to a deep-seated cultural contempt that makes it acceptable to turn our backs on women in labour and immediately after birth?

16

Young Adonis

'May Fair stall bookings, strawberry and wine evening, seventies, eighties, nineties disco. I think that's your lot,' Lucy said, pushing her forward-planning folder across the table to Jane Morris, who was going to reallocate Lucy's responsibilities as social secretary of the Parent–Teacher Association.

Good old Jane – in the end, it had been a suggestion of hers, rather than any of the agencies or jobsites with which Lucy had registered, that had provided Lucy with a route back into relatively permanent work. During the course of the Class 7 parents' pizza night out Jane had mentioned that a friend who worked for a charity magazine was about to go on maternity leave, and nobody had yet been recruited to cover for her. The magazine – which was circulated to members of the Countrywomen's Guild – had left it to the last minute, and was keen to avoid the expense of advertising or paying an agency if possible, and might

Lucy be interested? Lucy had duly applied, and, to her astonishment, had been asked to start immediately.

After a few weeks in the job, she had been relieved when Jane suggested she might want to consider standing down from the PTA. Let one of the other stay-at-home mums shoulder the burden for a change; she was working now, and could consider herself excused. If that meant the ornaments didn't get dusted once a week, and Clemmie's cake-sale offerings weren't home-made and Lottie didn't always get reminded to take in her swimming kit, that was just too bad.

Handing everything over to Jane was a relief not dis-similar to the final days of Lucy's stint at *Beautiful Interiors*, when, as the last day drew closer, it had ceased to matter whether she had mispriced the latest style of contemporary chandelier, and she had felt the burden of needing to prove herself, at least to that particular set of colleagues, gradually lightening, till eventually, as she left the building for good, it had completely dis-appeared.

When you were about to move on, all the day-to-day worries of the job began to reveal themselves for the transient chimera they were, and if anything went wrong you could just repeat the magic formula: 'It doesn't matter – I'm out of here.' As you approached the date when you would be officially liberated from your role, you were freed from the oppressive trajectory of your future responsibilities. It was only a fleeting freedom, though, because as soon as you'd started your next job you had a whole load of new performance in-dicators to worry about, but it was nice while it lasted.

So far the work at *Ladies' Circle* magazine had not turned out to be particularly demanding or oppressive. The editor was a manageable boss – neither depressive, bullying, frustrated, nor slave-driving – and when Lucy was shown round the office after her interview she formed an impression of people quietly pottering at their desks who would probably go straight back to internet shopping the moment the tour was over. Her new colleagues were, in the main, pleasant, middle-aged women who wanted to get away on time, with the exception of one or two young ones who were obviously champing at the bit to escape to a sexier, more cut-throat environment, where the subject matter would be a bit more glamorous than the Countrywomen's Guild annual Sponge, Jam and Pickle Competition, or the featured herb of the month, or the knitting patterns that they were all, on occasion, called upon to proofread.

The pay was modest, but it was enough to make a difference, and her financial situation had stabilized. It helped that Adam now had a decent income and was paying out a steady proportion of it as maintenance – he'd submitted to pressure from Emily and got a job as marketing director of a household-name nappy brand.

If she was careful, she could manage, at least for now – and as for the future, who knew? They were getting by. And maybe in due course she would earn more, and they would do better. In the meantime there would be no holidays, and she'd pared back the children's out-of-school activities, and renounced the bulk-bought booze, which she had come, for a time, to think of as a necessity.

It was traditional, at all PTA meetings, to open, and finish, at least one bottle of wine, but she hadn't had any to offer Jane, and had given her tea instead. She didn't have a drop of alcohol in the house; after the drama of New Year, she'd lost the appetite for it. She knew she'd been using it as a crutch and an escape, and that it wasn't much good for either; it provided temporary relief, but it didn't solve anything, and had been on the way to turning into a problem in itself. It seemed better just to allow herself to be sad.

It helped that she now had Pomfret, her beautiful Russian blue cat, for company. OK, so she was perhaps also unhealthily obsessed with internet dating websites, and Young Adonis might be just another manifestation of self-destructive risk-taking – but she damn well didn't care, she was going to meet him anyway.

It had been good to see Jane, a reminder of old times; she saw Jane as the sort of stay-at-home mum she had aspired to become herself, calm, efficient and contented, a serenely gliding swan whose dignified manner belied the frantic paddling going on underneath. With Jane, there was no whiff of competition, or of jealously thwarted ambition; she seemed to be quietly satisfied with her life, which made her very soothing company.

Still, Lucy was conscious that it was getting late, and she'd have to be up at six the next morning to sort out the girls and get to work.

The cat slid underneath the table and brushed against her legs, and she reached down to stroke him and tickle him on his favourite spot, underneath his chin. Before she straightened up she surreptitiously checked her watch. It was already nearly ten o'clock; definitely time to wind things up.

'Do feel free to come back to me if anything's unclear,' she told Jane, who had taken a sheaf of papers out of the forward-planning folder and was flicking through them. 'I may be stepping down, but I'm still up for helping out whenever I can.'

Jane put the papers back in the folder, but made no other move to go. Then she said, 'You're looking really well, you know. I think maybe being back at work suits you?'

Lucy had been so preoccupied with how her children would react to the change to their routines that she hadn't really given her own feelings about the job much thought. Luckily, the girls had adapted brilliantly. It was true that Clemmie hated being hustled out of the house and into the school breakfast club on Lucy's days in the office, but Lottie seemed not to object to her mother being distracted. Perhaps she had felt, in the old days, that Lucy was breathing down her neck all the time. Perhaps she'd had a point. On the plus side, both girls enjoyed seeing her mother in her new working wardrobe. (Lucy had found it necessary to invest in one or two January sales bargains.)

Come to think of it, Lucy liked dressing for work in the mornings too, and the job was a partial release from the gentle semi-purdah of her old life, the daytime world of mothers and retired people, the almost exclusively feminine club at the school gate.

'Well, so far so good, I suppose,' Lucy said.

'I've been thinking about going back to work myself,' Jane said with an apologetic smile.

Lucy thought: You're scared. You're good at what you're doing right now, and you know you can do it. You're not ready to face up to the fear that you've forgotten how to do anything else.

'Why bother if you don't have to? I wouldn't rush it if I were you,' Lucy said.

Jane shrugged sheepishly, and Lucy thought: No, not scared – she feels guilty for not working, and she knows when she does go back to work, she'll feel guilty for not being at home.

'I couldn't go back to nursing,' Jane said, 'I wouldn't have the stamina. I'd have to look for something else.'

'How about something more desk-based, but still in the health service?' Lucy suggested. 'And maybe part-time would suit you. I find it's quite a good compromise. Anyway, there's never any harm in looking.'

'True,' Jane said. She stood up and picked up the folder. 'Anyway, I'd better let you get on. It was lovely to see you. You will pop along to the next committee meeting, won't you? I don't think anybody would expect you to stay for the whole thing, unless you wanted to, but I think they'd all like the chance to say thank you.'

'Of course I will, and thank you again for letting me off the hook,' Lucy said.

After Jane had gone she went upstairs to check on the girls. Lottie's light was still on, but went off as soon as Lucy reached the landing – Lottie was speeding through the final instalment of the *Twilight* saga, and kept on reading it long after her official bedtime. Clemmie was sound asleep.

Lucy sat down at the computer to check her messages. And there he was: Young Adonis.

He was always succinct, but timely; she was never left wondering if he'd gone cold on her. Just as pleasingly, he didn't pester.

See you Saturday for night of sin in Cheltenham. Opt-out clause present and correct, of course, because if we knew for sure, what would be the point? Looking forward. xx.

She knew objectively that it was irresponsible to be plotting a weekend away with someone she'd met online, but never in the flesh. Not that it was a whole weekend – just one night, a Saturday, while the girls were with Adam and Emily. Nice old Mrs Meadows from across the green had a key and was going to feed the cat; all Lucy's charges would be taken care of. And surely she deserved a little romantic adventure? Perhaps that was a euphemistic way of putting it, but so what? Anyway, it wasn't just about sex – it was about going away, being in the company of someone new, someone young; it was about being wanted. And she'd just got through a particularly awful, icy, exhausting January. She was owed a treat.

It wasn't as if he was a total stranger, anyway. He was twenty-eight – about the same age as her sister, and her husband's girlfriend. Not all that young, really; it wasn't as if she was cradle-snatching.

He lived in Gloucester, made his living as a carpenter and was in a band she'd never heard of, and his

Facebook page was mostly photos of dirty-looking people in wellies at festivals. Meanwhile, he knew that she was separated with two children and worked in publishing. It was all above board. Of course, there was plenty that could go wrong – when it came down to it, he might not like the look of her, or she him – but she didn't think she was going to end up buried underneath his floorboards.

She hadn't told Adam exactly where she was going – she'd have her mobile on her, he could contact her if need be – and she had also decided not to tell Hannah, because sneaking off to a hotel with a stranger was such a reckless, Hannah-ish thing to do, yet Hannah was behaving in such a sorted, sensible way these days. It would be humiliating. Lucy was meant to be the one with common sense, Hannah the one who went in for chaos and sexual folly. Lucy couldn't bring herself to admit that she'd ceded her usual territory and was exploring the hinterland that Hannah had abandoned.

However, Lucy had taken the precaution of emailing Tina and Natalie, and giving them the contact details for the hotel that Young Adonis was taking her to. It wouldn't have seemed right to tell just one and not the other – she was still smarting slightly about Tina's decision to withhold the story of her affair with that man, the top-secret so-called Grandee, although she did understand why. In a way, Tina might have been right; it was possible that disclosure at the time might have led to an even greater rift than secrecy.

Lucy had phrased her account of what she was planning to do in the Old Rose Hotel in such a way as to obscure the fact that this would be the first time she and Young Adonis had met face to face. Natalie had sent a rather cryptic reply: *Well, be careful . . . but not TOO careful.* Cautiously giving her blessing, Lucy thought.

Tina was more inquisitive: *Who? How old? Where did you find him? How can you be sure he's not an axe-murderer, or a conman or some other kind of wrong 'un?* And Lucy had replied, *Because of the way he writes. He's literate, he's funny, and he doesn't do sob stories,* and Tina had responded, *Well, that's good enough for me. Happy hunting, Cougar.*

Thankfully, neither of her friends had tried to stop her, and they hadn't reminded Lucy of her responsibilities as a mother.

Lucy knew that when she dropped the girls off at Adam's new flat on Saturday morning Adam would gaze at her forlornly and give her his best wounded smile, which meant: I know. I fucked up. I'm a cad. Forgive me? They were getting on rather better these days. Clearly he was in no rush to get divorced – well, that suited her; but also it meant that he was in no rush to marry Emily. Emily had recently turned twenty-seven; Lucy thought Adam might be able to string her along for another four years, maximum, before he got set an ultimatum.

But that was Adam's problem. Lucy's next move was to recruit a lodger; after the uncertainty of the last year, she was determined to build up her financial reserves. A young, working woman, who wouldn't be there at weekends. She wasn't looking for a replacement for the au pair function Hannah had once carried out, though having someone else living in the house might stir up some ghosts. Not that Lucy had lost Hannah or anything, but that time, in which Hannah had lived under her roof and been her companion, was clearly dead and gone.

A lodger would be different; she would want a bit of polite contact, but on the whole, she would keep herself to herself.

People came and went, and you couldn't bring them back, but you might be lucky enough to find new people who would give you some of what you'd taken from the ones who had disappeared, and who would accept some of what you had to offer in return.

She had mentioned the lodger plan to Adam, who had oh-so-jokingly offered to take up the position himself. But he didn't really mean it. He was only kidding. Problem was, he never had had much of a sense of humour.

When they got to Adam's flat, which was in a prosperous but unpretty tract of south-west London suburbia, she said a passably cordial hello to Emily, who was hovering nervously, and said goodbye to the girls as quickly as possible. It was the perfect maternal double bind; she didn't want them to be upset that she was leaving, and she didn't want them *not* to be upset. Still, it was only for one night; and she hoped Young Adonis would be an effective distraction. But first she would have to steel herself to drive to Sunnyview.

The M25 was a long slow hell, but arriving at journey's end was not much of a relief; she still always dreaded these visits, principally because Ellen invariably made her feel guilty. Ellen was in her room, as usual, sitting with her back to the window, listening to a book on CD; she'd developed a taste for grisly murder mysteries, and Hannah and Lucy had bought her a good stock for Christmas.

Ellen took the headphones off and said, 'You look shattered.'

'I'm fine. It's just a beastly drive, that's all,' Lucy said, taking her coat off and perching on the end of the bed.

Ellen grunted. 'I know it isn't easy, trying to hold down a job and keep the household going. And it can't be very nice knowing your girls are enjoying themselves with Adam and his new woman. I expect he can afford to buy them lots of treats now he's back in work.'

'Well, that's a good thing, isn't it?' Lucy said. 'Anyway, I don't think they feel too hard done by. They did pretty well at Christmas. We're not quite so pushed for cash these days, especially now I've got a job too.'

Clemmie, predictably, had been enthralled by her Talking Walking Pet Wolf for all of half an hour, while Lottie had been quietly pleased with her newly pierced ears, and the clothes she'd chosen for socializing with her friends outside of school.

'Yes, but it's only a temporary contract, isn't it?' Ellen said. 'You need to be keeping your eyes open for something else. Something in an office with a few more men in it. You're not going to meet a new husband working on a freebie for old ladies, are you?'

'I'm not looking for a new husband.'

'Why not? Don't tell me you're going over to the other

330

side as well.' Lucy stared at her in bemusement. 'You know,' Ellen said, 'alternative lifestyles.'

Lucy realized that her mother was referring to Natalie. She had fallen into the habit of relaying stories from her friends' lives when she visited Ellen, as it gave them something to talk about other than the toxic subject of their own family. Sometimes she felt uneasy about this – it was gossiping, really, though the likelihood of Ellen passing anything on to anybody else was negligible. In the case of Natalie's doubts about her sexuality, Lucy had been careful to not give the name of the friend in question. Given the distaste with which Ellen had brought the subject up, it seemed that she'd been right to be cautious – although it would, of course, have been better to say nothing at all.

'No, I haven't got together with another woman,' Lucy said, 'though I have met a man on the internet, and I'm going to meet him tonight and shag him stupid.'

Ellen's expression shifted subtly into a new configuration that Lucy couldn't interpret. She shook her head. 'I'll thank you not to use that kind of language in my room.'

It was only then that Lucy identified Ellen's change of mood. The lines on the good side of her face had deepened, and that side of her mouth was curving upwards. She was smiling.

'You've had your hair done, haven't you?' Ellen said. 'Bit shorter than usual. It's much better – takes years off you. So what about this new man? I do hope, Lucy, that you're not about to make a fool of yourself.'

*

Back in the car and on the road, Lucy realized that her clothes had picked up the smell of the nursing home: decay combined with disinfectant. She had planned to get changed anyway, once she'd put a bit of distance between herself and Sunnyview. It would be as well to stop off somewhere – catch her breath, get herself into the right frame of mind.

She found a pub with parking, went inside and headed straight for the ladies': candy-stripe wallpaper, seashell-shaped hand soap, too cold for comfort. There she swapped her chinos, hooded fleece and plimsolls for stockings, heels and the party frock she'd worn to the cheese-and-wine fundraiser, the night she'd sat on Ian Morris's knee.

Her reflection in the spotty mirror above the hand basin wasn't so bad – certainly no worse than the photo she'd emailed to Young Adonis. She brushed her hair: *Much better. Takes years off you.*

She might as well go for it. While she still could.

She felt slightly foolish coming out of the loos in the outfit she had come to think of as her Dress of Disgrace, but told herself it was preferable to turning up at the hotel dressed as Casual Mum, and anyway, what did it matter if anyone had noticed her change of outfit? The pub was virtually empty anyway.

At the bar she ordered a coffee, then retreated to a corner table to drink it. She was startled when somebody came up to her to ask the time, and then went on, 'You look kind of familiar – you're not on the telly, are you?'

She had been approached by a spivvy-looking man in

early middle age, who was giving her his best blagger's smile, big on teeth, but sad in the eyes, defying her not to be charmed.

Suddenly it dawned on her: for the first time in fifteen years, she was being chatted up.

Her last first date had been with Adam. She'd just moved into the house on Brixton Hill with Tina and Natalie, and was temping while she looked for her first job in journalism. She spent a week in the marketing department of a big drinks company; he was one of the graduate trainees. One Friday night she was just about to go home when he said, 'Aren't you going to come for a drink? Just a quick one? We always go down the pub at the end of the week.' And he smiled at her and, just like that, she said yes.

She didn't make it home till Sunday afternoon. A couple of days later they went out for a meal after work, but she was shy and he was distant, and the mood was tenuous and uncertain. Right up until the moment when they were walking away from the restaurant under her umbrella and he stopped and kissed her, it had been impossible to tell whether the intimacy they'd already established was a one-off, or the beginning of something.

This time round, her only communication with the man she was about to meet had been via her computer. Would he be attracted to her? Would she be attracted to him? Would he turn out to be an axe-murderer after all? How on earth was she going to get through this without having a glass of wine, and if she did have a glass of

333

wine, would she decide that she needed another, and another, and would it then turn into a disaster anyway? And, after so long, what would it be like, to be with someone who wasn't Adam?

The light was beginning to fade as she skirted the centre of Cheltenham, pulled on to a B-road and then turned on to a long, secluded drive. Finally she parked in a grassed area edged by trees and occupied by a scattering of cars, one of which almost certainly belonged to the man she was about to meet.

But which? The red Ford Ka, the battered Peugeot, the white Nissan? Not the Beemer, surely; wrong income bracket. Young Adonis had been disarmingly open about how this hotel deal was a promotional giveaway.

She checked her make-up in the rear-view mirror and squirted on some more perfume (she'd thrown out the stuff Adam had bought her, and had reverted to an ancient bottle of Clinique Happy, which had probably gone off). Then she got her bag out of the boot and went off to check in, stepping carefully so her heels wouldn't sink into the soggy grass.

'Mr Hallam has already arrived,' the bored yet unctuous man at reception told her. 'Somebody will show you up in a minute.'

A teenage bellboy with fiery acne, dressed in a too-tight uniform, took her bag and she followed him up several flights of stairs with fleur-de-lis carpeting to a creaking upper corridor done up in dusty pink and old cream.

'Here you are, madam,' he said and rapped on the door.

The man inside the room called out, 'Come in!' and the bellboy pushed the door open.

Jack Hallam was reclining on the bed, barefoot, in jeans and a T-shirt, watching TV. He turned it off and looked up at her with a grin.

'Hello, you,' she said.

'Well, hello,' he said.

She remembered the bellboy – she should slip him a quid – but he had dumped her bag by the bed and had already disappeared.

An hour later Jack said, 'Oh dear. It wasn't that bad, was it?'

They were lying naked, face to face, on the rumpled bed, in the dim light cast by Jack's bedside lamp. The skylight overhead was dark and full of stars. She was crying, or rather, a sadness that seemed deeper than her, more universal, was welling up and spilling out as tears on her face, the hotel pillow and his and her inter-locked hands.

'It was lovely,' she said and smiled at him. There was a scattering of faded freckles across the bridge of his nose, and his eyes, which she had at first thought were green, were tinged with gold. 'I'm not unhappy. I mean . . . I forgot about everything. I lost track of time. And now it's done.'

She withdrew her hand from his, sat up, took a tissue from the box on the bedside table and blew her nose.

'My mascara's running,' she said, 'I must look like hell.'

'No, you don't. You look beautiful.'

'Thank you,' she said. 'So do you. Actually even better than your photograph.'

He smiled and wrinkled his nose at her, and said, 'You know what, I'm starving. Do you fancy ordering something to eat? We could get room service. We could get a bottle of wine, too. To celebrate.'

She drew her knees up to her chin and locked her arms round them.

'What are we celebrating?'

He raised his eyebrows at her. 'Well, apart from the obvious – which is what just happened . . .' He hesitated. 'Maybe I'm wrong, but I'm guessing that's the first time you've been with someone since you've been single.'

'OK,' she said, 'yes, it was. But I don't drink.'

'Well then,' he said, 'celebrate with a club sandwich. Or scones and jam. Whatever you fancy,' and he got up off the bed and went in search of the menu.

The bellboy who brought in their food was the one who'd carried Lucy's bag up an hour earlier. He didn't look either of them in the eye, plonked the food down on the desk and retreated as quickly as possible.

She realized that the room, which had previously smelt of pine toilet cleaner, now smelt overwhelmingly of sex. Plus, if any more of a giveaway had been needed, she and Jack were now both wearing hotel dressing-gowns.

They ate in a silence that struck her as surprisingly companionable. When he'd finished, he turned to her and said, 'I'm afraid there's something I didn't tell you.'

Her heart sank. 'Oh God . . . don't tell me you're married.'

'No, of course not. It's just – you were so straight up with me about having children, and I didn't tell you about mine.'

She was about as taken aback as if he'd suddenly offered to marry her.

'I have a little girl,' he went on, 'called Ivy. She's four. Lives with her mum. We split up when Ivy was two – her mum was seeing someone else. She's married to him now.' He smiled and shook his head. 'I know. It doesn't really go with the whole Young Adonis thing.'

Lucy reflected on this for a moment.

'No,' she said, 'but actually, I think I like it. I should have guessed – there's something quite gentle about you. A bit dad-like, if you don't mind me saying. I mean, I can imagine you pushing a swing and all that stuff. Do you see much of your little girl?'

'Oh, yeah. My ex has been pretty good about that. To be honest it's useful for her, too – she's got another one on the way. Want to know something funny? It's because of Ivy I got this hotel deal. First prize in her pre-school raffle. One of the other parents works for the chain.'

'Pretty good prize I'd say.'

'Yup.'

'And was there really absolutely no one else you could have asked to come here with you? No one more your own age?'

'Well . . . women my age tend to want commitment.'

'And women my age are grateful for what they can get,' Lucy said, 'before it's too late.'

Jack smiled. 'Come off it. You're not even forty yet. Plenty of life in you yet, I'd say.'

'I went to see my mother this morning,' Lucy said. 'She had a stroke last year, and she's stuck in a nursing home. It's always a salutary reminder of what's ahead.'

'But not just yet,' Jack said, 'with any luck.'

'You know what, I think I'm going to take a shower,' Lucy said. 'And then maybe we could go out and have a little stroll round outside? I know it's pitch black out there, but there's a full moon, and it looks like a beautiful clear night. And dinner's not till seven, so we've got a bit of time.'

'Sure,' Jack said.

She got to her feet, shed her dressing-gown, went into the en suite, turned on the shower and stepped under it.

A moment later Jack got in and stood behind her. His arms reached round her waist. She stiffened, then let her hands rest on top of his and allowed herself to lean against him.

She closed her eyes. She did think of Hannah and Adam in the shower together, but that seemed like a memory from another life, one that was beginning to lose its power to hurt.

They stood there for what seemed a long time, unmoving, as the water hissed and splashed and ran over and down and past them.

17

'Why are you here?'

Now that Matilda had a regular bedtime, Natalie and Richard were theoretically free to snuggle up together on the sofa in the evenings, talk, bond, make love and rediscover what had attracted them to each other in the first place.

In practice they invariably retreated from each other, usually to different rooms. Somehow they never went to bed early, and they certainly never went to bed together. Although the cot was now in the small third bedroom, Matilda still often woke in the night, and they had used this as an excuse for Richard to stick to sleeping in the guest room. Natalie doubted whether this arrangement was sustainable, but she didn't allow herself to look too far ahead. Meanwhile, they both continued to dance round a great unspoken row.

They got through Valentine's Day without too much difficulty. They had agreed it would be best to get their own presents, rather than bother with the rigmarole of providing lists, and so Richard had picked out some new cufflinks and Natalie, who could now fit back into a size 16, treated herself to a new pair of jeans. In the morning Richard went out to get the *Record* and came back with chocolates, which Natalie thanked him for even though she was trying to give them up; in the evening the babysitter turned up, and the restaurant had their reservation and hadn't put them next to the loos, and they made perfectly adequate conversation over dinner.

Natalie said she was looking forward to going to Cornwall at Easter; Richard said he wasn't sure if he could get away, and he should really keep on putting the hours in if he wanted to make partner. Natalie said she was apprehensive about returning to work, and Richard reminded her that they were letting her go part-time, and ten months off was a pretty good innings, and anyway, she seemed to be getting a bit fed up with being at home. Natalie wondered if she should have gone for a nursery rather than a quarter of a black-market nanny share with Jessie Oliver from antenatal class, and Richard said he was sure she'd done the right thing.

They made it through to the pudding menus before Natalie's mobile rang and the babysitter told her Matilda had woken up and wouldn't stop crying, and could they please come back.

They were not, had never been, a couple who went in for slaps and threats and tears and tempests, and Natalie's first clear warning that they were on unsafe ground was the timbre of Richard's voice – accusing, and rather louder than normal – when she got back from her Tuesday night yoga class to find him waiting for her in the living room.

He was still dressed in his work clothes: a white shirt, dark grey suit and blue tie, which had not been loosened. Next to him on the sofa was a large piece of white sugar paper, which had, until recently, been kept rolled up tight, and was now weakly trying to return to its previous shape.

Richard switched off the TV and said, 'Natalie, we need to talk.'

'Is Matilda OK?'

'Matilda is fine, she's asleep.' He picked up the drawing and opened it out. 'I found this today.'

Natalie reluctantly took in the big breasts, the heavy belly, the strong legs and the posture of frustrated, hampered waiting. Somehow, even though she was no longer pregnant, it was still true to life; Adele had seen her accurately, seen something more than the way she looked, and had captured it.

'I don't think you would have ever told me about this. Would you?' Richard said and let the drawing fall back on to the sofa.

'I just . . .' Natalie swallowed. 'It was just something she suggested. You know she was really into art, and painting and everything? I thought it would be . . .' She trailed off. What could she say? *Fun? Novel? Different? A way to pass the time?* Anything and everything would sound incriminating.

Richard crossed his arms and shook his head.

'Natalie,' he said, 'I know you're lying. It's blindingly obvious that something happened.'

Natalie grabbed for the piece of paper. 'Oh come on, like what? I was due to give birth any minute when she did this. I mean I was already overdue. But if it bothers you, I'll get rid of it, OK?'

She tore the piece of paper right across – straight down through her pregnant belly – and then quartered herself, bisecting her limbs and torso. Then she screwed the pieces up into a ball, marched through to the kitchen and slung them into the bin with last night's potato peelings and dirty nappies.

'There. All gone,' she said as she went back into the living room, slapping her hands against each other as if brushing off dirt. 'Happy now?'

Richard sighed. 'If I hadn't found it you would never have done that. You'd have kept it. As a little memento. A trophy. What difference does it make, whether it's in the wardrobe or in the bin? You still hid it.'

'I'd actually forgotten all about it,' Natalie lied. She sat down next to him and tried for a more jocular tone. 'So what prompted you to start turning out the wardrobe, anyway?'

Richard folded his arms. 'I wasn't turning anything out. I was looking for some painkillers. You finished up the packet in the bathroom cabinet and put it back even though it was empty, which is the kind of thing you do quite a lot, Natalie, because you're so wrapped up in yourself that half the time you're barely aware of what's in front of you. I know you sometimes keep a stash of medicine in the wardrobe, so I checked in there. And you know what? When I found that picture, part of me was shocked, but another part of me wasn't at all surprised.'

He adjusted his glasses again and peered at her, and she had a glimpse of what it would be like to be one of his clients. People came to him, she knew, when they were desperate, and often when bankruptcy had long since become inevitable. Yet, even at the crowded court hearings at which their failed businesses were wound up, they would often plea for more time – another two days; a creditor would come through; a new order would be confirmed – and the judge, weary of excuses, having heard it all before, would chivvy them along and call for the next case.

'Natalie,' Richard said, 'did something happen between you and that woman?'

For a moment Natalie was tempted to deny it, to prevaricate, to ask him to define his terms. Then she said, 'It did. Just the once. I'm sorry.'

She wanted to add, It was a mistake, a one-off; but she knew he would say, What, just like the time before? So instead she said, her voice trembling slightly, 'It didn't mean anything.'

'Can I ask when?' Richard asked.

Natalie swallowed. 'It was the night I went out with drinks for them, with the antenatal group mums, back in the summer. I went back to hers for a little bit afterwards. It was, you know . . . it was nothing really.'

Richard groaned something that sounded like 'Oh God!' and jolted upright and paced away from her. She stood too and moved towards him, and he spun round and shouted, 'How could you do that to me? How could you do that to all of us? Your parents were here babysitting and you took it as an opportunity to . . . How could you be such a fucking selfish bitch? I could kill you!'

He had grabbed her by the shoulders and his face was inches away from hers; she had never seen it so distorted by rage and hate. And then, as quickly as he had seized her, he let her go. He stumbled back to the sofa where he sat still for a moment before beginning to cry – awful, wrenching, unpractised gasps and sobs that made his shoulders shake and his face stream with mucus.

She sat down next to him and waited, not knowing what else to do. After a while he took a red spotted handkerchief out of his pocket – he always carried a handkerchief with him; it was one of the rituals of their relationship that he would pass it over to her whenever something got the better of her and set her off, because she never had one.

He took his glasses off and wiped his face and blew his nose. Then he dried his glasses and put them back on and looked at her.

'Richard,' she said, 'I know this sounds as if it can't possibly be true, under the circumstances, but—'

'Don't say it,' he interrupted. 'I don't want to hear it. Don't sit there and tell me that you love me, but you're not in love with me. Don't tell me that you love me like a brother, or that I'm your best friend. I'm not your brother and I'm not your friend.' He stared down at his hands and blinked as if to clear his vision. 'What have you done to me? I could have . . .' He looked up at her again. 'I could have hurt you, Natalie. I'm not sure I can do this any more. You're turning me into someone I don't want to be.'

'But it was nothing,' Natalie whispered.

'Oh, Natalie. If you can't be honest with yourself, what chance is there that you're going to be honest with anyone else? I don't want to spend years of my life wondering and then find out that you were just denying yourself all along. Don't cheat on yourself, Natalie. Don't sacrifice yourself. If you do we'll end up hating each other. And right now I don't hate you. I feel . . . sorry for you.'

'I'll go and talk to a counsellor,' she said. 'I'll work through it. I'll sort it out.'

'I suppose I should probably go too,' he said. 'Will you find someone? Find out what we have to do?'

'I will,' she said, and he nodded and another raw breath shuddered out of him, as if he was about to start crying again.

Did blessings always brighten as they took their flight? She had been tiptoeing round Richard for months and yet now she was suddenly reminded of how benign, how fair, how fundamentally reasonable he was.

If they did break up, and were open with their families and friends about why, he would be devastated, and at least part of his suffering, mixed in with grief, would be humiliation: the humiliation of being found wanting, and of becoming someone whom colleagues and acquaintances and fellow alumni would gossip about, for a season, and not always sympathetically.

But then how might his life take shape if she were to formally remove herself from it? He was the archetypal family man – affectionate, patient, decent, steady – and, despite his own misgivings, he was successful: he was a catch. Surely, by and by, someone would feel for him, and want to make it up to him: someone who wasn't perpetually thwarted, someone who would be happy to take care of him.

His family would welcome this new person with open arms, relieved that Richard had found someone suitable. Perhaps, ultimately, the newcomer would become his wife, a stepmother for Matilda. Natalie herself would be spoken of in slightly hushed tones: the first wife, the mother of Richard's first child – because probably there would be other children – someone of whom it wasn't quite right to speak ill.

He would always be a good father to Matilda, she was sure: kind, committed, just. And how, or who, would she be? She didn't know.

'I don't deserve you,' she told him, 'but for what it's worth, I do still love you.'

'I know you want me to say it back, but I can't, not now,' he said. 'I can't believe that love can feel like this.'

'I'm sorry,' Natalie said.

What more was there to say? She stood up and went slowly and heavily upstairs, got ready for bed, lay down in the dark and waited for sleep.

She listened to Richard's footsteps creaking on the landing below. He used the bathroom and went into the room she had begun to think of as his. After a while she heard snoring.

Something still didn't feel right.

She got up again and, as quietly and gently as she could, closed the bedroom door.

There was no couch in the counsellor's office, just two overstuffed pastel armchairs next to a coffee table with a large box of tissues on it. Natalie imagined patient after patient – no, client after client – blubbing, and Louisa Mead delicately nudging the tissues towards them until they took the hint and blew their streaming noses.

Louisa invited her to take the other seat and Natalie perched, edged her buttocks back, tried to relax, wriggled, fidgeted, felt squeezed. The armchair was simultaneously cushiony and difficult to sit on. Something smaller and harder would have suited her fine. This was already like being loved to death.

Like the furniture in her office, Louisa was soft-looking, substantial and dressed in spring green. She had a round face with worried brown eyes and a sensible iron-grey haircut that reminded Natalie of Bella Madden, though Louisa seemed gentler, less of a cheerleader, more subtle. So this was the kind of person who made a living out of patching up the woes of married couples: motherly but a little mournful, blending the nurse's dispassionate nurture with the tactful practicality of an undertaker.

'So, Natalie, how are things?' Louisa asked.

There was a large kitchen clock mounted on the wall by the door. Natalie's session had officially started at 3.00 p.m., and it was now five past, which meant she had already had nearly a fiver's worth of therapy.

'Not too bad, I suppose,' Natalie said, 'could be worse. Could be better, obviously.'

There was more she could have said: how she was living from day to day, trying to get out of the house and keep busy, but not quite able to forget that Richard would have to return from work eventually, and that her heart would sink as soon as she heard his key in the door. She knew he was furious and hurt and distraught, and she could understand why, but her only defence against pure self-loathing was to withdraw from the way he saw the world and regard him as a hostile presence to be resisted and ignored.

Preserving her equanimity took effort – an effort so great it was difficult to concentrate on anything else. While Richard suffered and Matilda fretted, Natalie was dazed and distracted; she dropped things and forgot things and went from confusion to muddle to mess. It seemed to be impossible to ever focus her thoughts on the task in hand.

Even food had lost its appeal. She had not consciously made any decision to eat less, but all her clothes were noticeably looser. She was shrinking.

She had dreamed the night before that she was pregnant, and nobody could believe it because she was so thin. In the dream it hadn't occurred to her to wonder how she could possibly be having a baby when she hadn't had sex since that solitary attempt shortly before Matilda's birth, which had not concluded in ejaculation. Still she'd woken up feeling surprisingly happy, until she'd remembered Richard was downstairs. Even in his sleep he emanated humiliation, anger and grief.

'Tell me, Natalie,' Louisa said, 'why are you here?'

What would be an acceptable answer? 'Because my marriage is in difficulty?'

Louisa nodded. *Phew! That was easy! I hope all the questions are like that!* Then Natalie realized that Louisa was going to let the silence drag on until Natalie filled it. A fiver's worth of complete non-communication was a distinct possibility.

Natalie shrugged. 'I'm here because Richard and I agreed that this was the best way forward.'

'You understand the rationale behind me seeing each of you separately before I see you together? It's so that you can speak freely about anything that is making you feel unhappy or uncomfortable or worried. Anything at all, whether it's to do with friendships, family relationships, work, or caring for your baby. It's Matilda, isn't it?'

'Yes.'

Louisa consulted the personal details form on her lap. 'Nine months old.'

Natalie nodded.

'Who's looking after her today?'

'A friend.'

Richard had asked Natalie not to tell Tina where she was going; he preferred not to disclose 'this difficult stage we're going through' to anyone outside the family. Natalie had not respected this, which was something else to feel bad about. But Richard didn't know that both Tina and Lucy had some idea of what had happened with Adele, and she couldn't bring herself to tell him – she'd let him down badly enough as it was. So

349

she'd told Tina about the discovery of the drawing, and the counselling, and it had been a relief not to have to come up with a lie.

Richard had pointed out that she could take some time off work, so that Matilda would be in the care of the nanny they were sharing with Jessie Oliver, but Natalie didn't think this would create a good impression, not so soon after coming back from maternity leave. As for Richard's suggestion that she could have asked her mother to babysit instead – could even have confided in her – no way.

She knew exactly how Pat would react if she told her; she would be angry, and distressed, and she would say, 'But are you sure? What brought this on? What about Matilda?' and then, if Natalie held her ground, she would start to blame herself. Natalie was going to need to be feeling very strong and sure indeed to face up to any of this.

'Tell me about your friendships,' Louisa said.

'I don't really see that as a problem area.'

'So would you say you have generally good relationships with your friends?'

'Yes, of course.'

There was a pause. Natalie added, 'We've had our ups and downs. That's inevitable, isn't it? Over time, you change, sometimes you need a bit of space, then you come back together. I've known some of my friends since university. You can't live in each other's pockets. You have to cut people a bit of slack.'

'Do you have any particularly close friends?'

'Well . . . I suppose my favourite friends, though

I don't actually see them all that often, are Tina and Lucy. They had a massive falling-out last year, but everything's kind of patched up now.'

'So do they often fall out with each other?'

'Oh no, that was very unusual.'

'And have you ever fallen out with either of them?'

'I like a peaceful life, personally. I don't get into fights with people.'

'So are you happy with these friendships?'

'Yes, I think I am. I think, you know, we're all very different, we're different personalities, but that's part of what's good about it. I mean, I'm the quiet one, really, the one in the middle. The other two are both quite strong characters. But they need me there. I'm sort of the jam in the sandwich.'

'So are you happy with all your friendships?'

The clock ticked for perhaps half a minute before Natalie said, 'I'm a little sad about one of my friendships.'

'Why don't you tell me about that,' Louisa said and waited.

How many minutes would it take, how much would it cost to explain who Adele was, what they had done, what it meant? Best to be brief.

'It's a friend I met through antenatal class. She's actually broken up with her partner now, and got together with someone new. He's a single dad. She met him through her son's nursery. Anyway, we were close for a time, and now she's back at work and in a new relationship and we've kind of fizzled out. Which, you know, isn't the end of the world; friendships come and go. But it's a shame.'

'So one of the relationships in a social network that you and Richard were closely involved in, that you joined for support, has broken down.'

'It has, but to be honest I'm not sure how much of a chance she and Marcus really had. They never seemed very together. They hadn't been together very long before they had the baby. I think he might have been a bit of an accident.'

'Would you and Richard have seemed to be "together", do you think?'

'Oh yes. We've been together for ages. More than a decade.'

Louisa glanced down at the form in her lap. 'So I see. And did you plan to start a family?'

'Yes. I was pushing for it for ages before Richard agreed. I thought it would . . .'

'Yes?'

Natalie shrugged. 'I thought it would satisfy me. I thought if I had a baby, everything else would make sense.'

'And did it?'

'I think it did the opposite. I wanted to change my life, and my life had changed, but it wasn't enough.'

'You mentioned that you miss your friend. What was it you liked so much about her?'

'Oh . . . I think I was really impressed by the way she was in the classes. If she felt something she didn't bother to try to hide it. She said what she thought, and she did what she wanted to do. She didn't care if people thought she was strange. She didn't feel she had to be cheerful all the time, either. Or nice. Or careful. I just

352

really admired her for being willing to live like that.'

This was all true enough, but she knew it wasn't the whole truth. She was selling Adele short.

She decided on a bold experiment: to see how it would sound out loud.

'She was beautiful, of course. I didn't see it at first. But then I did.'

'You were attracted to her?'

'I suppose I was. Especially once I knew that she was interested in me. I was flattered. And especially flattered that she wanted to draw me. I'm not exactly a remarkable physical specimen. But she made me feel like I was.'

'Would you say the relationship was more than a friendship?'

Natalie sighed. 'We had an encounter. A tryst. I suppose you might say she seduced me. A one-off. I didn't really expect it to lead to anything, though, and it didn't.'

'Were you disappointed?'

'No. Why would I be disappointed? What had happened was an absolute gift. She made me feel alive.'

'Does Richard make you feel alive?'

'Not in that way. No.'

'Did he ever?'

'I wasn't with him because he made me feel alive,' Natalie said. 'I was with him because he made me feel safe.'

'Safe from what?'

'I didn't want to be the person I might become if I crossed the line.'

'What line?'

Natalie exhaled. 'Why does it all have to be so public?' she said. 'Why can't it just be private like it is for everyone else, just two people in a room, in a house, in a café, seeing if they can get along?'

'All genuine relationships are ultimately private,' Louisa said.

'I know. I know they are. But . . . before you can be comfortable with someone, you have to go through all the sex and uncertainty to get there, don't you?'

'Is that a bad thing, do you think?'

Natalie hesitated. The clock ticked on.

'No,' she said eventually. 'It's what I want. I think. It's what I'm missing. It's what I've never let myself have.'

'All intimacy, all communication, involves risk,' Louisa said. 'The same goes for being here. But it seems to me that it's a risk you're willing to take.'

'But it's not. I haven't wanted to risk anything. Not for years,' Natalie said. 'What happened with Adele happened with somebody before, a long time ago. So long it seems like another life. I was travelling – I was in New Zealand, which is where my brother lives. People often do things when they're on holiday that they wouldn't do normally, don't they? I met this woman in a pub – we were staying in the same hostel. It was a complete fluke. I was only there because I couldn't get a bus to Auckland till the next day. Surely nothing really life-changing could happen that much by chance? I knew I'd never see her again. But still, when Richard and I went to visit my brother a couple of years ago I had this fear, which was really almost a hope, that I'd bump into her. But I didn't, of course. I remember reading *Fear of Flying* and thinking that she was my zipless fuck. But I didn't allow her to liberate me.'

There was another silence. Natalie remembered her mother saying: *Happiness doesn't mean you're immune to regret*. Then she rallied and went on.

'I was seeing Richard when I met her, too,' she said. 'But the stakes were much lower. We were just girlfriend and boyfriend. We had a chance to get out of it then. I did tell him, and we broke up . . . but . . .' She willed herself not to cry. 'I missed him. We met up a couple of times . . . it was just such a relief to be with him. That's when I decided he was what I wanted. I told him it was just something I had to get out of my system, and he gave me the benefit of the doubt.'

'And does he still?'

'This will sound odd, but I think the only way I can retain his trust is for us to make a clean break of it.'

'And is that what you want?'

'I have never really known what I want,' Natalie said. 'What I do know is what I don't want. I don't want to be on my own. I don't want to be a divorced single parent. And I don't want my parents to have to be ashamed of me.'

'Why should they be?'

'If they knew what had happened. What I've done. They'd be appalled. They'd be disgusted. They'd think I needed to get myself sorted out and save my marriage.'

'And do you?'

'If I don't, why am I here? If my marriage fails and it's all my fault they'll never forgive me.'

'A relationship that comes to an end is not necessarily a failure.'

'It will be in their eyes.'

'What about in your eyes?'

'How can I?' Natalie said. 'How can I abandon my family just because I suddenly decide it was all a terrible mistake?'

'Who says you have to abandon them?'

'That's how my parents will see it, however it turns out.'

'And do you believe your relationship with Richard was a mistake?'

'How can I think that when I wouldn't have Matilda without it?'

'If Matilda was an adult woman facing the same dilemma, what would you advise her to do?'

Natalie tucked her feet up on the chair, rested her forehead on her knees and clasped her arms round her legs. Then it occurred to her that it probably wasn't very hygienic to put her shoes all over the furniture, and she unfolded herself.

'I'd tell her that life is short, and happiness is worth hoping for.'

Louisa permitted her a small smile, and Natalie thought: So that's it. I really am going to have to go.

She'd been loitering in the garden of Eden: orderly, circumscribed, obedient and unsatisfying. Now she was about to get herself thrown out.

She and Richard almost never ate together now; he had started having his evening meal in the canteen at the office before putting in another couple of hours at his desk. That evening he got home around nine and came straight to the kitchen, where she was ironing a shirt ready for work the next day.

He asked her how it had gone, and she murmured something about how it had been interesting, but Louisa had suggested she avoid going into too much detail until Richard had been for his solo session and they were both on the counsellor's couch together.

'Did you tell Tina what you talked about with Louisa?'

'She didn't ask,' Natalie said, quite truthfully. 'I think she could see I was totally shellshocked.'

'Ah well,' Richard said, looking apprehensive. 'My turn next.'

Then, to her surprise, he gave her a quick, awkward hug.

'It was brave of you to go through with it,' he said. 'Look, maybe we haven't made such a good couple. But if we do come unstuck, we'll just have to make sure that we're the best possible exes.'

Then his eyes started to tear up and he beat a retreat.

At lunchtime the next day Natalie went to the canteen with Hannah, Lucy's little sister, who had fetched up in her department on a six-month admin contract. Natalie had never seen Hannah out of jeans and baggy jumpers, and it was interesting, even a little intimidating, to see her looking rangy and lean in an olive-green trouser suit.

But then Natalie told herself she couldn't allow Hannah to give her an inferiority complex. This was

Hannah: chaotic, untidy, disorganized Hannah, whose love life Lucy always rolled her eyes over, who was perpetually short of cash, running out of Tampax and let go from her latest job. This was Hannah, who'd slept with her brother-in-law and broken up her sister's marriage, and who was being very friendly to Natalie, but nervously so, as if she was either worried that Natalie knew and secretly loathed her, or didn't know and might one day find out.

Then they began to talk about work, and Natalie was reminded of a different Hannah; the one who had stoically run round after Lucy's children for all those years, who had helped to deal with A & E dashes and chicken pox and tantrums and tears and way too much laundry, and who, after each pointless one-night stand and dull clerical post, somehow picked herself up, carried on and started looking for the next one.

Natalie asked after Lucy and Hannah said, 'I think she's going to be all right. This new job seems to have boosted her confidence, and the girls have settled down.' Then she added, without looking at Natalie, 'I have to say, it's a load off my mind.'

Natalie wondered if she should say that she knew what had happened with Adam, but wasn't going to make an issue of it. She had decided that if Lucy had made her peace with Hannah, it was all right for her to be cordial too; it was really none of her business. But then Hannah started to talk about something else, and the moment passed.

They talked briefly about TV, and films, and places to eat – Natalie, whose experience of the outside world had been somewhat limited since she had Matilda, had few insights to offer about anything other than what was on the box, but it was pleasant to chat about things that she imagined she might, one day, be able to explore. Hannah spoke as if she half expected anything she volunteered to be pounced on and corrected. Her ruthless self-deprecation, hesitation and willingness to please were eerily familiar, and it took Natalie a while to work out that this was because all these qualities reminded her of herself.

Did being put upon make you more sensitive to other people's needs? It was good to talk with someone she could trust not to comment on the weight she had lost, or to ask her when she was going to have another child. Probably comments about her figure were intended to be flattering, and asking her about extending her family was a sort of veiled compliment too, since it demonstrated a benign assumption that she was sufficiently motherly to wish to repeat the experience of giving birth. But no: why give people the benefit of the doubt? Such remarks just compared you to the way onlookers thought you ought to be. It was enough to prompt you to get very, very fat indeed, and have your tubes tied.

Anyway, the conversation flowed readily enough, which was encouraging, because Natalie had been worried that she would find herself out of practice at this sort of casual chatting after all the months at home with a baby, especially as her recent exchanges with Louisa Mead and with Richard were still so fresh in her mind. She wouldn't have been surprised to find herself staring at someone with her mouth slightly open and nothing coming out but drool, like an old woman on the edge of decay.

It was partly because she wanted to avoid this sort of drying up that she jumped in as soon as there was a natural pause, a possible end point, and remarked that she really ought to be getting back to her desk.

'Oh, really?' Hannah said. 'But you've only taken half an hour.'

'Yes, well, I've got lots to get through, you know, lots to catch up on.'

'Lucy says you're much too conscientious,' Hannah said. 'Can I tempt you to come out for a walk? It's a beautiful day. I'm going to go down to the river.'

Natalie was about to say no, maybe another time; she couldn't have pinpointed exactly what it was that changed her mind. It wasn't really that she thought Hannah was attractive, and admired the sleek olive-green trouser suit, though those things didn't hurt. It wasn't even that she had, in the course of the last half-hour, come to think of Hannah as someone she could enjoy spending time with, and allow herself to like.

No; it was really the mention of the beautiful day, the river and the walk that clinched it. Natalie had come to think of walking as something she did to shed pounds and occupy Matilda; strolling and chatting with a friend was a luxury from a previous era. And she re-membered of old that one of the things she had always liked about the offices of the Department for Children, Schools and Families was its closeness to the Thames.

In the oppressive, overcrowded city, which Natalie

had lately come to think her mother was right about, the river was always escaping. Sooner or later, the sluggish but indomitable water would make its way out past the Thames Barrier and eventually disperse into the sea. Seagulls would wheel above it, and holidaymakers would photograph it, and watch the water shift and retreat and meet the horizon, and be gratefully reminded of their own insignificance, and the compensatory pleasure of having a companion with whom to stroll on the beach.

18

Comeback

Tina got the phone call she'd been dreading – the one that cast doubt over the security of her job – just after coming back from the park with William on one of the first sunny days of spring. She had even noticed a few belated daffodils coming up, and after the long dark winter the unfamiliar brightness was a boon she knew better than to take for granted, a permission to walk into a benign and generous future, in which people strolled and smiled rather than keeping their heads down out of the wind and scurrying past.

This new mood of optimism lasted just long enough for Tina to get home, take William's coat off and lay him down under his baby gym. Then the phone rang. The caller display said: *Work*.

She picked up immediately, thinking that it might be Dan. He was able to call her more openly from the office now that they'd agreed it was all right for their colleagues to know he was William's father, a disclosure which Dan said had been, just as he'd predicted, a ten-minute wonder, with half their colleagues claiming they'd guessed months ago, and most of the rest indifferent, apart from a small minority who had clapped Dan on the back as if he'd just scored one for the team. (Tina hadn't welcomed this detail.)

But instead of Dan saying, 'So how's my babymother today, and how's my boy?' she got Jeremy saying, 'What do you want first, the bad news or the bad news?'

'How lovely to hear from you. I'm very well, thank you, and you?'

'We've taken an editorial decision to bring the Vixen Letters to an end. Now, don't sulk. All columns die a death sooner or later. It's inevitable. Part of the natural order of things. This one you've just filed is going to be the last one. Send me a paragraph to add on at the end. Wind it up. Say thank you and goodbye. Over and out.'

'This is a surprise,' Tina said. 'You seemed to be happy with the way the column was going.'

'I was, but right now it's not going anywhere. You're scraping the barrel, Tina. Let me remind you of the original brief. You were meant to be writing about being single and childless and thirty-five, right? Well, you're not any more, are you? I can tell you're trying not to whinge, but, honestly, sleepless nights, nappies, struggling on, who cares? There's no story there. No drama. No news. It's just drudgery. So that's Bad News Part One. You ready for Part Two?'

'Go for it.' Tina's voice came out as a strangled croak.

'I need you to come in. Monday morning, eleven o'clock. We need to talk about your future in the department. Now don't get your knickers in a twist, cos we're going through this with everybody. Voluntary redundancy programme. Aim is to reduce headcount by a fifth.'

Tina cleared her throat. 'Somebody saw year end looming and panicked about the figures?'

'What can I say, Tina? It's not my idea. I'm just implementing the latest directive from the bean counters. I'm not happy about it either, believe me.'

Tina thought this was probably true; Jeremy didn't have any qualms about wielding the hatchet for his own reasons – if someone screwed up a few times too often, say, or just wasn't up to scratch – but he wouldn't like doing it to order, and he would not be pleased about his kingdom shrinking. Fewer underlings equalled reduced power.

'Monday at eleven it is, then,' she said.

'Looking forward to it.'

He hung up, and Tina put the phone back and allowed herself to cry.

She'd known, in principle, when she'd started the Vixen Letters that one day she would finish, just as she'd known, on the first day she'd walked into the offices of the *Post*, that one day she would pass the other way through the revolving doors and never return . . . and the first time she and Justin had gone up to a hotel room, it had occurred to her that there would be a final rendezvous too.

You couldn't let the inevitability of last spoil the sweetness of first, or put you off, or deter you. You could usually forget the conclusion altogether if the beginning was sufficiently seductive. But oh Lord, sometimes, when the ending came into view, it seemed like one hell of a price to pay.

But feeling sorry for herself wasn't going to help. She needed to work out whom to ask to look after William on Monday morning.

She balked at asking her mother, because she didn't want to have to lie, and she didn't want to tell the truth either. Up until now, she'd been able to square up to Cecily with her head more or less held high. She kept telling herself, I'll show them. It's all going to turn out fine. I don't need a husband to help me raise this baby, I can support him, I have a job. But if she lost her job, her situation would begin to look as unfortunate in her own eyes as it already did to her parents.

She decided to call Natalie, though she couldn't remember whether Natalie worked Mondays or not. As she explained what had happened she was aware that her voice was high and breathless, not far off hysterical.

'OK, Tina, deep breaths,' Natalie told her. 'Really – don't sweat it. You'll be fine. Bring him round on Monday morning. I'll be here, and hopefully out of my pyjamas.'

'Thank you,' Tina said. 'So . . . are you all right?'

There was a short, enigmatic silence, and then Natalie said, 'Everything seems to be shifting, and I don't know what's going to happen when it settles. I know that sounds evasive, but I can't really say much more right now.'

'So if I were to ask you if you and Richard are breaking up, you'd say you couldn't tell me?'

'That's about right, yes.'

'You sound as if you've made your peace with it anyway, whatever it is that's happening, or however it's going to turn out.'

'I don't know about that. Things seem a bit clearer, maybe. Though possibly only to me.'

They said goodbye, and Tina went over to the photo montage mounted above the mantelpiece and looked for Richard. There he was, in his wedding suit on the steps outside Marylebone Register Office, next to Natalie in her cream lace prom dress, both laughing as they were pelted with confetti.

She had known Richard almost as long as she'd known Natalie; they had always seemed so well suited. And yet now it turned out that they had been fundamentally incompatible from the start.

And as for Lucy and Adam, their wedding had been a much more traditional affair, complete with the big white dress, the July drizzle, the chilly church, the even chillier marquee in the grounds of a country house hotel, and the drunken and marginally inappropriate best man's speech.

There had been an undertow of family tension: Hannah had looked much too thin in her strapless bridesmaid's dress; Lucy's father had opted to leave straight after the church service to catch a flight back to Spain; and Ellen hadn't created a scene or anything, but had got so paralytically drunk that Richard had to help her up to bed at the end of the night. Adam's family, meanwhile, had been conspicuous by its absence; he had no siblings or cousins or uncles or aunts, and his father, the widower, looked frail and lonely.

Yet Adam and Lucy had been so completely happy. As if nothing could touch them.

There they were, a gorgeous couple; they could have come straight off the top of the cake. Adam was quietly proud, young love's dream with those tender eyes and the dark hair and that kissable, sculpted face, and Lucy looked as soft and pretty as a rose in bloom, and as treasured as a princess.

How could it all have gone so wrong? Damn it, Tina needed to be able to experience companionable love by proxy, if not at first hand . . . Surely somebody's relationship had to work out?

If she lost her job, she would sooner or later get another. She imagined that finding love after marriage would be an infinitely tougher challenge, and might bring much less certain rewards.

On Monday morning Tina got William fed and dressed, showered, put on her new Magic Knickers and squeezed into a navy-blue skirt suit, blouse, the obligatory tights and high heels.

She checked her foundation, mascara and lip gloss, and spritzed herself with perfume. Classic Chanel, nothing too sexy. What a palaver! How had she ever managed to do all this and get to her desk for 9.00 a.m.? How was she ever going to do it again? Every week-day and occasional weekends and Bank Holidays? And why did anyone say that motherhood made you glow? She wasn't glowing. She looked extinguished. And what was happening to her hair? She hadn't had it cut for ages – how was she ever going to make time to have it cut again? – and now it was coming out in handfuls every time she washed it.

Where once she'd been lean, fit and hungry, now she was exhausted, terrified and soft. She was in no fit shape to fight for her professional life.

She carried William downstairs at arm's length so he wouldn't sick up on her suit. She drove to Natalie's, and after she had dropped William off she nipped to the newsagent's across the road to bag a copy of that day's *Post*. Then she joined the post-rush-hour traffic, praying she'd be able to find a space in the *Post*'s small and oversubscribed underground car park.

It turned out that staff losses had an upside; she was able to park almost straight away. She was half an hour early. Just right. She'd wait in the car: it would be too painful to sit in reception, as if she was a potential tryout invited for interview.

If Dan had been in, she might have gone up to say hello, but he'd just flown out to interview a famously sexy actress, known for being significantly nicer to male journalists than to women, on the set of her latest film. Admittedly the film was being shot in the Scottish Highlands rather than somewhere hot and sunny, but still . . . hardly a chore.

Poor Dan, he'd spent hours talking her down, re-assuring her that neither of them were going to lose their jobs, that she wouldn't be forced to crawl to her parents for a handout, that she wouldn't end up on the breadline. There was no one else whose desk she would feel welcome to loiter at for any length of time, in the absence of having her own.

This was not how she had wanted to come back. Now that Dan's paternity was out in the open, she'd been planning to bring William in sometime, show him off, the way other mothers did with their new babies. It would have been much too weird to do it before, but now Dan could come and join in receiving the congratulations, it might be kind of fun. But this . . . this was excruciating – and totally surreal. It was almost enough to make her question if she still belonged here.

She put on the overhead light, opened the paper and started flicking through it, looking for the article Dan had told her was going in that day. He'd said it was something about becoming a dad, and his own father, and had asked her if she'd like to read it before he submitted it, but she'd been much too busy flapping about the prospect of redundancy to bother, and anyway, it had sounded pretty innocuous. She was much more interested in what he was planning to ask the man-eating actress.

There it was! Nice big photo – he looked pretty good. He was wearing the new jacket she'd encouraged him to buy when they'd gone mooching round the fag end of the sales; it was dark blue, well cut, but unobtrusive, and had the effect of making him look a bit more formal and high-minded than usual.

Next to the photo of Dan was a small black-and-white inset of an old chap standing barefoot on a beach, his trousers rolled to the knee, gazing at the camera with a rueful, absent-minded smile.

Why I'll Never Be a Match for My Father

by Dan Cargill

These days I find myself thinking about my own father in a fresh light. He never made much money; he worked as a hospital porter, and my mother was furious when she found out that he regularly donated small amounts of his modest salary to a range of charities, but he was a good man, fond of a pint, regarded with affection, loved by everyone who knew him. He had an otherworldly aura that comes across even in photographs – like the framed holiday snap that has place of honour at my bedside, joined, now, by a picture of my infant son, who, in this image at least, has much the same air of quiet, inexpressible knowingness.

Idealistic men do not always make good fathers, but my father was naturally interested in how children saw the world, and he seemed to enjoy playing with us as much as we loved playing with him. It wasn't all building dens, planting cress and floating paper boats on the pond, though. My mother worked full-time as a secretary and, as far as he was concerned, that meant shirking household duties wasn't an option – an attitude he got some stick for, both from his friends and from my grandparents. But he shrugged off their teasing. He cooked, cleaned, made up bottles of formula and changed nappies. His cooking was a bit hit and miss, but you can't have everything, and I don't think my mother will hold it against me if I point out that hers is the same.

I always thought that, at some point in the future – when I grew up – I would be as good a dad as Dad. And now I'm not, and never will be. You know what fathers of small babies look like: exhausted, but proud. My nights aren't broken by my son crying – he's yet to stay overnight – but still, oddly, I find it hard to sleep. I often wake with a start and wonder if it's because he has, if we are unconsciously connected. I think about him all the time, wondering what he is doing, and in place of pride, I have the sad, tired, niggling sensation of separation and loss.

This is what happens when you have distance where intimacy should be. I think this is what heartache feels like, and I've never known anything like it. It's different from grief, because the loss is not complete, but just like grief, it's a process of learning to live with what's not there.

My father died two and a half years ago. Afterwards, I threw myself into work; I guess I was belatedly trying to prove something to him. I still defer to his advice on difficult predicaments, and I've thought a lot about what he would have said to me about my current situation. I think it would probably have boiled down to: What can't be cured must be endured. I'm an absentee father. I have to accept it, make the best of it, and stick with it. There will be an answer. Dad was boundlessly optimistic, and often that's more helpful than looking ahead and seeing only gloom and doom.

My mother is going to meet her new grandson for the first time next weekend. I'm very grateful to my ex for facilitating this. Now she's a mother herself I think she knows how much it means.

I hope this means my ex and I can find a way to be a family, even if we can't be a couple. After all, marriages come and go, but she'll always be the mother of my child. So this Mother's Day, I'll be drinking a toast to mothers everywhere, and I'd urge everyone to do the same. But spare a thought for fathers, too.

Tina folded the newspaper and dabbed her eyes with a tissue. God! Crying again.

She checked her make-up in the rear-view mirror, turned off the light, got out of the car, remembered to lock it, smoothed her skirt and walked towards the lift. Her heels tapped smartly on the concrete. She'd spent months in slippers or trainers; it had been so long since she'd worn proper shoes that she felt like a little girl dressing up.

The interview, if you could call it that, took place in a small office with no window apart from a glass wall thoughtfully exposing whoever was in it to the scrutiny of passers-by. It was as if Tina had been summoned to take part in a non-optional reality TV show, and she half expected an authoritative regional voiceover to cut in and provide a commentary, making pseudo-scientific observations about her body language and speech patterns.

There were three of them present: herself, Jeremy and an HR woman called Frances, all sitting at one end of a long table that took up most of the space in the room. Frances looked exhausted, and had evidently done more of these sessions than was good for her; Jeremy looked well, but bored and restless. Tina took that as a good sign. If he had been poised to oust her she thought he would have looked marginally more engaged.

It quickly became apparent that this was more an information session than a sacking, and that Jeremy regarded it as a tedious formality. He treated Frances with barely disguised contempt, and Tina remembered

372

that he had always thought the HR department was superfluous. Jeremy reckoned editors should be able to hire and fire as they chose, unencumbered by internal bureaucracy and the patsies who administered it.

As Frances explained what Tina might be entitled to should she choose to leave she felt her breasts prickling and knew she was oozing milk. She didn't dare glance down to see if any of it had come through. It was hot in the little goldfish bowl of an office and she would have quite liked to take her jacket off, but she didn't dare do that either. She would just have to hope her breast pads were still in place. She could smell the sickly sweet odour of her deodorant, rising to combat the fresh reek of fear. She imagined herself looking redder and redder.

At last Frances glanced at Jeremy and said, 'I think that's everything, isn't it? Thank you for coming in, Tina. We'll let you get back to your baby now.'

Jeremy stood up and leaned across the table to shake Tina's hand. He said, 'Thank God that's over. For a minute back then I thought you were going to blub. You look all hot and bothered. It isn't hormones, is it?'

'No,' Tina said, 'you need to turn the heating down. It's not like it's the depths of winter any more. Save the planet and cut costs at one fell stroke.'

'You hear that, Frances?' Jeremy said. 'See, my writers do care about the bottom line.'

Frances raised her eyebrows at Jeremy to indicate that she wasn't done with him yet. Jeremy scowled and sat down again and Tina went out and took the lift without bumping into anybody.

She got out at the ground floor to go to the ladies'.

Only sales, circulation and partworks down here, so no one she knew well, and less risk of having to make conversation.

She changed her breast pads. Sopping wet, and there were spots of damp on her blouse, so it was just as well she'd kept the jacket on. She was already looking forward passionately to collecting William. Thank God for Natalie: dear, kind, steadfast Natalie . . . who had plenty of problems of her own.

Someone came into the stall next to her and began to pee. Tina was reminded of the awkwardness of sharing toilet facilities with people at work; one minute you were excreting next to someone, the next you were trying to psych them out with your professionalism.

The woman next to her flushed and continued to rustle. Changing tights? Tina decided to make a run for it. There was a social code for these occasions: high-ups usually preferred to pretend they hadn't seen you, equals and allies might chat, and underlings could be briefly acknowledged. But easiest of all was to avoid contact altogether.

She let herself out and washed her hands. God! She had an inch's worth of roots, and there was white at her temples – veritable white!

The door of the other stall opened and Julia McMahon came out, clocked Tina's reflection in the mirror and stomped up to the basin next to her.

'Hello, Julia,' Tina said. Oh God – could it be any worse? She took a paper towel and dried her hands. Quicker than the blower. She could be out of here in three seconds flat.

374

'What are you doing skulking round down here?' Julia asked, and Tina wished she'd gone for the dryer after all. She could have pretended not to hear.

She mumbled something about having popped in for a quick meeting with Jeremy, and Julia said, 'Ah. Yes. *That* meeting.' She looked at Tina more closely. 'Are you all right? You've gone very red in the face.'

'Yes, well, I'm the single parent of a nine-week-old baby and I've just had it explained to me that if I don't offer myself up for voluntary redundancy I'll probably have to reapply for my job and might end up losing it. I've had better days,' Tina said, dropping the paper towel in the bin. 'Still, it's a tough time for everybody, isn't it? I don't imagine morale is particularly high.'

Julia shrugged. 'I guess with any change there are winners and losers.'

'Oh come on. If a fifth of us are fired, who is that good news for? There's still the same amount of paper to fill. Those who are left will just have to work harder than ever.'

Julia hit the button on the blower and said loudly over the noise, 'Some of us don't mind hard work. Putting in the extra hours. Networking. I guess it's a lot easier when you don't have to rush back to do the pick-up from nursery. But then, maybe Dan will be willing to share that with you. If you're both still here.'

The dryer stopped.

Tina said, 'You seem very confident that you're going to be all right.'

Julia said, 'What can I say? Watch this space. The more senior you are, the more expensive you are. But

375

I'm cheap and I'm good, and I'm willing to step up. Disaster's always an opportunity for somebody. You know that as well as I do.' She pushed past Tina and let the door bang shut in her face.

Tina decided to leave it a couple of minutes, let Julia get well on her way to wherever she was going. Then she spotted the pink mobile phone sitting on the shelf above the basin.

Hah! So Julia wasn't quite so smart as she thought she was. Not too clever, really, to leave something like that in the loo with someone you'd been picking a fight with.

She hesitated, but only for a moment. And then she grabbed the phone and hurried out and along the corridor.

'Julia?'

Julia was already approaching the lifts, stopped and turned. 'What?'

'Is this yours?'

Julia's expression was horrified: *I can't believe I did something so stupid.* She reached for the phone rather gingerly, as if Tina might be about to jerk it away, leaving her foolishly clutching at empty air.

'Thanks.' More of a growl than an expression of gratitude, but Tina knew that she briefly had the moral upper hand. She decided to press her advantage.

'I'm sorry about you and Dan,' she said. 'I know me having William must have made things difficult.'

'It didn't help,' Julia agreed, 'but the real problem was you being you.'

Tina swallowed. 'Well . . . I know I'm not everybody's cup of tea.'

'It's not that I dislike you,' Julia said, 'though you're not my favourite person, obviously. It's that you have the things that I want. Or you used to.'

She held up the phone and added, 'Thanks for this. I'm expecting a call on it any minute. I'd have been scuppered if I'd lost it.'

They came to a standstill next to the lift.

'Up or down?' Tina asked.

'Oh, you take it, I'll go for the stairs. I could use the exercise. We can't all slob round and still have model pins.' She glanced appraisingly at Tina's legs and bounded off.

Tina pressed the button to summon the lift. She realized that she was almost happy. As if happiness was a golden state she'd left behind, but which was now beckoning, soliciting hope and gleaming with promise, though it was impossible to tell whether she was remembering or anticipating.

The Vixen Letters

The sisterhood of motherhood

Since I found myself unexpectedly pregnant last year, and began to write about becoming a mother, the number of letters and emails I receive has more than tripled. Some have been kind, not a few were exasperated, others offered useful tips and words of warning. Each and every message was written in the light of personal experience, though not all were from mothers.

Whether parent, childless, orphaned or estranged, married, single, bereaved or divorced, all of us have mums. Even when they are absent, they remain uniquely powerful in our hearts and minds. That power is a source of strength, but it can also seem like a threat – and the best way to cope with a threat is to knock it down. That's why teenage girls give their mothers hell – and that's why we all love to indulge in the blame game. If it's possible to find fault with Mother, it's likely that fault will be found.

We accept that children rebel against their parents and need to create space in which to become themselves – but don't parents, too, feel the need to escape, not so much from their children, but from the expectation that they should take responsibility for every aspect of their child's wellbeing and development? If, as an adult woman, I am unhappy, can it really ever be my mother's fault? If she is unhappy too, whose fault is that? We live in an age that deems it compassionate to shift the blame from the criminal to the criminal's upbringing. But is this really either kind or truthful?

When you're dealing with the weight of cultural expectation, from time to time you need to let off steam. You need to moan, mock, poke fun – and you need other women to do it with. Ideally, you need women who knew you when you were different – women who can remind you of the time when you were just you.

They say you can choose your friends, but you can't choose your family. That means you can unchoose your friends, too, but that's not a freedom to be used lightly. Beware of the contemporary vogue for friendship-purging, which means ditching all the connections that are apparently no longer of use to you, as if clearing out last season's cheap fashion hits from the back of the wardrobe. Friendship is not a commodity; you can't weigh the value of one against the other, and decide to keep this one and ditch the next. You decide that a friend no longer suits you at your peril, not knowing how you or she may change.

Friendship is a gift. It's the lightest and freest of bonds, but that doesn't mean that it is without obligation. And if you have friends you can quarrel with, or let drift and return to, you have friends for life. Few friendships are based on ties that are durable enough to survive the weight of acrimony. And fewer still are sufficiently strong for you to be able to turn to your friends at your moment of greatest need, when no one else is there, and count on them to help you and see you through.

It's a great thing, the sisterhood of motherhood, whether we're bickering or bonding. It's so often mothers who hold it all together – when fathers die, or live elsewhere, or work every hour God sends and crawl back home to sleep. Mums just have to keep on going, trying, sometimes failing, then trying again to do what's best for their children. We need all the help we can get.

Much has been made of the tensions between different

types of mother – the cake-baking home-maker and the briefcase-wielding careerist – and also between women with children and women without. (Which prompts me to ask, who stands to gain most from women fighting among themselves? Divide and rule is the oldest trick in the book. No wonder women still earn less than men.)

Why did the Working Mothers and the Yummies have it in for each other? I think each clan was secretly envious, and thought the other had it easy; and probably there were more than a few would-be defectors on either side. I have to confess that back when I was a Childless Career Woman, I was guilty of underestimating how much discipline and self-denial goes into being an old-school, fragrant, nurturing wife and mother.

Back then, I didn't have much sympathy for the Working Mothers either, but in another couple of months I'm going to join them. As I'm a single parent, there was never much chance of me becoming a Yummy. But you know what? Even if I had a husband around, I'd still want a job.

There's a wise old saying that you shouldn't put all your eggs in one basket. Being a dependant is OK as long as Hubby keeps his side of the bargain, which is to stay married and pay the bills. But what if you break up and he loses his job, and you're faced with trying to return to work in the throes of a downturn which is clearly far from over? If you'd been working all along people might have said your marriage hit the rocks because you neglected your husband, but at least you'd have the consolation of a pay cheque.

This is going to be the last of these columns, so it's time for me to say farewell, and to thank you for all your letters. With Mothering Sunday fast approaching, I'd also like to take the opportunity to say thank you to my own mother, who has been unfailingly staunch and supportive. I know I have disappointed her many times over the years, but she has never given up on me. I think it's fair to say that there are some subjects on which we will never agree, but I've realized that disagreements, even long absences, do not show that love is over, only that it is changing.

19

Salvage

With Lucy and Natalie on board for Easter at the Old Schoolhouse, Tina had decided to extend the invitation to Dan. He was much less likely to misinterpret it as a romantic overture if her friends and their daughters were there – and it was a confirmation that he, too, had become someone with whom she wanted to have a life-long, but platonic, connection. Besides, he had to meet Natalie and Lucy sooner or later. It seemed like a golden opportunity.

She knew that she'd been a lousy friend at least some of the time – self-absorbed, neglectful, and the now-defunct column hadn't helped. But the drama of William's birth seemed to have lanced any remaining unspoken bitterness about what she'd written, and now that everything was out in the open and the air was definitely cleared, she and Natalie and Lucy had been getting on better than ever. Which was just as well, because they all had plenty of other things to worry about.

She had learned that her job was safe, but Dan, after much deliberation, had decided to accept the offer of voluntary redundancy. 'The writing's on the wall for newspapers,' he had said. 'I want to try and get in on something new rather than go down with something that's dying. Might as well take the cash and cut my losses.' He was currently exploring various options, all to do with websites. Tina felt nervous for him, but she could also see his point, and she had come to have some faith in his ability to transform difficult situations into promising ones.

The fearsome features editor, Rowena Fix, had also opted to leave, and to Tina's slight chagrin Julia had been appointed in her place. Tina's one-time potential protégée had outstripped her; it was just as well that they had arrived at a truce. When she returned to work, she would be on general writing duties and, to a large extent, she would be at Julia's mercy; if Julia didn't give her decent features to write, she wouldn't be getting any bylines.

Losing her column had left Tina anxious and in-secure, and ready to get away from it all for a couple of days. Not that escaping was straightforward. It took for ever to assemble all the clobber she would need, and fit it into the car: the travel cot, the sterilizer, the packs of nappies . . . endless kit, none of it dispensable. There was no way round it, once you were a mother, you had serious baggage.

At least she had Dan around to keep an eye on William as she packed, and to help her lug stuff downstairs. They'd agreed to use her car – she'd refused to contemplate attempting the journey in Dan's, for if it made it to the Old Schoolhouse, it sure as hell looked as if it wouldn't be making it back again. Dan had briefly attempted to defend his shit-coloured, moss-sprouting rust-bucket, but almost immediately capitulated: 'Why are we even arguing about this? You're right. My car's a crock. Let's take yours.'

As she pulled away from the tall, narrow townhouse with her flat at the top, she felt the breath sigh out of her body, taking her worries with it. In the morning she would wake up somewhere else: somewhere softer, greener, cooler, with a hint of salt in the air.

Dan, who was in the passenger seat, turned to look back at William and pulled a series of increasingly idiotic faces to entertain him, then complained of a crick in his neck, whereupon she pressed play and *The Wheels on the Bus* CD started up.

Dan made a plaintive request for the Sex Pistols – 'If we don't educate him now, we might have years of this!' – and she told him to forget it. Dan groaned, then started singing along: 'She'll be coming round the mountain when she comes . . .'

Tina had never heard him sing before; it was a pleasant surprise to discover that he sounded OK – in tune, warm and cheery. The London streets and traffic flowed past and around them. Her spirits lifted as they always did when she was heading west, towards the house and the stretch of sea that never seemed to change, however much she did.

The place was filled with ghosts of her younger selves: loquacious child, stroppy teenager, restless twenty-something. But the effect of this superimposition of echoes and traces was not melancholy or eerie, it was affirming. The details of all her previous visits were blurred and softened, doubts and squabbles mixed up with pleasures and treats and good times. All that remained was a hazy intensity, an awareness that she had been both happy and unhappy there, and these emotions had made the lane and the house and the garden and the beach vivid to her, and were the source of her attachment to them. It wasn't somewhere she could ever stay for long – it was too remote from the rest of her life – but it was somewhere she revisited in her dreams, and felt soothed by. She knew that whenever she went back, she would always feel welcome.

She hoped it would come to serve as a reservoir for William's memories of growing up, too. Paddling in rock-pools; collecting seashells; playing card games on wet afternoons; being indulged or ignored by his playmates, the offspring of his mother's friends . . . The summers of his childhood presented themselves to her like the quick flicker of a pack of cards being shuffled.

She imagined herself walking, in a year or two or three's time, along the beach, with William at her side, his hand in hers. Would Dan be on the other side of him, ready to hold on tight, so William could swing suspended between them? She was surprised to find that she wanted it to be so – wanted it so badly that she felt tears come to her eyes.

'OK, he's asleep,' Dan said, and turned the music off. 'How about you give me a crash revision course on these friends of yours? The unofficial godmothers?'

'Well, you must at least be able to remember their names. I've talked about them often enough.'

'Sure, yeah, but how do I know which is which?'

'I showed you the photos, didn't I?'

'Well, yeah, but they're both going to have changed a bit since then, aren't they?'

She supposed this was true. Looking back at the photo of her with Natalie and Lucy on millennium New Year's Eve, she'd been struck by how they had all begun to undergo the peculiar metamorphosis of ageing, whereby the generic fresh-faced appeal of youth is replaced by signs of character and experience.

Lucy's unthreatening prettiness had given way to something more self-aware and challenging, with a hint of stubbornness in the set of the jaw and a flash of resilience in the big brown eyes. And Natalie – mild, approachable Natalie, with her sensual mouth and muted, patient expression, as if she was always daydreaming about something she knew she could never have – was now present and alert as she had never been before. Her wistfulness had come into focus, and been transformed into both regret and hope. There was also a new edge of dryness and toughness to her that sometimes caught Tina by surprise.

And as for Tina herself . . . she would like to think that she'd softened, but the truth was she probably looked even sharper and more cantankerous than before. It was hard to look gentle and benign after three months of broken nights.

'Lucy's the one with the hair,' she said, 'and the key thing to bear in mind, so that you don't put your foot in it, is that they've both recently broken up with their husbands.'

'Yeah, I remember that much. Not good news.'

'No, I know, it's dreadful, isn't it? Still, at least we don't need to worry about whether it's catching,' Tina said.

'True, but I hope that doesn't mean that I'm in for a whole weekend of you lot moaning on at me about how crap men are.'

'They won't, I promise you. Lucy seems quite happy now she's got the house and a job and a young buck to keep her satisfied, and Natalie's decided she's probably a lesbian, although she isn't out or anything, so watch what you say. Anyway, we do have other topics of conversation. Besides men, I mean.'

'I know you do, and I bet I can tell you exactly what they are. Babies, children, work, telly, other women you know, celebrities and shopping. Am I right or am I right?'

'Well, you know, and art, literature, philosophy and politics, in so far as they're connected to any of the other things you already mentioned,' she said.

He laughed, and she thought: This is going to be OK. Maybe even better than OK.

Traffic lights. While they were stopped . . . why not?

She reached across experimentally and rested one hand on his knee.

'I'm so glad you're here,' she said.

He smiled back at her. God, those blue eyes! He really was rather gorgeous. How come she hadn't realized that ages ago?

'There's no one I'd rather be with,' he told her.

Someone beeped her, and Dan said, 'Er, Tina . . . I think the lights have changed.'

A moment later both her hands were back on the steering wheel, and they were moving forward again.

'You know what?' she said. 'I'm knackered, and I'm really tempted to ask you to drive sooner rather than later.'

'Well,' Dan said, 'temptation's only any good if you give in to it.'

It wasn't what he said so much as the tone of his voice that persuaded her – the warmth of it, suggestive of un-tapped reservoirs of kindness.

And in that moment she finally allowed herself to fall for him, though there was no sense of plunging down towards a hard landing; it was more like easing into the comfort of a deep hot bath, and letting go of all the troubles of the day.

She flashed him another quick smile and fixed her attention on the road.

In the service station car park she turned to him and said, 'OK, all yours, but this doesn't mean I've turned into the kind of woman who lets a man do all the driving.'

'Of course not,' he said, and then she leaned across to kiss him.

*

Natalie hadn't been at all sure about the idea of setting off on the Thursday evening, straight from work, but Lucy had been adamant; she had no intention of spending Good Friday stuck on the motorway. Natalie had volunteered to drive at least some of the way, but again, Lucy wouldn't hear of it. Perhaps she wanted to prove that she could handle the journey just as well as Adam had once done – or maybe she just didn't fancy putting herself in the hands of a notoriously nervy driver. Natalie was generally feeling much bolder about tackling practical challenges – she'd told her parents that she and Richard were separating because she was gay, the M4 was quite unintimidating in comparison – but she would have to find some other way of putting her newfound faith in herself to the test.

It was nearly one in the morning by the time they reached Port Maus. Matilda, Lottie and Clemmie were all soundly asleep in the back, and had been for hours. Natalie was horribly sleepy too, but felt obliged to stay awake to help with directions, and chat to Lucy and generally be companionable.

The village was pitch dark; there were a few street-lamps along the three main roads, but the arterial lanes were unlit, and the inhabitants of the low thatched cottages were dead to the world behind their closed shutters. But it was a starry, moon-bright night, and as the road rose and fell it was occasionally possible to catch a glimpse of the black sea, shining and shifting under the still, dark sky.

'I hope Tina's there this time,' Lucy said. 'Remember when I turned up with Adam and Lottie for the millennium house party, and you two were still down the pub?'

'Ah. Yes, I do. You know what that was all about. Tina had just told me she'd got together with the Grandee. Her top-secret lover. I think he might have been some kind of politician.'

'Yuck. What possessed her to do that? Thank goodness that bit the dust and she ended up with Dan.'

'But I don't think she is with Dan, is she? She was very emphatic that they were just friends.'

'Oh, she's definitely smitten, even if she hasn't quite admitted it to herself yet. Bet you anything you like she gets together with him while we're in Cornwall. If she hasn't already.'

'She did sound very pleased that he was coming,' Natalie said.

Lucy shot her a sidelong look. 'It'll happen for you, Natalie, I'm sure of it,' she said. 'There's someone out there for you – someone who has no idea yet that you're out there for her, and that you're on your way.'

Natalie shrugged. 'Some of us just don't get lucky. Look at your sister.'

'Yes, but she's happy,' Lucy said. 'Right now she's about the happiest she's ever been. You can't knock that. She's very impressed with you, you know.'

'With me?'

'Uh-huh. Says you're really good at your job. She's amazed that, you know, you can be going through all this complicated stuff in your home life, and you just never let it show, you're always calm, always friendly. She thinks that even though you seem a

390

gentle sort, deep down you must be as tough as old boots.'

'Well, that doesn't sound terribly complimentary.'

'I think it is, though. She told me she was really grateful you never mention Adam – she does know you know about that, by the way. And she was touched that you trusted her enough to tell her what was going on with Richard.'

'It's nice to have someone at work to talk to about it,' Natalie said.

She and Richard were still living together, more or less amicably, though not for much longer. Richard had found a flat to rent in a Georgian square in Kennington, and would be moving out soon; she hadn't been quite so organized about finding somewhere, but had a few places in Lucy's neck of the woods to look at. Their house had gone on the market, and they'd had several viewings, but no offers yet. She thought it would be a relief to both of them to see the back of it; it had never felt quite like home.

'I told my parents why Richard and I are splitting up,' she said.

'How'd it go?'

'I was expecting a scene. And it was a bit bumpy, but it wasn't at all how I'd expected it. Dad went very quiet, and Mum wanted to know if Richard had been beating me up – she couldn't believe that I thought what I'd told her was enough of a reason for us to split. Then she wondered if I'd had some sort of breakdown and had I talked to my GP, and then she asked if we couldn't just quietly get on with whatever we wanted to get up to, and still stay married. After that she thought it over for a bit, and she talked about it to my brother, and then she said that all she and Dad really cared about was my happiness and Matilda's, and I could count on their full support.'

'Phew! Good for Pat. Are you relieved?' Lucy asked.

'I'm impressed with them, actually,' Natalie said. 'That probably sounds horribly patronizing. I expected moral outrage. But I think they only get like that about abstract things, and it's just a way of letting off steam – it's the great British hobby, isn't it, moaning about stuff, complaining that the country's going to the dogs? When it comes down to it, they're very pragmatic.'

'What about your brother?'

'He rang up from New Zealand and said better late than never, and he'd always thought there was something not quite right with me and Richard and he was glad that we'd finally figured out what it was.'

They reached the house. The gates were open, and a light glowed in one of the lower windows. Lucy pulled on to the driveway and parked behind Tina's hatchback.

'It really does look like a school,' she commented.

And it was true, the building was a little forbidding, but the effect was softened by the setting. As Natalie walked towards the door she noticed the hush and the coastal freshness of the air. She could just make out the red glow of the tulips blooming in the border in front of the façade.

Tina opened up before she even got to the front step. She was in her pyjamas and dressing-gown, but looked surprisingly fresh and wide awake.

'You made it!' she cried. 'I'm so pleased to see you. Come on in, you must be exhausted.'

They embraced, and Natalie stepped into the hallway. Earlier that evening she wouldn't have been able to recall it, and yet it immediately seemed familiar, and she knew it hadn't changed a bit: the black-and-white chequerboard floor, the wide staircase with the red runner, the faded watercolours, the umbrella holder, the shelving unit for flip-flops and welly boots, the mahogany coat-stand with Tina's padded jacket hanging off it – all exactly the same. The air had a static, closeted, anticipatory quality, as if the house had been waiting for them.

'I've tried to air it,' Tina said, 'but I'm afraid the last guests left a week ago, and it's still a bit stuffy.'

Lucy came in behind them. 'You know, at one point I never would have thought I'd say this,' she said, 'but it really is good to be back.'

They unloaded their luggage and put the children to bed. It transpired that Tina and William were in the master bedroom in the tower, and Dan was in the little single room next to it; or perhaps Dan was in the master bedroom, and William was in the single. Tina wasn't explicit – she merely gestured at the archway that led that way as they passed it, and said, 'The three of us are in there.' She looked so pleased as she said this that Natalie wondered if the getting-together Lucy had predicted had already happened. If not, it surely wasn't far off.

At Natalie's request, Tina had put her and Matilda in

393

the room she'd slept in when she'd come to stay for the millennium. It was at the back of the house and had bluebell wallpaper, on which was mounted a framed specimen of Tina's cross stitch, a childhood project: *Bless this house.*

Once Matilda was settled in her travel cot Natalie joined the others in the kitchen. There was an open bottle of wine on the table, and Tina said, 'Would you like some? Lucy's abstaining.'

Natalie glanced at Lucy in surprise, and Lucy said, 'Makes a change, doesn't it? I kind of decided I'd had enough of drinking.'

'Next thing we know, you'll be running the marathon,' Tina said.

'Actually, I have started taking tennis lessons. I thought it might be an idea to get fit,' Lucy said.

Natalie drank half a glass of wine and then felt so sleepy there was nothing for it but to say goodnight – she'd never known where the other two got their stamina from. She went up to the bluebell room and got into her nightie and leaned over Matilda's travel cot and listened to her oblivious calm breathing. As her eyes adjusted to the dark she could make out Matilda's plump cheeks and still, serene expression.

The curtains were stirring slightly in the breeze, and she realized that Tina had left the sash window slightly open. She pulled it right up and leaned out and breathed in deep lungfuls of clean air. The wash of the sea on the beach was clear and close, and she could hear Lucy laughing downstairs.

Then she shut the window and fell into bed and into

a deep sleep. Sometime before dawn, she dreamed that she and Adele were alone in the house, which was suddenly not the Old Schoolhouse any more, but had become her own home, though it was completely bare and empty.

The building was almost immediately overrun by marauders, who pressed on the windows, climbed on to the roof, and invaded from all sides. She and Adele fled to the beach, ran down to a little jetty she'd never noticed before, boarded a ship; but its sails were torn and marked and couldn't catch the wind, and their persecutors were now pirates, running amok, sinking them.

As the sea closed over their heads and they drifted down into the gloom she saw the fear in Adele's eyes and knew they were about to die . . . but Adele pressed her lips to Natalie's and breathed air into her, and then she couldn't see Adele any more, she was rising, rushing upwards, and the water was gleaming . . .

She surfaced to the sound of Matilda chortling and gurgling, and saw that she hadn't quite closed the curtains, and the room was flooded with light.

When Lucy came to she checked the clock and did a double take. It was eight thirty already! And the girls hadn't come in to find her! Well, that was strange . . . and a little perturbing.

Over the last few months, Clemmie had got into the habit of coming into her bed for a cuddle first thing every morning. Lottie was too old for that, but given that they were in an unfamiliar place, Lucy would have expected her to want her mother too – even though things had been rather strained between them of late.

Lottie had been keeping an exercise book in the old wooden box Tina had given her, and Lucy hadn't been able to resist the temptation to read it. She had been appalled to discovered coded tales of shoplifting and bullying and underage sex, enough to make your blood run cold. She had confronted Lottie and been all set to storm up to the school and hand it over to the headmistress as evidence, until Lottie had persuaded her that it was, in fact, a story, and the names didn't actually correspond directly to any of her classmates, and were merely figments of her imagination.

Lucy still had a bit of trouble believing this, but she had decided to give Lottie the benefit of the doubt. After all, the sex parts had been rather inexplicit, and she suspected that if Lottie'd had any more than the basic anatomical knowledge she'd obtained from her biology classes, she might have made use of it. And anyway, she wanted to believe her daughter was still innocent. To be able to make such things up did suggest that worldly corruption was on its way, but perhaps that was inevitable.

And Lottie was doing well at school, as was Clemmie, so there couldn't be all that much to worry about, at least for now. They seemed to have settled, to be coping, to not be about to go off the rails; they had even got used to Emily. They both said she was all right, but Clemmie said she wasn't a very good cook, and could only make pizza, pasta and packet burritos.

Lucy dressed and made her way downstairs. She could smell bacon and fresh coffee. She pushed open the kitchen door and, sure enough, there was Tina, pinny on, washing up while Natalie dried, a little radio chuntering away tinnily in the background.

Tina wished her a good morning and offered to fix her up some breakfast. Lucy, who couldn't remember the last time someone had cooked for her, settled at the table and said yes, that would be lovely.

'Clemmie and Lottie have gone into Port Maus with Dan, by the way,' Tina added. 'Dan wanted to get a paper, and I think Clemmie wanted some sweets. I hope that's all right.'

'Of course,' Lucy said.

What a blissful morning . . . a lie-in . . . breakfast all made for her.

It did occur to her to wonder how early on a Bank Holiday morning it would be acceptable to phone Jack, but five minutes later the girls came back, looking fresh and happy, and keen to get down to the beach, and she forgot all about him.

Tina seemed to have decided that Lucy shouldn't be expected to sort out any of the meals during the course of their stay. It was lovely to be looked after for a change, but when the time came to prepare the roast for Easter Sunday lunch, Lucy insisted it was her turn.

Natalie made the pudding in the morning – a pavlova, unusually ambitious – and Dan impressed all of them by baking a cake. When it came out of the oven Tina said, 'Wow, have you ever thought about becoming a house-husband?' and Dan said, 'Frankly, no. Who wants to be taken for granted?'

Then Tina cosied up to him and whispered something in his ear, and they looked at each other and exchanged a secret smile, and Lucy had to suppress a pang of envy. She was still getting used to the novelty of seeing Tina so publicly loved up.

But she should count herself lucky to have the ideal occasional lover. Maybe she could let Jack stay overnight once in a while, when the girls were at Adam's. Perhaps one day she would even introduce them to him . . . but then again, maybe not. What was the rush? She'd let him in when she was good and ready.

Anyway, she had to get her lodger sorted, and she needed to suss out whether the woman whose maternity leave she was covering was likely to return and, if so, she needed to find another job . . .

Besides, if she ever felt lonely, there was always the cat for company. Pomfret would never come any closer to infidelity than sneaking across the green to Mrs Meadows for extra treats, and could be relied on to give her and the girls a warm welcome when they got back home the next day.

First things first: she had Sunday lunch to see to and she was determined that it was going to be a feast. And it was. Even Lottie and Clemmie contributed, having baked and iced little fairy cakes to serve with coffee – spring colours, yellow, pink and blue.

It was early evening by the time they finally got round to going out for a stroll.

'Let's go down to the beach,' Natalie said, 'there won't

be time in the morning, will there? I know we all need to get away early.'

And so they followed the path that led down to the sea, and walked out towards the water's edge. The day was poised on the cusp of twilight, the colours fading and flattening as the sun withdrew, and the air was cold. The sky was clear and pale with a hint of stars; the sea was shadowy grey, its daytime blues and greens already gone.

Dan produced a camera and, ignoring all protests about wayward hair and general unpreparedness, marshalled them all into a group photo.

Lucy had taken Matilda, to give Natalie a rest; now she passed her back. She stood in the middle, with Natalie on her left and Tina, who was carrying William in a sling, on the right, and Lottie and Clemmie in front.

'OK,' Dan said, fiddling with the camera, 'everybody ready now . . .'

Lucy linked arms with her friends and did her best to smile into the camera, knowing that such photo opportunities didn't come along all that often, and it might be months or even years before all of them were once more in the same place at the same time, lined up in front of a lens; aware that the resulting snap would quite possibly find its way into albums and emails and frames, and come to stand for something: the preservation of a lost moment.

She imagined the years ahead of them opening up like a series of gateways, suddenly telescoped, and simultaneously visible: ten years from now . . . twenty . . . thirty . . . their lives would change, their jobs and addresses and love interests and maybe even their names . . . there might be more children, who knew? . . . grandchildren . . . and they would age, and stoop, and nobody who didn't already love them would ever think of any of them as beautiful. But they would remember the way they had once been, they would remember each other, and they would remember this; until eventually even memory lapsed, and was lost, and only mementoes remained, passing into curious or indifferent hands, little scraps and leftovers of life.

The camera clicked and flashed and whirred, and they moved away from each other, freed from the constraint of posing for the record. They crowded round Dan to inspect the image on the camera screen, and pronounced it good. Then they left the darkening beach and headed back to the warmth of the house.